Every Little
Piece of Me

Every Little
Piece of Me

New York Times Bestselling Author
LEXI RYAN

Cover design © 2020 by Hang Le

Cover photo © 2020 by Sara Eirew

Ebook ISBN: 978-1-940832-13-5

Print ISBN: 978-1-940832-14-2

❧ Created with Vellum

Nina, this alpha's for you.

ABOUT EVERY LITTLE PIECE OF ME

It's not every day you're invited to your wife's wedding . . . as a guest.

The first time I saw Brinley Knox, she was crying, draped in a ridiculous pink tulle dress for her sweet sixteen, and cursing the boy who'd broken her heart.

I was the hired help, a teenage charity case.

She was the daughter of the wealthiest family in Orchid Valley.

I knew a girl like Brinley was off-limits. That didn't stop me from kissing her. Or from promising that if she were ever mine, I'd never let her go.

The *last* time I saw Brinley, she was sleeping, tangled in the sheets of my Vegas penthouse, my diamond glittering on her finger.

I returned three hours later to an empty bed, the ring on the dresser, and a goodbye note.

We haven't spoken in the six months since, but I'm not the kind of guy who'd file for a divorce he doesn't want.

Until I got this damn invitation, it never occurred to me that Brinley didn't remember our impulsive Vegas nuptials.

It's time to return to Orchid Valley and remind the bride-to-be that I'm a man who keeps his promises.

Every Little Piece of Me is a sexy, standalone second-chance romance in Lexi Ryan's all-new Orchid Valley series. It includes the prequel, *Every Little Promise*, for your convenience.

NOTE FROM THE AUTHOR

First, thank you so much for buying *Every Little Piece of Me*! I'm so excited to share this new series with you. I hope you love the town of Orchid Valley and its cast of characters as much as I do.

I included *Every Little Promise* for your convenience. Please feel free to skip past it if you already enjoyed it as a free download. Or read it again if you can't get enough of Marston's Vegas seduction!

I hope you enjoy Marston and Brinley's story. Thank you for reading!

Love,
    Lexi

Every Little

Promise

CHAPTER ONE

MARSTON

*I*t's been more than ten years since Brinley Knox ripped out my heart, and I still see her everywhere—pumping gas in Orange County, waiting tables in Toronto, riding a Spin bike in a Manhattan fitness center, and, one desperately lonely night, working the pole at an Atlanta gentlemen's club.

Tonight, she's sitting at the bar at my favorite Vegas nightclub, wearing a little black dress and sipping a martini.

"Incoming," my friend Alec says, his elbow digging into my side. "Damn, she's fine."

I struggle to pull my attention off the sexy brunette—a doppelganger of my first love—and follow my friend's gaze. There's a blonde sauntering toward me with a martini in one hand and a glass tumbler in the other. She's hot as hell in a skirt that would test indecent exposure laws anywhere other than Vegas and has the kind of long, toned legs that should send my imagination running wild.

And I have zero interest.

"All yours," I tell Alec.

He grunts out a dry laugh. "She only has eyes for you, I'm afraid."

My attention's already back on the brunette at the bar, and I will her to turn around. The way she's sitting sideways in her seat, legs crossed at the knee, head turned away, I can see more thigh than face. While I typically wouldn't complain about the view, I need confirmation that it's not her.

I should let it go. It's *never* her. She's just on my mind because it's September twenty-first.

"The bartender told me you were drinking bourbon," the blonde says when she reaches our table. She offers me the tumbler.

From his post across the room, the bartender gives me a curt nod. His grin says it all. He thinks he did me a favor by sending this woman over. Maybe some nights I would agree, but tonight I'm too distracted by the Ghost of Christmas Past.

"It's Knox bourbon," the blonde says. "I thought you might want to get a taste of how they make it where I come from."

That gets my attention, and I frown as I swivel my gaze back to her. "What?"

"Knox bourbon," she says, her tongue dancing along the rim of her martini glass. "Black label. You'll love it."

I've spent the last ten years steering clear of anything with the Knox name, but if this woman is from the home of Knox bourbon . . .

I take the glass. "Thanks. What's your name?"

"I'm Savannah." She offers a delicate hand, and I shake it briefly and even manage a smile before swirling the bourbon under my nose.

Some people think all bourbon smells the same, but a true connoisseur can smell the difference in every variety. Knox bourbon smells like oak and pear with notes of first love, stolen kisses, and heartache.

"Savannah."

"My friends call me Savvy," she says.

I scan my memory for the name. "You're from Orchid Valley?"

"Well, from Atlanta originally, but I live in the OV now. You know it?"

I open my mouth to explain I lived there briefly in high school, but every word disappears from my mind when the brunette across the room finally turns. Once I see her full profile, the rest of the world falls away.

I'm not imagining things. Dark hair, high cheekbones, lips that can't possibly be as soft as they are in my memory. *Brinley Knox.*

"That's my friend Brinley," Savannah says, following my gaze. "Her parents actually own the Knox distillery in Orchid Valley."

"*The* Brinley Knox," Alec says, and now we're all staring at her. "She's *smoking hot*," he mutters.

I shoot him a look, and he holds up both hands, his face a mask of innocence.

"How do you know Brinley?" Savannah asks him. She turns to me. "Do you know her too?"

As if she senses our attention on her, Brinley turns

5

toward us, and her spine goes rigid. Her lips part, and when she meets my eyes, I can't *breathe*.

I'm already out of my seat and heading her way.

"Marston," Alec calls after me, "are you sure you should—"

"Marston?" Savannah scrambles to keep up with my long strides. She grabs my arm. "You're *Marston Rowe?*"

"Yeah. Now if you'll excuse me . . ."

She tries to hold me tighter, but I shrug off her touch, not taking my eyes off Brinley. *Fuck me. It's really her.* I keep my gaze locked on those blue eyes with every step closer, oblivious to everyone around me.

The sight of her after all these years is both a punch to the gut and a balm to old wounds. This is the bitter and the sweet. This is the freefall into memories of first love and regrets of things left unsaid.

When I step up to the bar beside her, her eyes are all over my face, my chest, and down to my waist before slowly roaming back up. It's as if she needs to catalog every inch of me to convince herself I'm real—or maybe that's what I want to believe, and she's really sitting there wishing me away. "Marston?"

"Brinley." Her name is a hushed whisper off my lips. The way you speak in church or after witnessing a miracle. Because damn. *It's really her.*

She hurt me in a way I never thought anyone could. I was too young and too proud to fight for what we had, so I let her go. I walked away, even when every part of me wanted to hold on. But now, taking in her big eyes and that soft skin, staring at those lips I spent hours worshipping . . . I'd swallow all my pride if it came with a taste of her.

But Brinley's gaze isn't like her friend's. Savannah was a

woman on a mission, ready to seduce and be seduced, whereas Brinley's appraisal is all about checking in on an old friend.

I allow myself an extra beat to take in the tan skin of her thigh, the low back of her dress, and her red-bottomed fuck-me heels.

"Brinley, look who I found." Savannah's practically panting as she smacks a hand on my shoulder. "I'd like to take a moment to make it clear I had no idea who he was when I went over there."

Brinley blinks away from me and smirks at her friend. "*Marston* was the . . ."

"The man candy I was ogling? Clearly!" Savannah shrugs and gives me a quick once-over. "I mean, can you *blame* me?"

Brinley gapes at her friend. "Savvy!"

Savannah chuckles and then backs away. "I think I'll go chat with Marston's buddy and give you two time to play catch-up."

The way Brinley bites her lip makes me think she's not sure this is the best plan, but her friend slips away before she can object. I don't miss her hard swallow as she turns her attention back to me. "If I'd known *you* were the one she'd set out to seduce . . ." I wait, wanting the rest of that thought, but she doesn't finish. "You look good." She laughs awkwardly. "As Savvy already established."

"So do you." My gaze dips to take her in again. "More beautiful than ever."

Her cheeks tinge red. Brinley Knox, only living heir to the Knox bourbon empire, has the world thrown at her feet, but she still blushes at compliments from the delinquent orphan who stole her first kiss. "Thank you."

7

"Happy birthday."

Her eyes widen, as if she didn't expect me to remember, which is . . . ridiculous. This is more than her birthday. It's *our* day. It's the day everything began for us. "Savvy surprised me with a trip to Vegas. We're only here for the weekend, but it's more than I've done in forever. She says I work too much, which is really code for me being boring, and she insisted . . ." She picks up her drink and takes a generous sip. "I'm rambling."

"I don't mind." The words come out rough and reveal too much. Like how glad I am to see her. Like how much I've missed her.

She looks around. "I'd invite you to have a seat, but this place is packed."

"You can come to my table. We reserved it, so it's ours for the night."

Brinley scans the room until she finds Savannah sitting with Alec in our semicircular booth in the corner. Alec's already gotten her a fresh martini, and as we watch, he whispers something in her ear that makes her laugh. "Is it just you and your friend, or . . . ?"

Another sentence I'd love for her to finish. Does she want to know if I'm here with a date? Does she wonder if I found love again after I walked away from ours? I've wondered the same about her a thousand times, but I always stopped myself from looking her up. Why pick at old scars?

But now that she's in front of me, I can't help myself. I inspect her left hand, fixated on that naked ring finger. It doesn't mean anything. Just because she's not wearing a ring doesn't mean she's not involved with someone. And it's not like one Vegas run-in means we get a second chance.

8

This doesn't change anything.

She slides off the stool, shaking her head as she hitches her purse over her shoulder. She's a few inches taller in those heels but still barely reaches my chin. "This is crazy. You don't owe me any answers, and no one would blame you if you hated my guts."

"Wait." I reach out to grab her by the wrist, but I remember myself and only let my fingers skim the delicate bones there. "Where are you going?"

She shrugs. "To tell Savvy I'm leaving, then to the room to have a meltdown and maybe room service?"

"Do you mind if I join you?"

She laughs. "For the room service or the meltdown?"

I exhale slowly. The reunion I fantasized about definitely didn't involve her having a meltdown at the sight of me, but hell—I'm not feeling particularly steady myself. "Either? Both?" I take a chance and step closer but shove my hands in my pockets to keep myself from touching her. The decade between us doesn't change the fact that she pushed me away. "It's been too long, and if I'm not going to see you again for another ten years, there's no way a couple of minutes standing at a bar will be enough."

The look in her eyes as she considers this undoes something in me. Is that hope? Is it longing? Because there's nothing in the energy snapping between us that makes me believe she wants me to walk away.

I swallow. "I'm not here with anyone else. Even if I were, I think we both know I'm enough of an ass that I'd choose to spend my night with you instead."

She scoffs, and she probably thinks I'm blowing smoke and trying to charm her, but every word is true.

"I have an idea." I watch her carefully. "If you can put

off the meltdown for a few hours, I can take care of feeding you. What if we share some drinks, catch up a little, and do that whole reminiscing thing without any of the awkwardness I'm pretty sure we're supposed to be feeling right now?"

She drags her bottom lip between her teeth in a gesture I've replayed in my memories a million times—Brinley in my arms, my fingers threaded through her dark hair, her eyes on mine as I lean in to sample what she's tasting. "What if I just want to sit across from you and pretend you never left?" That hits me like a blow to the gut. I left. It's true. But only because she begged me to. She must see something in my face at that, because she flinches and drops her gaze to the floor. "Sorry. That's not fair."

When she keeps her head bowed, I take her hand and skim my thumb across her knuckles. The contact is like a jolt of adrenaline through my system. *Can't you feel that?* I want to ask, but when she looks up and meets my eyes, I know she does. "Tonight can be whatever you want it to be," I say. *Just let it be with me.* "You make the rules."

She hesitates a beat, then smiles. "Okay then, let's go to your table." Pink blooms on her cheeks as if she's just agreed to spend the night in bed with me, and I have to physically stop my thoughts from going down that track of *what if.*

I mocked Alec mercilessly for reserving this table—it cost a small fortune—but as I lead Brinley through the packed room, I'm fucking grateful we have it. This all feels like a dream, and I'm afraid if I let Brinley out of my sight, I'll wake up and never see her again.

"Brinley!" Savannah says when we reach the table. She and Alec are on one side of the booth, and she's practically in his lap. "This is Alec Hayes, Marston's business partner and future father of my children."

I arch a brow at Alec. "You move fast, brother."

Alec smirks. "She said she wanted her kids to have eyes like mine, so I offered her my DNA."

I slide in the side opposite them. "Totally reasonable," I deadpan.

"You two have some sort of consulting firm, right?" Brinley asks, looking between us as she scoots in beside me. "You come in when resorts are in trouble and get them back on track?"

"Something like that." I fight back a smile. I might've refrained from looking up Brinley, but it seems she's kept tabs on me. I don't hate that. "Alec and I are working on a project at a spa off the Strip."

Savannah wrinkles her nose in my direction. "Sorry about earlier. I never would've come on to you if I'd known who you were. I wouldn't do that to Brin."

Brinley scowls. "How many of those have you had?" she asks, pointing to Savannah's glass.

Savannah shrugs. "Enough that my tongue's loosened a little, but not so many that I've lost control of it entirely. *You* need to catch up."

Brinley takes a small sip of her drink. "I'll pace myself. Thanks."

Savannah and Alec turn back to each other, returning to their conversation.

I settle into the booth and study Brinley. "You moved back to Orchid Valley after you finished college." It's not a question. Even if I hadn't put as much together from Savannah's introduction, I know Brinley well enough to know it's true. Or *knew* her . . . Can you know someone when you haven't spoken to them for ten years?

"I always planned to. Even with its faults, it really is the only place I'd want to raise a family."

Family. The word makes me bristle, but it doesn't come as a surprise. Brinley always wanted to be a mom, to raise half a dozen rug rats and let them wreak havoc on her parents' immaculate mansion. The image would make me smile if it didn't exclude me so completely. "And is that what you're doing there?" I shift my focus to that naked ring finger again. "Being the perfect wife and mother?"

"I'm not the perfect anything." She drains the rest of her martini and doesn't meet my eyes, focusing instead across the packed bar. "I need to run to the ladies' room."

I'm a dick. "Sorry. I didn't mean . . ."

"It's not that." She settles her glass on the table and gives me a tight smile as Savannah looks up and meets her gaze. "I'm fine. Really."

Savannah turns to Alec. "I'll be right back. Don't go anywhere."

My friend gives her his widest smile and slowly looks her over. "I wouldn't dare. Want another drink if the server comes around?"

She beams as she climbs out of the booth. "Of course! Get my girl and me each another lemon drop martini."

Brinley opens her mouth, and I think she's going to object, but instead she says, "If you don't mind."

Savannah gives Alec an air kiss then slides her arm through Brinley's as they walk toward the bathroom.

"So that's Brinley Knox," Alec says. He scans my face, and I know he's looking for shock or panic or some shit. "You okay?"

"I'm fine." *I'm a fucking liar.*

"You think she's intentionally evading the question about her marital status, or . . .?"

Right. *That.* "I'm not sure." But I intend to find out.

"Assuming she's single . . . you two just gonna pick up where you left off?"

Since we "left off" with Brinley pushing me away, I hope not, but I shrug.

Alec grunts. "Tone it down, Mars. You're way too vocal about your emotions."

"Shut the fuck up." I take a sip of my bourbon. Alec Hayes knows more about my life pre-college than anyone besides Aunt Lori, but that doesn't mean I'm going to spill my guts right now. "I'm still trying to figure out if this is really happening."

"It's happening." He pauses a beat, his gaze glued to the hall where the girls disappeared. "If you need me to keep the friend busy tonight, I can do that."

"Real fucking selfless of you."

Alec grins. "I'm giving like that." That grin falls away as he studies me. "I see that brain of yours working overtime. Dial back the introspection and enjoy yourself."

"That could be a recipe for disaster," I mutter, but it doesn't matter. Even if spending the night with Brinley is a terrible idea, I know I'll take every second she'll give me.

He takes a pull of his vodka tonic and sighs. "Consider it a gift—one night in Vegas with the love of your life."

"You're making a lot of assumptions there, Hayes."

"I'm not assuming shit. You'd have to be blind to miss the way she looks at you. And you've told me more than once how you feel about her."

"No, you're assuming I'll only get one night."

Alec snorts. "I have complete confidence that you'll get your night *and* turn it into whatever you want." He pauses a beat. "Have you thought about this, though? She kind of fucked you up, dude. Do you really want to ask for seconds?"

My emotions are a mess of regret and longing and hope. I can barely remember the anger I felt those first few years after she pushed me away. I want Brinley. If there was any doubt about it in my mind before, it vanished the moment I laid eyes on her. "I want it all."

I drain my drink. Bourbon isn't meant to be guzzled like a cheap beer, but I'm wound so tight and I just want to enjoy this night—this *chance*. One more chance with Brinley. Alec is right. It's a gift—one I never dared ask for.

CHAPTER TWO

MARSTON

September 21st, before

"When you're done scrubbing those pans, come find me in the dining room," Aunt Lori says. "I'll need your help to set up for tomorrow's breakfast."

I nod, not bothering to look at her. I'm half afraid she's going to renege on her promise to pay me for tonight. Ten dollars an hour to help cook and wash dishes for some spoiled teenager's fancy birthday party? It seems too good to be true. But even if she breaks her promise, it's not like I had anything better to do with myself.

I moved to Orchid Valley a week ago. I'd been living on my own in Atlanta. It was fine at first—better than being stuck with my mom and her carousel of bad boyfriends. But then I didn't make rent one month and was short again the next and found myself sleeping in the park. It was temporary. I just needed to save up enough for a room. Maybe I could have done it, but I didn't have a place to wash my clothes, and I couldn't use my car because I couldn't afford gas, so I lost my job. Then a reckless, desperate idea turned into flashing red and blue lights and a breaking and entering charge.

It wasn't Mom but Aunt Lori who got the lawyer to make the judge go easy on me. She turned Mom's addiction issues into a massive sob story. I hate pity, but it worked. A couple of days later, per court orders, I moved sixty minutes north to Lori's little place in Orchid Valley. And on Monday, per court orders, I'll attend my senior year of high school here with a bunch of rich kids. Not that I'm complaining about that—I know Lori saved my ass—but if the party happening down the hall is any indication, Orchid Valley is crawling with entitled, preppy-ass teenagers.

"Leave me alone!" someone shrieks from the hall, and I look up just in time to see a ball of fluffy pink tulle barreling through the double doors and into the kitchen. She turns around and gives me a shaky smile. "Do you mind if I hide in here for a minute?" Tears stream down her face, leaving sooty trails of mascara in their wake.

Shrugging, I drag my gaze off the girl in the ridiculous dress and focus on scrubbing the pan in front of me. "Don't care," I mutter. *Scrub, scrub, scrub.*

I'm aware of her walking toward me, but I don't look up. I'm good at being invisible, and that's all I want to be right now.

"I'm Brinley Knox. What's your name?"

Brinley Knox, the guest of honor. Funny that she asked if she could stay. This is her house, after all.

I feel her gaze on me and realize she's waiting for an answer. "Marston." I tense, waiting for her next remark. I get all sorts of shit about my name.

Brinley sniffles, and despite myself, I'm aware of her eyes on me, of every move she makes to close the distance between us. "Are you new here? I don't think I've seen you on staff before."

Staff. Her family has *staff*. Of course they do. They live in a freaking mansion and are throwing their daughter a sixteenth birthday party fancier than most people's weddings.

"I'm new." I rinse the pan and set it in the rack to dry before pulling the drain on the soapy water. I grab a towel and dry my hands. "Why are you crying?" I can't imagine ever crying if I lived in a house like this. But what do I know? Maybe her dad hits her. My mom always said dysfunctional doesn't have an income bracket.

She pulls her bottom lip between her teeth, smudging her bubblegum-pink lipstick. "It's my birthday," she says, as if that's any sort of explanation.

"Shouldn't that make you happy? It's your birthday, and your parents threw you this big party." The sneer I intended to wrap around my words is nowhere in sight. Whatever her problems are, they're real to her. I can't believe I feel sorry for the spoiled little rich girl.

"My boyfriend broke up with me. At my party." Her bottom lip trembles. When she meets my eyes, something hits me. She's *pretty* underneath that makeup and ridiculous dress. Really fucking pretty. Her dark hair is pinned in curls on top of her head tonight, but I bet it's long and soft when it's down, and her blue eyes . . . Well, even full of tears, those eyes are like a sucker punch to the gut. "He said I'm uptight, and he doesn't want to be with a girl who makes him wait for a kiss when we should already be doing . . . *other* things."

Jesus. "What a douchebag."

"You know what's funny? I was going to let him kiss me tonight. I've been looking forward to it all week, but I don't think he would have cared if I had."

I toss my towel on the counter and lift my chin in the direction of the party. "Point him out to me. I'll teach him a lesson." Only assholes try to manipulate girls into sex before they're ready.

Her watery eyes go wide for a beat before she smiles, and *damn* . . . That smile. She's more than pretty. She's take-me-by-the-nuts-and-own-me gorgeous. "You'd beat up *Roman Humphries* for breaking the heart of some girl you just met?"

She says his name like it's supposed to mean something to me, but I shrug. "Sounds like someone needs to."

She looks me over slowly as if she's seeing me for the first time. The black oxford and matching dress pants Aunt Lori said I had to wear tonight are new and easily the fanciest clothes I've ever owned. This girl probably doesn't wear anything from Target, and she sure as hell doesn't know what it's like to live on the streets. I feel my past written on every inch of my skin. Self-consciousness pricks at the back of my neck. "Marston, you said? You're the boy who moved in with Ms. Lori. You're on probation or something?"

I lift my chin. "What do you know about it?"

She treats me to another one of those soul-owning

smiles, and my stomach hitches. "Only that you're the most interesting boy in this town. Not that there's much competition." Her fluffy tulle skirt sweeps the floor as she closes the distance between us. She doesn't stop until she's a foot away, craning her neck to look up at me. She's close enough that I could wipe the smudges of makeup from her cheeks. Close enough to kiss. "You're tall."

I bite back a laugh. "You're short." And without realizing it, I'm cupping her face in my hands and wiping away the tear tracks. She gasps in surprise, and I drop my hands. "Sorry. You had . . . makeup or whatever. From crying."

"Oh. It's okay." She gives me a shy, crooked smile.

Really fucking pretty and really fucking off-limits, Marston. "You should get back to your party."

"Because you need to get back to work?" she asks, looking at me again.

Because I want to kiss you. Because I think you'd let me. Because I have no business kissing a girl who lives in a mansion *and has* staff.

But I don't say any of that. Instead, I say, "So you can tell Roman to get the hell out of your house."

She giggles, and I don't know if it's because she's scandalized by my use of the word "hell" or if she's maybe feeling the same contact high from being close to me as I'm getting from her. "My parents would kill me. *A good hostess takes disappointment with grace*," she says, clearly parroting a lesson she's been reminded of repeatedly.

"Then don't kick him out. Go out there and make it clear you don't need him."

She skims her fingertips across my knuckles before taking my hand. "Come with me somewhere?"

I should say no. But I couldn't refuse her, even if I wanted to.

Brinley leads me to the servants' stairs at the back of the kitchen. The stairwell is so narrow and her skirt is so big that I have to walk up behind her, but she never lets go of my hand.

We've climbed two flights when she opens a door and pulls me through it and down a dark, narrow hall.

"Where are we going?" I ask, because I should care. Because I shouldn't be willing to follow her anywhere.

Turning, she puts her finger to her lips and winks before pushing open a door I didn't even see. She leads me into a fancy room with the biggest piano I've ever seen. Tall bookcases line the three walls, and a balcony overlooks the ballroom below. Music, laughter, and conversation float up to us.

"Should I be here?" I whisper, even as she pulls me closer to the railing.

"If anyone catches us, I'll tell them I wanted you to set up refreshments for me and my friends." She gives a final tug on my hand before dropping it and turning to look out at her party. "When I was a little girl and my parents had parties, I'd sneak out of bed and watch them from up here."

"They didn't see you?"

She shakes her head. "No, not with the way the lights in the ballroom are. Mom said it was designed that way by my grandmother so she could spy on her guests."

With that bit of reassurance, I take the last step to the railing and look down at the party below.

The biggest party I ever went to was Aunt Lori's wedding when I was five or six. I remember thinking her husband, a

20

schoolteacher, must've been spectacularly rich to afford to feed fifty people for dinner. But Brinley's birthday party is at least three times that big, and everyone in the ballroom below is dressed in formal gowns and tuxedos. It doesn't look real. It looks like something from TV, and it's the perfect reminder that I belong back in the kitchen, not here with Brinley.

She growls softly, and I arch a brow in question. "See that?" she asks. She points to the dance floor, where teenagers and adults alike sway to Norah Jones's "Come Away with Me."

"Dancing?" I ask.

"No, the guy in the white tux eating the face off the girl in red."

The white tux makes it easier to single out the couple in question. They're on the dance floor, but dancing seems secondary to making out.

"That's Roman," she says. "Jerk couldn't even wait until after my party before moving on."

Roman's hands move up and down the girl's back before settling on her butt. "Total ass," I agree. "You can't tell me you really want to be with a guy like that."

"I . . ." She shrugs. "I guess I thought I did, but maybe for the wrong reasons?"

"What were those?"

She cuts her eyes away from me, as if she knows I won't like the answer. "My parents are friends with his parents. He's . . . a good match, as my parents would say."

"I can't pretend I know what it's like to have that kind of pressure. The only thing my mom expected of me was for me to leave the house when she had her guys over and that I didn't call the cops when she was dealing." As soon as

I see the sorrow in her gaze, I regret saying it. "Don't look at me like that."

"Like what?"

"Like you pity me. We all have bullshit in our lives. Mine's just a little less shiny than yours."

"I don't pity you." She gives a shaky smile. "If anything, I envy you."

I scoff. "Yeah, right."

"You know what I see when I look at you? *Freedom*. I'll never have that, not as long as I'm a Knox."

I want to argue that being on probation hardly makes me the icon of freedom, but I get what she's saying. There are expectations that come with this kind of money. More money, more problems or whatever. "That's pretty depressing."

She shrugs. "My parents are pretty depressing." She steps closer, and the back of her hand brushes mine. I hold my breath and tamp down the impulse to thread my fingers with hers. I have no business touching a girl like this.

Suddenly, the music goes quiet, and everyone turns to the ballroom entrance, where a frail girl with long red hair walks into the room. She's wearing a light blue version of Brinley's dress, and when she lifts her hand and waves like some sort of pageant queen, the room erupts in applause.

"Who's that?" I ask Brinley.

"My sister, Brittany," she says softly.

I frown. "Is it her birthday too or something?"

"No. But she . . ." She swallows. "She's been sick. It's kind of a big deal that she's even home right now, and a bigger deal that she's out of bed. She's spent more time in the hospital than out of it this year."

"I'm so sorry."

"Me too." There's more than *sorry* there in the anguished lines of her face—some complexity of emotion I can't read and don't dare try to interpret. "We're only eleven months apart, and we used to be best friends. People thought we were twins."

I look down at the redhead and arch a brow at Brinley. "Even with the hair?"

"That's a wig. She lost her hair after the chemo."

My neck and cheeks burn. "Oh, shit. I'm sorry." *I'm such an idiot.*

"She handled it like a champ. That's how she does everything. Knoxes keep their chins up."

Her fake smile draws my attention to something she said. "You . . . *used to be* best friends? You aren't still?"

She shakes her head. "I love her more than anyone, but she pushed me away after this last recurrence. It makes sense. On some level, she resents me. I get to live the life she thought she'd live, and I still get to have all the experiences she was supposed to have right alongside me."

That seems unfair. "But that's not your fault. Surely she knows that."

"Yeah. Of course, but it's normal. She's not trying to be cruel. She's just human."

"That's an awfully mature way to look at it."

There's something in her eyes when she looks at me—not quite a vacancy but a distant pain, as if this is something she's pushed way down. "There's no point in being immature about it. It wouldn't fix anything."

We both watch the party below as Roman pulls Brinley's sister onto the dance floor and spins her around in his arms.

"You think she knows he broke up with you?" I ask.

"Yes," she says, but she doesn't explain how. Maybe she

talked to her sister before she hid in the kitchen. Maybe her sister was the one she told to leave her alone.

"Does he have no shame? Dancing with your sister at your party, right after breaking your heart?"

She shakes her head. "No one will ever judge you for showing kindness to a dying girl."

What about showing kindness to you? "You should probably get back to your party."

She turns away from the crowd below and studies me for a long beat. Her cheeks are flushed and there's something almost lonely in her eyes. "I'd rather not."

My phone buzzes from inside my pocket. Since this is a brand-new phone and the only one who has the number is Aunt Lori, I know it's a text from her before I look.

Lori: Where are you? I need you in the dining
   room.

"You need to go?"

I nod as I type back a reply, letting Aunt Lori know I'm on my way. "Duty calls." I hesitate. "You feel better?"

Brinley releases a ragged breath. "Actually, I do. It wasn't the birthday I planned, but maybe this is all for the best."

"What did you plan?" It's a dumb question. Obviously, she planned to enjoy the party with her boyfriend, but I'm stalling now. I don't want to leave her.

Her gaze settles on my mouth when she says, "I thought I'd get my first kiss tonight."

Her *first* kiss? I won't be eighteen for a couple more months but . . . well, kissing is kiddie stuff at this point. Not that I had the best role models. But those blue eyes are still on my mouth. I thought I knew hunger when I was on the streets, but I've never felt anything like this need to kiss her. "Judging from the way he was kissing the girl in red, I think you would've been disappointed anyway."

"Maybe," she whispers.

This time when her gaze dips to my mouth, I let my own go to hers—to the smudged bubblegum-pink lipstick, to her soft, plump bottom lip. I think of my aunt talking to me after my hearing telling me that I need to learn my place, that I'll come to understand folks like us have to make do with less, that I can't take things just because I want them, and that life doesn't work like that. But in this moment, it does. I want to take this kiss, despite who I am and where I come from.

I move slowly as I lower my mouth to hers, giving her a chance to pull away. She doesn't. And maybe part of me knows she wants this kiss for all the wrong reasons, that I'm some tale she'll tell her spoiled girlfriends at parties—the night she kissed the bad boy from the wrong side of the tracks.

But I don't care enough to let that stop me, and when I lower my mouth to hers, I don't care about anything at all. Not anything but this. *This kiss. This moment.* The feel of her soft lips under mine and her sweet little exhale that feels a lot like relief.

I bring my hand to her jaw, and she opens to me with a gasp and threads her fingers through my hair.

She doesn't taste like bubblegum. She tastes like the fruit punch and champagne, sweet and heady. Intoxicating. And she doesn't kiss like she's looking for a story to tell. She kisses me like she never wants to stop—as if she wants to stay here in my arms all night. It makes me feel like Superman, but I have to end this moment.

Her eyes stay closed for a long beat. I take advantage of the moment to study her face, the sooty smudge of her lashes on her flushed cheeks, the dark curls my clumsy hands pulled free, the perfectly smooth skin where her shoulder meets her neck.

I want to kiss her there.

The thought hits me so strongly that I back away before I can give in to it. I shouldn't be here with her. I shouldn't be doing this. But I won't regret one second. "Good night, Brinley," I whisper, forcing myself to back away another step, even as every instinct begs me to stay close.

She opens her eyes slowly, bringing her fingertips to her lips as if she wants to hold the memory of the kiss there. "Thank you, Marston."

I crack a rare smile. Brinley Knox, spoiled little rich girl, just thanked this delinquent punk for kissing her. This night has certainly taken an unexpected turn. "My pleasure."

"Can . . . can I see you again?"

I might've been tempted if she hadn't looked over my shoulder to make sure no one was here before asking. That one little glance is all the reminder I need of who I am and where I stand. "Better you don't."

"Why?"

I arch a brow. "Because I'm not like him." I shift my gaze toward the balcony and the idiot ex below. "If you were mine, I'd never let you go."

CHAPTER THREE

BRINLEY

Present day

*M*arston Rowe still makes my insides flutter when he looks at me. He still makes my pulse buzz and my imagination run wild.

It's easy to tell yourself you've exaggerated the effect someone has on you. We do that with our memories— smooth them, finesse them, make people into two-dimensional versions of themselves. I've watched my parents do this with my sister until their memories of her were hardly recognizable to me. Instead of the kind, joyful, but humanly flawed girl she was, they remember a saint, a perfect daughter, and then criticize me for my failure to measure up to that fictional version of her.

In some ways, I thought I did that with Marston. Maybe a single touch from him *didn't* make my heart beat faster. Maybe seeing him again *wouldn't* make me want to turn back time. But he's everything I remember, validating every instinct that had me seeking him out and making all my reasons for not doing it sooner weigh heavily on my mind.

I push into the bathroom in front of Savvy, rushing past women touching up their makeup at the long counter and the ones washing their hands at the sinks. I race into the first open stall I see, and my heel snaps under my foot.

"Shit!" Before Savvy can say or do anything, I shut the door and throw the lock behind me.

"Brinley? Are you okay?"

I lean my forehead on the cool metal stall, my breaths short and jagged. "Fine. I just need a minute." I dig through my purse and find the bottle I'm looking for. If any moment called for anxiety meds, this is it. I clutch the bottle in my hand.

"Sweetie," Savvy says softly. Under the door, her black heels come into view. I can imagine her standing there, one hand on the stall, one clutching the tight muscles at the base of her neck, worry forming three little lines between her brows. "Talk to me."

"What did I think was going to happen?" I'm asking myself more than her. "What was I thinking?"

"I don't know, honey. What are you talking about? Your shoe?"

I laugh, but it comes out high-pitched. "Marston. Fuck the shoes."

"Did something happen while you two were at the bar? Did he say something that upset you? Do you want to leave?"

"No!" I take a breath. *Calm the fuck down, Brinley.* "I mean, with us running into each other. I thought this was what I wanted, but I'm totally unprepared for everything I'm feeling." I shove the pills back into my purse. I know they'd help, but they make me sleepy, and even as panicked as I'm feeling, I don't want to miss the little time I get with Marston.

"How were you supposed to know we'd run into him? You can't prepare for that."

I unlatch the door and let it swing open. "It wasn't a coincidence. I knew he'd be here."

She frowns. "How?"

I look around the bathroom and realize we're catching the attention of the women around us. While they're strangers who probably don't care about my drama beyond a passing curiosity, I'm a private person and hate the idea of them listening. "It doesn't matter how, but let's just say if fate brought us together tonight, I nudged it along."

Savvy cocks her head to the side and studies me. "You still have feelings for him."

"Of course I do. Does anyone really get over their first love?"

Her smile is gentle, but she nods. "Yeah. Yeah, sweetie, most people do."

Grimacing, I turn and lean against the side of the stall. "What am I doing?"

"Panicking in a Las Vegas club bathroom while a sexy-as-sin man waits for you at his private table. A sexy man, by the way, who looks as if he'd like to read your skin like braille. With his tongue."

I cut my eyes to her, scowling. "That's rather specific."

She shrugs. "You asked." She looks around then steps

29

into the stall with me, pulling the door shut behind her and throwing the lock. "You know he's probably sitting there thinking you have a husband back home. The way you exited that conversation was conspicuous as hell."

I wince. "I know. I wasn't ready to talk about Cami, and I panicked."

"Is this about her? Or is it about Julian?"

Neither. Both? I chew on my bottom lip because I can't deny that Julian's proposition is what had me looking up Marston to begin with. "I don't want to make a terrible mistake."

"Do you hear yourself? That's your red flag. Tell Julian thanks, but no thanks." She pulls her phone from her purse. "Want me to do it? I can text him now."

My eyes flick up to meet hers. "I meant tonight. With Marston. I wanted to see him, but being this close to him makes me feel like my world has spun off its axis—or like someone has yanked the reins to my future out of my hands."

"Would that be so terrible? Maybe you need a break. You work so damn hard and do everything for everyone else. Take tonight—just one night—to really enjoy yourself."

"I'm not sure a wild night of sex with my ex will solve any of my problems."

"It can't hurt." She tosses her long hair over her shoulder and smirks. "I'd also like to point out that I said nothing about sex. That was all you."

I ignore this. "I won't apologize for caring about what happens to The Orchid and to everyone who works there."

"We'll all manage." She puts a hand on each of my shoulders and squeezes gently. "Quit trying to fix everything. Trust that sometimes things work out, and even when they don't, the sun still rises. These shoulders carry enough without piling on everyone else's problems."

I drag in a deep breath and exhale slowly. My life might feel like it's on the precipice of disaster, but at least I have the *best* friends.

Savvy must take my deep breath as a sign that I'm pulling it together, because she smiles. "When you nudged fate along, what were you hoping for?"

"I was hoping seeing him would make it easier to decide what happens next." I shake my head. "I think it might just be making it harder, though."

She pulls me into a hug and whispers, "The night's not over yet."

WHEN WE WALK BACK to the table—or hobble, in my case —Alec and Marston haven't just gotten us drinks. They've ordered food—a *lot* of food. Soft pretzels, sushi rolls, and a charcuterie board fill the table. I know Marston said he'd feed me, but I didn't expect a buffet.

"I wasn't sure what you liked," Marston says. "There are other options if nothing here appeals to you. This was just what they could bring out right away."

Savvy looks at me and raises a brow. I'm not a mind reader, but I don't have to be to know what she's thinking: *Fuck that man silly.*

"I'm going to dance. You drink," she says. She takes Alec's hand and tugs him out of the booth. "Come on, pretty boy. I don't like dancing alone." As she saunters away, she throws a wink over her shoulder.

My heart swells. Some people are given a family to care

for and protect them by virtue of being born. The rest of us have to find our family in the friends who'd do more for us than our blood relatives ever would, and I thank God for mine every day. *We make our own family.* Those words came from my sister weeks before she died. They were both advice and a promise to the sister she was leaving behind.

With the other side of the semicircular booth empty, it'd be awkward to sit thigh to thigh with Marston now, so I slide into the booth opposite him and take a plate with shaking hands. I've been so nervous about tonight—hoping my plan would work and terrified that it might—that I've barely eaten all day. "Thank you for the food. You really didn't have to get all this."

He shrugs. "Alec gets cranky if he doesn't eat regularly, so the food really benefits all of us."

"When did you two meet?" I ask around a bite of pretzel.

"College. We interned for the same company junior year."

I look toward the mass of teeming bodies on the dance floor but can't spot him or my friend. "Can I trust him to be good to Savvy?"

"Without a doubt," he says solemnly. "I wouldn't have let her sit with him to begin with if I didn't think so."

I love that he takes the question seriously rather than mocking my protective instincts. "I appreciate that."

"I'm sorry if I upset you when I asked about your life," Marston says. "All the times I've thought of you, it never occurred to me that you'd still be single. I just assumed you'd be pregnant with a third kid by now. Married to . . ."

Somebody my parents approve of. He doesn't have to say it.

Before Marston Rowe blew through my life like a Georgia storm in springtime, that was exactly where I was headed.

He swallows. "Anyway, I'm sorry about how I asked. Ten years later, and the idea of you waking up next to someone else kind of turns me into a jealous prick."

My eyes widen at that—the idea that he cares enough to be jealous after all this time. "I'm not married." I let out a long breath at the pang of guilt that slices through me. Would he forgive me if he knew about Cami? Would he understand? "What about you? Did you ever find someone?" I already knew from internet stalking that he's never married, but that doesn't mean there wasn't someone special along the way.

"Oh, hell no. No one would want to put up with me." His smile is grim and does little to soften this declaration. He shrugs. "I travel all the time and work too much."

"A lot of people travel and work a lot."

"True." He swirls the amber liquid in his glass. "I guess I've never met someone who made me want to trade in my life for marriage and kids."

It's so hard to imagine that. Every memory I have of Marston is filled with his unconditional affection and protective and loving disposition. It was easy to imagine him with a family of his own. "Once, for a little bit, you wanted those things."

"Only with you," he says, his voice low and rough.

My laugh is half crazed. "I don't know if I've had enough to drink to return that kind of honesty."

He chuckles, then murmurs into his bourbon, "Me neither."

I take a sip of my fresh martini and resist the urge to guzzle it, but no amount of alcohol can compete with the buzz from those words. *Only with you.* "I can't believe I'm really sitting here."

Marston's chest swells as he draws in a deep breath. "I'm a little stunned myself. What are the chances?"

Our meeting would've been statistically improbable, but like I told Savvy, I helped the odds. She's the one who insisted we come to Vegas to celebrate my birthday, but I'm the one who planted the seed.

Last month I did a web search for Marston on a whim—something I don't allow myself to do more than a couple of times a year—and I saw that his consulting firm was over-hauling a Vegas resort and the grand reopening was scheduled for my birthday. I mentioned in passing that I wished I was the kind of girl who ran away to Vegas for her birthday, and Savvy took it from there. After that, it was as simple as a little social media stalking to see which Vegas clubs Marston frequented on prior trips to Vegas and . . . voila! "Coincidental" run-in.

"I mean more than running into you," I say. "I mean that I'm surprised you even want to sit here with me." Because when I last saw him ten years ago, I didn't just push him away—I shoved as hard as I could. The pain of losing my sister made me crueler than I thought possible, and the desperation of my grief and guilt fooled me into believing that if I cut him out of my life, I might be able to salvage my disintegrating family.

"I want to sit here with you," he says, piling food on his own plate. "Even if I didn't realize how much until I spotted you across the bar."

Emotion clogs my throat, but I swallow it down with more vodka. We eat in companionable silence for a few minutes, and I feel the alcohol work through me, loosening my muscles and locking away my worries for another time.

"I'm sure your parents are glad you're in Orchid Valley," he says, finally breaking the silence.

"They don't live there anymore, actually." I smile, ungrateful daughter that I am. "Too many memories, I guess? Dad always wanted to retire in Florida, and he finally talked Mom into it, so they sold the house and he spends his days golfing while she redecorates their place in Boca Raton."

He nods as if this isn't a surprise. It shouldn't be. My parents are a perfect fit in the world of Boca Raton socialites. "So, tell me what I've missed. No Mr. Perfect yet, but you went to college? And . . . let me guess, you're teaching now?"

I shake my head. "Not exactly. I ended up majoring in business so my dad would pay for school."

He winces. "Some things never change."

I know he doesn't mean it as a barb, but it burrows just beneath my skin anyway, festering there. I pick at a piece of sushi. "I guess not."

"You're working for him now?"

"No." And this is something I can be proud of. "I manage a day spa on the lake. It's called The Orchid."

His face lights up, and warmth spreads through me at the pride in his eyes. "A spa, huh? I might know a little bit about that line of work. You like it?"

"It's nothing as big as the places that hire you, but I love it." My words come out a little rough. "The Orchid is a space for women to relax—to treat themselves and be taken care of, because they spend so much of their lives treating and taking care of others. It's a place of luxury for those who can afford it, but when I came in, I decided every woman deserved a taste of that. So we also offer free yoga classes weekly and encourage the community to attend. Every quarter, we offer a series of free meditation classes. We also do wine tastings and girls' nights, and the only expense there is any food you buy or wine you want to take home. It's been a hit, and these community outreach efforts have improved profit margins rather than reducing them, like the owner's sons swore it would."

"Only you could find the intersection of good business practice and civic duty. It's perfect. They should interview you for the commercial."

"I don't mean to sound like a sales pitch. I just truly love it, and I love the people I work with and what we offer to the community."

"If half these places we work for had someone with your passion at the helm, they wouldn't need us at all."

I duck my head, blushing. He has no way of knowing how much that means to me. "Thank you."

I consider telling him the rest—that the owner is selling, and I want her to sell it to me. She's given me until next June before she searches for another buyer, but the bank won't give me the loan I need.

But that's all content under the heading of *Reasons I Shouldn't Be Here with Him*, so I say none of it and instead stare into my drink.

"What are you thinking?" he asks.

I slip off my heels under the table and lift the broken one up for him to see. "I'm wishing I hadn't tried to run in ten-year-old shoes. I wanted to cut loose this weekend, but dancing barefoot in a Vegas nightclub is on the other side of that line."

He laughs. "Fair enough. Let's run back to your room and get another pair."

The only other shoes I brought are the canvas sneakers I wore at the airport. They'd look ridiculous with this dress, but I'm afraid I'll sound shallow if I admit that. Savvy has Barbie feet, so anything she has will be too small. "Maybe I'll go to the boutique down the street and treat myself to a new pair." It'd totally blow my fun-money budget for the month, even with the cash my parents gave me for my birthday, but it *is* my birthday, and . . . I really do want to dance.

Marston picks up his phone, and for a jealous moment I wonder if he's already making plans with someone else, since I'm about to leave. Would it be too clingy to make sure he knows I'm planning on coming back?

Don't be that girl.

I grab my own phone and text Savvy that I'm going to the mall and I'll find her when I get back.

"I already messaged Alec to let him know," Marston says. He slides out of the booth and offers me a hand. "Let's go."

Maybe the vodka's getting to me, because it takes me a beat to put it together. "You bought this table for the night, and you're going to leave to go *shoe shopping* with me?"

"Getting it for the night means it'll still be ours when we get back." He turns his palm up and curls a finger. "Come on."

I slip my broken heel back on and climb out of the booth. "You surprise me," I say, taking an awkward hobble-step forward.

"I do?" He steps behind me, and I release a surprised

shriek as he scoops me into his arms and strides toward the door.

I throw my arms around his neck. "You cannot *carry* me all the way out of this club."

We get a few curious glances, but people turn away just as quickly. As crazy as his behavior seems—as crazy as it'd be anywhere else—apparently it's not gawk worthy in Vegas.

"I think I'm proving that I can," he murmurs in my ear, still weaving through the crowd like carrying me is nothing. He's not even winded. "Maybe we shouldn't bother with the new shoes." His breath tickles my ear. "I like having you this close."

Fireworks detonate in my belly, and I close my eyes and mouth, not trusting myself to answer. He smells different than he used to. The scent of detergent and whatever soap he used as a teen has been replaced with citrus and fresh water, like subtle, expensive cologne. The smell suits him. It's bold without being overbearing, interesting while still smelling clean. I'm intoxicated by it and want to bury my nose in his neck until I can imprint the smell on my memory.

When we reach the sidewalk, he strides straight to a black limo pulled up along the curb and opens the door. "This is us," he says, his voice a little deeper than before. My body brushes against his as he lowers me to my feet, and our eyes meet for a beat, his hands still at my waist.

Kiss me. I press my lips together to trap the wish on my tongue.

The next car in line lays on its horn and tears me out of my trance. I duck into the limo and take a seat.

Marston leans in the front and says something to the driver before sliding into the bench seat beside me.

The food and booze have me feeling loose and relaxed, and instinct has me leaning my head on his shoulder. "I remember when you were so intimidated by my parents' money, but now you ride around in a limo and order people around like you've done it all your life."

His eyes are hooded as he looks down at me. "I'm not the boy you knew in Orchid Valley." He sweeps two knuckles gently across my cheek then tucks a lock of hair behind my ear. "I worked my ass off to put as much distance between him and me as possible."

I swallow hard. "That's too bad."

"I disagree," he says, his voice tight.

I slide a hand to the back of his neck. "It's too bad, because I really liked him."

Marston's dark eyes are fixed on my mouth, and there's so much longing in his gaze that my skin heats.

I've spent ten years convinced any reunion would lead to heartbreak and thinking that he must hate me, that he *should* hate me. But he just carried me in his arms out of a nightclub and is looking down at me now like I'm the most precious thing he's ever seen.

"Is this real?" I ask.

He searches my face and shakes his head. "I'm still trying to figure that out myself."

"I missed you." Then, because I need it like I need air and because I realize he's holding himself back, I kiss him. It's a simple brush of lips that, between any other two people, could be nothing more than friendly affection. But we aren't just any two people. We're Brinley and Marston, and ten years later, it feels like we were never apart. Ten years later, and it feels like he still owns my heart.

He sighs against my lips, then takes control. He turns

39

toward me just enough to cup my face and tilt it toward him, but he doesn't devour me. He sips, tasting me in measured sweeps of his mouth. I shift too, angling toward him and pressing closer until I'm practically in his lap. I'm lost as his gentle exploration turns searching.

Yes, I think, *find me. I've been lost for ten years.*

He guides me to straddle his hips. My skirt slides up then bunches around my waist, and I rock forward and feel the hard length of him.

He groans and pulls away. "We're here."

I blink and look out the window. Sure enough, the driver has brought us to the circle drive at the entrance of an upscale mall.

I straighten and start to back away, but he holds me fast, his grip on my ass firm enough to make me think of a hundred ways we could spend the next hour right here in this limo.

"I missed you too," he says, voice gruff. "I thought leaving was the hardest thing I'd ever have to do, but it turned out staying away was so much harder."

My heart pinches, and I draw in a sharp breath. "Marston—"

He presses a firm kiss to my mouth. "Later. We'll talk later." He moves me off his lap just as the driver opens the door.

CHAPTER FOUR

BRINLEY

October 5th, before

"Come on," Liam says, stroking his hands down my arms. "I'll be real sweet. I promise."

I shrug out of his grasp and shake my head. Again. I've been politely declining the invitation to join him in his car for the past ten minutes, and yet we've somehow made it all the way from the dance floor in the middle of the gymnasium to the back door. "I said no. I'm not interested."

"You know what you are, Brinley? A cocktease. You make promises with those pretty eyes and short skirts, and then shut down when it's time to follow through."

Promises with my eyes? What does that even mean? My

cheeks burn, and I tug on my dress and glare. "I didn't promise you anything, Liam."

"Pretty soon that shit's going to catch up with you," he says. "Then you'll be sorry you didn't just give yourself to a nice guy like me." He doesn't wait for me to respond before turning around, pushing out the door, and heading toward the parking lot.

I nearly forget Liam when my gaze snags on the tall, dark-haired boy sitting on the hood of a beat-up Honda Civic and smoking a cigarette. He smirks when he catches me staring, and I blink at him as the door floats closed again.

I stand there and argue with myself. I could dance with my friends and tell them what an ass Liam was, but I'm afraid they'll say he's right and I should loosen up. Or maybe I should go home. I'd need to find a ride, since Liam's the one who brought me here, but if I did, I could keep Brittany company. The doctor wouldn't release her to come to the dance, so she and Mom are doing a movie night.

Neither option appeals to me. And maybe this makes me a bad friend or a bad sister, but what appeals to me is the guy sitting in the parking lot just beyond that door. Marston Rowe.

He's a senior at OV High, so I don't have any classes with him. But I've seen him in the halls since he started here last month, and he's barely acknowledged my existence. I'd say he's avoiding me, but that's ridiculous. I didn't do anything wrong. I'm not one of those popular girls who maintains her status by stomping on other people. I'm nice to everyone. But maybe . . . maybe he thinks I'm uptight too. Or maybe he hated kissing me?

I should stay away. If he wants to avoid me, that's his business, not mine. It was just a kiss. It probably didn't mean anything to him, and it shouldn't mean anything to me. But . . .

When I take a deep breath and push outside, I'm relieved to see he hasn't moved from his spot. He's not in dress clothes like the other boys. Marston's wearing torn-up jeans and a button-up shirt. He's undone the top buttons and rolled the sleeves to the elbows, exposing thick fore-arms and a tattoo around his right wrist.

I stride to him, pretending we're friends and he doesn't intimidate the hell out of me. "I'm surprised you came." I look over my shoulder toward the gymnasium doors. I didn't see him in there earlier, and I'd bet money he didn't set foot inside tonight. Since my attention goes to him anytime he's anywhere close, I don't think I would've missed him. "If you want some company, I could go inside with you and introduce you to some people."

"Nah." He takes a drag off his cigarette and turns his head to exhale a long stream of smoke. "I'm good."

I bite my bottom lip, then take a chance and hoist myself onto the hood beside him. "Hasn't anyone told you that's a deadly habit?"

When Marston turns back to me, he arches a brow. "Do you *need* something?"

The day was sweltering, but the heat faded with the setting sun. The October breeze is a welcome, cool caress on my hot cheeks. I shrug. "I was bored in there, so I might as well keep you company out here."

He stubs out his cigarette on the hood and tucks the butt into his pocket. "Are you always like this?"

My stomach pitches, and I tense in anticipation of some

43

sort of criticism. My father is Abraham Knox. I was raised on criticism. "Like what?"

"The welcoming committee? The one who makes sure everyone has a friend?"

"Who said I do that?"

He props his hands behind him and leans back. "We go to the same school. I see you in action. Little Miss Perfect is nice to everyone."

I slide off the hood and step away. "If you want me to go away, just say so."

He shakes his head, and a shadow of a smile crosses his face. "It wasn't an insult."

"It wasn't a compliment."

He chuckles. "Fair enough." His gaze sweeps over me again, stuttering for a beat where the hem of my polka dot dress meets my thighs. When he tears his gaze off me this time, it feels like maybe he doesn't want to.

Is Liam right? Does my dress make me a tease? "Is it too short?" I ask quietly.

Marston's eyes snap back to mine. "What?"

I swallow. "My dress?" I tug on it again. "I felt pretty in the store, but maybe it should be longer. Someone said it was too short, and . . . Never mind. It doesn't matter."

He shakes his head. "It's a dress, just like half the other girls are wearing. You shouldn't have to dress differently just because you're prettier than the rest of them."

I bite my lip, but my smile breaks through anyway. "You gave me a compliment."

He rolls his eyes. "You know you're pretty."

"But you called me the prettiest."

He turns his head, looking around the parking lot, at his shoes and the sky and anywhere but me. "It's true."

The red flush creeps up his neck, making me smile bigger. "I'm surprised to see you here. I didn't peg you as the type who'd come to homecoming dances."

"Aunt Lori wanted me to come. She feels like it's an important part of high school, and I didn't feel like arguing."

"And does Aunt Lori know you're spending the whole night sitting on your car and smoking?"

"What she doesn't know won't hurt her." He's silent for a beat, and when he finally looks at me again, his jaw is tight, his eyes narrow. "Your date probably won't like you sitting out here with me."

"My date left when I refused to let him feel me up in the back of his car."

He grunts. "Christ."

"What?"

"You sure know how to pick 'em."

I shrug. "Maybe it's not them. Maybe it's me." He's quiet, watching me as if he's waiting for me to explain what I mean by this. "I'm sixteen, and the only boy I'm interested in kissing avoids me."

"Happens to the best of us," he mutters.

I lean over, knocking his shoulder with mine, and whisper, "It's you, dummy."

His head snaps around and his eyes are wide.

"Don't look so shocked." I smile. I don't know why I feel more comfortable with this surly stranger than I do with any of the boys I've been going to school with for years, but . . . well, maybe that's just it. I like that he doesn't know me or my family. I feel like everyone else comes to me with a box they assume I should fit into, but Marston doesn't have any expectations. It's freeing and makes me feel bold in a way I've never experienced before.

"If you're here with me because you want to horrify your parents, I'll take you home and grope you in front of the security cameras. Save us both some time."

"Wow. What an offer," I deadpan.

"It would, you know."

"Would what?"

"Horrify them. Maybe even push them to stop treating you like a child. I'm not judging you for wanting out from under their thumbs."

He's not wrong about the way my parents treat me, but he's way off about why I'm sitting here. Is it so hard for him to believe I might be interested in him for reasons that have nothing to do with my parents or my need to be kind? I cling to that unfamiliar boldness. "I'd rather skip the security cameras and go somewhere no one is watching."

He studies me for a long time, and there's so much suspicion in his eyes that I expect him to tell me to get away. Instead, he wets his bottom lip and swallows hard before nodding. "Get in."

I should be nervous about getting into Marston's car, given how he could easily misinterpret what I just said. And I am nervous, but not for the logical reasons. I'm nervous because I want him to kiss me again. Because I like the way he looks at me and I want more of it.

The car has a beat-up leather interior, but it's clean and doesn't smell like smoke. I buckle in as Marston climbs into his side. He turns the key in the ignition, and the car slowly coughs to life. He shoots me a look like he's waiting for me to comment. When I say nothing, he says, "This is Aunt Lori's dead husband's car. It's been sitting in the driveway for two years, so I'm surprised it works at all."

"I'm not judging."

He smirks at this—because he finds that amusing or doesn't believe me, I'm not sure—but he doesn't mention it again as he pulls out of the parking lot and onto the main road. The windows are down, and the cool evening air whips through my hair, tugging strands free.

"You know much about the south dock at Lake Blackledge?" he asks.

"Other than that it's there?"

"It's a short walk from Lori's, and it's nice and quiet at night." He takes his eyes off the road for a beat to look at me. "I thought we could go there if that sounds okay."

My body is like a balloon slowly filling with helium. I might float. "Sure."

"I'm not going to kiss you again," he says.

And . . . *pop*. I fall. Hard. I'm not sure if it's embarrassment or hurt that makes me want to jump out of this car and run home. "Fine. Whatever."

He smirks at this but doesn't talk to me again until we pull into a parking spot at the dock. He turns off the engine, but when he climbs out of the car, he leaves the radio playing and the windows down. I stay where I am for a minute, watching him wander toward the water with his hands tucked into his pockets.

His back is broad, and his jeans hang low on his hips. He's tall but not lanky. He's got some muscle to him and could easily pass for one of the guys on the OV High football team. I heard the girls joking that he's so smart and ripped because he spent a year in juvie and all he could do to pass the time was work out and read. I don't know if the thing about juvie is true. The rumor mill at OV High is more based on entertainment than truth.

I want to shake off the awkwardness he threw over us when he said he wouldn't kiss me, but I can't. Not when I want exactly what he's said he won't give me. I climb out of the car and follow him into the gravel beyond the parking lot. The night is clear and the lake seems to sparkle in the moonlight.

"You like the lake?" I ask as I move to stand beside him. I shouldn't read too much into him bringing me here, but last weekend when I asked Liam to take me somewhere special, he took me to the football field and kissed me under the bleachers. Well . . . he probably wanted to do more than kiss, but I didn't let that happen. Maybe I am uptight. A tease.

Marston nods without looking at me. "Nothing in Atlanta is this pretty. At least not where I lived."

I have so many questions about his life before he came here, but I don't want to pry or make him uncomfortable. For some reason, it seems important that I like him without demanding details about his past, so I give him a little piece of myself. "I've lived here all my life. Most of my friends can't wait to leave, but . . ." I shrug. "I've traveled a lot, you know, and I like to go places to visit, but I love coming back. I can't imagine anywhere else feeling like home."

"You're lucky. I'm not sure I've ever had a place that feels that way." He turns around, finally, and a thrill washes over me as he devours me with that intense gaze. No one has ever looked at me like he does. And he doesn't want to kiss me. It's maddening.

"Where are your parents?"

His lips twist in a sneer. "Mom is probably strung out

and mooching off her most recent boyfriend. And . . ." He hesitates as if he's not sure he wants to share the rest, but then he shrugs. "I don't know my dad."

"You never met him?" The idea lights some traitorous fantasy inside me. My father works so hard for our family. He protects us and provides for us, but sometimes, his constant judgment and criticism make everything so much harder.

"My father is nothing more than a blank space on my birth certificate," Marston says, snapping me from my horrible thoughts. "Mom doesn't know which of her guys knocked her up and didn't care enough to figure it out."

"Oh." My cheeks are so hot. I shouldn't have asked. "I'm sorry."

"I'm just guessing here, Brinley, but there's a really good chance I'm better off without him." He studies me, and the silence stretches between us, like a tightening string trying to pull us closer. "I can't decide if you feel sorry for me or if I'm this train wreck you can't look away from."

I step forward. He's so tall and so warm, and I really wish he would kiss me again. "I don't think you're a train wreck. And if I feel sorry for you . . . well, it's no more than I feel sorry for myself."

The DJ on the car stereo gives a rundown of the weather, and then James Blunt's "You're Beautiful" starts playing.

He shifts awkwardly as he turns to me. "You want to . . . dance or something?" There's a nervous insecurity in his voice I haven't heard before.

"You'd dance with me?"

"Isn't that what you wanted to do tonight? Dance?" He

49

turns up his palm for a beat then seems to think better of it and drops his hand to his side.

Before he can turn away, I rush forward and clasp my hands behind his neck. A soft, surprised laugh puffs from his lips, and his eyes are smiling as he settles his hands on my hips.

His dark hair has grown out since that first night we met. What would it feel like to slide my fingers through it? We barely move. The only dancing we're doing is more about shifting our bodies fractionally closer and closer.

When I settle my cheek against his chest, he seems to relax. One hand shifts from my hip to the small of my back. "Why don't you ask me about juvie or my probation? It's all anyone else cares about, but you haven't asked me a single question."

I don't look at him, sensing he wouldn't want me to. "Do you want me to ask?"

"I don't like it hanging between us. It makes me wonder if you'd run away if you knew the truth."

For some inexplicable reason, those words make me want to cling to him. "How bad is the truth?"

"Could be worse, I guess. Could be better." The song ends, and he pulls away. "I don't want to kiss you again until you know who I am. What I am."

"You're Marston," I say. Feeling bolder after a whole song in his arms, I skim my fingers over his cheek and trace the strong line of his jaw. "The boy who kissed me on my sixteenth birthday and who danced with me by Lake Black-ledge in the moonlight."

"I'm a delinquent and a thief. And I spent most of last summer homeless." He drops his hands and backs away. My skin feels cold without his touch. "I'm not the kind of guy you should be looking to for dances or kisses or . . ." He turns away and drags a hand through his hair. "Fuck."

I place a tentative hand against his broad back. "Are you okay?"

"Get in the car. We should go."

A delinquent and a thief. I wonder if he really believes that's all he is.

CHAPTER FIVE

MARSTON

Present day

"Don't be ridiculous," Brinley says. "I'm not going to let you buy my shoes."

The shop clerk hands my card back, and I tuck it in my wallet. She was more than happy to take it and my whispered instruction that anything the birthday girl wanted was to be charged to me. "It's already done."

"Marston!" Even when she's exasperated, the way she says my name turns me on. There's just a little of that Southern honey on the first syllable, tugging down and making it a little longer.

"It's your birthday, and I didn't get you anything."

"You didn't even know we'd run into each other," she says, blushing.

I shrug, smiling. Ever since she kissed me in the limo, I can't *stop* smiling.

She stares at the new shoes and worries her bottom lip between her teeth. I normally don't care about shoes, but seeing Brinley in these heels with a skinny strap across her toes and another around her ankle, I can understand how a man might develop a fetish. It's impossible to look at her in these and not imagine her wearing them and nothing else.

I could tell she was trying to talk herself out of them, which is interesting, since I assumed she'd be rolling in family money by now. Hell, maybe she is and she's more frugal than her parents ever were. Either way, I wasn't about to let her walk away without them or let her pay for them herself.

"I love them," she says, "but I didn't expect you to buy me anything. This is too much."

"It's not. Consider it your Christmas present ten years late."

She lifts her head, opens her mouth, then snaps it shut again before finally saying, "Thank you."

We only had one Christmas together, and it killed me that I couldn't spoil her. I bought her a twenty-dollar necklace from Target and even felt guilty about spending that. I had a job with the groundskeepers at Brinley's parents' estate and worked in the kitchen with Aunt Lori sometimes, but I used most of that money for gas, insurance on Uncle Henry's old Civic, and money for Mom. I didn't feel right having a warm place to sleep and three squares while she was back home trying to clean up her act and struggling to pay rent on that shithole her slumlord called a house.

But now, everything's different.

"Come on, birthday girl," I say, taking Brinley's hand. "We're not done yet."

"You got me a present that Christmas, remember?" she says as we wander out of the shoe store. "It was a heart-shaped necklace."

Brinley's probably gotten thousands of priceless gifts in her life, and yet she remembers that necklace? Part of me wishes she didn't. "Not much of a gift, considering what you meant to me." My jaw twitches, and I don't say the rest. *Nothing compared to what* he *got you.* I was setting the dining room table for their Christmas dinner when Roman showed up with the small box. I was in the next room when she opened the diamond tennis bracelet, and I could hear her little sister and Mom going nuts over it. *"Oh my God, that's so romantic!" "Brinley, put it on! It's perfect."*

She squeezes my hand, as if she's right there with me, reliving those memories. "I never cared about the money."

It's easy not to care about money when you have it, but it's not her fault she was born into that world, so I shrug and pull her to a stop in front of a two-story jewelry store with lush carpets and chandeliers in the entrance. "I cared. And now it's my turn to spoil you."

Her eyes widen as she turns and sees where I intend to go next. "Stop it. No. You can't."

I release her hand and stroll inside, winking at her over my shoulder. "Can and will."

A saleswoman is quickly in front of me as if she can scent a man in the mood to spoil a woman. Brinley is right. I used to be intimidated by all this shit, but I learned over the years that if you walk and talk with enough confidence, the staff will kiss your ass and assume they're a sales pitch away from a fat commission check. "How can I help you, sir?"

Brinley's still in the hallway, hands on hips like she can talk me out of this if she's just stubborn enough, but I point to her. "That beautiful woman right there? It's her birthday, and I want to spoil her rotten. I'm thinking earrings and a necklace."

The saleswoman beams. "I'm sure we can help you, sir. Diamonds?"

"And pearls. She has a soft spot for pearls."

"Follow me. I have some options I think you'll love." She slips behind a long counter, and across the hall, Brinley wanders toward another store window. She doesn't have to come in here for me to buy her something, and yet, right now, I'm more interested in what's caught her attention.

I hold a finger up for the saleswoman. "I'll be right back."

Her face falls and I know she's worried she's lost me, but I'll make it up to her.

I head back into the hall and stop next to Brinley, who stands outside La Perla. The lingerie in the window is black and gray lace, and I immediately picture her in it—her skin flushed from arousal, her nipples taut against the lace bra, the way the high-cut panties would hug her ass.

Stripping her out of that lace is officially on my bucket list.

"See something you like?" I ask her.

When she turns to me, she's smiling. "Thank you for coming to your senses," she says, starting to walk away.

"Oh, no. I'm not done there. Just taking a little detour." I turn toward the window, taking my time as I imagine the showcased bra and panty set on her.

"You did *not* just ogle that mannequin."

I chuckle. "I did, but only because I was thinking of how it will look on you."

"What a line." She smacks my arm playfully. "You're ridiculous."

I arch a brow. "It's not a line. My only question is if you're going to stay out here or go in with me while I buy it." I stride into the store.

She chases after me and grabs my arm. "You don't need to buy me gifts."

"Oh. This isn't for you." Her face falls, and I realize she thinks I'm saying I'll buy this for someone else. *Seriously?* I dip my head so my mouth is right by her ear when I whisper, "Sending this home with you, knowing you'll think of me every time you wear it? That'll be a gift for me."

BRINLEY

Does he want me to drag him into a dressing room and jump him? Because the temptation is so strong that I'm considering it. But it has nothing to do with him buying me gifts and everything to do with the sweet things he's saying . . . the old feelings he's bringing to the surface.

I press my palms against his chest and push him back so I can see his dark brown eyes. "If I let you buy it for me, would you want to see it?"

His nostrils flare, but he pulls back instead of moving closer. "It's not a requirement, if that's what you're asking."

"That's not what I'm asking." I look him over as thoroughly as he was studying the mannequin in the window. "It might be worth letting you spoil me if you're spending the night thinking about what's underneath my clothes."

"Done," he says. He gets the attention of a svelte brunette salesclerk with little more than the lift of his chin, and she comes scurrying over like a puppy greedy for attention. He leans over and whispers in her ear. She nods and shoots me a smile. He tucks something in her hand—cash, a credit card? Hell, for all I know, he's handing over his phone number, but . . . no. I'm beginning to realize that, for tonight at least, I don't need to worry about other women.

"I'll get a dressing room ready for you," the clerk says.

When she disappears into the back of the store, Marston turns his attention on me again.

His eyes are so hungry as they skim over me that I feel five inches taller. I've dated on and off over the last decade, but my first priority has been and will always be Cami. Somewhere along the way, I stopped feeling desirable. I didn't realize until this moment just how much I missed that feeling. Or maybe I missed *him*.

"And what are you going to do while I try on lingerie?"

He shrugs. "I need to go run an errand. I'll meet you back here in fifteen minutes."

It's ridiculous, but my stomach sinks with disappointment. Never, ever would I think I'd be the kind of woman who'd model lingerie for a man in a public dressing room, but the way he was looking at me? The things he was saying? If he'd wanted to come back to that dressing room with me, I don't think I would've denied him. Instead, he's running an errand while I shop.

"Thirty-four C?" the saleswoman asks when she appears again.

"Wow. Yeah. How do you do that?"

She smiles. "Your husband. He had a few ideas, but he said you can get whatever you like."

"Oh, he's not—"

"Lucky girl," the woman next to me says, and I follow her gaze to Marston's retreating form. "A generous husband who looks at you like you're the object of his every fantasy and is *also* that fine? You've found yourself a unicorn. Don't let him go."

I swallow hard and dare to imagine—for a few beats of my heart—that it could be that simple. Just don't let him go. Just love him and let him love you. Just trust that what we once had is powerful enough to pave the way for forgiveness he doesn't know I need.

But looking too far down the road wakes my anxiety and makes panic claw its way up my throat, so I shake those fantasies off and focus on tonight.

I think of Marston with every piece of lingerie I try on. I think of him when the soft lace scrapes the sensitive peaks of my breasts and when I tie the little bow at the front of the bra. And I think of him when I ask the dressing room attendant if I can give her the tags and wear the lingerie out of the store.

"Ready?" Marston asks when I finally emerge from the dressing room. He tucks his wallet into his back pocket, and when I glance to the register, he says, "It's taken care of, Brinley."

My stomach flutters at the warmth in his eyes. "Thank you. I hope you didn't wait long."

"Not at all."

I wave goodbye to the saleslady and follow Marston to the hall. He takes the bag from me.

It should come as no surprise that Marston grew into a

man with impeccable manners. Even though he was raised without being taught any sort of etiquette, he was always a gentleman. And he still is today.

"Can I look?" he asks, parting the tissue paper.

I laugh. "You can, but that's just the stuff I was wearing earlier."

He arches a brow. "So you . . .?"

I grin and give a little shimmy as I head down the hall. "I like it," I call over my shoulder. "It feels good."

After he picks his jaw up off the floor, he catches up quickly. "Where to next?"

"Back to the club?"

"You sure? It's your birthday."

"I'm not going to spend my night with you in a shopping mall."

His tongue darts out to touch his bottom lip, and he takes in every inch of me. The heat in his eyes is so intense, it's as if he can see right through my clothes to the new lingerie underneath. "I'm enjoying myself."

"Me too." I grab his free hand in mine. "But now I want to dance."

CHAPTER SIX

MARSTON

October 12th, before

I'm on Aunt Lori's shit list. My crimes? Not being where I said I'd be, exploiting her trust, and—the worst, and possibly more foreign to me—*making her worry*.

I didn't think it was a big deal to leave the school. I'd be home before curfew, so what did it matter? But one of the girls who works for my aunt was at the dance and decided my absence merited a text to Lori. Which means that while I was driving Brinley to Lake Blackledge, Lori was driving into town to the high school. And while I was driving Brinley home and trying to do the right fucking thing for once in my life, Lori was searching for me and convincing herself I was dead on the side of the road somewhere.

We pulled into the driveway at about the same time, and she read me the riot act, complete with a guilt trip about how worried she was.

Now I'm grounded. Almost eighteen years old, and grounded for the first time in my life. Mom never cared enough to bother with discipline to begin with—and grounding me would've kept me in the house when she wanted our place to herself.

I always assumed being "grounded" meant you stayed home, but Lori said she wasn't rewarding me with laziness and told me I had to work with her all weekend. At the Knox house.

Fuck me.

I managed to stay in the kitchen through breakfast, and I'm currently using a mop to take my frustrations out on the floor. If it was up to me, I'd hide in here all day. I'd clean the floors with a toothbrush if that was what it took.

"I think that spot's clean."

I stop scrubbing but don't turn around. I dunk the mop in the bucket and get to work on a new area.

"It all looks clean, really," Brinley says, "which is great, since I need you for something else."

I tense. I'm trying to do the right thing and stay away from this girl. Doesn't she get that? "I'm working."

"I want to rearrange the furniture in my bedroom. Ms. Lori mentioned at breakfast that you'd be working here all weekend and could help me. So, I thought, no time like the present, right?"

I slop the mop back into the bucket and turn to face her. And . . . *damn*. Last weekend she stole my breath in that short polka dot dress, but today she's doing it in sweatpants and a loose T-shirt that's falling off one shoulder. Her hair's piled on top of her head, and she's wearing glasses. All things considered, her outfit says she's not trying to impress me, but she's still so fucking gorgeous that she doesn't have to try. "What do you want from me?"

She cocks her head to the side, unfazed by my mood. "Today or in general?"

"Brinley."

She sighs, then pastes on that sweet-girl smile. The one that's half saintly patience and half gracious hostess. "I want to move my bedroom furniture, and I'd love if you were the one who helped, because I like spending time with you."

"Why?"

Her smile falls away and she steps forward, toeing the line between friendly and intimate. "Hasn't anyone ever wanted to spend time with you just because?"

I look her dead in the eye. "The only friend I ever had was my mom's dealer when I was eight, but it turned out he just wanted me to be his drug mule."

Her jaw drops. "Oh, Marston. I'm so—"

"It's a joke, Brinley. I have friends. I just don't understand why you want to be one of them."

She folds her arms under her breasts and—dammit, I'm *not* going to stand here and look at her chest. "That's not very nice, you know."

"I never claimed to be."

"Marston," Lori says, pushing into the kitchen. My aunt is a big woman with chin-length black hair and the kind of eyes that always make it look like she's smiling even when she's not. I'd never guess she and Mom were sisters if I didn't know—and not just physically. It's hard to believe that two women so different could've grown up in the same house. "Oh, good. Brinley found you. I want you to help her cousin rearrange her bedroom furniture today, okay?"

I lift a brow. Her cousin?

"Smithy's a football player," Brinley says.

Smithy. Great. A rich jock. On the bright side, at least I won't have to endure the temptation of spending the day alone with Brinley.

"You'll like Smithy. Anyway, it's solid wood furniture," Lori says, "so you'll want the extra help."

This time, there's nothing about Brinley's smile that says "Little Miss Perfect." Instead, her lips curl into something more like a self-satisfied smirk. "Come on. I'll show you my room."

Lori shakes her head. "No, Brinley, honey, I'm sorry. Your mom wants to take Brittany shopping today, so she needs you to go to the nursing home and check on your grandfather."

❦

LORI WAS RIGHT ABOUT SMITHY—THE dude's cool. But "heavy lifting" doesn't quite cover the experience of moving Brinley's furniture.

"Oh, wow," Brinley says, eyes wide as she walks into her room. She must have changed when I was out front meeting Smithy. Her sweatpants and loose T-shirt have been traded for a pair of fitted jeans and a silky pink shirt with skinny straps. "You're done already!"

Smithy wipes his hands on his jeans and looks around at Brinley's white furniture now positioned in its new spots around the room. "You owe us big time. I about crapped myself lifting that bed."

Brinley wrinkles her nose. "Too much information." She looks to me. "If it was too heavy, you should've left it. I could've asked Mom to get the movers to come back. When she wanted the piano in the ballroom for her party last spring, she had them come take care of it. I'm sure they could've done this too."

"It was fine," I say, even though every muscle in my back disagrees. "We handled it."

Smithy rolls his head side to side. "Barely. I'm gonna go home and sit in the hot tub. Enjoy the new arrangement, Brin." He gives her a quick hug, then gives me a clap-hand-shake. "See you later, bro."

"Thanks, Smithy," Brinley says, smiling at her cousin's back as he leaves.

Then we're alone.

In her room.

"I'd better see what Aunt Lori needs me to do next." Well, I earn partial credit. I said the words, but my feet don't move, and Brinley does.

She smiles up at me. "I'm sorry I wasn't here to help."

I can smell her flowery perfume. I normally hate perfume, but whatever she's wearing is light and clean, and as pretty as she is. "It's no big deal." I swallow. *Move your ass.*

I don't move.

"Do you feel this, Marston?" She presses a palm to my chest.

"Feel what?" I ask, but I do.

She smiles. She knows I'm dodging. In truth, I've never felt anything like this before—this instant chemistry, complete awareness of her, of us.

"This," she whispers, brushing her hand against mine.

I want to close my eyes at that brief contact—to absorb it and relish it. But I keep them focused on her.

"You kissed me on my birthday," she whispers.

As if I could forget. "I shouldn't have."

"I don't agree." Her gaze settles on my mouth. "I'm glad you did. I just . . . I feel this thing every time I'm around you, and I think you feel it too, but I also think you want me to leave you alone."

This is it. This is the moment I tell her I wish she'd back off. This is the time to tell her it'd be better if she stayed away from me. But before I can open my mouth to say what I should, she lifts onto her toes and presses her mouth to mine.

My reaction is one hundred percent instinct. I slide one hand behind her back and the other into her hair. Mom was an addict, and I thought I escaped that curse, but now I'm wondering if this is how it feels—a magnetic pull toward something that can only end badly.

Brinley's mouth is so damn sweet under mine, and when I taste her lips with my tongue, she lets out this soft little moan that makes me crazy. She presses one hand against my chest, and just when I think she's going to push me away—since one of us should stop this—she fists her hand in my T-shirt and tries to draw me closer.

I guide her back without realizing what I'm doing. The next thing I know, she's against the wall and my hand is sliding up her side, under her shirt.

I still my hand at her ribs and break away, breathless. She looks up at me with those big blue eyes, her lips pink and swollen from my mouth. Tentatively, I tuck a loose strand of her hair behind her ear then graze my thumb down the side of her neck.

"Tell me what you're thinking," she whispers.

I'm thinking this is crazy and incredible and that it can't possibly be real, because I've never had anything this good for myself without stealing it. "I'm thinking you should stop trying to spend time with me." My thumb skims along the band of her bra, and she sways toward me.

"Brinley!" Her mother's sharp voice comes from outside the bedroom.

I jump away just before she enters.

Brinley smiles at her mom, but it's fake—because of her relationship with her mother, or because we were almost caught? "Hey, Mom. Like my room like this?"

Her mom looks back and forth between us, a frown turning her patrician face sour. "What are you two doing in here?"

"I was just thanking Marston for helping Smithy move my furniture."

"Is that right?" Mrs. Knox asks me.

I don't dare turn to look, but I can feel Brinley's eyes on me, can feel her panic at almost being caught. Does she think I'm going to tell her mom what we were really doing just now? "Yes, ma'am. My aunt asked me to help. Smithy just left a minute ago, and I was about to leave too."

The expression on Mrs. Knox's face as she looks me over is that of someone who's found a pile of dog shit in the middle of her living room floor. She sniffs. "If you're going to help your aunt out around here, I don't want you and Brinley alone together. It might not be a big deal where you come from, but it's considered inappropriate in our family."

My hands curl into fists and my chest churns with rage I can't do a damn thing with. My hackles are up, but half of me knows there's no fight here I can win, and that half wants to hide.

"Mom, the door was open," Brinley says, and I almost laugh, because the door *was* open and still I had her pressed against the wall with my hand up her shirt.

"Marston, you're dismissed," Mrs. Knox says, those sharp, angry eyes on her daughter now. "Please leave me so I may speak privately with my daughter."

It takes every ounce of my willpower not to turn around and look at Brinley, but I'm afraid her mother would see too much if I did. I don't know the punishment for "inappropriate behavior," but I don't want to risk Brinley suffering whatever it is.

I nod and walk out of the room.

I'm not three steps down the hall when I hear Mrs. Knox say, "Do you want everyone to think you're spreading your legs for some trashy *delinquent*?"

CHAPTER SEVEN

BRINLEY

Present day

"I think maybe I need some rules for tonight," Marston says.

"Rules?" My voice cracks. We're back in the limo and moving slowly through traffic on the way to the nightclub. I don't want rules. In fact, what's the opposite of rules? *That's* what I want.

Marston nods, his gaze flicking up to mine before dipping to my mouth again. "I don't know where the lines are, and I'm sitting here wondering if half the things I want to do and say are allowed."

I laugh. "You literally just bought me the nicest lingerie

I've ever owned. Say what you want." I scoot closer and trace the back of his hand with my index finger. His hands were always big and rough, but they're a little bigger and surer now, just like the rest of him. I wonder if they'd feel the same on my skin as they used to. "Do what you want."

His smile is tenuous, but his eyes are all over me. "Ten years later, and you're still the most beautiful thing I've ever seen. And I can't stop thinking about kissing you again."

My breath catches. "Yeah. You're definitely allowed to say those things." I shift forward and bury my face in the side of his neck, breathing him in, then skim my mouth up to his ear, nipping lightly and making him groan softly. "You're definitely allowed to kiss me."

His hand tangles in my hair and he brings his mouth to mine, kissing me deeply and with the kind of hunger that mirrors my own and only makes me want more. Something in the back of my mind warns me that I shouldn't be doing this until we have a conversation, until I come clean about what happened after he left, but I tamp that down. I kiss him back and funnel all of my fear and guilt and worry about the future into that kiss.

When he tears his mouth away from mine to kiss my neck, I realize there is some honesty I can offer, and the confession bubbles out of me. "I knew you'd be here. That's why I was at the bar. Tonight wasn't really a coincidence."

He looks into my eyes, and I want to pour my soul out on the floor of the limo, if only to be free of the weight of my secrets. But then his lips curve into a smile that reminds me so much of the boy I loved and lost that I know I won't say anything tonight that could hurt him.

"I looked you up and knew your latest project was

reopening today. And then I stalked social media to find out what clubs you liked in Vegas." I swallow. "I wanted to see you. You probably think I'm crazy."

He shakes his head, something like awe on his face. "Sometimes crazy is good."

I don't even realize we've stopped until the driver opens my door and offers a hand to help me out.

"You can leave those here if you want," Marston says, nodding to my bags.

There's a promise in that offer—our night doesn't end at the club—and the hours ahead glimmer before me with possibility. Reluctantly, I retreat from the warmth of Marston's arms, and he follows behind me. On the sidewalk, he holds me close, leading me around the line in front of the club and right to the door. He flashes his ID to the bouncer, who checks his list, then lifts the ropes to let us through.

Marston doesn't lead me to his table but toward the mass of dancing bodies. He pulls me into his arms, his hands slipping from my hips—lower. I can feel the hard length of him through his dress pants. Just holding me turns him on, and I know if he were to slide his hand under my skirt, he'd find the same was true for me.

"Tell me why you came," he says against my ear. His mouth brushes lightly there, and at first I think it might be an accident, but then his teeth skim across my earlobe and he sucks it into his mouth.

A shiver runs down my spine, and that touch of his mouth undoes me. Reaching up, I thread my fingers into his and roll onto my toes, bringing my mouth to his ear. "I couldn't stop thinking about you, and I decided it was time to prove to myself that I'd worked you up in my mind to be something you weren't."

He dips his head, pressing his hot, open mouth against my neck just below my ear. "Had you?"

I shake my head. "The second I saw you walking toward me, I felt it again." I try for a second to figure out how I can explain what I mean by that, but he just nods and returns his mouth to my neck.

"Tell me I get you all night."

"I don't want to be anywhere but where you are."

The song is somehow both fast and sultry, and it makes me think of silken sheets and frantic hands, candlelit bedrooms and desperate mouths, of the slide of sweat-slicked bodies and *passion*. I *miss* passion. My thighs clench together, and I squeeze my eyes shut.

When he twirls me around, I instantly miss his heat, but then he pulls my back to his front and presses his palm flat against my stomach. This is good too—the hard length of him behind me, the heat of his breath on my neck.

I don't know what I'm doing here or why I thought seeing him would help me figure out what's next for me at home, but I can't regret it. I've missed feeling this—adored and *beautiful*, a way only he has ever made me feel. Maybe it's as simple as chemistry, but what we have has always seemed more than attraction. Like the stars waiting behind the clouds. Like the promise of the sunrise after a long night. Like the sea rolling into the shore. *Inevitable. Fated.*

When the song ends, I step out of his arms. My whole body is tense with need, but it's a delicious kind of torture, and I'm not in any rush for it to end.

He nods to the table. "Drink?"

"Yes," I breathe, relieved to break the intensity of this moment.

We return to our booth to find all the food has been cleared away. Alec and Savvy are huddled together on one side. Alec notices us first, but doesn't bother putting any space between himself and my friend.

I catch Savvy's eye. "You two having fun?"

She grins. "Of course." The music's louder than it was when we left, and she has to shout to be heard. "Why would we choose anything else when fun's a choice?"

Marston holds my hand as he slides into the booth, pulling me in beside him and wrapping an arm around me. Savvy's eyes track the movement, and her smile stretches wider.

"Savvy's never played at a blackjack table before," Alec says, leaning toward Marston.

"Only the computer," she says with a shrug.

"You'd love it," I say, smiling. "Do you want me to take you to the casino?"

Savvy shakes her head and waves me off. "Alec's going to take me. I'm sure you two will be okay here," she says with a wink. "Text me if you need me."

"Same," I say, reaching out to squeeze her hand.

Savvy climbs out of the booth, Alec behind her, then stops suddenly. "But first, let me see the new shoes."

I scoot to the edge of my seat and stick out one foot.

She groans, hand to her chest. "Those are fucking *hot,* girl."

"Marston bought them for me." I throw a smile over my shoulder for the man in question. "Even though I told him not to."

"You lucky bitch!"

"She deserves it," he says.

Alec slides his arms around her, pulling her back to his front and whispering something in her ear that makes her grin.

"Shoe shopping and *then* the casino," Savvy announces. She waves goodbye with a wiggle of her fingers.

"Behave!" I call after her.

"Don't behave!" she calls in return.

"I think Alec is smitten," Marston says.

I shift around so I'm looking at him. "I hope so. Savvy deserves a night with a guy who treats her like a queen. She hasn't had enough of that in her life."

Marston quirks a brow. "What will you think if Alec takes her shopping and buys her shoes, designer clothes, and jewelry?"

"Can he afford it?"

He chuckles. "And then some."

"I'll think it's great. He wants to spoil her, and she deserves to be spoiled."

Marston tucks a lock of hair behind my ear before leaning forward and asking, "So why is it so different when I do it for you?"

I'm saved from trying to explain when the server appears at the table.

"What can I get you two?" he asks.

"I'll have a martini," I say. I started with vodka. Better to stick with it.

"The special edition Maker's," Marston says. "A double."

The server gives a sharp nod and then heads toward the bar.

Once we're alone, Marston looks at me with heavy-lidded eyes. "I assume you want to stay for a bit? We can always join Alec and Savannah in the casino."

"Staying sounds good. This is a change of pace for me." I look around the club. "Is this your scene? Wild nightclubs where you can barely hear yourself think? Women scoping you out from every side of the room?"

His lips quirk. "Jealous?"

I return his smile. "Not as long as I'm the one sitting here with you."

He looks around, as if he's barely bothered to register the space before now. "It's not how I spend all my leisure time, but I enjoy the scene with the right company."

I lean forward. I don't want to miss a single word he says.

"Can't hear me?" he asks.

"Barely."

He wraps an arm around my waist until I'm thigh to thigh with him. Any closer, and I'd be in his lap. "Better?" he asks against my ear.

I straighten as a shiver runs down my spine. He's so close I can smell his cologne. The heat from his leg warms mine. Memories of his hand on me commingle with my promise to spend the night with him, and it all tangles up in a ball of need that sits low in my belly. "Better," I say.

The server returns with our drinks, and I take two long swallows of mine.

Marston settles one hand on my thigh and cradles his bourbon with the other. He watches me from over the rim of his glass as he sips.

"What else can I get you, sir?" the server asks.

Marston's hand slips under the hem of my dress, his fingers curling around my inner thigh. The feel of his warm, calloused hands tugs on that knot in my gut—loosens it until all that fear and heartache and hope and longing unravel.

In this moment, ten years ago doesn't matter. Tomorrow doesn't matter. Only this.

"I think we're fine for a while," he tells the server, his voice low as his hand drifts higher.

I know the server can't see us, but he's standing right there, and my cheeks burn with the knowledge of where Marston's hand is headed.

"Of course, sir," the server says.

Marston sets down his glass and angles toward me in the booth, his hand creeping a little higher on my thigh. He studies my lips for a long moment before slowly lowering his mouth toward mine. "I'm going to kiss you again," he whispers.

"Good." I'm the one who closes the distance between our mouths, and I moan at the contact. His kiss is a sweet relief. I didn't work him up to be better in my mind. I'd *forgotten* the electric charge between us, that *rightness*.

He cups my jaw in his big hand and tilts my head back, taking my mouth fully in a heady exploration of tongues and lips and need. I'm entirely his.

His hand slides farther up my skirt, and when his fingers brush against my panties, I know exactly where I need this night to go. I need this and him. I need . . . *more*.

"You wanted me to think about you in these?" he asks, tracing the scalloped edge of the lace with his fingers. "I can't stop thinking about it."

He kisses his way from my mouth, along my jaw, back to my ear, and those fingers slide into my panties. He hisses out a curse when he skims my wet center.

My thighs part in invitation. *Yes. This. Please.*

"Is this what you came for, Brinley? Is this what you needed?"

I meet his eyes. It's dark in here, but not so dark that I can't see the hunger in his expression. But I don't need any light at all to know. I can feel it in the way he strokes me.

He holds my gaze as he slides a finger inside me. My breath hitches. My body squeezes around him. He pumps in and out, his palm giving me delicious pressure against my clit. He's barely touched me, but I'm so close, sitting on the razor's edge of pleasure and release and unsure which way I want to fall.

Part of me is aware of the club music booming around us, but I can hardly hear it because every one of my senses is wrapped up in him—the way he smells, his powerful arm braced between my legs, the sound of his breathing growing rougher from nothing more than touching me.

I'm not the kind of girl who gives a man free rein of her body in the middle of a club. Not the kind of girl who can get off in a dark corner when anyone might look over and guess what's happening under the table. But tonight, I want to be. If the man is him, I want anything he can give me.

I reach for him and trail my hand along his powerful thigh, higher.

He nips at my earlobe. "Not yet," he growls. He slides a second finger inside me, and my muscles clench tight around the welcome intrusion.

My mind flickers to the first time he touched me like this—at the creek on my parents' property, the trees the brightest shade of green all around us, the smell of spring flowers in the air. I was clumsy—nervous and inexperienced

—but so in love. It was new and exciting and as exhilarating as this moment.

This is so different . . . and yet, at the root of the arousal, at the root of the pleasure, it's the same. It's *him*. It's the inevitable and the impossible.

"You feel so good against my hand," he says. "You're so fucking wet, I'm liable to make a fool of myself right here."

My lips part, and I drag in a ragged breath as my whole body goes tighter.

"That's it, baby," he murmurs, giving me a fraction more pressure. "Let go. Let me feel you come."

"I can't," I whisper. I don't know what I'm objecting to —where we are, how crazy this is, or what I should be doing this weekend instead of being here with him.

"All you have to do is enjoy. I'm losing my mind thinking about tasting this sweetness I feel on my fingers. Are you going to let me do that? Can I strip you bare and kiss you here?"

I don't know if it's the words or if my body just can't hang on anymore, but suddenly, I slip. Dive. Fall. Every muscle goes tight, clenching, then pleasure shoots down my spine so violently that my hips buck off the seat.

"Fuck, you're so beautiful." He kisses up and down my neck.

I survey the club. It's dark, and no one's looking our way. But still . . . "I can't believe we just did that." I bury my face in his neck and laugh. "Holy shit."

He strokes me gently again, and I shudder with aftershocks of pleasure. "I'm ready to crawl under the table and get a taste of this."

My cheeks blaze at the thought—not from embarrassment but from the shock of realizing I just might let him. "Are you this wild with all your girls?"

He stiffens then pulls back. "I'm not going to pretend I've been celibate all these years. Have you?"

I swallow hard. Thinking of the days after Marston left, of college, of boyfriends and disappointing one-night stands, of Julian. "No."

He shakes his head as if he can see the shame on my face. "Don't do that. We've had lives while we've been apart, and neither of us needs to feel guilty about that." He kisses the corner of my mouth. "But no," he whispers, skimming his mouth along my jaw to my ear. "To answer your question, I've never done anything this crazy. Never felt as wild for anyone as I feel for you."

Swallowing, I cautiously step into the treacherous waters we've been dancing around all night. "I always wondered what it'd be like to see you again," I say. "I thought you might come back one day."

"I did. Once," he says, and everything inside me freezes. "I'd finished my first year of college and I caught a Greyhound to Orchid Valley all the way from California. You were having some sort of party at your house. The back patio was full of people, and there you were in this pink sundress, your hair pulled up, holding someone's baby."

Holding someone's baby. He saw me holding Cami. She was the first baby I'd ever held. The only one I held for years. In those first few weeks, my inexperience was terrifying, but by the time Marston would have seen me, holding Cami was second nature. "You were there?"

"Boys like that move from one girl to the next, Brinley," Dad said. "He's already forgotten about you. And even if he hadn't, you

think he'd want you now? This is the worst nightmare for a boy like that."

I never fully believed those words, but they must've taken root on some level for this revelation to shock me so much.

"You looked absolutely stunning, and I was so distracted by the sight of you that I didn't even notice your dad coming up beside me." He draws in a long breath. "He told me if I cared about you at all, I would leave town and never come back. He said he'd lost a daughter already and he'd sooner cut you off than lose you to me."

The blow I feel at those words is as familiar as my father's sneer. His threats to cut me off worked for years—until I finally cut myself free—and I can't help but wonder what would have come of my life if Marston had called his bluff.

"I argued at first. I'd come all that way and . . ." He looks down at his bourbon, his jaw twitching. "I left the house and went into town, thinking I'd catch you later, but his words kept echoing in my head. I decided I needed to go. It'd been a year and you looked so happy. You were doing fine without me, and I didn't want to ruin your plans."

"So you left." I don't mean for my words to sound like such an accusation, but they do. I was incredibly lonely during those years—isolated from my friends, trying and failing to prove I could hack it as a mother. If I looked happy, it was because I was holding Cami. She was the only light in my life. Even now, when life has gotten so much better and there's so much good around me, she still shines brightest.

"It was the right choice, wasn't it?" he asks. If I tell him the truth—that I wish he'd stayed, that I wish he'd at least

79

let me know he'd cared enough to come—it might break something in him that I have no right to break.

I offer a small truth instead. "It was the only choice."

"I thought that—" He cuts himself off and shakes his head. "Never mind. I don't want to talk about that tonight."

Me neither. I lean forward and press a kiss to his throat. "What do I have to do to talk you into taking me somewhere more private?"

CHAPTER EIGHT

BRINLEY

October 19th, before

"So, tomorrow night?" Roman asks, tugging on a lock of my hair and smiling.

I take a sip of my mocha. "I still need to ask my mom, but if she says yes . . ." I smile. I'm trying to convince myself it'd be nice to go out with Roman again. It would go a long way to getting Mom off my back, and maybe it would help me get over Marston.

Until Roman decided to be a dick at my birthday party, I really liked him. He apologized the next day, and if it hadn't been for Marston, we probably would've gotten back together. But instead of throwing myself into Roman's arms when he said how awful he felt, I accepted his apology and went about my day.

I was too preoccupied with the first boy who kissed me to give much thought to the guy who missed his chance. But since Mom found us in my room, Marston has made it clear that he wants nothing to do with me. Meanwhile, for the past week, Roman has been waiting at my locker with a mocha every morning and after swim practice to walk me home every evening.

Isn't it healthier to spend my time and energy on a guy who's interested in me in return?

"If she says yes, then what?" Roman prods, inching closer. "I want to hear you say it."

"Then I'll go to the drive-in with you."

The first bell rings, and he grins and pulls away. "I promise she'll say yes. I'll make sure of it." He smacks my butt lightly then walks away toward his first-hour class. "See you after practice."

I wave goodbye, but his words echo in my head. *I'll make sure of it.* That probably means his parents are going to talk to my parents about this potential date. That shouldn't annoy me—that's the way things work in my family—but it does. I want to date boys who are sweet, regardless of what my parents think of their social standing. Boys who like me despite my family's influence and not because of it.

I grab the books for my first two classes from my locker and slam it shut. When I spin around to head to first hour, Marston is standing in my way—shocking, since it seems like I can look for him all week and barely catch a glimpse of him, but now that I'm determined to move on, here he is.

"The drive-in?" he asks. The hallways are clearing out as everyone tries to get to their seats before the tardy bell.

"Hey, Marston."

His scowl might have intimidated me if I didn't know he was such a nice guy deep down. "Why doesn't he just come right out and ask you to give it up to him in the back of his car?"

I bristle. "Why do you care?"

"I don't." He lifts one shoulder in a lopsided shrug. "Do what you want. I'm just surprised that you're dating him after what he did to you on your birthday."

"He apologized. He was upset about a fight he'd had with his parents and took it out on me."

"A good sign that he's a dick."

"He's not . . ." I shake my head. "I'm not doing this with you. You kiss me and then avoid me for weeks. You don't get to weigh in on who I do or don't date."

I stomp off to class, but I barely hear a word in my first three classes. At lunch, I'm too sick to my stomach to eat, and I don't even know why. Is it because of what Marston said about Roman? It doesn't matter what Marston thinks about the guys I date. But the feeling follows me through the rest of my day, and instead of getting a snack between the final bell and swim practice, I tell the coach I'm not feeling well. I would head home and hide in my room, but Dad's working at his home office today, and he'll chew my ass out if he realizes I'm missing practice, so I linger. I chat with a few friends in the parking lot, declining half a dozen offers for a ride home. Only when everyone's cleared out do I start walking—the long way.

When I pass the marching band supply shed, someone grabs my arm and pulls me inside, away from the view of the cars merging onto the road. Marston has the same scowl from this morning on his handsome face as he kicks the door closed. The shed is crowded with old props and plywood scraps, and the only light filters in from high, dusty windows.

"What the heck, Marston?" My objection comes out too weak. It's the objection of a girl who knows it's bullshit to be treated like this but who's so desperate for the attention that she doesn't really mind. I am *pathetic*.

"We need to talk," he says through gritted teeth.

"Normal people do that in less creepy places. Maybe over coffee or, oh, I don't know, when they're already hanging out together at the lake. *Not* in the supply shed."

"I can't exactly have this conversation anywhere it might get back to your parents that you're talking to a *delinquent*, can I?"

Guilt punches me in the gut. *He* did *hear Mom that day in my room.* "Marston . . ." What can I say? She didn't mean it? She absolutely did.

He leans his head back, frustration all over his face. "What do you want me to do, Brinley? Watch you date an asshole and pretend I don't care?"

"It's not like *you* want me," I snap . . . and immediately realize my mistake. The right response would've been to defend Roman or to tell Marston he doesn't get to have a say in who I date. Instead, I made it about us. Not that there really is an *us*.

I'm an idiot.

He swallows hard. "It doesn't matter what I want." The words are so soft that I can barely hear them. Maybe he hoped I wouldn't hear them at all.

"It does to me." I step forward and lift a hand to the

side of his face. He closes his eyes as if he's been starved for my touch and he's afraid this isn't real. "I like you, Marston Rowe. I'm just trying to figure out if you like me too." I wait with my palm pressed to his cheek, my body a breath from his. I wait for him to kiss me or push me away or tell me I'm a stupid girl.

Instead, he takes three deep breaths before finally opening his eyes, and when he looks at me, I see so much anguish in his expression that it makes my chest ache. "Roman is talking about how he's going to sleep with you at the movies."

"What? No way! How would you even know that?"

He blows out a breath. "I was using the weight room over the weekend when the football team showed up for conditioning. His friends were giving him a hard time for not being able to close the deal with you. He's apparently decided he needs to get between your legs to protect his reputation."

I drop my hand. I don't want to believe it, but . . . well, I'm close enough to Smithy to know how the boys at this school talk, how they prove themselves.

"You deserve better." He stares at me for a long time before ducking his head and turning to the door.

I step in front of him before he can reach for the handle. "I know." I swallow and force myself to meet his eyes. "I know I deserve better."

"Then . . ." He shakes his head. "Why?"

"I'm lonely. I know that sounds ridiculous, but if you knew what it was like to live with my dad, you—"

"No, it doesn't. It doesn't sound ridiculous. It sounds human . . . to search for connection." He scans my face as if he's trying to read my mind. "Your sister's sick, and your parents are ass—" He grimaces and searches for another word. "Your parents are hard on you."

I drop my gaze to my shoes. The glossy black finish is covered in sawdust from the shed floor.

"And you and Brittany probably share friends too, am I right? I hear them bombarding you with questions about her. I bet you don't mind either, but I never hear them ask how *you* are."

"I *don't* mind," I object softly. I feel like he's seeing right through me, like he's found all the ugly, rotten, spoiled parts I keep hidden. The parts that resent my sister for her cancer, even when I know it's not her fault. The parts that resent my parents for all the times they seem to forget about their healthy daughter. It's like he can see even the parts I don't want to see myself, and I can't decide if it's terrifying or . . . a relief.

This is why I've felt sick all day. Not because I'm worried Marston will judge me for dating Roman and not because I think Marston's right and Roman might hurt me again. My stomach has been in knots because where everyone else sees Brinley Knox, good girl and perfect daughter, Marston sees *me*. I've never felt so vulnerable. "How do you know all that?"

His lip twitches. "I'm bored. I've had some time to think about what makes you tick."

My eyes widen. "You've been thinking about me?"

"A little."

"Enough to psychoanalyze me." Now I'm smiling. Smiling because he knows I'm screwed up and selfish—what the heck is happening here? "You've been thinking about me *a lot*."

"Not in a creepy way."

I chew on my bottom lip. "Maybe I wouldn't be so lonely if I had a friend who thought about me in a not-creepy way. Then maybe I wouldn't need to go to the drive-in with Roman."

He grunts, but it sounds like he's trying not to laugh. "You're bribing me to be your friend?"

"Only if it'll work."

"Friends." He shakes his head. "Your parents would freak out on both of us."

"I think I need something in my life that my parents *don't* control . . . and the only parts of my life they don't control are the ones they don't know about."

CHAPTER NINE

MARSTON

Present day

*H*aving a limo drive me around Vegas is all about swagger. I'm much more comfortable driving my own damn self or grabbing a Lyft if I'm drinking. But I've made my business successful by always appearing to be and have the best. The limo makes the right kind of statement, even if I find it obnoxious.

Tonight, as I cruise down the Strip next to Brinley for the third time tonight—her in my lap, my hands on her thighs as she makes a mess of my hair and kisses my neck—I realize it's growing on me.

Her phone buzzes in her purse beside me. Groaning, she digs for it then grins when she looks at the screen.

"What is it?" I ask.

"Savvy and Alec ended up in some club that has pole dancing."

I cough out a laugh. "Pretty sure that's called a strip club where I come from."

She shakes her head. "Not for strippers but for the customers." She grins, eyes bright. "Savvy teaches a pole fitness class at The Orchid, and she wants me to go try out some moves with her in the club."

I slide my hands to her ass and squeeze. "That's something I wouldn't miss. Want me to give the driver the address?"

"Not just yet," she says, sliding off my lap and to her knees in front of me. The smile on her face as she unhooks my belt is devious, and I want to imprint it on my memories.

"Or we could go to the room first," I say. But I'm already shifting in my seat, making it easier for her to free my cock from my pants.

I'm hard as hell, and *Christ*, her hand. Her grip is firm as she slides up and over the wet tip of my cock—her lips parted and her eyes wide. She watches her hand move over me, and my cock grows even harder. *So fucking hot.*

"I don't want to wait." Her gaze returns to mine for a split second before she resumes watching her hand. *So hot.*

She lowers her head and drags a slow, wet path along the underside of my cock. It's all I can do not to thrust up into that heat, that perfect mouth, but I somehow manage to keep my hips still.

She slowly lowers her mouth over the head of my cock, and I don't dare blink, don't dare look away.

We never did this before. I thought about it. *Christ*, did

I think about it—then and since. But until that last night together, we took things slow. She was so innocent and eager to hand me all her firsts. But we're not the same people we were then, for better or worse, and tonight I'm no longer the delinquent kid who needs to worry that Brinley's life will fall apart around her just because she's associating with me. And she's no longer the girl who jumps at her father's shadow.

She works her way down my shaft slowly—torturously—but I love every fucking second. She squeezes the base with one hand and works her mouth over me.

I was already so turned on from touching her in the club, and now I'm on that edge too fast.

I slide a hand into her hair, and she lifts her gaze to meet mine. This, *this* is the hottest thing I've ever seen: Brinley Knox on her knees before me, eyes on mine as she sucks my cock.

I don't guide her with my hand. I don't want to know what she's doing next or lead her into the next touch. I just want to feel exactly what she wants to give.

She works me over, again and again, until I think I can't hold on anymore. Then she pulls her mouth off me and teases me with her tongue before doing it all over again. It's bliss and torture and something between dream and fantasy.

When she finally takes me there, she ignores my warning and moans around my cock. I come with her name on my lips.

She crawls back onto my lap, straddling me and looping her hands behind my neck. She leans her head against my shoulder and releases a contented sigh. "I don't want tonight to end."

"Me neither." And sitting here with her, it's easy to forget we needed that decade apart. I needed to get where I am, but part of me will always see it as a stolen chunk of our lives. Time we could've been together. "I still can't believe you tracked me down," I finally say. My voice is a little shaky. I have a lot of questions about that. *Why now? What does this mean? Do you still let your parents rule your life?*

But those are landmines, and I can't risk destroying this night for answers that can wait until tomorrow. Not when I have to fly to L.A. in less than twenty-four hours. Not when I still need to convince her that this—tonight, *us*—needs to be more than a blip in the timeline of our lives. We need to hold on and make it more.

She presses a kiss to the spot just below my ear. "I'm sorry I didn't do it sooner."

"Maybe I'm glad you didn't," I say. "Maybe I needed a chance to become a better man." How do I explain that everything I did, I did to be good enough? I didn't want to be the person everyone looked to first the moment something went missing. I needed to prove myself—to her, to her parents, to the world. I needed to believe I wasn't that kid who had to be saved by his widowed aunt, the charity case and the thief.

"When I look at you, I still see the boy I fell in love with," she says, and my gut twists tight. Her eyes skim over every inch of my face, and her gaze is so intense that I feel like she alone can see past this façade of money and luxury and all the way to the broken man beneath.

"I'm not, though." I grab her by the hips, pulling her tight against me.

She frames my face in her hands. "Still tough on the

outside and gooey sweet on the inside." She grins. "Still irresistible."

"With one important difference," I say, voice gruff. "I don't need a damn thing from anyone anymore."

She squeezes her eyes shut for a beat before looking at me again. "I don't think that's true, either. You've always needed someone to *see* you. I bet you still do. You've always needed more—deserved more—and all this money doesn't change that."

I don't know if I *deserve* shit, but I *want* her. Fuck, right now, I *need* her.

I knot a hand into her hair and guide her mouth to mine. Her kiss is open and hungry and . . . giving. It's simple and complicated. Just like us.

"I bought you one more present," I say, reaching into my pocket and pulling out the small velvet box. "Happy birthday, Brinley."

"Marston." She shakes her head as I place it in her palm. "You've already spoiled me too much. I can't."

My fingers brush hers as I open the box. "You can."

The box holds a pair of pearl-and-diamond earrings and a matching necklace. The diamonds sparkle in the low light coming in through the windows, and the pearls seem to glow.

She keeps her eyes glued to the jewelry when she asks, "Why don't you hate me?"

"I don't have it in me." I lift her chin until she's looking in my eyes. "Never have. Never could."

Her gaze dips then lifts. Back down. Back up. "Marston . . ."

I run a finger down her bare shoulder. "What is it?"

She shakes her head and gives me a sultry grin. "I want to cram everything we can into tonight. Starting with that club with Savvy."

"Anything you want."

CHAPTER TEN

MARSTON

October 27th, before

*N*othing feels better after a day of working in the Knoxes' endless gardens than diving into the cool waters of Lake Blackledge. The sun is low in the sky, and the warm late-day light makes the water's surface sparkle. Everyone thinks it's too cold to swim, but I don't mind it. In fact, I prefer the lake without all the people from school crowding the beach. I like the quiet. The solitude.

"What are you doing out there?" someone calls from the shore, and it's the only voice I want to hear right now.

Treading water, I squint in Brinley's direction.

I swallow hard at the sight of her. She's in a dress that comes down to her knees with a little sweater on top. Even from a distance, I can tell she looks beautiful. But she *always* looks like that. In the shed at school last week, we decided to be friends, but I haven't seen her since. Friends, we decided. But I have no idea how to be friends with *her*.

"Hey," I call, heading to shore. "What are you doing here?"

"I saw your car," she says. She kicks off her shoes and tiptoes into the water until it laps at her shins. She shudders. "Are you trying to freeze to death?"

I grin, still moving closer. "It's not that cold."

"It's not *warm*, either." She wraps her arms around her waist.

Once my feet hit the bottom of the lake, I walk toward her until the water's barely up to my waist. "It feels warmer if you get all the way in."

"I'll take your word for it." Her gaze dips to my chest then farther down before snapping back up. "You're not even wearing swim trunks."

I laugh. Under the water, my cotton boxer briefs cling to me. "I didn't have any with me."

"So why did you get in?"

I shrug. "I wanted to."

She looks over her shoulder toward the beach and the small parking lot beyond.

"Don't worry," I say. "No one's out here to see you talking to me."

She licks her lips then turns back to shore.

That ended quickly.

But when she reaches her shoes, she doesn't put them

back on. Instead, she takes off her sweater, then unzips her dress and lets it fall to the sand.

I can't speak. Can't breathe.

She shivers, but when she faces me again, she has a big smile on her face.

Her underwear isn't any more revealing than a bikini—hell, I came to the more popular part of this lake when I first came to town, and there were girls in bikinis that exposed way more than Brinley's lacey white bra and cotton panties—but there's something about this that's so much sexier. Maybe it's knowing I'm not supposed to know her like this. It's like she's letting me in on a secret—showing me more of herself than I'm supposed to see.

"If I get hypothermia, I'm counting on you to bring me to shore and warm me up."

My eyebrows shoot into my hairline. "Oh, really?"

She seems to realize how that sounded, and her cheeks glow pink. "Oh my God, I didn't mean it like that. Get your mind out of the gutter."

I hold up my hands. "I didn't say a thing."

"Okay. I'm coming in."

I grin. "Sure you are."

She takes a deep breath and takes off in a run into the lake, splashing water everywhere. She stops beside me, the water lapping just below her bra, and squeaks. "So. Cold."

I take both of her hands and back us into deeper waters. "It's better if you get your whole body in."

She lifts onto her tiptoes then dunks down to her neck in the water. "Still cold!"

I laugh and bend my knees to sink deeper with her. "Give it a minute."

Little by little, she relaxes until she lets out a long

breath and lifts her face toward the sky. "Okay, this actually is really nice."

"See?"

She turns in a slow circle. Following her gaze, I take in the view of the trees and the water, the way the setting sun peeks between the trees and sends dappled light dancing on the water.

"Do you like it?" I want her to. I *like* Brinley, but I have no idea how to impress a girl who has everything, and somehow, that makes it that much more important that she likes what I like.

"It's gorgeous." She swims in circles, and I follow, enjoying the way the water moves over my sore muscles. I spent my whole weekend trimming shrubs and shoveling mulch, and while I don't mind working with my hands, I'm not used to doing manual labor for eight hours at a time.

When she stops swimming, I can touch bottom, but Brinley has to tread water. She keeps her gaze cast on the opposite shore. I wait, giving her the time she seems to need to process her thoughts, but when she finally turns to me, her face is sad. "We're friends, right?"

I don't let my gaze dip beneath the surface of the water as I contemplate this. I've had friends, but never one I've so desperately wanted to see in wet underwear. I swallow. "Sure."

"I don't want to go home."

A surge of protectiveness washes over me. "Why? What's going on?"

She shakes her head. "Brittany's in the hospital again. I just went to visit her, and she was . . ." She drags her bottom lip between her teeth and seems to search for the word. "She didn't want me there."

"I'm sorry, Brinley."

She shakes her head. "No. It's fine. She's struggling to stay optimistic, and she's sick of being sick all the time. She *hates* the hospital. But . . ."

I can't pretend to know what that's like. I used to wish I had a brother—someone to get through the hard times with —but to have that and then feel like you might lose it any day? I can't imagine how lonely that would be, and Brinley's loneliness makes my heart ache. I've felt it in her since that first night. Maybe that's what's always drawn us together. "Why don't you want to go home?"

She looks to where the sun is disappearing into the trees. "Because she asked me to do her a favor, and I don't know if I can."

Only after a long silence do I ask, "Do you want to talk about it—the favor—or . . ."

She shifts in the water and floats toward me.

She loops her arms behind my neck, and my breath catches in my throat, but then her legs come around my waist, and I'm done for. "What are you doing?"

She licks the water off her bottom lip. "Throwing myself at the boy I like."

"Why?"

She shakes her head, her eyes fixed on my mouth. "Why what?"

"Why—" *Fuck it.* I don't need to know. I slide a hand into her wet hair and bring my mouth down to hers. I kiss her gently, and she answers my tenderness with intensity. I can practically taste the need to escape on her lips. She clings tighter and tighter to me, her breasts pressed against my chest, her hands tangling in my hair.

I tear my mouth off hers and kiss my way down her

neck, licking and sucking lightly until she's arching into me and moaning softly in my ear. I kiss across her collarbone up to her ear.

I think about this constantly. Brinley in my arms, kissing her, touching her. I think about it in bed at night. In the shower every morning. In the middle of fucking calculus. I've never been so gone for a girl. I keep telling myself it's because she's off-limits, but I know it's more than that. I am so fucking done trying to talk her out of this, trying to pretend I don't want her with everything I am.

When I lift my head, I draw in a ragged breath. Her eyes are closed and her head's thrown back, as if to give my mouth access to every inch of her neck. She slowly opens her eyes, and the hunger I see there makes me want her even more. "I don't want you to be with anyone else," I say. "Not with Roman or Liam or even some guy who's actually good enough for you. I want you to be with me." I swallow. "And I know your parents would lose their minds, so I'm not asking you to tell them, but I'm saying *friends* isn't going to be enough for how I feel about you."

Her lips part. "I can't stop thinking about you."

"Same." I look around. It's gotten dark, and the only lights come from the rising moon and the houses along the lake. "We should go."

"I don't want to go home," she tells me again.

I shake my head. "We'll go get dressed and then talk. You go home when you want. I'm not here to boss you around."

"Good," she says, but she doesn't pull back or unhook her legs from my waist, and I don't try to push her away.

"Are you really mine?" I ask.

She cocks her head to the side. "Depends. Are you mine?"

"Fuck yes."

Her smile is so big and bright and just for me that I feel like I've won the lottery and gotten superpowers all in one fell swoop.

CHAPTER ELEVEN

BRINLEY

Present day

*T*he room is dark and silent when I wake up, and my head aches.

I listen for Cami, for the soft sounds of her watching art tutorials on YouTube in the living room, but then I remember. My birthday. Savvy's insistence that I do something for myself and make my dream weekend in Vegas a reality. Running into Marston. Kissing Marston. Touching Marston. The lights on the Strip. We met Savvy at that club with the poles. I watched Marston as I danced, drank shots, laughed, and . . . everything gets fuzzy after that.

I fumble for my phone on the bedside table and turn it over.

When I first see the numbers 10:34, I close my eyes again. I wish I could sleep all day, but I need to call Savvy. If we're going to try to make it to our noon spa appointments, I need to get a shower.

I look at my phone again. I missed a call from my mom. *Shit.*

I sit up in bed, and my stomach heaves in protest.

Note to self: move slowly.

I fumble with the lamp and light floods my room—no. Not my room. A massive luxury suite. Marston's suite.

"Mars?" My voice is thick with sleep, but I don't feel rested at all. My head is heavy. "Marston?" I close my eyes against the light, push the sheets back, and carefully swing my legs over the side of the bed. I shiver when the cold air hits my bare skin. Because, of course, I'm naked.

Fuck. Shit. Damn.

Not that I mind the idea of spending the night naked with Marston—I've imagined it many more times than I care to admit. It's just that the reality is so much messier, and I wish I at least had some memories to take home with me.

I put the back of my hand to my mouth, and something hard tears at my lip.

A diamond.

On a ring.

A diamond ring on the ring finger of my left hand.

I extend my arm in front of me and stare. My internal organs can't decide if they want to sink or surge into my throat or tangle all together, and my pounding head is giving me *nothing* to go on here.

Yep, memories would be great. Details like how that

ring got on my finger would really come in handy right now. As would knowing the location of the guy who put it there.

My head pounds as I gingerly rise from the bed to hunt down my clothes. My breath comes faster and faster, and I start to count the beats of my inhales and exhales to force myself not to panic.

Did we have a clichéd drunken Vegas wedding?

I shake my head, then brace myself on the bedside table when the room spins. I never would have married Marston. That's a childhood fantasy, and there's too much at stake to indulge such whims now. And him? No, He wouldn't risk his fortune on a whim.

Just one band, Brinley. Just an engagement ring. This isn't good, but it could be so much worse.

I find my shoes at the foot of the bed, my bra and dress on the walnut dining table in the main part of the suite, and my panties . . . my panties are nowhere to be found.

I vaguely wonder if I lost them in the suite or long before we made it back here.

How much did I drink last night? Did someone slip me something?

I wriggle into my dress and loop the straps of my heels on two fingers. I need to get out of here. I sigh in relief when I see my clutch on the desk and find my wallet inside.

Where is he? And why didn't I get his damn phone number?

But maybe it's a blessing he's not here . . . and that I have no memory of last night or his proposal. Maybe it's easier this way.

I grab a pen and piece of hotel stationery and scribble a note to leave on the dresser.

Marston,

I'm so sorry. I don't know what I was thinking last night, but I can't. We can't.

Please forgive me.

Love,
    Brin

When I pull the ring off my finger, I swear something tears loose in my chest, unraveling years of pent-up emotions. I shove them back down and drop the ring on top of the note.

The room spins, and it's so tempting to go back to bed. Wherever he is, he'll be back soon.

But my daughter is waiting for me at home, and if Marston knew about her, he never would've put this ring on my finger.

MARSTON

I practically race to the elevator to get back to my room.

I'm not sure I've ever seen anything more gorgeous than Brinley tangled in my sheets, naked, with my ring on her finger. Except maybe her smile last night when we said our vows in that quiet little chapel, the way those blue eyes brimmed with happy tears when I said *I do*.

Alec told me I could skip the meeting this morning, which said a lot, since he knows I never miss out on business. Hell, if he'd known Brinley and I ended up getting married last night, he probably would've insisted I skip it. God knows I considered it.

I woke wrapped around Brinley, one leg thrown over hers, one hand between her breasts. She was clinging to that hand in her sleep, and I didn't want to pull away. But this is who I am now. A man who's true to his word. A man respected by the best in the business. I need to be that man now more than ever—to prove to her, to myself, that I'm not the screwed-up kid I used to be, that I'm worthy of her and this life we're going to build together.

The elevator dings as the doors slide open on my floor, and I smile, imagining crawling back into bed. I hate that I had to leave her the morning after our wedding, but making it up to her is something to look forward to.

I slide my key into the card reader and push into the room. The hair on the back of my neck prickles, and immediately, I know something's wrong.

"Brinley?" I walk through the suite, looking for any sign of her, but even before I see the ring on the dresser, I already know she's gone.

Every Little
Piece of Me

PROLOGUE

MARSTON

"I hope you're going to wipe that pissy look off your face before our dinner with the Gamble team," Alec says from my office door. He scratches his dark beard and fails to hide the amused twitching of his lips.

I toss the invitation across my desk. "Given what just came up from the mailroom, I'm not sure you want me there."

Alec strolls toward me and swipes up the linen-and-lace card detailing the upcoming Orchid Valley wedding. His eyes widen. "Is this—"

"Yes."

"But . . ." He scrubs his free hand over his neatly trimmed beard. "Do you know if—"

"All I know for sure is my wife is getting married and has invited me to her wedding. Thoughtful, no?"

When I first opened the invitation, I was sure it was

some sort of joke—a quirky way to apologize for walking away from me six months ago.

By the third time I read it, I wondered if it might be real. I don't keep tabs on what's happening in Orchid Valley, but the internet's a thing, so it was easy enough to pull up the *Orchid Valley Times*, do a quick search for Brinley Knox, and . . . there it was. The evidence stared at me in bold print at the top of last month's society page.

Brinley Knox and Julian Hallison announce engagement

My first instinct was to send the invitation through the paper shredder. It would certainly be satisfying, considering the care that was so clearly put into its production. The inner envelope is linen, tied with a thin lace bow, and the stationery is written in the finest calligraphy. Not computer-generated script—that wouldn't do for a Knox—but meticulous hand lettering. How many of these are floating around in the world if the Knox family deigned to invite the punk kid who worked for them one year? Or maybe they invited me as a jab. I can just imagine Brinley's mother insisting they send an invitation to the old town charity case. Not because I've made something of myself over the last eleven years, but because the old woman would want me to know Brinley's off the market. She'd want to announce—in the most respectable way possible—that her daughter will never be mine.

Joke's on you, old hag. She already is.

"Has she filed for a divorce?" Alec asks. He keeps rereading the invitation, as if the words might change. I might find it comical if I hadn't just done the same damn thing.

"Not that I know of."

"I told you not to let her walk away." He waves the invitation in front of me. "See what happens when you don't grow balls and go after the girl, Marston?"

"Glass houses and stone throwing, asshole."

"This is *different*. She thinks she's marrying this guy. In *May*."

"I'm aware." Just two months from now. The spring wedding high-school Brinley always dreamed of. I push out of my chair and straighten my tie. "Give the Gamble team my apologies. I'll be in touch."

A smile slowly stretches across Alec's face. "Finally."

Once, I promised Brinley that if she were mine, I'd never let her go.

I guess it's time to return to Orchid Valley and remind my wife that I'm a man who keeps his promises.

CHAPTER ONE

BRINLEY

"*D*on't look now," Abbi Matthews says across from me, "but the world's most beautiful man is standing at the bar, and he cannot take his eyes off you."

We met up at my cousin's bar tonight. Smithy's is our favorite outside-of-work spot. It's popular without being too loud or crowded, always clean, and my favorite idiot cousin owns the place and takes good care of us.

"Like, nine-out-of-ten fine," she continues. "You're so *lucky*."

"I'm off the market, remember?"

"Hmm." She frowns, her attention still on the other side of the bar. "That's cool—I'll take him for myself. If he ever stops staring at you."

I laugh. If he's looking at me and not her, he's gotta be incredibly near-sighted. Abbi's the kind of curvy beauty that inspires country songs and makes men stop in their tracks.

I wave the catering paperwork in front of her again. "Can we get back to business here? My wedding? The menu? You're the one who insists I need to make some decisions, so *heeeeelp*." I punctuate my whine with a smile, but she only laughs at me. Abbi and I have known each other since high school, but we were never super close until she dropped out of college and moved back to Orchid Valley. Once we found ourselves both working at The Orchid, we quickly became friends. She's been by my side ever since.

"Do you realize you haven't made a single decision about this wedding on your own?" She finally pulls her eyes off the hottie behind me to give me her attention. "What does that tell you?"

"If it were true, it would tell me that I'm not a big wedding person, but it's *not* true. I've made all kinds of choices. That's why I need you now. I have decision fatigue." I slide the paperwork across the table until it's in front of her. "*Please*."

"Name one."

"What?"

She folds her arms and flashes me her easy smile. "One decision. Name one decision you've made yourself."

"I don't know. They all blur together." She stares harder, and I throw up my hands. "Fine. The venue. I chose to have the wedding at the Chapel Valley Church."

She grunts. "That doesn't count. Your mom said, and I quote, 'If you get married anywhere but our family church, you'll be dishonoring your dead grandmother.'"

"It was still my choice," I say, but I know it's a lame defense. I don't care about this wedding. In fact, the part I'm looking forward to the most is the part when it's *over*.

Tossing her long, dark hair over her shoulder, Abbi grabs her martini glass and licks the sugar off the rim before taking a sip. "Try again."

Lemon drop martinis are historically our girls' night favorites, but I've been cut off for the next two months. I nearly salivate at the sight of hers, but the trainer my mom hired has me on a strict diet until the wedding. This means no booze, which normally wouldn't be a big deal, but since wedding planning involves extra time with my family, it's been *torture*. "I picked out my dress."

"You tried on half a dozen dresses and agreed to buy the one your bridal party cooed over the most."

Trying to pretend it's vodka, I take a long pull on my iced water—I haven't hit today's eighty-ounce quota anyway. In truth, I hated dress shopping. When I was younger, I imagined what it'd be like to wear a white dress and say vows to the man of my dreams. I haven't idealized weddings or marriage since I found myself knocked up and alone at seventeen.

"You didn't choose the invitations or the reception location. You didn't choose the flowers or even the song you're using for your first dance," Abbi says. She doesn't say, *"You didn't even choose your groom,"* but it's at the root of this conversation. It's the elephant in the room. My big secret, known only to two of my closest friends. "Can you think of something you truly chose on your own?"

I chose to invite Marston. And holy hell, I still can't believe I did that. Wedding planning has made me lose my mind. There's no other explanation for it. But after we looked over the hundreds of invitations from the calligrapher and approved them, I snagged a couple. *"For my memory box,"* I told my mom, and she had to wipe away tears. I did put one in my memory box. The other I carefully addressed to Marston Rowe, president and co-founder of Rowe and Hayes, International. I dropped it in the mailbox myself.

If Savvy and Abbi knew about *that* little moment of insanity, they'd say it was a cry for help. Savvy already thinks I'm nuts for walking away from Marston after the night we spent together in Vegas. I'd prefer to think of that night as a gift to my younger self—the one who kissed the new boy after knowing him for minutes, the one who stripped down to her underwear and swam in the cold October water of Lake Blackledge with him, the one who believed *maybe* her life could be her own.

I don't know what I expected Marston to do when he opened the invitation, but he should've gotten it by now, and I haven't heard a word. Maybe he burned it.

I'm being dramatic. "Okay," I concede. "I'm not into making wedding plans. I'll admit it, but let's not pretend this is a bad omen. If anything, it makes my life easier. You and I both know Mom will veto anything she doesn't agree with. It's better if I'm not too emotionally attached to any choice."

"Or to the groom," Abbi mumbles behind her glass.

I glare. "Say what?"

"Huh?" She takes a dainty sip then looks over my shoulder again. "Oh, hell. Mr. Hottie is coming this way. Lord help us."

"Have at him, girl."

"I'm afraid I'm already taken."

The familiar deep voice has me spinning in my chair and looking right into the eyes of Marston Rowe.

"Marston." I don't say his name so much as breathe it.

When his lips quirk up in response, his dark eyes scanning my face again and again, I feel transported back in time. To high school, when my loving housekeeper's orphan nephew was the biggest act of rebellion I'd ever managed, and the only thing I could think about. I think of stolen moments in the woods, at the lake, of dancing together outside the senior prom. I think of six months ago when I went looking for him in Vegas. I went to that club because I wanted to see him again, yes. And because . . . because I was lonely and panicking about the future, and I knew he'd wash that all away.

Most of the time, I'm grateful I came to my senses less than twenty-four hours later, but sometimes I wish I'd stretched out that indulgence just a little longer.

"Marston Rowe?" Abbi squeaks. "Holy hell, Mr. Self-Made Man, you look even better than you did in high school. I didn't even recognize you."

Marston swivels his attention to Abbi. "My apologies, I don't remember . . ."

"We never officially met," she says.

"In that case, I'm Marston." He offers her his hand. "You're . . . ?"

Abbi blinks, looking him over in a way that'd be super creepy if anyone else did it. She's just too cute to be a man-eater—which is why they never see her coming.

"Abbi Matthews," I supply when it appears my friend has lost her capacity for speech. "One of my best friends."

She blinks a few times before turning her gaze on me. "You . . . He . . . Does he know you're engaged?"

If he somehow didn't, he does now. But I don't let my grimace show. I lift my chin and meet Marston's eyes. "I'm not sure. Did you get the invitation?"

"You invited him to your *wedding*?" Abbi screeches, and half the bar turns in our direction.

"She did," Marston says, his voice low and gravelly. I swear, this man was born with bedroom eyes and an intonation most guys can only manage mid-coitus or first thing in the morning. Is it any wonder I ended up in his bed in Vegas?

And engaged, Brinley. Don't forget that ring.

"You didn't tell me that." Abbi sounds too damn giddy, so I shoot her a look. "What? Most girls would consult their best friend before inviting their first love to their wedding."

"A little louder so the folks in the back can hear, Abbi?" I snag her half-full martini, and it sloshes over the rim and onto my hand, cold and sticky. "You're cut off."

She bites her lip and her cheeks blaze red, but her bright eyes give her away. She doesn't feel even a little guilty.

Marston's lips twitch again. *Of course.* I'm endlessly amusing. "It's nice to meet you, Abbi. I think I like you."

Abbi flutters her lashes dramatically. "And I like *you* . . . or at least everything I've heard." Her wink suggests graphic details I haven't shared with a soul, but Marston's cocky enough that he doesn't balk at the suggestion of me spilling all his bedroom secrets. "But seriously? She didn't mention me at all when you saw her in Vegas?"

Marston cuts his gaze to me for a beat, and I see the question there. *What does she know about Vegas?*

Seeing as how I can't even remember half the night, Abbi got more details from Savvy than from me. I drain the martini and shrug.

Marston treats Abbi to a full smile. "We didn't do a lot of reminiscing. You know how loud Vegas clubs are." He winks at her, all sexy, smooth charm, and jealousy rises so hot and brilliant in my chest that I wish Abbi had a second martini for me to steal.

"Right." She nods. "That makes sense."

"Are you still living in Orchid Valley or just visiting?" Marston asks.

I'm glad they're hitting it off so well, but I'd really love for them to hurry past the pleasantries and get to the part where Marston explains what brought him back to Orchid Valley for the first time in ten and a half years.

"I left for a couple of years, but I'm a lifer. What's kept *you* away so long?"

If that question causes him any angst, Marston doesn't show it. "Work's been good. It keeps me busy." He flashes me a smile. "But I'm here now."

"I didn't expect to see you . . ." I'm not sure how to finish that sentence. I didn't expect to see him before the wedding? I didn't expect to see him *at all*. I didn't really think he'd come, but why did I send the invitation? "Why *are* you here?"

He scans my face for a long moment. "We need to talk."

"Oh. Right, of course." Abbi hops off her chair and steps away from our table then nods toward where her brother and his friends are gathered at the back of the bar. "I'll go. I'll see if the guys have any room for me at their table so you two can just—"

"You don't need to go," I say at the same time as Marston says, "Not here. In private."

"That's not necessary." I wave to Abbi's now-vacant chair. "Have a seat."

Abbi's worried gaze ping-pongs between us—it's only now occurring to her that maybe she shouldn't leave me alone with my greatest weakness since salted caramel gelato. She puts her hand on my arm. "Do you want me to stay?"

"Yes," I say, and at the same time, Marston says, "No."

"Considering I'm engaged to another man," I say, trying to appeal to Marston's reason, "I think it would be more appropriate for us to have someone with us as we talk."

Marston's jaw tightens. "I thought it might be more comfortable for us to talk privately about that *engagement.*" The word seems to detonate when it hits the air, and his eyes flash, exposing his first real sign of emotion since he approached us.

Okaaaaay. So he's pissed about the wedding. On the one hand, this is unreasonable. He and I haven't been a couple for eleven years. I can marry whomever I want. On the other hand, I was wearing *Marston's* ring just six months ago, and if you don't consider the fact that we were drunk off our asses and only engaged for a matter of hours, it's understandable that he might take offense to me getting married so soon after.

He looks around the room. "This isn't the place."

I stiffen when I realize how right he is. There are already eyes on us, and I'm sure the gossip mill is going nuts with news of Marston Rowe being back in town and talking to *me.* Any second, someone could walk up and ask about my daughter. Or Julian could drop by Smithy's for an after-work beer. If Marston saw us together, would he immediately know my relationship is a sham? Marston knows what I'm like when I'm in love, and I can't begin to fake that level of connection with Julian.

So talking here is a bad idea, but I can't leave with him without causing a stir, either.

Why did I send him that invitation? What was I thinking?

Nausea washes over me, and my skin feels too hot. "Excuse me. I need to use the restroom." I sway a little as I push to my feet.

Marston steadies me with a hand on my arm. "Are you okay?"

"Want me to go with you?" Abbi asks.

I shake my head. "No. I just need a minute."

I feel like every person in Smithy's bar has their eyes locked on me as I walk to the restroom. Keeping my steps slow and measured, I don't let my face fall until the door closes behind me.

I run the water cold and brace myself on the sink.

Everything is okay. This is just one moment. Inhale and exhale, and move your way through it.

Once my breathing evens out, I splash cold water on my face and blot it dry with a paper towel. I'm definitely overreacting. There are a thousand reasons he could be in town and want to talk to me alone. Thousands of reasons that *don't* begin with the words *"You're the love of my life. Please don't marry anyone else."*

Because I'm almost positive I don't want to hear those words. Mostly.

When I step out of the bathroom, Marston is waiting there, leaning against the wall across from the ladies' room, arms folded, jaw twitching with aggravation. *The picture of tall, dark, and pissed off.*

When Marston sets his mind to something, he gets it, and tonight, apparently that something is talking to me alone.

"Sorry." I smooth down my pencil skirt. "That vodka didn't sit right." I turn toward the main room.

He catches me around the waist and spins me so fast that I'm trapped between the wall and him before I can blink. "Give me one minute." He braces his hands above my head and leans forward.

I swallow hard. Not because I'm scared. Marston's never scared me. But looking up at him when he's this close is stirring up all kinds of memories. I don't know if I'll ever be able to look at him without part of me wishing for the future I longed for at sixteen. I place a firm hand on his chest. "I don't think this is a good idea."

"Was Vegas a joke to you?"

Of all the questions I expected him to ask, that wasn't anywhere on the list. "What? Of course not. Vegas was . . ." *Hot. Impulsive. Crazy. Amazing. Wild . . . everything.*

He dips his head until his lips hover right above mine. "Don't you dare call it a mistake," he growls, his warm breath tickling my skin.

I ache to close the distance between our mouths, ache to feel his kiss again. I'd never call Vegas a mistake. Maybe I should, but I can't.

"Fuck, you smell so good. I couldn't get the smell of you out of my mind for weeks after you left me that damn note. Do you know how crazy that made me?"

My hand is still against his chest. If I pushed, he'd back off. He'd give me the space to clear my head. But when he shifts his mouth from above mine to my ear, I don't want to push him away. I want to pull him back. "Marston—"

"Is this why you sent me that invitation? Did you want me to come here and remind you what it's like between us? How it feels when we're close?" He takes a full step back, and my hand falls to my side. His cold gaze settles on my ring finger and the diamond winking in the low light. It's a family heirloom, given to Julian by my mother and father when he asked them for their blessing. My grandmother wore this ring until the day she died.

"I don't know why I sent it," I admit.

"Do you really love him?"

"I . . . I mean, he's . . ." I swallow. "Of course."

The corner of his mouth curls into a sneer. "It's a wonder more men aren't fighting for your affection with declarations like that."

I lift my chin. "I love him. I wouldn't be marrying him if I didn't." The words taste like lies on my tongue and send a new wave of nausea rolling over me. I shouldn't have chugged that martini.

"And such a faithful heart, too. Did you even have a full day between being in my bed and putting on his ring? Or were you already with him when you tracked me down in Vegas?" He surveys every centimeter of my face. "I thought you were better than that."

His implication is like a smack in the face. "I don't care what you think." I sidestep him to return to my table, but he takes me by the shoulders before I can get far. In a breath, he has me pinned against the wall again, and his mouth crushes against mine.

Fireworks explode in my stomach. All at once, the floor is falling out from under me and I'm floating.

The kiss doesn't last long—I don't let it. I tear my mouth away before it can swallow me whole.

I shove him back, my lips tingling. "You can't *do* that." The kiss was everything I remembered, everything that's missing when I kiss Julian. Everything I've been trying to

123

convince myself I don't need. But if someone would've seen us, it would be a mess.

He cups my jaw in his warm hand and strokes the rough pad of his thumb across my bottom lip. "That's not what you said in Vegas."

A sob rises in my throat, hot and insistent. I have to close my eyes to try to steel myself against his touch, but it doesn't help. I don't want to pull away. I want to lean in. "That's not fair."

"You want to talk about *not fair*? How do you think I felt when my wife sent me an invitation to her fucking *wedding*? I'm surprised you didn't save yourself the postage and include it with the divorce papers."

My head swims. Note to self: guzzling vodka when you're on a strict low-cal diet is bad news. The room seems to tilt on its side. The floor is a little wobbly beneath my feet, and I could swear he just said . . .

"I let you go when you ran out on me the morning after our wedding." His lips brush mine with each word. "But last I checked, bigamy is illegal in this country, and if you think I'm going to give you up without a fight, you don't remember me at all."

Wife. Divorce. Wedding. "What are you talking about?" Vegas. All those missing hours. The ring on my finger when I woke up in his bed. Did I really . . .? Could I have?

He straightens, his eyes narrowing. "Vegas? Ring shopping at midnight? That sweet little chapel you said reminded you of the church on Lake Blackledge?"

I shake my head. "I'm sorry. I . . ." I dig through my memories of that night, but everything gets fuzzy at the second club—blips and blurry images of Savvy dancing and laughing, of Marston watching me with hot, hungry eyes as

I did a thigh hold-spin on the pole. And I have no memories after that.

"You really don't remember?" He staggers back a step and drags a hand over his face. "You'd had a few drinks, maybe had a good buzz a couple of times, but you never seemed drunk."

"No, but I . . ." I shake my head. "I have bad reactions when I mix alcohol with my anxiety meds. Some people get sleepy, but I just . . . get happy and then forget everything from the night—sometimes even stuff that happens before I take my pills. It happened at Christmas, and I realized I can't drink at all on my meds."

He turns away and tucks his hands into his pockets. "And you took anxiety medication that night?"

"I don't remember," I admit, though I can imagine needing it. I was on an emotional rollercoaster seeing Marston again.

"You woke up with my ring on your finger. What did you think that meant?"

"I thought I'd lost my mind in Vegas and gotten engaged." Apparently, I was half right. "I have to go," I whisper.

He shakes his head. "No. We need to talk about this."

But I'm already running toward the door.

CHAPTER TWO

MARSTON

*B*rinley doesn't remember our wedding.

As hard as it's been to wrap my mind around that, it explains a lot, and maybe—just maybe—it means I haven't lost her yet.

I park in front of The Orchid and climb out of the Bentley I rented after my plane landed in Atlanta. Tucking the package from Aunt Lori under my arm, I grab the two coffees I bought at the local coffee shop on my way here—black coffee for me and a butterscotch latte for Brinley.

I would've liked to chase after her when she ran out of the bar last night, but I knew she needed space to digest the news. I resisted the urge to show up at her place and demand she talk to me, knowing it'd end badly—likely with my fist in her unsuspecting fiancé's face. I imagined him answering the door and looking at me like all the rich pricks around here used to do. Julian, pronounced the American

126

way, with a hard *J*—even his name makes him sound like some rich asshole born with a silver spoon in his mouth. As anxious as I was to talk this out, I didn't want to see the evidence of the life she's built with him or risk losing my shit if I had to watch him touch her.

Maybe it makes me a callous asshole, but I don't want Julian to be part of the conversation Brin and I need to have.

I still can't quite wrap my head around the idea that she *forgot* that night. It's a gut punch, even if what she says makes sense. Xanax and alcohol don't mix, and after about five minutes with Dr. Google, it became clear to me that she's not the only one who loses chunks of time when she mixes the two. But why did she take Xanax in the middle of everything? Was she already engaged? Or at least in deep enough with Julian that guilt had her reaching for her prescription? Bottom line is she doesn't remember, and I can't do anything to get those memories back for her.

After deciding against showing up at her door, I drove around town and kept driving until after midnight. Some part of me assumed Orchid Valley would be the same as it was the day I drove away, frozen in time, but of course it's not. The city's grown, with new developments along the lake and up into the mountains. I drove past Brinley's parents' place and saw it's been turned into a vacation spot for tourists. Downtown has grown and flourished, and the high school has at least a few new wings.

Now it's been twelve hours since I broke the news to my wife and saw her face pale with horror, and I'm done waiting.

The Orchid is a two-story stone building right on Lake Blackledge, set against a backdrop of the southernmost part of the Blue Ridge Mountains. It's clear from the moment I step in the front doors that Brinley runs a topnotch spa. From the soft music playing overhead to the minimalist decor to the subtle greens and blues on the walls, the space hits all the right notes for ultimate relaxation. I'm in places like this all the time, but I'm not immune, and some of my frustration melts away.

The brunette behind the counter is wearing teal scrubs and a white medical jacket. She greets me with a smile. "Good morning. How can I help you?"

I glance at her nametag and return her grin. "Hello, Wren. I'm here with Brinley's coffee. Could you point me to her office?"

A blush creeps up her neck. "Of course. Just follow me."

That easily, I'm in, led through a service door and to an office at the far end of the hall.

Wren pokes her head in the door. "You have a visitor."

I hear Brinley's confused "Who?" but I step around Wren and toward Brinley's desk before Wren can answer.

Brinley's eyes go wide. "Marston, what are you doing here?"

I place her coffee on her desk in front of her. "I'm bringing you coffee. A butterscotch latte." I pull the package out from under my arm and place it on the desk beside her coffee. "And Aunt Lori's chocolate oatmeal breakfast cookies."

Wren twists her hands. "I'm sorry, Brinley. I thought you knew he was coming."

I wave her off and take a seat. "Not your fault at all. I made it sound like that was the case."

Brinley stares at the package for a long beat, then shakes her head as if she's trying to snap herself out of a stupor.

"Wren, thank you. It's fine. Please close the door on your way out."

"Sorry again," Wren whispers, then the door clicks closed.

Brinley pushes the coffee and cookies to the far side of her desk and folds her arms. "You can't just show up at my office. I'm working."

"Would you have rather I showed up at your house last night?" I ask, and she pales. Right. I'm not the only one who thinks it would end badly if I had to see her playing house with another guy.

She grumbles something that sounds an awful lot like "pigheaded male" then leans back in her chair and stares at the ceiling. "What do you want?"

"I want to talk to my wife."

She presses her palms against her eyes and rubs. "Please don't use that word so loudly." Her distress shows on every inch of her face. I almost want to promise to leave and make this all go away.

Except she looked just as stressed last night when she was talking to her friend Abbi in the bar, and the dark circles under her eyes are the kind you get after weeks of not enough sleep, not after a sudden shock.

My jaw goes tight. "You're still wearing his ring."

She drops her hands and gapes at me. "You've had six months to mention we were married. Six months, and you haven't made any effort to reach out to me, but you think that because you show up and tell me about some vows I don't remember taking that I'm just going to . . . What is it that you expect me to do, Marston? Cancel my wedding? Tell Julian, *Oops, turns out I'm already married?*"

"For starters," I say softly.

Her gaze drops to my left hand and her brow wrinkles. "You're not wearing a wedding band."

I blow out a breath. I've worn the brushed platinum band for six months, but on the flight to Atlanta, I decided to take it off. "I'm here to fight for you, not to ruin you. I'll put it back on when you put on yours."

"I . . ." She presses her palms into her desk and exhales slowly. "You're sure it was real? Like, whatever we did, it was a legal marriage?"

I pull the copy of our marriage certificate from my back pocket and hand it to her. I knew something wasn't right when I got that invitation, and I came prepared.

She stares at the document. "This is real?"

"It's a copy, but yes. It's real. We've been married for six months."

She laughs, but the sound is more maniacal than joyful. "And you thought it was totally normal for your wife to not so much as *speak* to you during that time? Seriously?" She flicks her gaze up to my face. "Why didn't you tell me?"

"I assumed you regretted it." *I was afraid if I contacted you, you'd ask for a divorce.* "If I'd realized . . ." I blow out a breath. "I wish I'd known."

"Yeah, you and me both." She squeaks, her eyes back on the paper. "This is a mess."

"It doesn't have to be." Standing, I open the box from Aunt Lori and unwrap a pile of breakfast cookies. Back when Lori worked for the Knoxes, she'd sometimes bake these for the girls, and they were always Brinley's favorite. When I told my aunt I was coming to Orchid Valley for a visit, she insisted on sending cookies for Brinley. I pluck a napkin from the box and pile three cookies on it before sliding it across the desk. "You look exhausted. These might help."

"Of course I look exhausted," she mutters. "I didn't sleep."

"Up late talking to the fiancé about your marital conundrum?" I know venom drips off the word *fiancé*, but I don't care. She's my wife.

"No." She shakes her head, sighs, then reaches for her latte. She pops the lid off, smells it, then whimpers. "That's sugar."

"Butterscotch. Your favorite."

She worries her bottom lip between her teeth. "Since I didn't drink butterscotch lattes in high school, I'm guessing this is something I told you in Vegas?"

It shouldn't hurt that she doesn't remember. It's not as if she intentionally forgot. Nevertheless, my stomach muscles contract at the blow, and I have to clear my throat before I can talk. "After we left the chapel, the sun was rising, and I took you to breakfast. You asked the server if she could make you a butterscotch latte. You said it was your favorite because it reminded you of when you were little and your mom would sneak you butterscotch candies to keep you quiet when your dad was on an important phone call."

She scoops foam onto her index finger and brings it to her mouth, moaning softly as she sucks it off.

I can't take my eyes off her. "Are you trying to turn me on because you want me to fuck you against that desk or because you want to torture me?"

A blush crawls up her neck and across her cheeks. "You can't talk to me like that anymore."

I circle the desk, take her hand, and pull her out of her chair. She stands and sways toward me. "Ah, but I can. And you know it." I tuck a lock of her hair behind her ear. "You liked me talking to you like that."

"Marston . . ." My name is a plea on her lips, and it twists my gut.

"I'll stop." Her eyes lift to meet mine, and I wait a beat, holding her gaze. "But only if you want me to. Not because you think I should."

"What's the difference?"

"You," I whisper. "The difference is what you truly want versus what you *think* you should want."

She turns away and steps toward the big window at the far wall of her office that overlooks Lake Blackledge. "I can't think straight when you stand that close."

I don't smile at this. There's no victory in anything that has her pulling away. "You said you weren't up late talking to your fiancé. Does that mean he took the news about our marriage well?"

She shoots a look at me over her shoulder. "We don't have a marriage. We have a piece of paper."

I grit my teeth. "And what did Julian think about your *piece of paper*?"

"I haven't told him yet."

I'm torn between offering to pick up the phone and deliver the news myself and doing a little fist pump. At the bar, she pretended our vows meant nothing to her, that it was little more than a pesky technicality she was going to have to pay a lawyer to deal with. But this . . . If she didn't tell Julian yet, could it be she's still trying to decide what to do? "He deserves to know sooner rather than later."

"Yeah, I can't imagine what it must be like to have something like that kept from you." She treats me to

132

another over-the-shoulder frown before giving me her back again. "I'll tell him."

"Does he make you happy? Will a life with him be a dream come true?"

She squeezes her temples. "In some ways, yes."

I didn't realize I was standing on a cliff until she shoved me over the edge with those words. It's going to take more than that to get me to give up. "But in other ways . . .?"

She finally turns around and leans against the window. "What do you want from me, Marston?" Her eyes are so sad. I see more than exhaustion there. I see loneliness—and why the hell is she marrying this guy if he leaves her feeling like that?

"Why did you leave that morning? In Vegas?"

"I told you. I didn't know we'd gotten married. I saw the ring and thought we were *engaged*."

I flinch and shake my head. "What made you decide to disregard that decision? What made you walk out the door without saying goodbye?"

She opens her mouth, but before she can manage a response, her eyes well with tears and a sob bursts from her lips.

"Fuck. I'm sorry." Pulling her into my arms is instinctive. It's not a choice but a need, like taking my next breath. The sight of her tears wrecks me, but feeling like I'm the cause breaks my heart.

Her sobs are quiet. Her whole body shakes against mine, and my shirt goes damp with tears. I hold her through them like I always did. I hold her until the shaking subsides and her breathing evens out. I hold her until she pulls away, and when she does, I feel the loss in my chest.

"What do we do now? Do we need lawyers, or can we just find a judge and explain this was all a mistake?"

I wonder if she knows how much that word hurts. *Mistake*. I cup her jaw in one hand and tilt her face up to mine. How can she be even more beautiful to me? We've only been apart six months this time, but her blue eyes are more vivid than I remember, her lips fuller. "There was no mistake. You might not remember our wedding, but you wanted to do it. We're meant to be together, Brinley, and I'm here to remind you of that."

Typically, I pride myself on thinking through every action and reaction, but there's none of that with Brinley. Only instinct and impulse and need. I don't think as I lower my mouth to hers again. I don't question my next move or how a kiss right now will work for or against me.

My lips touch hers, and the only reason I don't kiss her longer and deeper, the only reason I end it before pouring all of my heartache into the kiss, is because she's shaking.

She brings her fingers to her lips. "You can't just kiss me, Marston. I'm marrying someone else."

I lift her left hand, studying the ring again. I want to pull Julian's off and replace it with mine. But I won't. That's a decision she needs to make. And I won't slide mine on next to his, because that's not the way this works. Every decision needs to be hers—taking off his ring, putting on mine. So I pull the ring we picked out together from my pocket and tuck it into the palm of her hand, closing her fingers around it. "The night we met, I told you that if you were ever mine, I wouldn't let you go without a fight. I meant it. Nothing's changed."

"You didn't even know me when you made that promise."

I tuck an errant lock of hair behind her ear. "Sometimes I think I knew you better after five minutes than anyone at that party did. You were . . ." I shake my head, looking for the word.

"A spoiled little rich girl."

I bring her fist—the one holding my ring—up to my chest. "My heart."

She squeezes her eyes shut and draws in a ragged breath. "This is such a mess." She laughs, but fresh tears well in her eyes, and I know if I don't give her some space, she might break.

"You need some time to process."

She nods. "I . . . As much as I might want to, I know we can't just push this under the rug. We have to deal with it, but I . . ."

"I should've called you sooner." I brush her tears away with my thumbs. If I'd come after her, she wouldn't have had a chance to get engaged to Julian. *To fall in love.* "I should've come after you the moment I read that note." I push my luck and brush a kiss across her forehead before dropping my hands and backing away.

I'm one step into the hallway before she speaks again.

"Why didn't you?"

When I turn, I see she's followed me to the door. She's leaning on the jamb, arms crossed, and she looks so damn beautiful that I can't speak for a moment. "You left me that letter and walked away. I thought if I contacted you, then you'd get the ball rolling on ending it. I wasn't willing to lose you completely. Even if all I had left was a piece of paper."

CHAPTER THREE

BRINLEY

"*W*as that Marston?"

At the sound of Savannah's voice, I tear my eyes off Marston's retreating form. "Hey, Savvy."

My friend looks over her shoulder at Marston's back until he pushes through the door to the lobby and disappears. "What's he doing here?"

I return to my desk, trying to figure out how to answer that question. She follows me, eyes narrowed as I collapse into my chair.

Do I want to tell her? *Yes*. Do I want to keep the situation with Marston a secret from everyone—especially friends who might be *delighted* by my current marital status? *Also yes*.

"What's this?" She snags the marriage certificate from my desk, and her eyes go wide as she scans it. "Well, fuck me silly. It *wasn't* just an engagement ring." She grins up at me. "That dirty dog got you drunk and married you. My belated congratulations."

I lean my head back. "Savvy, this is not a cause for celebration."

She glances over her shoulder toward the door. "Shouldn't you two be hashing this out?"

I shake my head. "There's nothing to talk about."

"Looks like y'all need a whole lot of talking," Savvy says, waving the marriage certificate. "Like, a *whole* lot."

I snatch it back from her and shove it into a desk drawer. "I didn't ask you." She's trying to hide her smile behind her hand. "Woman, my life just imploded. You are not allowed to take pleasure in this."

Dropping her hand, she takes a deep breath. "I'm not. I'm sorry. My knee-jerk reaction to any difficult situation is to make light of it. I'm a bitch, and I'm sorry. Tell me what you want to do. We can talk this out, or we can play hooky and go do some serious day drinking. It's your call."

I fold my arms. "Can you go back to being a callous bitch? Being annoyed with you was a nice distraction from my problems."

"And would you say your biggest problem is being engaged to Julian, or being married to Marston?" I scowl, and she throws up her hands. "I'll behave. We only talk if you want to."

"There's nothing to talk about," I say. "I'm marrying Julian. This thing with Marston is just . . . It's . . ."

She arches a perfectly shaped blond brow. "Just the perfect way out of a bad decision?"

"Stop that."

"You know I haven't been a fan of this marriage-of-convenience plan of yours from the start. I'm not going to rewrite history and pretend I ever liked it. Marriages need love."

"I love Julian," I snap, a tad too defensive, since I screwed that one up already last night.

She scoffs. "They need *passion*."

"Julian and I have passion."

"He was your convenient fuck for six years. Your booty call. Your friend who scratched an itch. That's not passion. Passion is you and Marston in Vegas. It's the look in your eyes just now when you watched him walk away. It's hot, and it's full of vivacity, and you deserve it."

"I'm a mother and a workaholic. The passion you describe only works on wild weekends in Vegas or for single twenty-somethings without baggage. I don't have the energy for that."

She frowns and stares at my hand. "What are you holding so tightly?" She takes my hand, and I open it, revealing the ring Marston just gave back to me. "Oh, Brinley."

"What?"

"Girl, that guy is mad over you. He came here to claim his woman but calmly walked away so you could think about it. Even if you don't *have the energy* for that, don't you think it'd be worth it to find some?"

I swallow. "That's not the life I want, Savvy." I hate the disappointment in her eyes, but I understand it.

She nods. "Okay, girl. Whatever you want, you know I'm behind you."

❧

WITH RARE EXCEPTION, I never take a lunch break, but

today I give myself thirty minutes to run home. I should use the time to eat something healthy and trainer-approved, or to do any one of the dozens of real-life tasks that always seem to get pushed aside, but emotional exhaustion hangs on me like two hundred pounds strapped to my back, so I collapse on the couch and close my eyes.

I'm used to an empty house in the middle of the day, but when I hear the sound of heavy steps coming into the living room, I know Julian's here. He doesn't live in my condo with Cami and me—I insisted we wait until after the wedding—but he owns the building and is the only reason Cami and I can afford to live here.

His smile is as warm as his hazel eyes when he steps into the room. "Hey, beautiful." He's a sight to behold in pressed slacks, a dress shirt, and tie, his sandy-blond hair artfully tousled, but I'm too tired to fully appreciate how good-looking my fiancé is.

I sit up and rub my eyes. "Hey, babe. What are you doing here?" I try to force a little enthusiasm into my voice, but judging by his confused smile, I'm not all that successful.

"I stopped by The Orchid to see you, and they said you went home. Are you okay?" He takes me by the hands and pulls me off the couch, wrapping me into a big hug, and some of my tension melts away. Julian is warm and always smells like his clothes just came out of the wash. Back in his arms again, it's easier to remember why we're doing this. We're good together. Stable. *Solid.* We can make a good life together.

"I'm fine," I say, closing my eyes. "Just tired."

He pulls back and tilts my face toward his with one big hand. "You don't have to pretend with me, Brinley."

I try to swallow, but gratitude and guilt make a logjam in my throat. "Between wedding planning, long hours at work, and family stuff, I can't keep my head above water these days."

He strokes his hands down my arms, a pinch of worry creasing between his brows. "You don't have to do everything yourself, you know."

I shake my head. I want to bury my face in his chest again, but I'm afraid if I do, I'll lose the courage to talk. Already, I feel the words fading away. This feels like a crazy dream, and I don't want to make it all real by speaking the truth, but I need to tell Julian about Marston. Last night, I walked straight home, paid the babysitter, and checked on my sleeping daughter.

By the time I settled into bed and called Julian, I'd already decided I couldn't tell him over the phone. While I'm not sure of the standard protocol for telling your fiancé that it turns out you're already married, I'm pretty sure it's a conversation best had in person.

But now Julian's here, and I'm out of excuses. "It's not just that." I head to the kitchen and busy myself preparing a new pot of coffee.

"What is it, then?"

I lift my gaze. Julian moved to Orchid Valley and set his sights on me immediately. He got me into bed with his charm the first night we met, but he could've just as easily done it with his looks. In the years since, I've learned everything else I need to know. He listens when I talk, cares about my daughter, and works as hard as I do. He'll be a good partner, but is that enough? "Are we about to make a terrible mistake?"

His gentle smile falls away, and I'm aware of his attention with every move I make. He's an attentive guy. I think that's what drew me to him. But Julian has never been the issue in the Brinley-plus-Julian equation. It only took him one drink to talk me into joining him in bed, but it took him six years to talk me into being his wife. And now I have to tell him I'm already married.

"There's nothing about marrying you that feels like a mistake to me," he says.

There it is. I squeeze my eyes shut as guilt lodges in my chest. This isn't a massive leap of faith for Julian. His feelings go deeper than they should if we're really planning on making this a temporary arrangement.

"Hey." He turns me so my body's square with his and gently squeezes my shoulders until I open my eyes again. "We're already friends, and we're good together—in bed and out of it. I'm not worried."

"Not even a *little*?" My voice cracks, and I feel so damn guilty for my lack of faith that I hide my face in his chest.

"Nope." He smiles sweetly then lowers his mouth to my ear. "What's the worst that can happen? We discover we're poorly suited roommates? Surely we can tough that out for a few years. Personally, I'm looking forward to waking up next to you every day."

"Marston Rowe's back in town." I spit the words out before I can convince myself to hide them instead. "I saw him at Smithy's last night. Then again at my office this morning."

"Marston the ex? The one you ran into in Vegas?" He releases me and grabs the coffee pot to fill it with water.

I busy myself with grinding the beans. "Yeah."

"What brings him to town?"

"Me."

Julian flashes me a smile then looks me over slowly. "No doubt. What did he say when he found out you were getting married?"

I press the button on the grinder, and the room fills with a loud whirring. When I release it, I breathe deeply. Funny how the smell of a stimulant can be so relaxing. "He's not happy about it." I'm such a coward. *Just spit it out. Rip off the Band-Aid.*

Julian makes a noncommittal hum, but I already know he doesn't like Marston. It's just jealousy, but that's ridiculous when I'm marrying *him*.

I take the now-full pot of water from him and pour it into the machine.

After I position it under the drip spout, Julian takes me by the hips and turns me to face him. "How did it feel to see him again? This was the first time since your escapades in Vegas, wasn't it?"

"Confusing." I wince. This is all so unfair to Julian, but if we have anything right between us, it's honesty. I don't want to change that now. "I panicked when I woke up in his room in Vegas, and that ring . . ." I let my gaze drop.

I keep thinking about what it was like to wake up with Marston's ring—the thrill of it and the dire realization that we'd never work together. I can't take back the decision I made in his Vegas hotel room when I decided to walk away, and I can't change the reasons it was the right choice, yet I feel myself second-guessing it anyway.

Julian squeezes my hips, drawing them forward until our bodies are flush. He leans down, touching his forehead to mine. "The what-ifs in life can be brutal."

"Get out of my head," I say, laughing.

"Don't let him spook you." His dark eyes search mine. "Okay?"

I wrap my arms around his waist and nod. "I'll try."

"I thought I'd make dinner tonight, since Cami has dance. What do you say? Maybe your favorite lasagna, and we can share a bottle of wine."

I force a laugh. "My trainer wouldn't approve of this plan."

He grunts and slides his hands around to squeeze my ass. "I don't approve of your trainer. Can't he see you're already perfect?"

"Hardly." The coffee pot beeps, and I nudge Julian away so I can pour myself a cup, knowing even as I do that I won't enjoy it. Trainer Matt, thief of joy, has made me swear off half-and-half as well as all the fun carbs. I forced myself to toss Marston's butterscotch latte into the trash after he left—just to prove to myself that I *do* still want to look my best at my wedding in two months.

"Is that a no?" Julian asks. I don't miss the worry in his voice, and I want to reassure him that seeing Marston meant nothing but again, honesty matters.

"It's a *no* to the wine and lasagna, but a yes to dinner." I take a sip of my un-doctored, utterly disappointing black coffee, and face my fiancé. "I can make myself a salad."

He grins. "It's a date."

"I'll put it on my schedule." Easy. Steady. Rock-solid. This could be a good life.

"I need to get back to work," Julian says, taking my coffee from my hands and setting it on the counter. "But first . . ." When he lowers his mouth to mine, I do everything I can to turn off my brain. I don't want to think about Marston right now. I don't want to think about my friends' warnings that my reluctance to plan this wedding has some greater significance. I want to lose myself in Julian's lips and the sweep of his tongue across mine.

I try, and little by little, it works.

By the time Julian pulls away, we're both breathless.

"Before you leave . . ." I place a hand on his forearm so he won't go too far. "I have more I need to talk about. Marston's return complicates things."

Julian's face falls, and he takes a step back. I wonder if he even realizes he's retreating. I would too. *Run. Run fast from this disaster you're about to marry.*

"Remember what I told you about Vegas? How I thought he proposed to me that night?"

"Then you came to your senses the next morning." He takes my hand and squeezes. "You made the right choice to walk away. You told me yourself that the two of you can't be together."

I nod. "The thing is . . . I woke up with his ring on my finger and thought I'd agreed to marry him, but I was wrong. He didn't propose that night." I let my gaze shift to the marriage certificate sitting on the counter. I brought it home from work, and now I'm not sure what to do with it.

Julian turns to try to see what I'm looking at, but it's not legible from here. "What is it?"

"I married Marston Rowe." I hate myself for every bit of shock, horror, and hurt that crosses over his beautiful features. "That's a copy of our marriage certificate from Vegas."

He strides to the counter and picks up the paper, studying it like it's one of his real-estate contracts.

"He thought I knew."

Julian drags a hand through his hair. "You don't even

remember that night. How do you know he didn't drug you and drag you into some seedy wedding chapel?"

"Because Marston wouldn't do that." I've been honest with Julian about my history with Marston and about everything we went through together. Julian should know Marston's not that kind of man, so the implication irks me a little.

Julian ignores this and pulls out his phone, tapping quickly on the screen. "It only takes thirty-one days to get an uncontested divorce in Georgia. Looks like most divorces are settled in sixty days, so we'll be well under that if we pull some strings to move things through faster." He lifts his head and gives me a tender smile. "We can fix this."

"He kissed me," I blurt. "Last night and again this morning."

At this, he freezes, his whole body tensing and his jaw going tight. "And did you kiss him back?" he asks, his voice deadly soft.

"No. Of course not. I'm marrying *you*. He just . . . did it, and I wouldn't feel right not telling you."

"That motherfucker," he mutters. He drops the paper and his phone and comes back to slide his arms around me, holding me tight against his chest. Normally, this is comforting, but right now, his arms feel like a cage. "Jesus. You scared me. I was worried for a minute this was making you have second thoughts about our wedding."

I squeak. I was way past second thoughts before Marston showed up, and Julian knows it. He had to campaign hard to talk me into this marriage, and while I haven't shared every moment of panic with him, I have kept him up with my fears and doubts. "I mean, I can't get married if I already am, but we just have to figure out what the next steps are."

"We'll work on this together. Call your dad's lawyer. I bet he knows someone who can push the paperwork or whatever through quickly." He buries his face in my hair and draws in a long, ragged breath. "Scared the shit out of me."

"I'm sorry. I didn't mean to."

He grips my shoulders as he pulls back. "Have you said anything to Cami?"

"What? No. Of course not." I shake my head. "I'm still trying to make sense of my thoughts."

His shoulders sag. "Okay. I'll do a little research today, and we'll make a plan over lasagna and wine."

"Over salad and water for me. Gotta fit into that wedding dress." I force a cheerful grin and hope it hides my doubts. As in, will we be able to fix this fast enough that there'll still be a dress to fit into?

"Tell me Trainer Matt goes away after the wedding," he says.

I smile. "Of course. I'm not going to be the woman who gets up at four a.m. for personal training for the rest of her life."

"Good. Because feeding you is in my vows, and I won't let anyone stand in the way of those." He gives me one final kiss, and we both know he's not just talking about Matt.

CHAPTER FOUR

BRINLEY

October 20th, before

My favorite time of the week is the time I get with Marston. It doesn't happen as often as I'd like, but moments with him still feel like a breath of fresh air after years of being trapped underground.

We have to be creative when we see each other. Sometimes we go to Lake Blackledge, sometimes we hike, and sometimes we drive out of town—miles away and back in the same night just so we can eat dinner or go to the park someplace where we're free to talk and hold hands. It took some convincing to get Marston to drive my car, but mine is better than his, and the highway doesn't scare him like it does me.

Tonight was a drive-for-hours night, and we talked about everything and nothing. My parents believe I'm at Stella's house, because she's the best friend ever and insists on covering for me any time I need it. *"Your house has become half prison and half shrine to a dying girl. Get the fuck out of there!"*

I squeeze Marston's hand when he takes the exit to Orchid Valley. "Why does it always go so fast?"

He flashes me a tentative smile. I know he wants more time together as much as I do, but the more I try to think of a way to tell my parents about this relationship, the more I know they'd freak out. Last week, I discovered they were reading my texts—something I'd suspected but hadn't known for sure. It's like the sicker Brittany gets, the more they need to control me. "We could go to the lake for a few minutes before I take you back to Stella's."

I lean across the console and kiss his shoulder. "Yes, please."

And with the promise of just a few minutes more with him, my mood lifts, and I fill the rest of the drive with happy chatter.

Marston never complains when I ramble. He says he likes knowing what I'm thinking about and wants me to feel like I can tell him anything—from the most trivial thought to the most awful. While I haven't been quite brave enough to share the ugliest and scariest thoughts that lurk in the darkness of my mind, I've never felt judged by a single thing I've shared with him. He might be the only person who doesn't look at me and try to evaluate me. When he looks at me, he sees me as I am, and that's who he wants. *Me*—not some prettied-up version.

It's nearly dark when he pulls into the small parking area by the loading dock, and I know our time here will be brief.

There's another car in the lot, but it probably belongs to someone who's watching the sunset from their boat on the lake. We'll have plenty of privacy by the time we slip into the woods.

We step out of the car and hold hands as we cut across the grass to the trail that runs along the water. We've walked it so many times that we could probably navigate it with our eyes closed.

"Stella's going to be so jealous when I tell her you bought me ice cream," I say.

He laughs. "I offered to bring her along."

"She doesn't want to intrude. She thinks——"

"Brinley? Is that you?"

A light bobs at the trailhead, and then Roman Humphries steps out of the trees and comes into view.

I don't know the name of the girl on his arm, but I recognize her from school. She's a freshman, and she clings to him, laughing at some shared joke before she says, "You said no one else comes out here."

"They usually don't," Roman says, coming closer. He flashes the light in our faces, and I squeeze my eyes shut against the blinding glare. "No fucking way. Brinley, what are you doing out here with Death Rowe?"

Marston's head snaps back at the verbal blow, but he steps forward. "What did you just call me?"

Roman chuckles, delighted with himself. "Your last name is Rowe, right? Death Rowe."

My stomach cramps as I look back and forth between Roman and Marston. "Don't call him that."

Roman sneers in my direction. "It won't make a difference. That's what everybody calls this guy. Seems appropriate for a kid who's on his way there."

Marston is so still and so quiet beside me, but I feel the fury rolling off him. This is a disaster in the making. Fear that it could end with trouble for Marston sticks like a bramble of thorns in my throat. I take his arm and tug him back toward the car, but he doesn't move. "Come on, Marston. Let's get out of here."

"What's the rush?" Roman pulls something from his pocket. A cigarette? He puts it between his lips and lights it with the other hand, taking a puff before strolling toward us and offering it to Marston. When it passes in front of me, I smell skunk. *Pot, not tobacco.* "Want a hit, *Death Rowe?*"

Marston's entirely still except for the tic in his jaw.

"Silly me. I forgot." Roman takes another drag before leaning forward and blowing smoke into Marston's face. How could I have ever liked someone like that? Why did I ever believe he was worth crying over? "You're on probation. They catch you with this in your system, and it'll be back to juvie for you."

"Back off, Roman." I tug on Marston's arm again, but he's immovable.

Roman blows in his face one more time and laughs. "Hope I didn't disrupt your plans with this one," he says, nodding to me. "I'll go so you can enjoy her. I know I did. Just last weekend, actually." He winks, then takes a single step around us before Marston's fist connects with his face with a sickening *thwack.* Roman collapses to the ground, face in his hands. "Fuck."

"I'm calling the cops," the freshman girl says.

"Don't!" Roman growls.

"I should." Her eyes blaze with anger as she sneers at Marston. "He can't just go around punching people."

Roman whips his head up and glares at her. "I have all that weed in my car. Do you *want* me to go to jail?"

"Marston, come on." This time when I tug on his arm, he takes a few steps back, but he doesn't turn to go.

His angry eyes bore into Roman. "Don't talk about her like that again."

I lace my fingers through his and squeeze, trying to communicate with the grip of my hand. *He doesn't matter. He doesn't know us. Don't let him ruin this.*

As if Marston can hear what I'm so desperately trying to telegraph, he finally turns toward the car and we walk away, hand in hand.

I don't speak until we're on the road again, headed, I realize with a sinking heart, to Stella's. "It's not true."

He doesn't take his eyes off the road or reply.

"Marston, I need you to look at me and tell me you believe me. It's not true. I've never let Roman touch me. Not last weekend. Not ever."

He slows down and pulls into the dark lot of a service station. After throwing the car in park, he leans back in his seat and closes his eyes. "I know." His voice is gruff, thick with emotion and repressed anger. "But that's the shit he's going to spread about you just because you're with me. You don't deserve that."

After unbuckling my seatbelt and then his, I crawl across the console and into his lap. I take his face in my hands and relish the feel of his scruff beneath my fingertips. "Look at me."

When he opens his eyes, he pulls in a deep breath and lets it out slowly. The rage seeps out of him, the firm set of his mouth softening, the tension in his shoulders melting away.

"Do you want to be with me?" I ask.

"Guys like Roman—"

"Screw Roman. Do *you* want to be with *me*?"

"More than anything." He lifts a hand and skims his thumb along my jaw. "You know that."

"Remember the night we met? You told me if I were yours, you'd never let me go. Did you mean it?"

He grabs my hips and pulls me tight against him. "I'd never let you go without a fight. Not as long as part of you was mine."

"I'm yours." Smiling, I shake my head. "And I don't mean part of me. I mean every little piece."

CHAPTER FIVE

BRINLEY

Present day

When I get home from work, the condo smells like heaven. The scent of garlic bread and Julian's red sauce meet me at the door. I follow the smell to the kitchen, where I find Julian at the counter chopping vegetables.

It's easy to imagine a life with this guy. He helps around the house—he's handy with tools and good in the kitchen. He's good to Cami and has always treated me right. Savvy's so hung up on passion, but passion makes you reckless. It makes you break your parents' hearts when they're grieving. It makes you get married in Vegas to someone who doesn't want the same life as you. What Julian and I have might not be passionate, but we've always had chemistry. Over the last six months, we've ventured into new territory and found we're compatible in more parts of our lives than just the bedroom. Instead of casual hookups, we started dating and spending more time together, and it's been good. Steady.

"How was your day at work?" Julian asks, flashing me a grin.

"It was all right. Kace came to bid the steam room remodel, but I already know Mrs. Wright is going to shoot him down. He threw out some numbers while we were talking, and there's no way." I shake my head and lean on the island opposite him. "That's tomorrow's problem, right?"

He pops a piece of raw carrot in his mouth and smiles around it. "That's right."

"How was your day?"

"Nothing special. Met with one of my property managers and went over some plans for the apartments on Spruce."

The front door whooshes open, and the walls rattle as it's slammed again just as quickly. "Mom, do you know where my dance shoes are?" Cami calls, jogging into the kitchen. Like it always does, my chest swells at the sight of her—dark hair in a high bun, that ever-present smile curving her lips.

I look to Julian. "Duty calls," I whisper. "I think they're in the laundry room." She sprints in that direction, and I follow her. "How was your afternoon with Mia?"

"Fine. We learned a new TikTok dance. Mia recorded us doing it, but she's going to send it to me." She bends to drop her jazz shoes into her dance bag. "I can't believe I'm missing lasagna night." She straightens and hoists her bag onto one shoulder before rubbing her stomach. "It smells so good, and I want to dive face-first into it."

"That might result in some painful burns, so I don't recommend it," I say, and my mood improves tenfold at the sound of her giggle. "And anyway, there'll be plenty of leftovers."

"Save me half the pan!" She grins. She looks just like her father when she smiles like that. The reminder of him used to make me sad, but I've long made peace with the fact that my daughter spent the first ten years of her life in a one-parent household.

"Of course," I promise, returning her smile. "How was school?"

"Good, but I just want it to be spring break already." She wriggles with excited energy.

"Just a few more days." I do my best to sound cheerful, but it's hard. She's spending her spring break and her birthday at Disney with her dad, and I'm dreading an entire week without her. "How'd your math test go?"

"It was easy, but Kellan got caught cheating off Mia and had to sit in the principal's office until his parents came to have a talk about it."

I wrap my arm around her shoulders, and we head to the front door. We carpool to dance classes, and it's my week off. "That's why it's never a good idea to cheat."

"He's dumb, though, Mom."

"Don't say that. Everyone has something they struggle with in school, Miss Smarty Pants. Just because you haven't found yours yet doesn't mean you won't."

"No, I mean he's dumb because he cheated off Mia, who's doing independent math and doesn't even take the same *tests*. He said he did it because he *likes* her. How does that even make sense? Why do people get stupid when they fall in love?"

Good question, sweetie. "He's ten. He's more likely *infatuated* than in love."

She shrugs. "Whatever. He's still dumb."

"Can I walk you down tonight?"

She tenses. "We agreed that you wouldn't! No one's mom walks them to carpool anymore. We're not *six*."

I want to push, but I know what it's like to be a kid hungry for some freedom. I promised myself the day she was born that I wouldn't be like my parents. I kiss her forehead. "Have fun at dance. I'll see you when you get home."

"Bye, Cami!" Julian calls from the kitchen.

"Bye!" she shouts over a shoulder. "See ya, Mom." She opens the door and bounds down the hallway toward the stairs.

"I love you," I call after her.

"Love you too!" she shouts, and throws me a kiss.

I toss one back at her and go to the window to look down at the street, where her friend's mom waits in their red minivan. I watch until Cami pushes out onto the sidewalk and climbs in.

"Finally alone," Julian says as he comes to join me in the living room. He wraps his arms around me from behind and trails kisses up and down my neck. "I've been thinking about you all day."

I stiffen and then force myself to relax. *This is my future husband.* "It smells great. I might cheat and have just a small bite."

He hums against my neck. "It needs another forty minutes in the oven." He gathers my skirt in one hand and strokes my hip with the other, tracing the edge of my underwear. "Care to pass the time with me in the bedroom?"

I squeeze my eyes shut, but all I can see is Marston looking at me with those hot eyes when I sucked the latte foam from my finger. *"Are you trying to turn me on because you want me to fuck you against that desk or because you want to torture me?"*

I shiver at the memory, and Julian shifts his hips and grinds his erection against my back, no doubt thinking my reaction was for him. "Julian, I can't," I whisper. "My mind's a mess right now."

"Just relax. This is exactly what we need." He cups me between my legs, and I jerk forward out of his grasp.

"Stop." I spin around to see him backing away from me, hands in his hair. "I'm sorry," I blurt, but I instantly want to take the words back. I don't need to apologize just because I'm not interested in sex right now. Swallowing, I offer an apology I won't resent later. "I'm sorry about how I handled that, but I'm not in the mood. It's been a long day, and I've had a lot on my mind."

He sinks onto the couch, rests his elbows on his knees, and looks up at me with narrowed eyes. "Is that really it? A long day, or you're thinking about *him*?"

"What if I am?" I press my hand against my stomach, where I'm pretty sure the nerves and stress of the last twenty-four hours have burned a hole. "What if I'm sick to my stomach because I *married* someone and can't even remember it? What if my fear and embarrassment over my future—*our* future—has made sex the last thing on my mind?"

"Am I supposed to keep my hands off you until this divorce or annulment or whatever goes through?"

"I never said that."

"But you don't want me to touch you now? Just because you got drunk and stupid?"

"Don't talk to me like that." My voice is low, but clear enough that I know he can hear every word. "I spent the first seventeen years of my life listening to my father berate me and knock me down with his words. I'm not about to let you or anyone else do it now."

He stands up and stares at me. "I just found out my fiancée is already married. You think you're the only one dealing with fear and embarrassment? I've been played before, Brinley. This feels . . . way too familiar."

My heart sinks. Julian's last serious relationship ended when the woman ran off with her ex-boyfriend and a bunch of Julian's money. "Julian, I'm sorry, but this is different."

"I've been here. I've been your friend, your lover. I've helped you out when money was tight."

I want to remind him I never asked for that help. I want to remind him I pushed back when he insisted Cami and I move into this condo. I can't afford even a small unit in this building on my salary, let alone this one, with three bedrooms and every offered upgrade. But he insisted I move in and pay just a fraction of the rent. *"We're getting married. Let me take care of you."*

But the truth is that I've been so caught up in my own whirlwind of emotions that I haven't given much thought to Julian's feelings, and that's unacceptable, so I don't say any of that.

"I've been here, and I've been mad about you all this time," he says, quieter now.

"I know." I draw in a long breath. "But be fair, J. I've

been honest about my feelings and my reservations from the beginning."

"I know." He swallows. "And maybe that's why it hurts so much to know you married him after a few hours in Vegas. And you're second-guessing *us* after he shows up out of the blue. I've been here, and I've promised you I'll always be here. What's he promising you?"

"It doesn't matter." I shrug. "I'm going to fix this."

"Then why haven't you called your lawyer?"

I bow my head, embarrassment and shame heating my cheeks. "I don't know." I look up. "Wait—how did you know I hadn't?"

His lips twist into a sneer. "Just a hunch." He grabs his keys off the counter and shoves them into his pocket. "I set the timer for the lasagna. Just pull it out when it's done. Let it cool before you put it in the fridge or . . . Fuck, throw it all away if that's what you're into tonight."

I feel helpless. We've never fought before—nothing more than minor disagreements—and I don't know how to handle this side of him. Is this how he'll act any time things are tough? "You're being cruel."

He shrugs. "I'm human, Brin. And you're fucking hurting me right now."

He walks away, and the walls shake as he slams the door behind him.

❧

MARSTON

"Marston!" Smith calls from behind the bar the moment he spots me. "Get your ass over here, you rich prick."

Grinning, I make my way toward him. When I was here last night looking for Brinley, her cousin wasn't around. Probably for the best, since I was in no mood to catch up, but tonight, nothing sounds better than a drink with my old friends, and when I called Smithy, he promised to make it happen.

Grant Smith, or Smithy to anyone who knows him, looks pretty much the same as he did in high school. He's thicker in the shoulders and chest and has a little more facial hair, but I'd recognize him anywhere. His light brown hair's a little longer, just past his chin now, giving him a hipster-stoner vibe.

It's so easy for me to remember the bad shit about Orchid Valley. For years, my strongest associations with this place, aside from Brinley, were the shame and embarrassment that came with being Aunt Lori's pity case, and I've forgotten about the good parts. I made some great friends during my time here, and I'm an ass for not doing my part to keep up with them.

I tap the knuckles he holds out for me. "Smith, nice place."

"Thank you. Nothing compared to all your fancy-ass resorts, but I like it. Fuck, man, I can hardly keep up with running this place. I don't know how you do it."

I grunt. "I don't run them. I run the company that gives those resorts *advice*."

"Is there a difference?"

I laugh. I can't imagine Smithy would be as impressed with my job if he realized that at the root of it all, I'm just a geek with a spreadsheet. "Countless differences, but the biggest is I pay other people to do all the real work."

"Hell yeah." He bobs his head. "Teach me how to do that before you go, okay?"

"Sure thing." I nod to the plentiful selection of taps. "What's good and local?"

"I assume your drinking is more refined than it was in high school?"

"A little." I grin because his happiness has always been contagious. "Remember when we got that case of Busch Light and drank it by the river?"

"Those were the days. No Busch Light on tap right now, though. I have a local wheat that's pretty good, nice and light, kind of like a Blue Moon with a bit of vanilla on the back end."

"Sounds perfect. Thanks." I lean against the bar rather than sit, and scan the room. Smithy has a couple of tables for pool—a favorite pastime of mine—a few pinball machines, bookshelves stacked with old board games, and even a Skee-Ball machine by the back hallway. The place isn't packed, but it's got a nice crowd for a Tuesday night, and the posters on the wall advertise Thursday night trivia. All in all, Smithy's is everything we would've wanted if we'd been allowed to go to bars when we were seniors.

It's funny. I always imagined that coming back to Orchid Valley would feel like a high-school reunion and that I'd be constantly surrounded by all the judgmental assholes I escaped when I turned eighteen, but I don't know most of the people here. I stayed away for years for all the wrong reasons. I should've come back sooner—should've come back for Brinley even before she found me in Vegas.

"Kace is already waiting in the back," Smithy says when he comes back with my beer. He hands it to me and tilts his head in that direction before grabbing another two beers—I assume for himself and Kace.

As I weave my way around tables toward the other side of the bar, Kace Matthews spots us and pushes out of his seat, tucking his phone into his pocket. "Mars!" Kace gives me a fist bump before pulling me into a one-armed hug. "Been too fucking long, man."

"It really has," I say, taking a seat across from him. "Thanks for meeting up tonight."

"Thanks for inviting me," he says. "But I can only stay for one beer, and then I have to head out."

"No problem." I shake my head as I look around the bar. "Nothing in this town is like I remember it."

"Let me guess. You remembered it as a prison full of entitled punks?" Smithy says, plopping into the seat beside me.

"Possibly," I admit with a grin. "But I never held that against you."

Kace smirks. "*Burn.*" He chuckles. "What brings you back?"

I hesitate. Obviously, I'm not going to throw Brinley under the bus by telling everyone in her hometown that while she might be engaged to Julian, she's *married* to me, but that doesn't mean I can't be honest about *who* I'm here for. Even if I leave out some details. "Honestly, Brinley."

"I fucking knew it," Smithy says, smacking a hand on the table. "Damn. Marston and Brinley. You two were *epic* together."

I grunt. "I have no idea what that means."

"Romeo and Juliet, man. Pyramus and Thisbe. Guinevere and Lancelot."

"So we're bound to die tragically if we follow our hearts?" I deadpan.

"*Right?* Epic," he says, nodding, as if this is something to aspire to. Smithy's always been half genius, half airhead. It's comforting to know some things don't change, though if I had to guess, I'd bet my old friend has upped his daily cannabis consumption since high school.

"You probably know this already," Kace says, taking his beer from Smithy, "but you're a few months too late. She's marrying Julian Hallison."

"They're not married yet." I watch him over the rim of my glass as I take a sip of my beer.

Kace shakes his head. "Does *she* know why you're here?"

"She knows." These guys were my best friends at Orchid Valley High School. Smithy's a distant Knox cousin, meaning he had a connection to the family without the luxury of the Knox Bourbon money. Because he was always close to Brinley, he knew about our relationship when only a couple of other people did. I worked with Kace and we were friends, but he didn't find out about it until later—when everything imploded and Brinley begged me to walk away from Orchid Valley and leave her behind. "What do you know about this guy she's engaged to?"

"Julian is a real-estate guy," Kace says. "Commercial investment stuff, mostly. You've probably seen the Hallison Way signs around town. That's his company. They buy, sell, remodel, and rent properties in Orchid Valley."

Smithy rubs his thumb against his index and middle fingers. So Julian has money. Luckily, that doesn't intimidate me anymore. "He's been chasing Brinley since he first moved to town, but she'd never been more than just an occasional hookup, no matter how much he tried to impress her. Then, six months ago, suddenly everything changed and they weren't just a couple—they were looking at engagement rings and talking wedding plans." He puts his fists on either side of his head, opening them dramatically to indicate his head exploding.

I look at Kace for confirmation, and he shrugs. "Smithy's got a better handle on the gossip around here than I do, but I never got the impression that my sister was a fan of the change in their relationship."

"Your sister?" I ask.

"Abbi Matthews. She's the chef at The Orchid's restaurant and one of Brinley's best friends."

I nod. "I met her last night."

Smithy grins. "Right. I hear you cornered Brinley in the hall, and she ran out."

I turn to him, brows raised, because seriously, we were alone in that hallway.

Smithy points to the tables by the front window. "Those spots have a great view of the bathroom hallway and people around here like to talk. There's not much that happens in my bar that I don't know about."

Kace snickers and shakes his head. "Let me get this straight. You show up all macho rich guy after not seeing her for a decade, corner her in the hallway, and tell her you're here for *her*, and she runs away from your cocky ass like you're some sort of creeper." He chuckles again and sighs. "Jesus, that's good."

"Thanks for the support, Kace," I say.

He stills his beer halfway to his lips and shakes his head. "What? Did you really expect her to wait for you all this time? That's not how these things work."

Smithy leans forward. "Yeah. How'd you even know if

there'd still be a spark there? What if she'd gotten ugly or developed some sort of unidentifiable stinky cheese smell?"

Kace and I both blink at him. "That's oddly specific," Kace says, brow arched.

"Happened to a girl I knew once." Smithy shakes his head sadly. "She was a tiger in the sack, but that smell was always *right there* beneath the surface."

"How . . . unfortunate," Kace says.

Smithy shrugs. "She got married recently. I can only assume her new husband has sinus troubles. Either that or he also smells like Limburger." He sighs. "Anyway, obviously Brinley doesn't stink and is still the stuff of wet dreams, so—"

"Dude, she's your cousin," Kace says.

Smithy turns up his palms. "By marriage and whatever. You can't tell me you don't think *Abbi* is fuckably hot."

Kace chokes on his beer, then returns it to the table with a *clunk*. "What the hell, asshole. She's my *sister*."

Smithy rolls his eyes. "Objectively speaking."

Kace turns to me with a pained expression that seems to say, "*Can you believe this idiot?*" but I can only laugh.

"I think what Kace is trying to say, Smithy, is that for most of us, there are certain women in our lives we can intellectually see as beautiful, but our brains don't connect them with sex."

Smithy makes a face. "Huh."

"And if you ever refer to my sister as *fuckably hot* again," Kace says, nodding in Smithy's direction, "I'll punch you so hard in the nuts, you'll feel 'em when you brush your teeth the next day."

"Noted," Smithy says, but his grin reveals he's not really worried. He turns his attention back to me. "What I'm saying, man, is that's a lot of faith to come back for Brinley out of nowhere."

"It wasn't out of nowhere." I look at Kace, wondering how much his sister tells him. Of course, I don't know how much Brinley told Abbi about the last time we met. "I ran into Brinley in Vegas in September. We spent—" I almost say "spent the night together" but catch myself. I don't want to start Smithy down that path. "We spent some time together."

Kace frowns. "Right, Abbi said something about Savvy and Brinley going to Vegas for Brinley's twenty-seventh birthday."

"And one week later, she had Hallison's ring on her finger," Smithy says. He must see the shock on my face, because he cringes. "Sorry. That probably sucks for you to think about. Like, how much did you fuck up that night together if she came back here and hitched her horse to the guy she'd been passing on for years?"

Kace calmly lifts a hand and covers Smithy's mouth. "Excuse him. We've looked into it, but there's no known cure for this mouth."

Did she get engaged because of what happened in Vegas? Or did she come to Vegas because she was trying to make a decision about the engagement? And if it's that, then why the fuck did she come home and say *yes*?

I don't believe it's all just a coincidence. Brinley doesn't make decisions impulsively—save for one Vegas wedding she can't even fucking remember.

I push my beer away, my stomach suddenly too sour for even a sip.

Smithy peels Kace's hand away from his mouth. "At first, we thought maybe she was pregnant, but then they started talking a May wedding and she never got a bump, so clearly not." Smithy shrugs, then his eyes go comically wide. "What if she got knocked up with *your* kid?"

Kace rolls his eyes. "I don't think that's what we're dealing with here, Smithy. I think maybe she's just ready to settle down. In which case . . ." He reaches for his drink and takes a long slug then wipes his mouth with the back of his hand.

I set my jaw. "Spit it out, Kace."

"Fuck, man. I don't think I should say."

"Say what?" Smithy cocks his head to the side as he studies Kace.

"Out with it," I mutter.

"Is this a pride thing? Like, you need to prove you can have the girl you could only have in secret back in the day?" When I don't give that bullshit the benefit of a response, he goes on. "Because if that's all this is, let her be. She could be happy with Julian. He's a solid dude, and he works with her life here. Do you really want to be the reason that all falls apart?"

I can't fault Kace for asking. I haven't been in touch, and for all he knows, I've gotten my money from screwing over everyone I can. But it still burns that he thinks I'd ever put my ego ahead of Brinley's happiness. "It's not about pride." I blow out a breath. "If it were about pride, I would've left town already."

"Okay," Kace says, nodding. "I respect that."

Smithy props his elbows on the table and leans forward, his gaze intense. "So what *is* it about?"

"I'm in love with her, you idiot."

Smithy grins. "Damn good thing she's *not* pregnant again, huh?"

Smithy's words hit me with the force of a Mack truck.

Kace frowns at me over his beer. "You look like you've seen a ghost."

I stare at Smithy. "You said good thing she's not pregnant *again*, which implies she's been pregnant *before*."

Smithy's eyes go wide and he looks at Kace, who just shakes his head.

"Brinley has a kid? Julian's?" Jesus. That would explain a lot.

Smithy opens his mouth and then snaps it shut, so I turn to Kace.

"Her name's Cami, and she's not Julian's," he says, but when I open my mouth, he holds up a hand. "Any other questions you have, you need to take to Brinley." He gives Smithy a hard look and says, "This is Brinley's to tell."

Brinley has a kid. A little girl. Brinley has a little girl and is engaged to be married to some guy who's clearly happy to step into the role of Cami's father.

"You okay?" Smithy asks.

I blink at him. My heart pumps too hard and too fast, and my chest aches under the weight of all my unanswered questions.

I don't want to give a single shit about this Julian guy or what he *thinks* he can give Brinley, but suddenly it feels like Kace's warning is right. I thought I was coming here to claim my bride, but suddenly it feels a lot more like I'm here to upend her life.

CHAPTER SIX

BRINLEY

I'm curled up on the couch when the door creaks open, and two sets of heels tap toward the living room. I don't get up. I figure I only have another half-hour, max, before Cami gets home, which means only thirty minutes left to sulk and feel sorry for myself. I'm going to make the most of it.

"Oh, *fuckmydiet* it smells so good in here." I know it's Savannah, because no one else says "fuck my diet" like it's one word and a working part of their vocabulary.

I open one eye to see her plopping brown paper bags on the coffee table. *Someone's* been to the liquor store.

"You don't need to diet," Abbi says, stopping by the couch to toe off her shiny pink ballet flats. "You're perfect."

"Um, *obviously*," Savvy says, "but 'perfect' takes effort for most of us."

I smile despite myself and sit up.

Savvy pulls bottle after bottle from the paper bags. I'm pretty sure she bought the whole liquor store. "Not all of us can be like you and have a hot little bod, despite never visiting the gym."

"Aw, I didn't know you thought I was hot," Abbi says. "Thanks, Savvy. You're a sexy kitten too."

Savvy winks. "Meow."

I nod to the collection of booze covering my coffee table. "Are you going to open a bar in my living room, or were you just planning to give me alcohol poisoning?" Baileys, Godiva liqueur, peppermint schnapps, vanilla vodka, and Kahlua.

"I need all of this to make the martinis we're having tonight," Savvy says. "I tried one for the first time in this little beach town in Michigan."

"There's a beach in Michigan?" Abbi asks, already reaching for the shaker.

"Um, yeah. Lake Michigan?" Savvy shakes her head. "At least you're pretty."

Abbi flips her off, and Savvy blows her a kiss.

"Anyway, the bartender called it the Kitchen Sink Martini, but I thought it tasted like the kind of thing you need to drink when you're heartbroken, so I call them Heartbreak Martinis."

"I'm not heartbroken. I'm stressed," I snap, but then soften when my bitchiness makes my friends give me puppy-dog eyes full of sympathy. "Sorry, but there's a difference."

Savvy points at me. "There is. And feeling stressed and not heartbroken when your wedding might fall apart should tell you something." Spinning on her heel, she heads to the kitchen and pulls my martini glasses off the shelf before filling a bowl with ice.

"Did I miss it?" someone calls from the door.

"Is that Stella?" I ask. I swear the stress and worry I've been carrying all day lift from my shoulders. My girls are here. *My family.*

"Of course it is!" Stella strolls into the room in a little white-and-yellow sundress with a flared skirt and bright orange heels. Oversized rock-star sunglasses hold back her red hair. I haven't seen her for a week, and I swear, my heart swells at the sight of her. She hoists a grocery bag from her shoulder and into the air like an offering when she sinks onto the couch beside me. "I brought the junk food."

Abbi wanders into the kitchen and peeks under the foil-wrapped lasagna pan cooling on the stove. "Junk food, sugary booze, and lasagna." She rubs her hands together. "Life is good."

"Who made lasagna?" Stella asks.

"Julian," Savvy says. She plops the bowl of ice in the center of the coffee table and positions the glasses around it. "How are you, Stell? How was Jamaica? Full of fun and hot sex?"

"I'm . . . single." Stella shrugs.

"What?" the rest of us say in unison.

Stella shakes her head. "You know what? Let's not do me. We can do me another night with another collection of booze and food. Tonight is about Brinley."

Savvy's smile falls away. "What happened?"

"Talk to us, Stella," I say. She was so into this guy that she'd been *living with him*, even though the commute from Atlanta is a bitch. And suddenly it's over?

"It's nothing." Stella lifts her chin in a familiar stubborn gesture then points at me. "Focus."

"Well, you look beautifully sun-kissed, whatever else is going on with you, bitch," Savvy says, waving to the fresh freckles dotted across Stella's shoulders and cheeks.

"Aww, thanks, baby boo."

I sag into the couch. Selfishly, I want hours with my girls, but that's not in the cards tonight. "You guys did all this, and Cami's going to be home in no time."

"No, she's not," Abbi calls from the kitchen. "My brother's on his way over. He's going to take her out for dinner and ice cream with Hope."

Abbi's brother, Kace, has been friends with my cousin Smithy since high school. He and Stella's brother, Dean, are as much family to Cami and me as these girls are. Kace has a four-year-old daughter Cami adores, and this certainly wouldn't be the first time Cami hung out with them for a couple of hours.

"Thanks, Abbi," I say, knowing she's the one who arranged it.

"So that means Kace is going to be here later?" Stella asks, waggling her brows.

"Stella!" Abbi abandons the lasagna to stomp into the living room and wave a finger at her. "He's still an emotional wreck from his divorce. He's in no place to be seduced."

Stella presses a manicured hand to her chest. "I swear, you climb into bed with a guy *one time* . . ."

Savvy cackles, and I feel even lighter. *These girls.*

"Lord *help* us," Abbi says.

Savvy rolls her eyes and gives Abbi a pointed look. "Kace can handle himself. He's a big boy."

"Yeah, he is," Stella says under her breath.

Savvy guffaws, and I bite back my smile.

Abbi shakes her head and grabs the bottle of vodka from the table. "You drive me to drink, woman," she mutters, and we all laugh.

I scan the piles of snack food Stella's pulling from the bag. Doritos, donuts, Milano cookies, and a box of Godiva chocolates. "I'm pretty sure we have enough here for all of us to have an emotional breakdown and still have leftovers."

Stella kicks off her heels and tucks her feet under her on the couch. "Someone catch me up."

"What do you want to know?" I'm dreading any kind of recap, because every time we run down the facts on the mess that is my life, I feel like a bigger idiot.

Stella opens the bag of Doritos and passes them to me. "The text from Savvy said, 'Julian's being a dick. Marston back in the picture. Intervention in thirty.'"

I turn to glare at Savvy. "Really, Savvy? Intervention?"

Savvy takes the shaker from Abbi and drops ice into it with a clunk. "Seemed appropriate."

"Weren't you going to be on vacation until tomorrow?" I ask Stella.

Stella sticks her bottom lip out in a pout. "I left his ass at the resort and flew home early."

"You *left him?*" Abbi screeches.

Stella rolls her shoulders back and ignores the question. "So, Julian? Marston? And I'm assuming y'all mean Marston Rowe, as in high-school Marston? As in *hotel-mogul* Marston?"

"He's not a hotel mogul." I grab the cookies. Trainer Matt can kiss it. "He's a consultant."

"Whatever. The interview I saw with him and his business partner in *Forbes* made it clear he's hot shit, whatever he's doing," Stella says.

"He *is* hot shit," I say, giving Savvy a pointed look. "And his hot-shit job means he won't be around long, so he's not 'back in the picture' so much as visiting the picture. *Briefly*."

"Or until you get a divorce," Savvy says.

"Wait." Stella hops off the couch and the bag of Doritos falls to her feet. "Why are you planning on divorcing Julian before you even *marry* him?"

"Before I marry Julian, I need to divorce *Marston*," I say, and she blinks at me, her jaw unhinged. "Apparently, I got drunk in Vegas and we got married. The engagement ring I found on my finger the next morning? Turns out it was a wedding ring."

"How long have you known this?" Abbi asks, plopping down into a chair across from me.

I sigh. "Since he cornered me in the hallway at Smithy's last night." Was that just last night? *Longest day ever.*

She bows her head, and I can practically see her talking herself out of being mad at me. "You've had so many chances to talk to me since then."

"I'm sorry, Ab. I'm kind of a mess right now."

She nods. "But you've told Julian?"

"Yeah."

"And how's he handling it?" Stella asks. Stella, the only one who doesn't know my reasons for agreeing to marry Julian.

"Not well." I pop a cookie in my mouth to buy myself some time. When I swallow, I say, "He's partly justified in his anger, but partly just being an ass."

Savvy arches a brow. "Sounds like a good reason to cut ties with him and stay married to Marston."

"Savvy," I groan.

"You're already married, goober. You don't need to marry Julian anymore. Collect your trust and end this sham of a relationship."

I open my mouth to explain, but Stella holds up a hand. "Wait. Why are you acting like one husband's as good as any? Like, I get that she and Marston have history—seriously, I was there—but she's engaged to Julian for a reason. The trust is just a silver lining." She studies my face for a beat, then frowns. "Isn't it?"

These girls are my family, and I don't like keeping secrets from them. But I've been keeping one major secret from Stella. She's been busy with Bobby, so we haven't been spending as much time together, but that wasn't the real reason I didn't confide in her. I knew she wouldn't agree with my choice. Stella might be a ballbuster, but deep down she's a romantic. She would want me to marry for *love*—nothing more, nothing less. "Julian knows I needed to be married to access my trust, and it turned out one of his investments wasn't going to pan out unless he was married. Remember Ms. Hilton from high school?" I ask Stella, who nods. "She owned an apartment complex with her husband their whole marriage, and she's determined to sell it to a married couple, not just 'some slick single guy.'"

Stella nods slowly, like she's trying to focus on someone speaking a language she can just barely understand. "Okaaaay . . ."

"So a couple of weeks before my birthday, Julian suggested we enter into a . . . marriage of convenience."

"Like, in a romance novel?" Stella says. "Honest to Christ, I didn't think that shit actually happened in real life."

"I know. And I really thought about it before agreeing. But the truth is, we work great together."

Stella glares at Savvy, then Abbi. "You two knew about this? And you let her do it?"

Abbi hangs her head. "She's stubborn."

"You guys, stop," I say. "I'm not marrying a stranger. I care about Julian. He cares about me. We've been friends for years and . . . well, doesn't it mean something that I always end up back in his bed?"

"Yeah, it means he's familiar dick," Stella says. "You don't *marry* familiar dick."

Abbi snort-laughs. "Oh my God, she's right."

Savvy shrugs then pours her sugary chocolate concoction between two glasses. "Actually, that makes a lot of sense."

"Excuse me," I say, snatching one of the drinks from the table. "Can someone please tell me what *familiar dick* means?"

Abbi sighs. "You know, the guy you always call when you want sex—not because it's particularly mind-blowing but because he's a sure thing and you don't have to worry about him turning out to be some psycho. *Familiar dick.* It's not great dick, but it'll do."

"Sounds like a campaign slogan," Stella says, lips twitching into a smirk.

I take a moment to direct my best "upper-management scowl" at each of my friends, but they erupt into laughter. "You guys are the worst."

"We're just jealous," Savvy says. "What I wouldn't give for a little familiar dick in my life. Hell, I'd settle for mediocre dick at this point."

There's a knock at the door, then the sound of heavy steps coming toward us. "It's just me, Brin," Kace calls.

Stella turns to Abbi. "Speaking of mediocre dick."

Abbi throws a pillow at her face and Stella catches it. "I cannot believe you just said that. Yuck."

The room goes quiet as Kace enters. He has the same dark hair as his younger sister, but the resemblance ends there. Where Abbi is all feminine sweetness and curves, her brother is all masculine scruff and muscle. Testosterone drips off this guy. If he weren't Mr. Good Guy, I would've definitely enjoyed that during my wilder days. "What's up, ladies?"

Stella presses the pillow against her face and snickers.

"Not much, Kace," I say, peering around him. "Where's Hope?"

"She's at Mom's still. We're actually going over there for dinner and dessert, if that's okay with you. Mom would love to see Cami."

Again, I'm buoyed by that lightness that comes with having friends who truly support me. "Of course. Thank you so much. Cami will love it."

"Anytime." He waves a hand to the drinks and food filling the coffee table. "What's the occasion?"

"Sex-toy party," Stella says, turning in her seat and grinning up at her old crush.

Kace's cheeks redden, and he coughs. "Hey, Stella." I shouldn't be delighted by how uncomfortable he gets around her, but I can't help it.

Stella grins. "Next time, we'll get you a sitter and you can join us."

Abbi shoots her a look. "Behave, Stella."

Stella shrugs and gives her the sweetest smile. "But I don't know how."

"So this has nothing to do with Marston being back in town?" Kace asks.

I stiffen. I love Kace, but I'm beginning to feel like too many people know my business. "What have you heard?"

"I saw him at Smithy's. When I asked him why he was in town, he said he was here for *you*."

The girls *aww* in chorus, and I want to hide under a rock. They're not making this any easier.

He arches a brow. "But you're still marrying Hallison, right?"

I give my friends a death glare. "That's right."

"I'm home," Cami calls from the front door.

Relief washes over Kace's face. *Poor guy.* Every bit of this conversation makes him uncomfortable.

"Kace!" Cami says, wrapping her arms around his waist. "Where's Hope?"

He musses her hair. "At Nana Matthews'. Want to go over there and have dinner with them?"

Cami beams. "Mom, can I?"

"Yes, sweetie. Have fun. I'll see you in a couple of hours."

As if just noticing the other girls, Cami goes around the living room, running the circuit of hugs to her honorary aunts. "Okay," she says to Kace. "We can go now."

"I'll see you all later," he says. He turns toward the door then stops with a grimace and throws me a wary look. "Listen, I don't know what's between you and Rowe, but you two should probably clear the air if nothing else." Kace holds my gaze for a long beat. "See you in a couple of hours." Then he follows Cami out.

When the front door clicks shut behind them, Abbi tosses another pillow at Stella. "I don't want to know anything about my brother's skills in the bedroom, *thankyouverymuch*."

"Nah, I don't know anything anyway," Stella says. "The only thing remarkable that happened that night was Kace's head exploding when he realized who was reaching for his dick. It just makes me feel better to imagine he's bad in bed, since he totally rejected me."

Abbi rolls her eyes. "You were seventeen. And *drunk*."

"Can we get back to Brinley's problem?" Savvy asks.

"Yes," Abbi says. "Brinley, the bitch, who has a fiancé *and* a husband, when I can't even find a date for Friday night."

"Hear me out," Savvy says. "I'm not telling you to end your relationship with Julian or to start a real one with Marston."

"Our lives don't work together," I say. "Please take Marston off the table."

"First of all, I'm not sure about that," Savvy says. "Second of all, I'm saying this has all happened really fast, and this marriage might mean you can slow it down. Collect your trust, buy The Orchid, then figure out what you want."

I snag one of the martinis off the coffee table and wince when the intense sweetness hits my tongue. "That's not an option."

"Why not?" Abbi asks.

Because my parents are controlling jerks. "Because marriage isn't the stipulation for getting my trust before I turn thirty. I only get it early if I marry someone my parents approve of."

"Oh, fuck," Savvy whispers, and the other girls look

down at their laps. Everyone in this room knows my history with Marston, and that a marriage to him won't get me the money under those terms. Not only do my parents not approve of Marston, they'd rather see me and their grand-daughter on the streets than welcome him as part of their family.

CHAPTER SEVEN

MARSTON

December 25th, before

There are moments where the divide between the relationship I have with my girlfriend and the one I want feels so vast that I wonder if we're just fooling ourselves. This is never as apparent as on days like today, when I'm setting the table for her family's Christmas dinner and pretending we're not even friends.

"Marston," Lori says softly from the opposite side of the table.

I pull my eyes off the double windows at the front of the dining room, ignoring the car that just pulled into the Knoxes' circle drive so I can focus on the place setting in front of me. I don't really want to see Roman sucking up to

Brinley's parents anyway. Not that he needs to. It seems like he's earned their unconditional approval just for being born rich.

"You keep focused today," Lori says quietly. "I know this isn't easy."

I meet her gaze. What exactly does she know? "I don't know what you're talking about."

She scoffs. "I'm in this house as often as you are," she says with a purse of her lips. "You're playing with fire like you're the only one who'll end up hurt."

"I'm not . . ." I shake my head. I don't want to lie, and I don't want to get Brinley in trouble. So, like always, I choose secrets. "I'll do fine today. I promise."

Lori gives me a quick nod of approval and then goes back to filling water glasses.

"Brinley, Roman's here," Mr. Knox calls from the front door. "Roman, you should really stay for dinner."

"Coming," Brinley calls from the den. I can't help but look as the sound of her steps come closer. She flashes me a smile as she passes the dining room with her sister, Brittany, hot on her heels. There's so much in that smile—our secret little language—that for a second I almost forget how much I hate the guy waiting for her at the door.

Aunt Lori clears her throat, and I get back to work.

"I wanted to bring you a present," Roman says from the foyer, and I stiffen.

"You didn't need to do that," Brinley says. I wonder if she sounds so uncomfortable because she really wishes he hadn't or because she knows I can hear their conversation.

"Of course I did," Roman said. "Christmas is about spoiling the people who matter to you."

I clench my teeth so tightly my jaw aches. He's really laying it on thick for her parents.

"Open it, Brin," Brittany says.

I focus on lining up the knife with the opposite fork and try to ignore the sound of tearing wrapping paper.

"Oh my God, that's so romantic!" Brittany croons. "Brinley, put it on! It's perfect."

"What a beautiful gift," Mrs. Knox says. "Roman, this is so thoughtful. Brinley, this'll look just stunning on you."

I reach for another wine glass, trying to hide what a fucking mess I am, but I feel like I can't breathe while I wait for the sound of Brinley's voice. When it finally comes, it's quiet, but not so quiet I can't hear. "Thank you, Roman. You shouldn't have."

"Why don't you two go to the study for some privacy?" Mrs. Knox says.

Glass shatters at my feet before I realize what's happened.

I dropped it. I dropped a wine glass.

Mrs. Knox runs into the room, eyes wide as she stares at the shattered crystal at my feet. Roman and Brinley follow shortly behind, and Roman smirks at me. The message is clear in that one little expression. *You're the help.* I'm *the one they want to see their daughter with.*

"Marston," Lori says. "What happened?"

"I just . . . It slipped. I'm sorry."

Roman puts a hand on Mrs. Knox's shoulder. "It's hard to find good help these days, isn't it? My parents are struggling with this too. One second they're careless with the china, and the next, the silver is missing."

My face is so hot, and I hate Roman more than I've ever hated anyone—for making this moment worse, for being such a dick every time I see him, but mostly for being the kind of guy Brinley's parents want for her.

"Roman," Brinley says. "This was an accident."

Mrs. Knox lifts her eyes, and her lip curls as she looks at me. Roman's message is clear. I can't be trusted. I'm not just beneath them—I'm so low I'm not even worthy to *serve* them.

"I was standing right here, ma'am," Lori says, her gaze flicking to mine. "It slipped."

"This is my good crystal," Mrs. Knox says, "and I'll be taking the funds to replace it from your wages."

I bow my head. "I understand."

Mrs. Knox gives Lori a cold stare. "I suggest you be more selective on who you bring in for seasonal help. Just because he can do the physical labor required in the gardens doesn't mean he's a good fit for *in-home* help." With that, she stomps away.

"Real smooth, Death Rowe," Roman says.

Brinley gasps, and I look up in time to see her glaring at Roman. "You promised you wouldn't use that name."

You promised? I didn't think it was possible to feel any smaller. When was Roman making Brinley promises? How often does he come over with gifts for her? How often does her father convince him to stay for dinner?

Lori looks back and forth between us. Seeming to sense that this interaction can't go anywhere good, she leads Brinley and Roman from the room. "I think your mother wanted you two to have a chance to visit in the study. Let's go then, and I'll make you some fresh coffee."

Brinley stays behind, scanning the mess at my feet before looking up to meet my eyes. "I'm sorry."

That's when I see it—the new bracelet on her wrist is

covered in diamonds. I could never afford anything like that in my wildest dreams. Hell, I probably can't even afford the wine glass I just broke.

I swallow—my pride, and the fucking shards of my heart. I never wanted to fall for a rich girl, but here I am. "Why are you apologizing? *You* didn't break it."

But she knows. It's all over her face that she too sees this divide today—between the couple we are and the couple we want to be. And when she walks away to join that asshole in the study, I have to press my palm to my pocket. The velvet box that waits inside holds my gift for Brinley: a twenty-dollar necklace from Target that feels like it's devouring what's left of my pride.

CHAPTER EIGHT

BRINLEY

Present day

I reread the most recent texts on my phone for the third time in the last ten minutes, still unsure how to reply.

> Julian: I was completely out of line tonight.
>   Can you forgive me?
> Julian: I'm an ass.
> Julian: I love you, but this whole thing . . . I
>   panicked.

He was, and I can, but I wasn't exaggerating when I told him I wouldn't let anyone push me around anymore. Part of me—possibly the least mature part—wants to make him stew for a bit.

A knock sounds at my front door, and I stiffen. I got Cami into bed an hour ago, shortly after all the girls left. I know I need to talk to Julian after the way we argued tonight, but I'm too exhausted.

The knock sounds again. "Brinley. We need to talk."

Marston. I open the door a crack. He rocks back on his heels and looks me over with those intense brown eyes. He looks gorgeous . . . and angry. I'm exhausted just thinking about another fight tonight. "You shouldn't be here."

He looks over his shoulder, glancing up and down the hall. "Because you're afraid someone might see us together, or because you didn't want me to know about Cami?"

My stomach lurches. Honestly, I'm surprised he didn't find out sooner. I guess I can thank his decade-long avoidance of Orchid Valley for that. I'm not ready to answer his questions, but I dodged the truth the whole time we were together in Vegas, and look where *that* got me. "Who told you?"

"Not you," he says, jaw twitching. "Why didn't you tell me?"

"Vegas wasn't about that."

He drags a hand through his hair and bows his head, like looking at me is just too hard. "Is she the reason you left that morning?"

My heart squeezes. "Partially."

He blows out a breath and lifts his gaze to mine. "How old is she?"

"She turns ten next week." I close my eyes and wait for him to do the math. A little chunk of my heart breaks off, knowing he'll never look at me the same. Maybe we were officially broken up, but I understand Marston well enough to know he'll see my behavior as a betrayal to him. It even felt like one to me while I was doing it.

He's quiet for too long, and when I open my eyes, his gaze is burning into me. I don't know what he's looking for, but it's as if he doesn't know me at all and he's trying to figure me out. "Is she mine?"

Those three little words are a knife twisted in my chest. I spent my entire pregnancy terrified he'd come back to Orchid Valley and ask me that, terrified I'd have to admit what I'd done. "No." My voice warbles on the word.

"But she's turning *ten*," he says, "which means she's mine and you're lying to me, or you—the girl who hadn't even kissed anyone before me—moved on *real* fucking quick."

That knife in my chest drags deep, and it guts me. It's not his words as much as the expression of sheer heartache on his face. I throw the door wide and turn back inside to grab a framed photo off the foyer table. "She's not yours." I shove it into his hand.

Cami's smiling broadly in this school picture, her dark hair pulled into a high ponytail, and when Marston looks at it, I know he's not going to see what I do. He won't see the freckles she got by spending hours at the pool last summer. He won't see that the crinkles around her eyes are absent— the tell that this isn't her real smile. He won't see the girl who's always a silly joke away from a giggle or the fourth-grader who cares so deeply about her friends. He'll see Roman Humphries' green eyes and the perfectly even top and bottom lip that look just like her father's.

"Who's the father." It's not a question. It's a demand for me to speak the words I owe him.

I would climb mountains and cross deserts to not be

responsible for the look on his face right now. "Marston, can we not—"

"You fucked *Roman* right after I left?" His raw voice is like razorblades to my conscience.

"I fucked a lot of guys right after you left." No reason to sugarcoat it. "My sister died, my boyfriend moved to the other side of the country, and my parents were like zombies."

"You *wanted* me to move. You *wanted* me to leave." He shakes his head. "I would've done anything for you, but *you* pushed me away and told me to stay gone."

If I close my eyes, I can remember the day I told him to go. My sister's body had just been lowered into the ground. My grief was a living thing, eating me from the inside out, my guilt right at its side, but the birds were chirping and the sky was blue. Down was up; left was right.

I can't expect him to understand, and I'm not sure I want him to. He endured enough suffering of his own during those years. "That summer almost destroyed me," I whisper. "I was a mess, and when I gave up on trying to make my parents love me, when I was consumed by grief over losing my sister . . . over losing *you,* I found escape in partying. In rebellion and booze and . . . sex." I swallow hard, remembering those awful weeks. They're little more to me now than a blur of shots, frat boys, broken curfews, and yelling matches with my parents.

"How could you?"

I can't expect him to understand what that was like— how I'd just lost my sister and felt like I'd lose my parents too if I did one thing wrong. But after Marston left, I spent a week walking on eggshells and trying to be the perfect daughter. When my parents still wouldn't look at me, I snapped. I got pregnant with Roman's baby, but it could just as easily have been someone else's. That Cami had Roman's DNA was one more reason I could never be with Marston again.

He shakes his head. "*Roman?* Did you even wait for me to get out of town before you let him in your bed?"

Once, those words would have broken me, but I'm not the girl I used to be. "If you want to stand there and slut-shame me, go ahead, but know that my father's ahead of you by almost eleven years."

❦

MARSTON

She has a kid.

Brinley has a *child*.

I left her house before our fight could grow into something more. Something *worse*. The moment she suggested I was trying to slut-shame her, I knew I needed to get out of there and ended up at Lake Blackledge. No surprise. This was always where I came to think when I lived in Orchid Valley, always the place where I could calm my mind enough to think clearly.

But *this* is a bombshell.

I guess I should blame the booze or the meds she was taking or the combination of the two, but she didn't breathe a *word* about her daughter the night we were together in Vegas. She somehow didn't think it was necessary to share that Roman fucking Humphries had gotten her pregnant within weeks after I left town.

That part burns. It's not the thought of her having other

partners, but the idea of her giving herself to *him*. It makes my blood run hot with rage. I was gone, but did she do it to hurt me on some level?

She has a kid.

My phone buzzes in my pocket. I want to ignore it, but I promised Alec we'd catch up tonight, so when I see his name on the screen, I answer. "Hey."

"From the tone of your voice, I'm guessing it's not going well?" he asks.

When I texted him last night, I was all cocky self-assurance. Brinley *loves* me. She *wanted* to marry me. It was only a matter of time before we figured this out—before we somehow made it work. "She has a kid," I say, and even out loud, the words still don't sound real.

"With the guy she's marrying?"

Thank Christ not. But fuck. Julian probably thinks of Cami as his by now, and how much worse would tonight have been if he'd heard me at the door and come to see who Brinley was talking to? *This is a fucking mess.* I blow out a breath. "No. She had her daughter in high school. Right after I left."

"Well, shit. Yours?"

"No." And I still can't decide if that hurts more or if it's a relief. But it was never really a question. Brinley may have kept her daughter a secret, but she never would've kept a child from *me*. She would've known I needed to be the father my sperm donor wasn't, needed to prove I was better than a blank spot on a birth certificate.

"Fucking hell," Alec says. "That's . . . Shit."

I sink onto a bench and look out over the water that's sparkling from the lights all around the lake.

"What are you going to do?"

"I came here for my wife, not to suddenly find myself the stepdad to a ten-year-old kid, but they're a package deal and . . . Fuck, I have to figure out how I feel about that before I push her on this marriage again."

"No one would blame you if it changes things, Marston."

I lean back and close my eyes, imagining the life I came here to fight for, the love I've never been able to cut from my heart, no matter how hard I tried. "Honestly? I don't think it changes anything."

CHAPTER NINE

BRINLEY

"You keep making faces like that, and I'm going to encourage you to take up day drinking," Savvy says, pulling a hoodie on over her open-backed tank top. She snuck in between personal training sessions and brought me coffee—and not just black brew but one of the concoctions from the kitchen with steamed milk and caramel. Since I've given myself permission to screw the diet for the time being, I'm enjoying every sip.

"What?" I ask. "Is my RBF flaring up again?"

She rolls her eyes. "You couldn't pull off resting bitch face if you tried. I'm talking about the *panic* in your eyes."

I look down at my planner, and that familiar dread coils in my stomach. "My parents are coming to town this weekend."

Savvy tenses. "Well, that should make this whole situation even more . . . interesting."

"First it was just supposed to be Mom coming to meet with the caterer, but then she and Dad decided they wanted to take Julian and me to dinner so he could meet some of their friends, and now it's a whole *thing*." I blow out a breath. "I can't believe I forgot, but with everything else. . ." I shudder as I imagine facing Mom and Dad with the news. *Surprise! I know you're here about my wedding, but first I need a divorce!*

"You look flushed. Are you sure you don't have a rare but possibly deadly new virus? You might need to be quarantined for exactly . . . however many days your parents will be in the OV."

I laugh. "You're so awful."

"What? I'll vouch for you." Smiling, she tilts her head to the side and studies me. "Did your fiancé come by to grovel yet?"

I shake my head. "He's texted, but the in-person groveling has to wait. He's in Atlanta meeting with a client and won't be back until tomorrow."

"Hmm. So the fiancé is out of town. What about the husband? Has he been by today?"

I grab the nearest pencil and fling it at her, but she dodges, and it hits the window and falls harmlessly to the floor. "Bitch. Don't call him that."

"Sorry. I meant to say have you talked to *Marston* since he showed up at your door last night?"

"Since he found out I could've starred on *Teen Mom*? No." I look out at the lake and watch a black bird with a long beak dive for a fish. "I don't even know if he's still in town."

"Oh, sweetie. This whole thing . . ." She shakes her head. "What a mess."

"A mess I created myself." When she opens her mouth—no doubt to object—I hold up a hand. "I know it's not entirely my fault that I don't remember my wedding, and it's understandable I'd be cautious about telling Marston about Cami, but come on, Savvy. I screwed up. A lot. If I don't own that, I'll just feel like shit about it for longer."

She folds her arms and huffs. "I don't want you to feel like shit at all."

"I'll get over it. Just let me wallow a little."

"Brinley?"

I look up and see Stella standing in the doorway to my office, her arms folded, her bottom lip trapped between her teeth. I know that look. That's the look my friend has when she's about to give me terrible news. She had that look on her face when the pipes in the steam sauna froze over. She looked like that when one of the staff members suddenly came down with the stomach flu and threw up all over a bridal party during their spa day.

She had that look on her face when she told me my parents knew about Marston.

"What is it?" I ask, already out of my chair.

"There's someone here to see you." She looks back and forth between me and Savvy. "Mrs. Wright's family decided to bring in a . . . consultant."

My shoulders sag. It's a touch insulting, considering all I've done for this spa in the past five years, but I can deal with this. Unless she wants to fire me, in which case—no. I won't get ahead of myself. "Okay. Show her in."

"*He* asked if you would meet him outside. I think he's afraid you're going to be pissed when you find out he's here."

Consultant. Him. "It's not— He wouldn't . . ."

"Oh, yeah." She nods. "He definitely did. Mrs. Wright hired Marston Rowe to figure out what to do with this place."

Marston Rowe is a legend among those of us who own and operate resorts. He swoops in and either saves them or tears them to the ground so the owner can sell off the parts.

My stomach knots. Marston may hold my fate in his hands.

"Is this bad?" Stella asks.

I wipe my hands on my pants and take a deep breath. "Not necessarily. He's really good at this stuff, and maybe he'll have some ideas. The Orchid isn't failing. It's thriving. Let's keep that in mind." *That's right. Think positive.*

"And he'd never do anything to hurt you?" Stella says, but it's a question more than a declaration. The question is fair. After the way he looked at me last night, after finding out that I had *Roman's* baby, I don't know.

We were madly in love once. Our relationship may have been a secret, but it was no less intense, no less real than anyone else's love. At the time, it was the only thing in my life that didn't feel like some sort of bad dream.

But that was more than a decade ago, and now, I'm not the girl he loves. Now, I'm nothing more than his future ex-wife.

"Do you think he took this job just to be closer to you?" Savvy asks.

I frown, considering her question. No matter how much Mrs. Wright's family claims to care about the future of The Orchid after its sale, I can't imagine they'd hire Marston if he charged them his normal fees, which I know a little about, thanks to the *Forbes* article. A place like Orchid Valley doesn't get the same volume of customers that vacation hotspots like Las Vegas, Sedona, or Lake Tahoe do. "I guess that's possible." *Likely*, even, but the question is *why*. He knows I don't want this marriage, and now he knows about Cami and Roman. Why on earth would he take a job in a town he hates just to be closer to the girl who broke his heart all those years ago?

Regardless of his reasons, this is going to affect me too. How am I going to repair things with Julian if I'm seeing Marston every day? I don't know how I can, yet if I had to choose, I wouldn't want Marston to leave. Not yet. He might be complicating the shit out of my life, but the idea of never seeing him again hurts too much.

"Looks like he didn't run away at your big secret after all," Savvy says.

I sink back into my chair.

"You okay?" Stella asks, stepping into the room.

I grab my coffee with a shaking hand and take three long gulps, practically scalding my mouth, but I barely notice. I need something to give me backbone for this conversation, and I'm hoping the caffeine and sugar are up for the job.

"Do you want me to ask him to come back later? I can tell him you're busy or that I forgot about a phone conference or . . .?"

I shake my head. "No. I need to do this. It's fine." *Think positive. Think positive.* "We're lucky to get Marston. He'll see things we didn't notice before and make this place even better. Some stranger might totally screw us over, but at least we *know* him." *Please let me be right, Marston. Please.*

"Better the devil you know?" Savvy asks wryly.

I shrug and smile at my friend. Then I focus on putting one foot in front of the other and walk out of the office. I pass the bathroom and force myself to keep walking. Do I *want* to fuss with my hair and lipstick before facing Marston? *Yes.* But I'd only be disgusted with myself if I gave in to the urge.

Marston's on the back patio of The Orchid. Our restaurant, The Patio, is named after this open-air dining area, though we have indoor dining as well. It's really one of the prettiest places to eat in all of Orchid Valley, especially at this time of year, when the heat isn't chasing everyone indoors to the air conditioning. The patio overlooks the lake, and meticulously manicured gardens line either side of it. If I stand on the far side and squint, I can just barely make out the little beach where I once stripped down to my underwear to swim in the cold water with seventeen-year-old Marston.

Marston reclines in a wrought-iron chair, legs crossed at the ankles. He's staring out at the lake, but I get the impression he's too lost in his thoughts to really see it. I wonder if he, like me, looks out at Lake Blackledge and sees the past.

"Good morning," I say quietly, not wanting to startle him.

He pushes himself out of his chair and turns to me. His eyes are red-rimmed like he hasn't slept, and his jaw is rough with stubble. He drops his gaze slowly from my face, over my belted sheath dress, and down to my toes, and leaves a trail of tingles in his wake. "Morning."

I almost expect him to make a comment about my appearance. When we were together in high school, he said repeatedly how beautiful I was. I took it for granted.

He doesn't say it today, and when he turns back to the lake, I tell myself that's a relief. "It's beautiful out here."

"Thank you. I sure think so. The view makes it popular,

but Abbi's an excellent chef too. It's really all about finding the right balance between mood, location, and price point, and . . ." I bite my lip. *Don't ramble.* "I'm surprised to see you here."

"You shouldn't be. I already told you I'm not going down without a fight."

"So you're working for my boss—why? To spend time with me?" He shrugs as if to say, *Worth a shot.* I fold my arms. "I'm engaged to be married."

"You're already married. To me."

But would I be if he'd known about Cami? His reaction last night confirmed my fears, and yet here he is—beginning a job he most definitely doesn't need and admitting he's here to be close to me. "This is a bad idea."

He quirks a brow. "Afraid you can't resist me?" Now his crooked smirk stretches into an all-out grin as he moves closer, and *fuck me*, because he looks damn good in a smile, and I swear I can feel his warmth as his body blocks the breeze off the lake.

I roll my eyes. "I have no trouble resisting you."

"I remember it differently," he murmurs.

I gape. "Of all the guys I've been with, you have absolutely the biggest—"

He stops me with his fingertips to my lips. "You don't need to say it."

"Ego!" I say, laughing. "The biggest *ego*."

He grins, but when his eyes burn into mine for a beat too long, I have to blink and look away. "I meant, I'm surprised the Wrights hired you. The family's notoriously tight with money and planning to sell soon. I wouldn't have expected them to invest in someone as . . . high-demand as you."

"Let's just say I had personal reasons for wanting the job, so they're getting a hell of a deal." The corner of his mouth twitches. "Mrs. Wright tells me you're the one who's responsible for bringing this place back from the brink of ruin."

I shrug. "It's been a bit of a passion project of mine."

He shoves his hands into his pockets. "We should talk about last night."

I shake my head. "Not here. Just tell me what you need to do your job."

He stiffens then rolls his shoulders back as if trying to shake it off. "Okay. Why don't you show me around, and I'll explain the process?"

&

MARSTON

My job is partially in tours and interviews and inspecting amenities, but most of my time is spent with spreadsheets, numbers, and statistical models. After five hours with my laptop and some key files in an empty office at The Orchid, my shoulders are tight, and I'm mentally exhausted from dodging thoughts of Brinley all day. I offered this evaluation to the Wright family to help Brinley and get to know her world.

I understand why she doesn't want to hash out our personal issues at work, but I suspect if I don't catch her while she's here, I'll never get the chance to talk to her alone. She's not in her office when I go searching, but a member of her staff catches me looking and suggests I check out the gym. I find her in the pool, swimming laps, and watch, mesmerized, as she glides through the water, her dark hair trailing behind her, her limbs pulling in long, even strokes. I don't know how long I stand there, but when she stops and clings to the edge of the pool, she's gasping for air, and I snap out of my trance.

"You swim like you're trying to escape demons," I say.

She smooths her hair off her face. "Yeah, well, I've found myself planning a wedding and a divorce all at once. It's been a little overwhelming." She gives a tentative smile. "Everything going okay?"

I tuck my hands into my pockets. "I wondered if I could have a few minutes of your time before you head home." *To Julian,* I mentally add, if only to remind myself.

She hoists herself out of the water. "I'm sorry. I thought Stella gave you all the files you needed. Is she gone for the day?"

"It's not about the spa." I take a deep breath. "It's about us."

She drops back into the water. "There is no *us*, and if you don't have any questions in your capacity here as a consultant, I'll get back to my workout." She goes under the water and pushes off the wall, returning to her laps.

I glance down at my jeans and dark gray Oxford shirt. I wasn't planning on getting in the water, but if she's not planning to get out . . .

I unbutton my shirt and toss it on the chair, then peel off my undershirt before unzipping my jeans and shoving them down my hips. I'm in nothing but my boxer briefs and headed toward the ladder when she emerges again, panting at the deep end of the pool.

Her eyes are wide. "What are you doing?"

I jump off the ladder into the water, letting myself sink

to the bottom before pushing back to the surface. I wipe my face and grin at her. "I don't mind talking in here. Some of my favorite memories are of being in the water with you."

Her cheeks redden and she swims toward the ladder, no doubt to run from me—from this conversation. "I don't think this is a good idea."

"You tracked me down in Vegas, gave me the hottest night of my life, and married me, but we can't swim in the same pool?"

She glances back at me, and her gaze snags on my bare chest. I fucking love the way she looks at me, even when she's trying not to. I wonder if she knows her tongue darts out to wet her lips.

"Stay," I say, swimming to the ladder to stop her. "Please. Last night was . . . I had no idea. I needed to process everything."

Brinley looks around like she's trying to make sure no one's watching and then sinks back into the pool with me.

I try not to think about joining her in here under different circumstances, but it's too late, and I'm glad I'm already underwater, because the memories alone have me half-hard. I clear my throat. "How was your day?"

"A little bit of an emotional rollercoaster. Yours?"

"Same." I swallow. "I can't stop thinking about you being a mom."

She studies me wearily, blue eyes wild and defiant.

"If you want to stand there and slut-shame me, go ahead, but know that my father's ahead of you by almost eleven years."

"I'm sorry about what I said last night. I was hurt and shocked, but you don't owe me any explanation for the choices you made."

She blinks, as if my apology takes her by surprise. "Thank you," she whispers.

It was a blow to realize she got pregnant right after I left, but so much of that pain was knowing she shared that with Roman. But now? After thinking it through and cooling off a little? I want to pull her into my arms and promise I'll never treat her like her father. I'll never shame her for doing what she had to do to cope. But I can't hold her. I can't whisper in her ear. Because despite the vows we spoke in Vegas, she's not mine, and she doesn't want to be.

"I wish I could've been here for you," I say instead, and it's such a weak fucking substitute for the things I want to say that it leaves a knot in my gut. "And I wish you would've felt like you could tell me about her. We talked about family in Vegas, but you . . ." Fuck, she probably doesn't remember that, either.

She turns away and shifts in the water until she's floating on her back and looking at the ceiling. "I remember that part."

"Why didn't you tell me?" I ask. She closes her eyes and draws in a long breath. "You thought I'd judge you?"

She turns her head and scans my face, searching for the truth. "Don't you?"

I shake my head. "I don't judge you. It would've hurt, yes, but I think it hurt more to find out last night, to know you weren't being completely honest with me in September."

"I wish I had been." She rolls to her stomach and swims to the ladder. She focuses on her fingers wrapped around the rails instead of looking at me. "If I would've been honest, we wouldn't be in this mess."

"How do you figure?"

She climbs out of the water and grabs a towel off a chair, rubbing herself down. I watch every move and make no effort to hide it. She's drying her hair when she faces me, lips twisted. "You'd never have ended up in a Vegas wedding chapel with the mother of Roman Humphries' baby."

"Is that what you told yourself when you left me that note?"

She shrugs, as if it's irrelevant, then turns toward the door.

"It wouldn't have made a difference," I say as her fingers curl around the handle. "I would've married you anyway. I'd marry you today."

She bows her head for a beat, but she doesn't look back to me before heading out the door and walking away from me—like she's done again and again since coming back into my life.

CHAPTER TEN

BRINLEY

"*K*nock-knock."

I look up from my computer to see Julian standing at my door. He's dressed for meetings today in a plum shirt and pressed black slacks. His sandy-blond hair is artfully messy in a sexy-casual look that takes him a special blend of three hair products and ten minutes in front of a mirror. I push out of my chair, relieved to see him after our fight two nights ago. "Hey, I didn't think you'd be back until tonight. How was your trip?"

Grinning, he strides into my office, hands tucked into his pockets. "It was good, but I decided to come back early and take my fiancée out for lunch." He peeks over his shoulder then lowers his voice. "I heard you've had a rough couple of days."

My stomach sinks. From the moment Stella told me Marston was acting as a consultant for The Orchid yesterday morning, I expected Julian wouldn't like it. I've been preparing for the conversation but didn't think I'd have to have it here. I school my expression and cock my head to the side. "Where'd you hear that?"

"The grapevine." He rocks back on his heels. "Mrs. Wright's eldest is an acquaintance. When I ran into him in Atlanta, he mentioned that Marston's consulting for them. He was crowing about it, actually."

"It was a bit of a shock," I admit, "but it hasn't been bad. In fact, if I'm looking at it objectively, having Marston's critical eye on The Orchid for a few weeks will only strengthen *my* future business." I force a smile, but the harder I try to cling to our plans—get married, buy The Orchid, live a simple, happy life—the more they feel like they're slipping through my fingers.

"I hope so," Julian says, a wrinkle forming between his brows. "I'd hate to think he took the position to have some power over you."

I open my mouth to explain that Marston wouldn't do that then snap it shut again, afraid any defense of Marston will be salt in the wound for Julian. "Lunch sounds good." I grab my purse. If I want to make this work, I need to start giving my fiancé more of my attention and energy, and that starts now.

Julian beams. "You just made my day."

It takes so little to make this guy happy. I'm a total jerk for not trying more often. "Where do you want to go?"

"Let's see what the specials on The Patio are." He misses my frown as he takes my hand and heads in the direction of The Orchid's in-house restaurant.

I've suggested The Patio for a quick lunch many times, but Julian always said there was no point in taking a lunch break if I wasn't even going to get away from work. "I can leave," I say, quickening my pace to keep up with his long strides. "We don't need to eat here."

He slows his steps and narrows his eyes. "Are you ashamed to be seen with me?"

I blink at him. "Wha— Why— No. Of course not." He looks so wounded that I can't even laugh this off. "Julian, we're getting *married*. Of course I'm not ashamed to be seen with you."

"Good." He gives my hand a gentle squeeze and resumes his path toward The Patio, if a little slower this time, and I wonder if this visit is really about us or if it's about Marston.

❧

"THANKS FOR HAVING LUNCH WITH ME," Julian says, stopping just outside my office.

"Thank you for taking me. It was a nice surprise." I hope my smile hides any untruth in these words. Lunch was good. Okay, well, the *food* was delicious. The company was . . . awkward?

The whole time we were eating, I felt like Julian was focused on how he looked interacting with me, rather than actually interacting with me. He didn't bring up Marston working at The Orchid, and neither did I—more of that conversation can wait until we're alone—but something was definitely off with him.

His gaze locks on my mouth for a beat. "I wish I could take you home with me."

I laugh. "We both need to work," I remind him, because it's true. Also because nothing's changed since he stomped out of my condo on Tuesday. I'm not ready for us to be physical again.

The door down the hall clicks open, but before I can turn to greet whoever's coming our way, Julian takes my face in his hands and lowers his mouth to mine. This isn't his typical "have a nice day" kiss or even his typical "I hate to leave, but if you insist, I'll go" kiss. This is deep and searching, and I'm so surprised by it that I just stand there. When I do pull away—because, *hello*, I work here—he holds me tight and doesn't make it easy.

"What's gotten into you?" I laugh.

"Can't a guy kiss his fiancée before he goes back to work?"

Not like that. But again, I'm hit with a wave of guilt over our mismatched feelings. I love Julian, I do. But I love him as a friend, and as someone I've agreed to have a partnership with. Though our relationship has involved sex from the beginning, it's never been *passionate*. It's weird to feel like he's making it into something it's never been before. I guess that's a conversation we need to have when we're alone.

When I don't answer, he backs away a few inches. "Let me come over tonight. I'll make you and Cami dinner. She's been begging me to make chicken and noodles again." He holds up a finger. "And before you say anything, I'll make you a salad."

Right. No excuses. But I shouldn't be looking for excuses. I should be looking for ways we can spend more time together to prepare for our marriage. "I'd love that. Thank you."

"Great. See you then." He kisses me on the cheek then

turns to go. Only then do I see Marston, stopped halfway down the hall and staring lasers at me.

"Hey, Marshall," Julian says as he passes, offering his fist to bump.

I shake my head. Julian knows his name and got it wrong to piss Marston off. I'd bet The Orchid on it. I don't care for this side of Julian, and the list of issues we need to hash out before the wedding is growing by the day.

MARSTON

I ignore Julian's offered fist and open the door for him in my best silent *get the fuck out*. It's one thing to know this asshole regularly puts his hands on *my wife*. It's quite another to see it for myself.

"Later, babe," Julian calls one last time before finally heading out into the lobby.

I let the door close behind him before slowly stalking toward Brinley. "Was that little show for me?"

"What?" Her lips are swollen from his kiss, but there's nothing in her eyes that says she was swept away by it. A curl of satisfaction twists in my chest.

I take another step closer. Then another. "He knew I'd be here, right? So he practically dry-humped you in the hall?"

She shakes her head, cheeks blazing red—not from Julian's kiss but from me. "You're one to talk," she snaps.

"Me? I haven't touched anyone but my wife since we were married."

She laughs. "Bullshit."

I stop in front of her and slowly look her over. I want to be disgusted, but what I feel when I look at Brinley isn't even in the same galaxy as disgust. "No. Just the truth. How many times do I have to tell you I keep my promises?"

She swallows, and the pulse point in her neck flutters faster.

I move closer until her breath catches. There's less than an inch between our mouths. I could close that space and remind her what it's like to kiss a man she can lose herself in. I wonder if she'd even stop me this time. "Does he make you as wild as you feel with me? Do his kisses make you forget who you are? Where you are?" I skim the bridge of my nose along her neck and breathe in the smell of her there. "Does his touch make you so wet you spread your legs in public? So wet you beg him to make you come in a dark corner?"

She's so still, eerily so. Until she's not.

I don't even see her hand coming until her palm connects with the side of my face—so hard and fast I feel every fingerprint.

She backs away, eyes blazing. "Don't speak to me like that again."

She spins on her heel and stomps into her office, slamming the door behind her.

I cradle my cheek in my hand and head to the kitchen for ice, focusing on the sting to distract me from the pain of seeing her kiss him and the feeling that I've already lost her.

CHAPTER ELEVEN

BRINLEY

"*J*ulian's coming over tonight," I tell Cami as we pack up to leave for the day. "He's making us chicken and noodles."

Her eyes go big. "My favorite! Is he making dessert too?"

Laughing, I throw my purse over my shoulder. "Don't push it, missy!"

She giggles and slides her backpack on as she follows me out of my office.

On the days she doesn't ride the bus to gymnastics after school, Cami rides the bus to The Orchid. I used to send her to an afterschool program, but now that she's older, I'd just as soon have her at work with me. I have a small desk for her in my office, and she does her homework while I wrap up emails and phone calls for the day. On the days I have meetings, she hangs with one of the girls—either in the kitchen to help Abbi with prep, or the group fitness room to help with Savvy's fitness classes. Sometimes, she joins Stella at the front and plays receptionist. If I lose The Orchid and the new owner isn't understanding about me having Cami here, we could lose these extra hours together. And *that* is assuming the new owner doesn't fire me altogether.

"Quit stressing," Cami says, narrowing her eyes and sticking her lip out in a pout.

I open the door to the lobby and hold it for her. "Who said I was stressing?"

"I always know when you're stressing. You get this little wrinkle right here." She points to her forehead. "Grandma says it's because you need Botox."

I grunt. *Thanks, Mom.* "Grandma might think I need Botox, but the kind of Botox she's talking about is never a *need* thing. You get it if you *want* it, not if you don't. I don't. I'm okay with my wrinkles."

"Good. Because you're perfect as you are."

I freeze in my tracks, but Cami spins around and grins. "Who are you?"

Marston's footsteps grow louder, closer, and tension ratchets tighter in my gut. *Please be kind to my girl. Please don't say anything about her father or our little drunken wedding in Vegas.*

By the time I will myself to turn around, Marston is standing in front of Cami with his hand extended. "I'm Marston Rowe. I was a friend of your mom's in high school, and I'm working at The Orchid as a business consultant for the next couple of weeks."

My daughter takes his hand in hers and shakes it so hard that I have to bite back a laugh. "Camille Knox. I'm a jack-of-all-trades around here, and I know my mom from when she became my mom."

Marston laughs, and Cami grins. After nearly ten years of being adorable, she struggles to maintain any semblance of modesty. "A jack-of-all-trades, huh?" He tucks his hands into his pockets and rocks back on his heels. "This is the kind of thing I need to know about as I evaluate the business. Tell me what all you do at The Orchid."

Cami begins to tick jobs off on her fingers. "I dust my mom's office because she won't let housekeeping in there, and she gets so absorbed with her work she doesn't even notice when there are dust bunnies piling up on her monitor."

Marston flashes me a smile. "Is that so?"

I shrug. "Guilty."

Cami goes to her second finger. "I teach yoga with Savannah on some Saturdays, and I'm actually better at a lot of the poses than she is. She can't even do full splits."

"Can you?" Marston asks.

"Yeah, I take gymnastics and dance." She goes to her third finger. "I help Abbi take inventory when she needs it, even though it's *freezing* in those walk-ins."

The corner of Marston's mouth twitches into a grin. "That's important stuff."

"I also help with the baking sometimes. That's my favorite, but Abbi's a control freak in the kitchen, so she doesn't let me help with much."

"You *are* a jack-of-all-trades," Marston says.

"I don't do massage because . . ." She shudders. "Just ew. No, thank you. I want to help with the facials—I give them to myself at home with face masks and stuff—but Wren said I have to have a special license for that. And I can't

213

answer the phones and make appointments until I'm sixteen."

Marston's eyes are bright when he turns to me. "Looks like you have an assistant-manager-in-training right here."

I'm a jumble of mismatched emotions, and I hold his gaze, hoping my eyes can communicate what I can't put into words. All these years, I believed Marston would see Roman when he looked at my daughter, and I believed that was all it would take to blind him to how amazing she is. Guilt lodges right beside pride in my chest—because she's so amazing that no one would ever miss it, especially not Marston. There's another emotion there too, one that begs me to pay attention to how good he is with my daughter. One I can't let myself examine much. One that won't matter by the time the divorce is finalized and Marston has returned to his life in L.A.

It doesn't matter that Marston likes Cami. It *shouldn't* matter. Then why do I have this lump in my throat and this pulling sensation across my chest?

"Mom, come on," Cami says, going for the exit. "We have to go. Julian's coming over to make us dinner, remember?"

The mention of Julian clears all the amusement from Marston's face. His shoulders tense, and he finally breaks eye contact.

"You should come too, Mr. Rowe," Cami says as I step up beside her at the door. "Mom says Julian always makes enough to feed an army."

I rest my hand on Cami's shoulder. "Baby, I don't think—"

"Unfortunately, I have other plans tonight," Marston

says with one more look my way. "But it was very nice to meet you, Cami."

"You too, Mr. Rowe. If you have any more questions about what I do here, you can find me in Mom's office after school and sometimes the kitchen."

Nodding, he holds the front door open for us. "Thank you. That's very helpful."

Cami walks out first, and I follow, pausing just outside the door. I dig my key fob from my purse and click the button. "It's unlocked."

She waves and climbs into the car as I turn to Marston.

"She's a good kid," he says, and there's something in his voice I can't nail down. Grief? Reluctance? Regret? Hell, I can't even figure out my own emotions. I don't know why I'm trying to understand his.

"I know." I exhale slowly and make myself meet his eyes —even though it'll make it that much harder to walk away. "Thank you for that."

He quirks a brow. "For what?"

"For making her feel special. She's grown up at The Orchid. It's important to her."

"It was nothing."

It was everything.

"Julian's . . . *coming over?*" he asks.

I shrug. "Yeah."

"Meaning he doesn't live with you," he says, searching my face.

I swallow. I don't want to stand here while Marston analyzes my relationship. It feels too flimsy under the heat in his stare. "That's right."

He cocks his head to the side. "Interesting."

I want to squirm under that knowing gaze, but there's

no way Marston can know the truth, and even if he did, it's none of his business. "I won't keep you. I know you have plans, but . . . have a good night." I turn to go, but his fingertips graze my wrist and I stop.

"I owe you an apology for earlier," he says, and slowly, I turn. "Seeing him touch you . . . kiss you?" He shakes his head and cuts his eyes away from me to watch the cars pass on the street. "There's no excuse. I was out of line."

"I shouldn't have slapped you."

"Nah." He backs away and gives me a grim smile. "I deserved it."

❦

BRINLEY

I hold my wine glass between both hands and lean one hip against a freshly scrubbed counter. True, this wine has calories that won't help me fit into my wedding dress, but tonight it's serving as a much-needed emotional crutch. Without it, I might burn the wedding dress and run far, far away.

I take another sip and bow my head, trying to clear away all the doubts and fears about my wedding that seem to multiply any time I see Marston. And this afternoon? Seeing him smile at Cami? I'm a mess.

True to his word, Julian made chicken and noodles for Cami and himself, and a salad and roasted chicken breast for me.

It's easy to imagine our life like this. Julian cooking us dinners so Cami and I don't have to rely on carryout, Cami entertaining us at the dinner table with tales from her day, cleaning up the kitchen with Julian after dinner while Cami watches TV, and then crawling into bed each night.

This isn't how I imagined a marriage of convenience would be. I imagined coldness, awkward conversations, and celibacy, but life with Julian won't be any of those things. It'll just be . . . a *marriage*.

"What are you thinking about so hard over there?" Julian comes up behind me and wraps his arms around my waist. He's warm, and his embrace should be a comfort. Instead, it makes me tense.

I don't want him to ask to stay over. I don't want him to try to touch me right now. I don't want to admit that both of these truths make me even more fearful about what happens next for us.

He nuzzles my neck and slips a hand under my shirt. "How's the wine?"

"Good." I will myself to relax and lean into his embrace. "I needed it tonight."

"I feel ya." He blows out a breath and pulls me closer still. "It's been screwing with me—knowing you're working with him now."

I had a feeling that was what the little show in the hallway today was about, but I didn't expect him to admit it. I should've given him more credit than that.

"Then I had a meeting with Ms. Hilton, and I swear, that woman's going to make me do literal backflips before she signs these contracts."

I frown. Ms. Hilton owns the apartment complex Julian's trying to buy. "You already have contracts?"

"Yes, but we've gone back and forth so many times, pretty soon the legal fees alone are going to make this investment a loser. But I think we're finally wrapping it up tomorrow."

I put down my wine and turn in his arms so I can see his face.

He presses a kiss to my collarbone. "Thanks for having me over tonight. I love spending time with you."

Guilt pulls tight in my chest. It's a constant presence, even when I try to push it away, but there's always been something else with that emotion. A suspicion about this arrangement. "She's going to sign before the wedding?"

His smile wavers, but he recovers quickly. "Well, maybe. I think we've got her convinced."

"Julian? I don't want us to lie to each other. We can't. Not if this is going to work."

He closes his eyes, then releases me before pacing the kitchen. "She likes that I'm with you. It matters to her that she's selling to someone she believes will take care of her tenants, and she likes you so much that you helped my case for buying her out."

"You said she wanted the buyer to be married." I swallow hard. "That's why this was going to work. We would *both* get something out of this marriage."

"I don't need anything more from this marriage than *you*." He shrugs. "I never did."

"But that wasn't what you said when I agreed." My heart is racing and a wave of nausea hits me so hard that I worry I might lose my lunch. "I wouldn't have agreed if I'd known—"

"If you'd known what?" His voice cracks, and his eyes blaze with emotion that blows me over. "That I love you? I already told you that, but you said I was misinterpreting a friendly love for something else. Or maybe you wouldn't have agreed if you'd known that I actually *wanted* to spend my life with you? But then, I've been honest about that too. But maybe you mean you wouldn't have agreed if you'd known he was going to come back into your life. Maybe you need to be honest with *yourself* and admit that your worries about this marriage have nothing to do with what we have and everything to do with *him*."

"That's not fair." But guilt and reason collide with my defensiveness, and I know on some level he's right.

"I've spent the last six months planning my wedding to a woman I love, and suddenly, I found out she was already married. You really want to talk about *fair* right now?"

Cami walks into the kitchen, her gaze ping-ponging between me and Julian. "Mommy, what's wrong?"

Julian steps away from me and braces his arms against the counter, squeezing his eyes shut and taking deep breaths.

"Nothing, baby. Julian and I were just having a little argument."

Cami bites her bottom lip. She's not used to this. The few disagreements Julian and I have had, we've had away from her, and he's never raised his voice at me.

I pull her into a hug and kiss the top of her head. "Sorry if we scared you."

She shrugs. "People fight sometimes. Daddy and Victoria fight, but Daddy always sends me out of the house with Rosalie if he thinks I can hear."

I swallow hard, wondering what kind of fights she hears at her father's house and how many times she's been sent away with the housekeeper.

"We can do this another time." Julian rubs the back of his neck. "I'm sorry."

"Julian . . ."

He meets my eyes from across the kitchen and waits for what I have to say, but I have nothing.

I'm sorry I married someone else and have no memory of it.

I'm sorry you've always loved me more than I've loved you.

I'm sorry I'm so confused right now.

"Walk me out?" he asks.

I nod. "Cami, I'll be right back, okay?"

"Sure. Thanks for dinner, Julian." She waves at him and runs back into the living room, clearly unconcerned about what she overheard.

I follow Julian to the hall and pull the door shut behind me before leaning against it.

"Have you even filed for divorce yet?"

I stare at my feet, too frustrated with him and myself and this whole situation to admit that I haven't done more than look it up online to see if I could even get a divorce if my husband doesn't want it. Turns out I can. "I still need to do the paperwork."

"I guess I should've known." He barks out a dry laugh and squeezes the back of his neck. "Brinley . . . can you at least tell me if I have a chance here?"

Guilt and sorrow and frustration twist like a ball of thorns in my gut. "Everything is happening so fast. Changing so fast. I can't get my bearings."

He shakes his head. "Nothing has changed. I'm still the guy who wants to spend his life with you. I'm still the guy you trusted enough to say yes—without being dragged drunk to a chapel." He blows out a long, slow breath. "I'm the guy who's here. The one you can count on. The one who isn't going anywhere."

"I know." And those are all the reasons I should protect

220

what we have, all the reasons our plans were perfect. But *perfect* is starting to feel like a trap.

"I'll pick you up at six tomorrow for dinner with your parents." He brushes a kiss across my forehead.

As he walks away, I realize that nowhere in his speech was the argument that he's the guy who can convince my parents to give me my trust. The trust has never been more than a superficial part of his reasoning. Julian's case for us has always been rooted in everything else. I'm the one so obsessed with finally feeling secure and independent that I couldn't see anything *but* the money. And if I can't appreciate the rest of what he's offering, I'm not sure I deserve any of it.

CHAPTER TWELVE

BRINLEY

February 21st, before

*A*nother day, another visit with my sister, another round of the silent treatment. She's barely looked up from her phone since she saw me walk in the door of her hospital room.

Every round of treatments, she looks less like the vivacious little sister I grew up playing dolls with and more like a hollowed-out shell of her old self. She's pale and painfully thin, and she sleeps so much I find myself staring at her wondering if this'll be the time she doesn't wake up. But when she's alert and I'm around, she uses her limited energy to ignore me. I don't know which is worse.

"I'll leave you alone," I finally say, pushing out of the lumpy chair by her bed.

"Wait, Brin." She drops her phone onto her sheets. "Don't go."

Swallowing, I turn. She's five feet away, but I feel like there are oceans between us. And maybe there are. We're living completely different lives. Or—I'm living, and she's surviving.

"Tell me something," she says, tilting her head to the side. She doesn't have her wig on today, just a pink bandana, tied in the back. She calls it "cancer chic" and hates the look as much as she hates the hospital gown.

"Like what?" I ask, but I sit back down. She doesn't believe me when I say it, but I *want* to spend time with Brittany. I miss her laugh and her smiles. I miss her friendship.

"Anything. Tell me about the last time Dad was a jerk, or what the gossip is at school, or who Stella's making out with." She gives me a weak smile. "Anything. Just talk to me."

I bite my lip and study her. "I'm still seeing that guy I told you about."

She smiles, actually smiles at me, which she hasn't done in way too long. "Are you ever going to reveal the identity of this mystery man?"

"Marston Rowe." I'm nearly giddy at just the sound of his name from my lips. He's my favorite secret.

Brittany gasps. "The ex-con?"

"Oh my God, that was a rumor. He got in a little trouble and was put on probation, but he's never been to *jail*."

She shrugs. "Still. Bet he's more interesting than *Roman*."

223

I bite back a laugh, but my smile falls away when I admit, "I'm in love with him."

"Aww! Brinley! Oh my God!" She's all smiles. "I told you those machines work!"

"What machine—are you seriously going to use my relationship with Marston as a way to justify your obsession with those fortune-teller machines?"

"Remember the fortune you got this summer? It said, and I quote, *This is the year you find great love—right when you need it most.*"

"The fortunes are all generic. It's a total money grab."

"So you *wouldn't* call this great love?"

I draw in a sharp breath. Because I would, but I never realized love could be so scary. "If Mom and Dad knew . . ."

She grabs my hand and holds it so tight it hurts. "*Don't* let them rule you. You see what happens when they get to make the choices?" She waves a hand, indicating her chemo-ravaged body. "This."

I shake my head. "Britt, they're trying to *save* you." My eyes brim with tears because I know where this conversation is going, where she's taken it before, and it hurts to even hear her ask.

"They've been pumping me full of poison for years. I just want to be done, Brinley." She shakes her head slowly. Her big eyes look almost cartoonish on her gaunt face. "And they won't let me go."

"Tell the doctors again. Maybe they'll listen if you ask to stop the chemo. Maybe if—"

"They won't. I need to do it myself, and I need your help."

I crawl into the bed beside her, tears rolling down my

face. "I don't want to lose you. You're the only family I have that *sees* me."

"Don't look for that from Mom and Dad. Go to Stella. Go to Marston." She strokes my hair. My little sister, sounding so wise. My *dying* sister, comforting me. "We make our own family."

꧁

MARSTON

"I don't want to move," Brinley says, her head on my chest, her legs tangled with mine. "Can we stay here forever?"

I look at the clock. It's nearly four in the afternoon, and she and I have had a rare full weekend afternoon alone together. "Not forever, but you aren't expected home for another few hours."

Aunt Lori is at the Knoxes' all day, and I managed to weasel out of catering duties. Brinley told her parents she'd be at the library studying for her chemistry final. I hate that she has to lie so much to be with me, but we both know they wouldn't bend on this. Asking for permission would only lead to them keeping a closer eye on her, and her parents—her father, particularly—are too controlling as it is.

"Brittany asked me a favor again."

I stroke her back, unsure what else to do. This is the third time she's brought up her sister wanting her to do her a "favor." The first time was at the lake, another time when we were driving around for hours, and now. She's never told me what the favor is, and I haven't pushed. Honestly, I think I already know, and I don't want her to have to say it out loud.

"You don't have to do anything you don't want to," I say softly, because I want to protect her from this—from the pain of losing her sister and the heartache of being asked to shoulder a burden no one should have to.

"It's easy to say that, but she doesn't see it that way." Brinley swallows and snuggles closer. "She doesn't want to keep fighting. This is her fourth round of chemo, and she gets sicker and weaker every time. She doesn't want to fight anymore."

I close my eyes and tighten my arms around her. "Has she told your parents?"

"Yes, but she's a minor, so they get the final say." She gives a shaky smile. "And my parents . . . She's their baby, and they don't understand that this is no way to live."

I kiss the top of her head and sigh. "I'm so sorry, Brinley."

"There's a guy at school who sells narcotics and sleeping pills. She knows exactly how much she needs, but he knows why she wants them. He knows what she's going to do and refuses to sell to her."

"So, she wants you to do it?"

"I'm the only one she can ask, but I just . . . I don't know if I could live with myself if I knew I was responsible for that."

"It's not fair of her to ask. That's too much. She has to know you'd carry it with you forever."

She turns her face into my chest. "I've spent the five years since her diagnosis completely helpless. I keep my grades up and do everything my parents ask of me so they don't have to worry about *me* on top of everything else. I visit Brittany as often as she'll let me, but none of that matters. None of it gives her a break from the grueling nausea, the infections that land her in the hospital, or the bone-deep exhaustion. None of it will give her her life back."

"It's not your job to do that—and you couldn't anyway. You take this all on your shoulders because you love her, because you're her big sister, but no one but the doctors can fix this, and even they have limits."

"It's just so heavy," she whispers.

"I know. I wish I could help."

She swallows hard and trails her fingers up my chest, across my shoulders and then down my arm. When she reaches my hand, she laces our fingers together. "You can. Kind of. Brittany told me we make our own family, and I realized you're that for me. The good kind of family."

I hold her tighter and say a silent prayer that I can always be that for her.

"Will you hold me like this while I sleep?"

My chest feels too heavy and too tight. Everyone looks at Brinley Knox and sees a spoiled rich girl with the perfect life. They have no idea how much she carries on her shoulders. "I'll hold you as long as you want."

CHAPTER THIRTEEN

BRINLEY

Present day

I don't look up from my computer when I hear Wren come in for our weekly meeting. "Just let me finish this," I say, typing out the end of my email.

"Take your time."

I do look up at the sound of Julian's voice. We haven't talked since he left my place last night. I tossed and turned thinking about our wedding and the way he misled me about Ms. Hilton. I stared at the ceiling as I thought about all the reasons I'd agreed to the marriage. All in all, my thoughts didn't get me anywhere, and I'm not quite sure I'm *ready* to see him again. "What are you doing here?"

He places a cup of coffee on my desk before settling his

messenger bag in Cami's chair. "I missed you, and I hated that we argued last night."

It's more than that, and we both know it. He's here because Marston's here.

I push away from my desk and get up to close the door. Everyone around the spa—especially Marston, who's in temporary residence in the office down the hall—is too invested in what happens with me and Julian, and I don't need eavesdroppers on top of everything else right now.

When I turn back to Julian, he's grinning. "I have good news."

"Yeah?" Relief washes over me. Maybe he *does* have a reason for being here beyond jealousy. "What is it?"

"My administrative assistant is pregnant, and she's decided not to come back after the baby's born."

"Well, that's exciting for her. What are you going to do? I thought you loved her?"

He steps forward and takes my hands in his. "She was great, but this means I don't just need her to train a temp. I need her to train her replacement. It means there's a position opening in my company."

I frown. I still don't understand how this is good news unless . . . *Oh. Ooooh.*

"You and I make such a great team. You can leave here. You won't be at the mercy of Mrs. Wright and her kids. You could start training right away, and I wouldn't have to go crazy knowing you're spending your days with your ex."

My mouth tastes sour. "You want me to leave this company and work for you just so you don't have to think about me having a few conversations—*business* conversations—with Marston?"

"Brinley." His face is a study of patience, but there's a

spark of frustration in his eyes. "This whole thing is nuts. They don't pay you nearly what you're worth here, and you work fifty hours a week. With me, you'd have an easy nine-to-five with better pay, better benefits, and we'd get more time together. You could focus on being a wife and a mom instead of giving all your energy to this place."

I pull my hands from his grasp and step back. My head is spinning. "Did you forget the whole reason we're *doing* this? I *love* The Orchid. I'm good at managing this place, and I don't want to leave. My dream is to work for myself. To be completely in charge of my own life for once. That's why I need my trust."

"But wouldn't it be nice to have that trust and use it for something else? Save it for Cami's college and buy a house. Spoil yourself for once. I already have a business. We don't need another." He searches my face. "And working for me, well—isn't that the next best thing to working for yourself?"

I shake my head. "No. It's completely different." My skin heats, and I can't take a full breath. "I know you don't know what it was like for me to grow up under my father's thumb. You don't know how he kept tabs on me even after I graduated from college. You don't know how hard I fought to escape that feeling of being a prisoner in my own life, but I need you to try to understand: I'll never be happy if I feel like someone else is controlling my fate."

His smile falls away and he tilts his head to the side. "That seems a little dramatic. This isn't an effort to control you. I just want to give you a good life."

"I believe your intentions are pure. I do. But that's not the life I want."

"Which life don't you want?" His face hardens and his

nostrils flare. "The one where you work for me, or the one where you marry me?"

The words hurt me only because they're so riddled with his pain, and I know that's my fault. "You *knew* why I agreed to marry you. You knew and you lied to me to make me believe we were after the same thing."

"We agreed to work together to make both of our lives better. That hasn't changed. Nothing that *matters* is different here."

"Everything's changed." I feel like he just pulled the rug out from under me and doesn't understand why I'm scrambling. "We had a plan, rules, and now you're completely changing the game. I don't want to hurt you, Julian, but you're not playing fair."

"Is *he*?" he asks, his voice rough. "Coming in here, being part of this place you love so much more than me. Is *he* playing fair?"

"Are you off the hook for lying to me because Marston's in town? Is that how this works? Do I have to give up my job and be your secretary because my ex is going to work beside me for a couple of weeks? Is that my punishment?"

Julian prowls forward, slow and angry. I back up and hit the wall, and he cages me in with a hand on either side of my head. "Your ex? Is that what he is to you? Does that mean you filed the paperwork? Tell me yes, and I'll walk out of here and won't say another word about him being in town and working with you. He can move in next door for all I care. Just tell me you filed."

I open my mouth to explain that I've been busy this week, that a divorce is a big deal, that I'm going to get to it soon. But I don't need to say any of those excuses out loud to recognize them for what they are. Julian deserves raw honesty. "I haven't."

He flinches, face contorting, and the evidence of the pain I'm causing tears me in two. "Do you want a life with him?"

L.A., fancy cars, fancier homes, leaving everything I love here and tearing Cami away from her family? Destroying my relationship with my parents forever? Regardless of my feelings for Marston, the answer is obvious. "I don't."

"Do you want a life with *me?*"

"Julian . . ." His name comes out in a raspy croak. "I don't know."

Julian stumbles back as if I've hit him. "Figure that out. Sooner rather than later would be nice. My parents are planning to fly in for the wedding." He opens my office door and slams it behind him as he walks away.

I lean back against the wall and press my palms to my eyes, but my tears leak out anyway.

$\maltese$

DIVORCE PAPERWORK ISN'T that complicated for a no-fault case like ours, but I stare down at the papers I printed off this morning and can't make myself pick up a pen.

Cami must've sensed my mood when she got off the bus, because she finished her homework quickly and asked if she could go hang out in the kitchen. I agreed, not wanting to poison her good mood with my brooding one.

It's good she's not here. It gives me a chance to get this done. Then again, I wish she were here and I had an excuse to avoid it.

"When I find myself hesitating to make the simple decision, there's usually a reason," Savvy says from the doorway.

Instead of looking up and acknowledging her, I fold my arms on the desk and drop my head. "It's called self-sabotage," I mutter.

I hear the soft scuff of her sneakered steps as she walks into my office, then a gentle hand is combing through my hair. "You're still trying to process that Julian lied?" she asks. I was able to give her the quickest debrief over coffee after her morning spin class, but she's been busy with clients all day, so I haven't seen her since Julian stormed out of here midmorning.

I lift my head and draw in a shaky breath. "He showed up this morning and told me he wants me to quit my job and work for him."

"He did what now?" She folds her arms and rocks back on her heels, her *oh, no you didn't!* stance.

"Am I crazy?"

Savvy bites her bottom lip and wrinkles her brow. "Can you be more specific?"

I gape at my friend. "Thanks, bitch."

Savvy grabs the chair on the opposite side of my desk, drags it next to mine, and sits down. "You're not crazy for wanting The Orchid for yourself. You run this business in a way you should be proud of. Never be ashamed of wanting more control, given all the work you do here."

"But . . .?" I swallow. As someone who grew up under constant criticism, I usually shield myself from it these days, but right now I need someone with some perspective to give it to me.

"You know I was never in favor of you marrying Julian just so you could get your trust."

"That wasn't the only—"

She holds up a hand. "I know. He's your friend, you make a good team, you don't want to be alone forever, and the sex is all right. I get it. There are days I'm so sick of going home to an empty house that I'm ready to take Smithy up on one of his random proposals."

An unexpected laugh bursts out of me. God, Smithy does love to proposition Savvy, but the idea of my hotheaded go-getter best friend with my stoner cousin is so absurd.

"I know you don't want to lose The Orchid, but I think the question you need to ask yourself is this: if Mrs. Wright sold this place to someone else tomorrow, and there was no chance of you buying it—trust or no trust—would you still want to marry Julian?"

I drop my gaze to my hands. When laid out so succinctly, it seems like it should be an easy decision.

She scoots the stack of divorce paperwork toward me. "Figure out that part first. Then tackle this question."

I throw myself back in my chair and whimper dramatically. "When did my simple life get so messy?"

She cracks a smile. "When you dared to let in the good stuff. Messy is okay. There's nothing here that can't be fixed."

I think of Julian's face when he left my office, and I'm not so sure that's true.

Standing, Savvy winks at me before returning the chair to its spot on the other side of the office and heading out. "Oh," she says, hand on the doorjamb. "Marston's in the kitchen baking with your daughter. Thought you'd want to know."

CHAPTER FOURTEEN

MARSTON

*C*ami slides the tray of puff pastry into the oven and closes the door. "Twenty minutes, and the dough should be perfectly flaky. Then we'll take them out and dust them with powdered sugar."

"Impressive," I say, meaning it.

She waves me off. "I love to bake, but someday I'll make Abbi teach me the really complicated stuff."

Clearly, this kid got nothing of her father's asshole genetics. She's fun and sweet and pretty knowledgeable in the kitchen. When I look at her, I can't help but think about Brinley's years as a single mom. She has Julian around to help now, but how did she do it before? She managed to get through college and build a career while raising an awesome kid. Was Roman around? Did they try to make it work?

"Hey, Mom," Cami calls right before I hear the sound of

Brinley's heels on the kitchen tile. "I'm teaching Marston how to make lemon poppyseed pinwheels."

After our encounter in the hall yesterday, I decided I needed to give Brinley space, and I've avoided her side of the building so much today that this is the first time I've set eyes on her. She's a knockout in her fitted black dress with a purple lightweight sweater, but it's the sight of her shoes that makes my mouth go dry. One skinny strap across her toes and another around her ankle. I'd recognize the shoes I bought her in Vegas anywhere.

She might not remember half the night, but I'll never forget it—the way she looked after the night was over, after we'd said our vows and celebrated too hard, and finally made it back to my suite. She slid out of her black dress and stood before me in nothing but the lacy bra and panties I'd bought her and those hot-as-fuck shoes.

The bra tied at the front with the most delicate silver ribbon. I kept my hands on her ass as I kissed my way across her collarbone and down between her breasts. I can still remember her quiet little whimper and the way she swayed toward me as I untied it with my teeth. After the bra fell away, I made my way to the little ties on each of her hips until her panties fell to the floor.

"Are you okay, Marston?" Brinley asks, pulling my attention off her shoes. "You look like you saw a ghost."

I shake away the memory. Was Vegas just a fluke? Will this all end with her filing for divorce and spending her life with Julian? I try to ignore the ache in my gut at the possibility. "I was just noticing your shoes."

Brinley's eyes go wide, and red colors her cheeks as she looks down at her feet.

"Those shoes are Mom's favorite," Cami says. "She *loves* designer shoes but can't afford them anymore."

Abbi clears her throat from the other side of the kitchen. "Cami, would you come to the storeroom and help me put away the new order?"

Cami looks to her mom. "Would you mind pulling the pinwheels from the oven when the timer goes off?"

"Sure, sweetie. That's no problem."

Brinley and I watch Abbi and Cami go before I turn back to her. "Your daughter's a very talented baker."

Brinley smiles. "She loves it. I think she'd be in here all the time if I let her."

My gaze flicks down to her shoes again. "She said you can't afford designer shoes."

She releases a stiff laugh. "I mean, can anyone, really?"

I prop my hands on the stretch of stainless-steel counter behind me and study her, unwilling to let her evade the subject so easily this time. "When we were in Vegas, I thought maybe your parents had squandered their fortune somehow, but that's not it, is it?"

"It's not their job to provide for me. I'm an adult now."

"They could, though. One would think that with the kind of money they have, they'd insist on making sure their only living daughter and only grandchild had everything they needed and more."

Sighing, she leans against the counter opposite me and crosses her feet at the ankles. "I'm not going to give you my rich-bitch sob story if that's what you're looking for. I like nice things, but I can manage without them too."

"I doubt it's a sob story," I say softly. "But I want to hear it either way."

She exhales heavily. "They kept tabs on me all through

college. I'm talking strict curfews, designated study times— Dad even went so far as to schedule my classes." She shakes her head. "I figured it was a small price to pay. I was a single mom, so they weren't just covering for my apartment and tuition. They paid for Cami's daycare and my car, my insurance, my spending money. Everything. Most single moms I went to school with were trying to juggle full-time jobs, school, and mothering, and still taking the deep dive into student loan debt. I didn't like feeling as if my parents were holding the reins to my life, but it seemed like a small price to pay, considering all they were doing for me."

"All that was barely a drop in the bucket for them," I remind her.

"That's not the way I was raised to think about it. Money has value, even when you have a lot of it. I *did* appreciate it. I still do. I'm grateful I was able to simultaneously get an education and prioritize my time with Cami." She grips the counter, her knuckles turning white. "When we were in Vegas, I told you that I wouldn't work for Knox Bourbon, but I didn't exactly get there right away. When I moved home after graduation, Dad gave me a position with the company. It was a joke. He had one of his guys following me around all the time, reporting every move I made to him. If I took a long lunch break, Dad knew. If I stayed late at work, Dad knew. And God forbid I tried something different in the company, like tweak our branding or bring in a new product line. I couldn't stand it, so one day I said *enough* and quit."

I see the angst from that decision on her face, the weight of it. I know her father well enough to know there were consequences before I ask, "What did he do?"

"The same thing he would've done when I was a child,"

she says with a bitter smile. "He took away my privileges. The car I'd been driving since high school? It was in his name, and he took it back. The house I lived in and all the furniture in it? In his name. The savings account I pulled from when money was tight? All of it was in his name. As much as I'd told myself that I didn't take any of it for granted, I'd always thought of it as mine. But it wasn't."

"And the asshole just took it all away." Of course he did. That's Abraham Knox's MO. Own everything, and you can control everything. In her darker moments, Brinley used to joke that he was pissed his money couldn't make cancer answer to him.

She shakes her head. "I thought I'd be fine on my own. Everyone else buys their own cars and pays their own rent. Then Dad started sending me monthly bills for the education and accommodations he'd paid for. He said that since he'd paid for it with the understanding that I'd be working at his company, I had to pay him back."

I feel my hands ball into fists. "He really hasn't changed."

She scoffs. "Not at all. But he didn't think I'd pay it. He thought I'd bend to his will and go back to how things were —me right under his thumb where he wanted me. But I was too proud and wanted to prove I didn't need him. I made that payment every month, with interest, even while it meant my other debts piled up. By the time I got my first paycheck at The Orchid, I was already buried by credit card debt. I needed a car to get Cami to school and myself to work, and I needed groceries and a roof over my head, some basic furniture for the one-bedroom apartment I was renting . . ." She shakes her head, eyes out of focus as she looks at the floor. "He took away everything, and I thought

I could start over, but it was so much harder than I'd ever imagined."

"But you did it," I say, and I'm so fucking proud of her. She always wanted to get out from under his thumb, dreamed of it the way other people dream of the kind of fancy possessions she had when he ruled her life.

"I didn't do a very good job with it. The first car I bought in my own name was repossessed, because once I realized I didn't stand a chance of making the payments, I had no idea what to do. Then I missed enough credit card payments and incurred enough late fees that I wanted to go back and shake twenty-two-year-old me. I'm better with money now. I know where to scrimp and save, but the consequences of those early days still follow me."

I stare at her for a long time, thinking through everything I know about her relationship with Julian and how quickly things changed between them after Vegas. "Brinley . . ." Sighing, I step forward, then tuck my hands in my pockets. Having her this close makes touching her far too tempting. "You know how things have changed for me. *I* could take care of you, and any of these lingering financial worries. With a combination of hard work and great luck, I've managed—"

"I don't want your money." She steps around me and walks to the oven, checking on the pastries inside while putting distance between us.

"Is that part of the reason why you agreed to marry *him*? For the stability?" I need her to say *yes*. I need this to be about what Julian can provide for her and Cami, but she stiffens, and when she spins on me, her eyes are blazing.

"No. I don't want Julian's money. Jesus, Marston, what do you think of me?"

"I didn't mean it as an insult. You've struggled so much, and I could see the appeal of letting him—"

"Well, you're wrong. That's not the life I want."

I swallow hard. I want to pull her into my arms so badly that my hands are shaking. "So it's really love, then? You spent one night with me and then came back here to kick-start your life with *him*? What the fuck, Brinley? How's that supposed to make me feel?"

She stares at me, that angry spark in her eyes flaring brighter. "How is this about *you*?"

"Can you really not remember, or is that just some bull-shit you're shoveling because you don't want to be held accountable for the decisions you made that night?"

Her whole face hardens, and when she opens her mouth, I brace myself for a verbal lashing. I *want* it. Anything that will help me understand.

Instead, she snaps her mouth shut and walks away.

※

BRINLEY

"You okay, Mommy?" Cami asks as we walk into the condo.

I toss my keys on the foyer table and hang my purse from the hook. "Yeah, baby. Why?"

"You were quiet the whole way home." She frowns. "Was it okay that I showed Marston how to make lemon poppy-seed pinwheels?"

The knot of worry in my chest loosens as I take in her worried green eyes. I smooth back her hair. "That was just fine. I'm sorry I'm being so quiet. I have a lot on my mind."

"About the wedding?" she asks quietly.

I swallow. One of my biggest concerns with this whole marriage is how it will affect Cami. I wouldn't have considered it if she and Julian didn't have a great rapport or if I thought our marriage would negatively impact her life at all. Before I agreed to Julian's proposal, I sat down with Cami, and we talked about what it would mean for us. I needed her to be on board too, or I couldn't do it. She was excited about the prospect of having a stepdad, and that seemed like enough. But still, Julian and I always said that if things didn't click for us as a married couple, we'd get divorced after Cami left for college, and I can't deny that a divorce would affect her—especially after living with him for that long. "A little," I admit. My phone buzzes in my purse, but I ignore it. "Do you ever think about it?"

She nods. "I think it'll be good for you not to be alone all the time."

My heart. "Honey, you don't need to worry about me."

"I know. You're fierce and you can handle anything," she says, parroting the words I've told her so many times when she's struggled. "But I thought Julian might make it so you don't have to work so hard."

I pull her into a hug and stoop to bury my face in her dark hair. "I kind of love working hard," I whisper. "It feels good to know I can do it on my own."

Not one for long snuggles these days, she withdraws from my arms and meets my eyes. "Whatever you decide, Mama, we're gonna be just fine. We always have been."

I nod and swallow hard, hoping those tears I feel rising can be pushed back down. "You're a pretty cool kid, you know that?"

She grins. "I know." Just like that, she turns and runs into the living room, the conversation over.

I grab my phone and wander toward the kitchen as I unlock it to read the text I missed.

> Marston: I'm sorry. I fucked up that
>   conversation. For the record, I hate that
>   you can't remember.

There's a video attached to the message, and I glance toward the living room before tapping play. Cami has her sketchbook in her lap and is already pulling up her favorite YouTube channel.

The video is low resolution, probably condensed before it was sent, but I can make out Marston and me at the front of a softly lit chapel. Marston's holding my hands, and a tall man in a dark suit stands before us.

I gasp, realizing what I'm seeing. This is our *wedding.* I'm simultaneously desperate to watch and scared that seeing it will confuse me even more.

Marston looks to whoever's holding the phone. "Ready?" he asks.

"We're rolling," the woman behind the camera says. "You both look great."

"Marston," the officiant says, "would you like to start with your vows?"

"Let me go first?" I ask, my voice nearly squeaking. "I don't want to forget what I planned."

I squint at the pixelated video, trying to determine how drunk I am. The excitement in my voice might be tipsiness, but I imagined myself stumbling down the aisle with Marston, and I don't *sound* drunk. Whatever made me decide to say these vows and put on his ring, I can't blame it all on the alcohol, which doesn't make any sense to me.

What was I thinking? How did I ever think we could work?

He leans forward and whispers something in my ear the phone's mic can't make out, but I laugh, fist his shirt in my hand, and pull him down for a long kiss.

"It's not time for that part yet," he says, amusement in every word.

I look to the officiant, and when he nods, I take a deep breath. "Marston, you're the first man I loved. When you came into my life, you saw *me* when no one else bothered." I bow my head, and the sounds of my ragged breaths are clear even if the picture isn't. "I'm not marrying you because I think it will be easy. I'm marrying you because I want to be the kind of mother who shows her children that the best things—the *right* things—are worth fighting for." I take his hand and squeeze. "I'm sorry I didn't fight for you sooner, but you're mine now and will be for as long as you give me the honor of holding your heart. Wear this ring, and let the circle be a symbol of our love. Something that has no beginning and no end—just as what we feel for each other seemed to exist before we met. Even a decade apart won't end or weaken it."

"Mommy, who are you talking to?" Cami calls from the living room.

My heart skips a beat and I pause the recording. "Just watching a video on my phone, honey."

"Sounds like you," she says.

I swallow and lower the volume before pressing play again.

Marston looks into my eyes and shakes his head solemnly. "When I realized it was really you sitting at that bar tonight, Alec told me I should consider another night

244

with you a gift. I told him that one night wouldn't be enough. From the moment I saw you in that ridiculous tulle dress at your sweet sixteen party, I thought you were special. Then you smiled, and I knew you were the most beautiful girl I'd ever seen. I talked a big game, but back then I didn't believe I deserved you. A lot has changed in the last ten years, and now I can finally take care of you. I can give you anything you need, buy you any luxury you want."

I shake my head a half-second before the image of me on-screen does the same. "I don't need luxuries."

"I know. I see that. But I need to be able to give them to you. Because you're what matters most to me." He brings my hand to his mouth and kisses it before sliding the ring on, and my heart tugs with longing. I want to be the woman who can wear his ring. I want to be the one who's confident enough to promise forever. But the girl on that screen must've forgotten who she was and what scared her. "Wear this ring, and know that the diamond is a symbol of our love. It's you and me. It's what we have. We can withstand anything and come out on the other side stronger."

I watch as I throw myself at him and bury my face in his chest.

"Brinley, do you take Marston to be your lawfully wedded husband?" the officiant asks.

Marston chuckles at my muffled "I do!"

"And Marston, do you take Brinley to be your lawfully wedded wife?"

He looks down at me, and I wish the angle of the camera allowed me to see the look in his eyes. Wish this video would let me zoom in all the way to what I saw in that moment, wish it could have recorded my thoughts and feelings so I could understand. "I do," he says softly.

"For as much as Brinley Knox and Marston Rowe have committed to each other before myself and the witnesses here, Brinley and Marston are now husband and wife in accordance with the laws of the state of Nevada."

The woman holding the camera cheers, and Marston cups my face in his hands and lowers his head. The video ends as his lips brush mine.

I turn down the volume and immediately push play on the video again, as if it might trigger a memory. I'm watching myself kiss him before our vows when a message from Julian flashes on the screen.

Julian: Running a little late. On my way.

The text is immediately followed by a knock on the door.

"Stella's here!" Cami says, racing to answer. Because tonight, Julian and I have dinner with my parents and their best friends from Orchid Valley to celebrate our upcoming wedding. And I was so caught up in watching the footage of my prior wedding that I forgot.

I rush to the sink and brace myself on the edge as I run the water cold.

"Hey, kiddo," Stella says. The click of her heels across the hardwood floor grows closer. "What are we going to do tonight?"

"We could Netflix and chill?" Cami asks.

Stella snort-laughs. "Just call it watching Netflix."

"Why?"

"Well, Netflix and chill is kind of something people say when they're, um, *dating*."

"Oh." Cami giggles. "Really?"

"Really." When Stella steps into the kitchen, I'm splashing cold water on my face. "Brinley, baby."

"Mom's stressed about the wedding," Cami says quietly.

"I can see that." Stella's steps soften and grow closer as I pat my face dry. Her hand is gentle on my shoulder. "Cami, honey, can you go to the living room? I'll meet you there in a minute."

Breathe. Just breathe.

I turn and wrap my arms around her, needing the reassuring hug of my oldest friend. And it helps. God, does it help. Stella, Abbi, Savvy—these girls are my family now. If my parents find out about the mess I'm in and disown me, I won't lose my girls. Their love has never been contingent on a damn thing.

"Is this about having dinner with your parents, or is it about Julian?" she asks softly, hugging me back.

"Both."

She strokes my hair. "Want me to see if Kace can babysit so I can go with you tonight?"

Pulling back, I manage a shaky smile. "You really want to face my parents again?"

She scoffs. "Well, no. I don't. But I will if it helps you."

The clunk of the front door is followed by the sound of heavy steps toward the kitchen. Julian's here.

I shake my head. "I've got this. Cami would be heartbroken if I took away her night with Aunt Stella."

She grins. "I *am* pretty cool."

"But are you cool enough to get her to finish packing for

Disney?" I ask, pressing my hands together as if I'm praying.

She laughs. "Sure. I'm guessing you made her a list?"

I grin. "Of course. It's in her room."

"Hey, Stella," Julian says, joining us in the kitchen. "Thanks for watching Cami tonight."

She gives him a tight smile. "No problem."

He looks me over and frowns. "Ready?" He no doubt recognizes I'm still in the same clothes I wore to work, never mind the mess I undoubtedly made of my makeup when I rinsed my face. If he's thinking my mother would never approve, he's right.

"I need five minutes to freshen up." *And pull myself together.* I jog to my bedroom and kick the door shut behind me. I unzip my dress and shimmy out of it even as I'm digging through my closet for a fresh one. I tell myself I don't care about my parents' opinion anymore, but everyone knows that's bullshit. I don't want them to be disappointed in me, and I know if they are, that disappointment will dog me for days. If changing outfits and freshening my makeup is going to keep my mother from making some snarky comment, it's worth it.

In less than five minutes, I'm heading back to the kitchen, where I find Julian leaning against the counter and staring at his phone. No—*my* phone.

"Brinley and Marston are now husband and wife in accordance with the laws of the state of Nevada," the voice from the video says.

Julian lifts his eyes to meet mine, and his pain is so clear there. The words *I'm sorry* sit heavily on my tongue. I *am* sorry. But I don't like that he looked at my messages without asking. I *am* sorry. But saying the words won't get us out of this awful limbo we've found ourselves in.

He straightens and hands my phone back to me. "You don't even sound drunk," he says, and the words sound like an accusation.

I take it and drop it into my clutch. "I know."

He studies me for a long time before dipping his head and pressing a kiss to the side of my neck. "Don't let him ruin us."

CHAPTER FIFTEEN

BRINLEY

March 4th, before

"Y ou're going to get us caught," Marston says, but I feel his smile against my mouth as I tug him into my room. He smells a little like sweat and grass clippings from working with the yard crew for the last few hours, but the earthy rawness of him only makes me want him more.

"My parents are gone until six tonight. The only one here is Lori, and she's cleaning carpets downstairs today." I kick the door closed and begin unbuttoning my shirt. "But you can go if you want."

He growls and nudges me to the bed until the backs of

EVERY LITTLE PIECE OF ME

my legs hit the mattress. Giggling, I lie down, grab a fistful of his V-neck, and tug him closer. He crawls on top of me, his knees on either side of my hips, one hand behind my neck and the other sliding down into my shirt to cup me through my bra, too impatient for me to finish undressing.

His kisses are searing and hungry, on my mouth, my jaw, my neck, behind my ear—all the places he knows I like the feel of his lips. I arch into his touch as his thumb skims my nipple in slow, torturous circles. "You're sure?" he asks.

"Hurry."

He chuckles against my neck. "I thought you said we had plenty of time."

"Not long enough." I take his hand and guide it down to my skirt and between my legs. He strokes me through my panties, and I draw up one knee to give him better access, rocking into him.

"Brinley!"

Marston jumps off the bed before I fully register the sound of my father's voice.

"What do you think you're doing to my daughter?" Dad's eyes are wide, his nostrils flared as he stalks toward Marston, and I freeze, paralyzed by fear.

Marston hangs his head and deflates. The guy I love. The guy who loves me but doesn't believe he's good enough —he *deflates* under my father's anger, and the sight of that breaks something inside me.

I scramble off the bed, stepping between Dad and Mars. "Daddy, it's fine."

"This is between me and Rowe." Dad palms my shoulder and pushes me to the side. "I give you a job, and you repay me by assaulting my daughter?"

"He didn't assault me! I brought him in here. I *love* him."

It happens so fast I don't even see it coming. The sting of my father's slap is so sharp that I expect to find blood on my face. I drop back on my bed, cradling my face in my hand.

"I won't let my daughter act like some low-class slut."

"Don't touch her!" Marston lunges at my father as my mom walks in the door. His fist connects with Dad's jaw with so much power that my father's head snaps back. He stumbles into Mom, and she loses her balance and knocks her head on the doorframe.

I hop off the bed and wrap my arms around Marston from behind, pulling him back to keep him from going after Dad again.

"Harriet, call the police," Dad says. His lip's bleeding, and Marston's knuckles are bright red.

"Yeah," Marston says, "call them and let them know you hit your daughter."

Tears roll hot and heavy over my throbbing cheek. "No. Don't. He'll leave. It's fine." My voice shakes. "*Please.*"

Mom searches her pockets and finally comes up with her phone, but she scans the room instead of dialing. "I don't understand."

"Of course you don't. You let your daughters get away with everything." Dad yanks her phone out of her hand and starts to dial.

I lurch forward and grab it from him. "Marston is *leaving.*"

There's panic in Marston's eyes, but his jaw is set, determination written in the hard line of his mouth. "I don't want to leave you with him. He hit you, Brinley. That's not okay."

"It wasn't anything. He didn't mean it. Just go. Please." My whole body shakes, and I beg, "Do it *for me*."

CHAPTER SIXTEEN

BRINLEY

Present day

*M*y father stands at the end of the long table at Orchid Valley's finest restaurant, looking like a king ready to speak to his subjects. Every eye in the room is drawn to him even before he clears his throat to get their attention. Abraham Knox has that effect on people—whether they love him or hate him, they all fall into line.

He hoists his champagne flute in the air. "I'd like to propose a toast to my daughter Brinley, for finally finding someone who'll marry her."

Uncomfortable chuckles sprinkle throughout the room. Maybe a few of those laughs are sincere. I tell myself Dad's friends are the only ones who'd find that joke funny, but people are assholes, so who knows. Beside me, Julian shifts uncomfortably, and I flash him a grateful smile.

"You've done well, Brinley," Dad continues, "and I know that somewhere, your sister is looking down on you and she's proud. She would have wanted you to be happy. Remember how much she loved weddings?" His face crumples, and he bows his head for a beat. Mom reaches up to squeeze his hand. "Brittany would've been such a beautiful bride, but life isn't fair, so I'll only get to watch one daughter walk down the aisle. Only watch one daughter say her vows."

All I can do is focus on my breathing. A deep breath in, a long exhale. In through the nose, out through the mouth. This is the cost of being the daughter who lived. Nothing's ever really about you again. It's always about the child who was lost.

"But we take the good with the bad," Dad continues. He shifts a bit to focus on my fiancé. "We're so proud to invite you into our family, Julian. I know you'll take good care of Brinley. You'll be her rock when she's unsteady. You'll be her brain when she misplaces hers."

Everyone laughs at *this* "joke," and my stomach cramps.

"As long as you're by her side, I'll know I don't have to worry. And I thank you for that." He lifts his glass a little higher and smiles broadly. "To the happy couple!"

"To the happy couple," everyone choruses.

Julian takes a sip of his champagne before reaching under the table to take my hand. "You okay?" he whispers.

I nod. Nothing unexpected here. But tears well in my eyes anyway.

The woman next to me leans over and pats my shoulder. I don't remember her name, but she was a regular at Mom and Dad's parties back in the day—always wearing diamonds and kissing ass. "We all miss Brittany, sweetheart," she says. "Just try to put on a smile for your parents."

I take my napkin and dab my eyes, smiling as she's so graciously suggested. "Thank you," I say, as if she just offered me profound advice. As if people haven't been telling me that for the last eleven years. *Just smile. Be strong for your parents.* And, the platitude I hate the most: *Everything happens for a reason.*

I turned that last one back on them when I got knocked up at seventeen. Most of them didn't get my point—that they only say such things when it suits them—but it shut some of them up.

"Excuse me." I push my chair back and stand. If I sit here one more minute, I'm at risk of either vomiting or screaming at the whole table. Maybe I'll *really* make a statement and do both. "I just need a minute."

Julian's chair squeaks against the tile floor as he pushes back and stands next to me. "I'm coming with you."

I want to be alone, but we've already attracted too much attention, so I take his hand rather than risk making a scene. Hand in hand, we wind our way around the table and toward the front of the restaurant. I try to keep my steps even, to let Julian set the pace, since I'm apt to run.

The host rushes forward and opens the door for us, and when the night air hits my face, I draw in a long, deep breath.

You're okay. Just breathe. In through the nose. Out through the mouth.

The early spring evening is mild, and when the door closes behind us, trapping the cacophony of the restaurant inside, it's like finally breaking the surface after being held underwater.

Julian rubs his big hands down my bare arms as if he's trying to warm me, and I have to take another deep breath to keep myself from swatting his hands away. "They don't mean to hurt you, Brinley."

I'm not sure that's true. "It's not that." And it's not. Dad's barbs hurt. They always do. But the anxiety pressing down on my chest has more to do with the wedding than with my parents.

Julian pulls me close and trails soft, leisurely kisses down my neck. His mouth is sweet, his kisses tender, but his touch does nothing to melt away the anxiety that has me in knots.

"What's going on out here?" Savannah asks in a singsong voice behind us, the click of heels on the sidewalk growing closer.

Julian groans as he lifts his head. "I would think that was obvious, Savvy. I was trying to seduce my fiancée."

"Right here on the street? You should at least put out a bucket for tips."

I turn around in time to see the annoyance on my best friend's face. Savvy was Team Marston before she ever met him. "Don't worry," I say. "We're keeping it PG-13 so we don't offend innocent eyes like yours."

Julian chuckles softly, and Savvy shifts her purse into her other hand to give me a one-armed squeeze. "I'm sorry I'm late."

Julian frowns at me. "You invited Savannah?"

I shrug. "Strength in numbers."

"Did I miss anything good?" Savvy asks.

"My dad gave a speech about how I'm a dumb, incompetent woman who's lucky a man like Julian is willing to take me on as his charge."

Julian grimaces. "It wasn't *that* bad."

"The way he talks, everyone in that room probably believes I'd electrocute myself making toast without supervision."

Savvy wrinkles her nose. "At least he's consistent?"

I give her an exaggerated fake smile and add, "It was fine. Everything's fine. I'm so happy my parents came to town to show off my fiancé to their friends." I throw out some jazz hands. "Yay!"

Frowning, Savvy looks at the door and back to me. "Tell me they're at least paying for the booze."

I slide my arm through hers. "Let's go order the most expensive steaks and competitor bourbon."

"You're so devious, and *I love it!*"

Laughing together, we head back into the restaurant. I look over my shoulder to make sure Julian's coming, and he schools his expression into a smile—but not before I see the twist of his frown and the irritation in his eyes.

He doesn't like that Savvy interrupted our moment. I get that and respect it, but the way he looks at her like she's the enemy? That doesn't help this sinking feeling in my gut.

❦

"INVITE ME IN," Julian says, squeezing my hand when we reach my door. "I know tonight was hard for you. Let me come in. It's been over a week since we've been together."

I tense. "I can't—"

"Or we could just . . . unwind together."

I nod, but not because I think the conversation we'll

have will be relaxing. I know what I need to do, and it's not fair for me to put it off any longer. "Okay. Come on in."

Stella's yawning when she meets us at the door.

"Hey, Stella," Julian says before stepping inside and pointing toward the powder room. "I'm going to use the facilities. I'll be out in a minute."

"I'll pour the wine," I say.

"Night, Julian," Stella says. She waits until he disappears down the hall before turning back to me. "I know it's barely past nine and I should be taking my newly single ass out to find a man, but I'm going home to crash. Don't tell my twenty-one-year-old self. She'd disown me."

I laugh quietly. "Your secret's safe with me. You know you don't need to rush into a new relationship, right?"

She waves a hand. "I know, I know, but I miss *sex.*"

I snort. "You and Bobby broke up less than a week ago."

She arches a brow. "And what does that have to do with how long it's been since I've been properly fucked?"

"Oh." I make a face. "Was that why . . .?"

"Still not talking about it," she says, but she softens the declaration with a wink.

Someday this girl is going to open up about what happened with Bobby, and I'm going to be ready. In the meantime, I'm just glad to have her back in the OV, even if it means she's had to take up temporary residence in her mom's guest room. "How'd it go with Cami tonight?"

"Awesome, of course. That girl wore me *out*, but we had fun." She stretches her arms overhead and yawns again. "What about your night? Did your parents openly mock you for having flaws, or did they stick to the subtext burns tonight?"

"A little of both." I grin, knowing she understands

without explanation. "It sucked, but that's nothing compared to how much it's going to suck when I talk to them tomorrow."

"Tomorrow?" She searches my face then seems to get it. "Oh, baby girl."

I swallow hard, but I can already feel the tears burning my eyes. "I really wanted it to work. He's a good guy, Stella."

She nods. "He's been good to you, but . . ."

"But I can't marry him just for The Orchid," I say, finishing the thought so she doesn't have to. "That's not fair to him."

"It's not fair to *either* of you," she whispers. "What can I do?"

"Remind me it's not the end of the world when my parents threaten to never speak to me again? And remind me I can climb out of debt and be independent *without* their stupid trust?"

"Done and done," she says.

"I'll pour the wine," Julian calls from the kitchen.

"Thanks!" I reply over my shoulder.

Stella blows out a breath. "I'll get out of here so you can . . ." Her gaze drifts toward the kitchen, and she swallows.

"Yeah." I open the door for her. "Thank you for babysitting, and everything else."

"Love you, boo."

"Love you too." I close the door behind her and head to the living room. The second I sink into the plush cushions of my sofa, my eyes float closed.

I listen to his heavy footsteps coming into the living room and force my eyes open.

He sets a glass of red wine on the coffee table, then drops something from his palm beside it. I can practically feel the air in the room chill. "Can we talk about why you even have this?"

Marston's ring.

I swipe the ring from the table, then blink up at Julian, my resolve hardening. "You looked in my jewelry box?"

"Yeah. And since you're hiding another man's ring in there, I'm glad I did."

"You looked at my messages without asking and then searched through my jewelry box." I shake my head. "What the hell, Julian?"

"Why. Do. You. Have. It?"

I stare at the ring where it sits in the palm of my hand.

The one Julian gave me is a family heirloom. When he told my parents he planned to marry me and asked for their blessing, Mom took him straight to Orchid Valley Bank and Trust to pull it from their safe deposit box. When he put it on my finger, he told me how my mom cried when he agreed to use it in his proposal, and I imagined how pleased my grandmother would be to see it on my finger.

The one Marston gave me is less familiar, and in no way an antique, but somehow it's no less precious. I wonder if we picked it out together that night—if he held me from behind, my back to his front, while I peered into the jewelry case and oohed and ahhed over the beautiful choices—or if he excused himself at some point during the evening and picked it out himself.

I stare at this piece of jewelry we both used as part of our vows and wonder how I was ever strong enough to take it off and walk away.

"Why do you have his ring?" There's no denying the anger in Julian's voice. I can't blame him for it, either.

I finally lift my gaze to his. "Because he gave it to me. The night he came back into town, he gave it back to me."

Julian's jaw twitches, and I count the flutters in that little muscle as I wait for his response. "Why did you *take* it? Why were you keeping it in your jewelry box like it's something you plan to *keep*?"

"Can we talk about you invading my privacy?"

"We're *getting married*." He paces the living room and drags a hand through his hair. "I'm in limbo here and getting nowhere with you. You barely let me touch you anymore—but, hey, why worry about me? I'm just the schmuck who wants to take care of you."

"We're not having sex, so that gives you the right to spy on me?"

"I don't want to find shit out from your text messages or by digging through your room. I just want you to *tell* me what you're thinking."

I only control you when I need to. I only cross the line when you behave badly. I've lived that life. I've lived with the man who can be lavishly generous only to yank it all away the second you step out of line. Living with that kind of "love" nearly destroyed me. I'm not living it again. I pull his ring off my finger and drop both of them onto the table. "I can't marry you."

Julian snatches Marston's ring and hurls it across the room. It bounces off the wall and lands on the floor in front of the fireplace. "This is such bullshit!"

I shake my head. I don't even recognize the angry man pacing in front of me. I feel like I'm dreaming. This is all so . . . *Surely* this isn't real. But when I force myself to meet Julian's eyes again, I see the hurt there. "Julian." I should never have agreed to this. I resisted for six years for a reason. I knew I'd end up hurting him. "I'm sorry."

He sinks to his knees in front of me. He picks up his ring, presses it into my hand, and closes my fingers around it. His grip is tight, and the stone digs painfully into my palm. "We'll be fine," he says, burying his face in my chest. "I'm sorry I'm panicking, but we can do this. We can get through this."

I shake my head, but he can't see me. I shove him back by his shoulders. "Listen to me." I wait until he lifts his eyes to meet mine. "I can't marry you."

"You're choosing him?"

I'm choosing me, but I don't let myself say it.

"What about The Orchid? Buying that place is your dream."

I shrug. "Everyone has dreams, but just because it's my dream that doesn't give me the right to act carelessly in my pursuit of it." I pull my hand from his and uncurl my fingers. "I can't marry you for business reasons when you're marrying me for personal ones."

"You *love* me." He presses his hand to his stomach as if I've plunged a knife in there, and I have no choice but to twist the blade—to end this with the truth before I hurt him more.

"Not enough to marry you."

CHAPTER SEVENTEEN

MARSTON

*A*braham fucking Knox is in town.

When I spotted him walking into the Spotted Duck tonight, it was every reminder I needed of why I stayed away from Orchid Valley for so long. To add insult to injury, I learned the Knoxes are in town for some sort of engagement party for Brinley and Julian.

At some point, I'm just going to have to accept that she's not going to break it off with him. Maybe her reasons are bullshit or maybe they're the right ones, but at the end of the day, she's the one who gets to decide.

And she's never led you to believe she's going to choose anything but a life with Julian.

I came straight to Smithy's to drown my sorrows. My old friend's behind the bar tonight and keeping me entertained with stories from his short career in the NFL. I'm pretty sure half this shit isn't true, but at least it's taken my mind off Brinley and our just-on-paper marriage.

"How much longer are you going to stick around?" Smithy asks, plopping on the stool next to me.

I stare at my beer. "I'm not sure. I'm meeting the Wright family in Atlanta on Monday afternoon to report my findings on The Orchid, so that's almost wrapped up." Brinley laughed in my face when I gave her a rundown of my suggestions for the owners. Every update on my list is something she's been after them to do for years. For her sake, I hope they'll listen to me. Good management will only take the company so far before an unwillingness to put money back into the business will backfire on them.

"What about my cousin?"

"Good question." If Brinley still wants to be Mrs. Julian Hallison, then maybe I need to fucking accept it and move on.

The only problem is that I don't know how.

One second, my beer is in my hand, and the next it's shattering on the floor and there's a fist flying toward my jaw.

I block it without thinking and turn to see the glassy eyes of the man it's connected to. *Julian.*

He smirks at the mess of broken glass and spilled beer at my feet. "Hey, Smithy," he says, swaying on his feet, "you gonna let this bastard make a mess of your bar?"

Smithy slides off his stool. "Julian, you're drunk. Cut it out."

"I'll call him a cab," the redhead behind the bar says, pulling a phone from her pocket.

Julian's eyes are bloodshot, and I wonder if getting this plowed is normal for him. "You think you're hot shit since you have all this money. Think you can swoop in and just take her? Well, guess what—her parents will never accept you. It doesn't matter how much money you have. They know who you really are."

Smithy takes Julian by the forearm. "Come on, man. Let's go cool off outside."

"You don't give a damn about anyone but yourself," Julian says, sneering at me. He looks me over, not budging even as Smithy tugs him toward the door. "Now she thinks she can't marry me. All because you've fucked with her head."

My breath leaves me in a rush. *She did it. She broke up with him.*

I don't realize I'm smiling until he swings at me with his free arm.

I dodge, and Smithy wraps Julian in a bear hug from behind, pinning his arms down at his sides.

"She can't even remember that night." Julian's practically spitting his words. "I asked around. I know all about your past, and you haven't fucking changed. You're a thief who thinks he can take anything he wants. And now you think you can come back to town and steal *my family*."

"Come on," Smithy says. "Out you go."

I'm barely aware of the people around me as I watch Smithy and a couple of other guys from the bar lead Julian outside.

Kace appears at my side. "Hey, Marston," he says, but his attention's on Smithy, who's wrangling Julian into a cab on the other side of the window. "Let me buy you a drink. You earned it after that shit."

I shake my head. "I have somewhere I need to be."

Kace grins slowly. "Are you going to Brinley's?"

I smack him on the shoulder and don't bother to answer. "See you later."

❧

BRINLEY

Marston: Can I come over? We need to talk.

I ROLL to my back on the couch and reread Marston's text. It's after eleven, so I'm pretty confident that whatever he wants to talk about doesn't involve The Orchid.

Me: I don't know if that's a good idea. Julian
was here earlier and things got ugly.

I wait ten minutes, and when he doesn't reply, I unlock my phone to text him again.

The doorbell rings.

Because I'm a coward, I pull up the app for my home security system to see who it is. I'm not ready to face Julian right now. I've never seen him as angry as he was tonight, and while he was entitled to his feelings, his rage scared me.

The camera shows Marston, head bowed as he waits, and I smile despite myself and go to answer it.

When I open the door, his head snaps up and he looks me over with fierce intensity, and I realize my mistake. I'm in my pajamas. They aren't the kind of thing I'd choose to wear if I knew Marston would be seeing me, but that doesn't seem to matter to him. His gaze skims over my thin white tank top and settles on my black cotton shorts before coming back up. A classier woman would've thought to put on a bra before answering the door, but something about motherhood took all the class out of me and replaced it with an endless need for comfort. Judging by Marston's flared nostrils and parted lips, he doesn't mind at all.

He's wearing the same dark gray shirt from work today, but he's discarded his tie and rolled the sleeves up to his elbows, revealing the tattoo around his right wrist. He swapped his dress pants out for jeans at some point. His hair's a little mussed and he's breathing hard, as if he ran all the way here. Holy hell, he's hot when he's a little undone.

He scans me—top to bottom—once, twice, a third time. "You're okay?"

The worry in his eyes makes my heart squeeze hard. "I'm fine."

"Did he hurt you?"

Oh, shit. He thought I meant . . . "No, Marston. It wasn't like that. I just mean it was upsetting. He left angry and hurt, but he's never lifted a hand against me." I swallow hard. "In fact, all these years, I've always been the one hurting *him*."

"I saw him at Smithy's just now. He was drunk and looking for a fight. When you said things got ugly . . ." He looks away and blows out a long breath.

"What happened at the bar?"

He shakes his head. "Nothing. It's fine."

"Obviously not nothing." It's my turn to look *him* over, but he doesn't appear to be injured.

"He took a couple of swings at me, but he missed." His eyes search my face then drop to my bare ring finger. "You broke up with him."

I shouldn't like that he came right here. Shouldn't relish

the intensity in his voice. Shouldn't be shaking in anticipation of his touch. "Yes."

He steps into my condo and kicks the door closed as he prowls toward me. The heat in his eyes tells me exactly what he wants, and I want to give it to him.

I had to call off the wedding. I had to break it off with Julian. And tomorrow I have to tell my parents. If I can't convince them to give me the trust anyway, I may very well have to give up my dream of buying The Orchid. I had to be strong earlier, and I'll have to find even more of that strength later. But right now, I want to lean into someone else's strength, if only for tonight.

His gaze locks on my mouth. "You canceled the wedding."

"Yes. But Marston, I still don't—"

He covers my lips with his thumb and shakes his head. "Let me have my moment, woman."

I'm surprised to hear my own laughter. I'm so drained from today, so confused from seeing that video with Marston, and so worried for tomorrow, that I didn't expect to have any laughter in me tonight. But there it is, and when he smiles, I'm glad for it. Marston Rowe's smile is a thing of beauty.

I don't fight it when he lowers that smile to my lips. I don't fight *myself.* I let him kiss me, and I kiss him back.

I shouldn't. Everything's a mess and this won't help, but his mouth is hot and hungry, and it feels so damn *right* to let him touch me that I give myself this moment of weakness.

He nudges me until my back's against the wall, then slides his hands up my sides under my tank top. I let him. I moan into his mouth, knowing the sound will goad him on —wanting it to.

When Marston cups my bare breasts, he groans against my mouth. My nipples tighten under his warm palms, and he rolls them in soft, torturous circles, making the muscles between my legs clench tight.

My feet are on the ground, but I still feel like I'm floating. I need to get my head out of the clouds and focus. "We shouldn't." I gasp as he latches on to my neck, and my objection sounds even weaker.

"Tell me you want me to stop," he murmurs against my neck.

"I don't." I tangle my hands in his hair, holding him close. "But this is going to make everything harder."

His hands drop from my breasts, leaving them cold and aching. "You're right about that." He grips my hips and hoists me up, pinning me between himself and the wall and guiding my legs to wrap around his waist. The thick length of him presses into me through his jeans and my thin shorts.

I rock, desperate for the friction to relieve the growing ache between my legs. He tears his mouth off my neck and peels off my shirt, tossing it to the side before he cups a breast in one hand and lowers his mouth. He flicks my nipple with his tongue before sucking it into his mouth. He's rough and then tender, sucking and then kissing, pulling and then licking, and I rock against him and thread my fingers through his hair again and again. I need more. I need to feel him on top of me, inside me, everywhere. I just want to lose myself and forget. I want . . .

I force my eyes open as reality descends. Nothing has changed, and the more of myself I give to him, the more it's going to hurt when the inevitable end comes. "Marston, stop."

He releases my nipple from his mouth and slowly kisses his way up to my collarbone. As he lowers me to the floor, he trails his mouth across my skin and up my neck before finally pulling back and looking at me. His eyes are dark, and he's as breathless as I am—more so.

"We can't." My objection sounds weak even to my ears.

"You're my wife. If you want this, we fucking *can*."

I swallow. "We still need to get divorced."

Marston steps back and shakes his head. "We don't."

"You don't understand. My life is here. Cami goes to a great school, and I love my job and my friends. Everyone at The Orchid counts on me, and I like knowing I provide them with the security they need." *For now,* I think, but I push back that thought. It's tomorrow's problem.

His gaze drops to my left hand and my naked ring finger. "If that was all you wanted, you wouldn't have broken up with him. Why were you two even engaged to begin with?"

I bow my head. "It doesn't matter."

"You're right. It doesn't." He cups my jaw and lifts my face to his, eyes searching, looking for answers. "There's a reason you decided to marry me in Vegas. *That* matters. And we're going to figure it out."

I will steel into my veins to resist leaning into his touch. "There isn't anything to figure out. It was a crazy, impulsive decision, and now we're going to undo it."

"Married or divorced, it won't change the way I feel about you."

There's an insistent tug in my chest, a magnetic pull toward him. But if I follow it, I know everything else will fall apart. "You should go."

CHAPTER EIGHTEEN

BRINLEY

"Are you excited about your vacation with Daddy and Victoria?" I ask when Cami finds me in the kitchen Saturday morning. "Everything's together? You have your phone and your special pillow with your suitcase?"

"Yes," she says, rolling her eyes in exasperation. "You already told me."

I grin. "I'm a little jealous. I wish *I* got to visit Mickey Mouse this week."

"And you'll miss my *birthday*," she says, propping her hands on her hips.

My iron will is the only thing keeping my smile in place. It will be the first time we've been apart on her birthday, but when Roman asked if he could take her to Disney for her tenth, I knew it'd be selfish to say no. "I don't *want* to miss it," I say. "In fact, maybe you should tell your dad you're just going to hang out here."

"Disney or bust!" She waves her arms around in her favorite TikTok dance. "But first, breakfast with Grammy and Grampy."

Laughing, I tug gently on her ponytail. "Yes. It's up to you how you want to do your hair, but fair warning—if you wear it up, you'll get Grandma's lecture about how much prettier your hair is down and how important it is to make yourself look your best."

Cami pats her hair then shrugs. "I'll deal with the lecture. I like it up."

That's my girl. "I wish I'd had even a fraction of your backbone when I was your age."

"I know Grammy and Grampy love me, even if they don't approve of everything I do."

I smile, but my heart twists at how sure she is in this. For so much of my life, I wasn't. When I think of what I need to tell my parents this morning, it's clear I'm still not. But one person I am sure of is my daughter.

I take her hand. "Sweetie, I need to tell Grandma and Grandpa something today, but I wanted to tell you first."

"Is it about the wedding?"

My heart squeezes hard. *I love this girl so much. Please, God, let me do right by her.* "Yeah. Julian and I broke up last night, and there won't be a wedding." I smile, wanting her to see I'm not falling apart. "But he still cares about you, and this won't change that." I'll kick him in the nuts if he makes a liar out of me. Before I agreed to marry him, I made him promise he wouldn't let whatever happened between *us* affect his relationship with Cami.

Cami pats my hand. "That's okay, Mommy. You're fierce, and you can handle anything."

My smile turns genuine. "So are you."

LEXI RYAN

"Are you going to marry someone else, then?"

I choke on nothing. "No plans right now," I say lamely. "Do you have any other questions?"

She looks at the ceiling then shakes her head. "I don't think so. Are Grammy and Grampy going to be mad?"

When it comes to my parents, I have to walk a thin line for Cami. On the one hand, I pride myself in being honest with my daughter about everything—with the current awkward exception of my marital status. On the other hand, she adores her grandparents, and I don't ever want to say anything that would jeopardize her relationship with them. "They might be," I finally say. "But they'll be okay."

"It's not their life anyway," she says.

Amen, sister.

❧

I'm a ball of nerves as I drive to the Orchid Valley Country Club. Cami and I are meeting my parents for breakfast at nine, then after we eat, I'll have mimosas on the patio with Mom and Dad while Cami attends the "dining room etiquette" class the club offers for kids once a month. I grew up going to those things and detested them. I'd never force Cami to endure the rigid and often sexist lessons, but she says they'll be useful when she runs for POTUS, and I can get behind that.

Mom and Dad are punctual if nothing else, and they expect the same of everyone around them, which is why Cami and I arrive ten minutes early, but we've barely been seated when my Mom arrives.

"Where's Julian?" Mom asks the moment she reaches

274

the table. She stares hard at the seat next to me, as if she's willing him to appear.

"Gonna cut right to the chase, then," I mutter, but my words are completely muffled by Cami's sprint toward her grandmother.

"Grammy!" she shouts, jumping out of her chair.

As disappointed as my parents were to find themselves with a pregnant teenager, they truly love my daughter, and my daughter loves them. Cami is probably the only reason I still have a somewhat functional relationship with my parents. I keep the peace for her—even if my parents and I don't always agree on . . . *anything*.

Mom stoops down to hug Cami then whispers something in her ear that has her running to the kitchens, where I'm sure she's chasing down some delicious baked goods my mom instructed the staff to have on hand for her.

I arch a brow at my mom, who pulls her most innocent face. "Just one tiny treat won't ruin her meal," she says.

Sighing, I rise to hug my mother. "Julian's not going to make it today." I force a smile and lie through my teeth. "Last-minute work meeting."

Mom gives me a hard look. "He works hard and he looks at you like you're a prize. Maybe we should move up the wedding to make sure he doesn't get away."

I fight back a grimace and take my seat. Sometimes the best thing I can do is not respond. I'm thankful Cami is still busy in the kitchen when Dad finally makes it to the table. "Where is Julian today?" His eyes land on my hand, and his lips twist. He's spotted what Mom somehow missed. My naked ring finger.

"He can't make it, but I actually need to talk to you and Mom about the wedding," I say, shifting under his scrutiny.

I'm twenty-seven years old, and he can still make me feel three inches tall when he looks at me like that.

The air in the room grows stiff with his tension. "What did you do, Brinley?" Dad asks sharply.

Mom takes a seat and lifts her glass of ice water with a shaking hand. "Let's at least hear her out before we get upset, Abraham."

Dad frowns and sits beside his wife.

I take a deep breath and focus on Mom as I say the words I'm sure she's already anticipating. "Julian and I broke up last night. We're canceling our wedding."

Mom gasps. "What?" Okay, so maybe she *hadn't* figured it out. "You're kidding. Tell me you're kidding."

It's Dad who doesn't look shocked. "You're always determined to make fools of us all, aren't you?" He shakes his head. "Do you ever think of anyone but yourself?"

I drop my gaze to my hand and my bare ring finger. "I'm so sorry for the position this puts you in."

"What about Cami?" Mom asks. "I was so proud of you for finally doing right by her—giving her a strong male influence in her home—and now you're just throwing that away. And why? Do you even have a good reason for this?"

I lift my chin and roll my shoulders back. "The truth is, I never had a good reason to marry him."

"Ridiculous," Dad grumbles. "You have no sense."

"It's true. Julian and I are good friends, and we care about each other a lot, but not enough to get married." I swallow and try to muster my courage. "Cami and I are doing fine on our own, but I was hoping you'd consider releasing my trust to me early even without the wedding. I wonder if the provisions in the trust might allow for exceptions if—"

"Why would I do that?" My father's face is red, as if his anger is literally making his blood boil beneath his skin. "You've just proven exactly how irresponsible you are, and you want us to shell out a bunch of cash for you to play nail salon for the rest of your life?"

I swallow, bracing myself for an uphill battle. "I understand why it might look that way, but I'm only asking for the money so I can make an investment. You know I planned to buy The Orchid after the wedding, and I still want to do that. If I don't buy it before June, I'll lose my chance, and the family will sell to someone else."

"Maybe you should've thought about that before you destroyed your chances with a good man," Dad says.

Mom places a hand on his arm. "Abraham, let's slow down. Maybe we could consider this investment." She turns to me. "Your grandfather decided the terms of your trust, but maybe we could talk to our advisors and consider buying The Orchid ourselves—that way you don't lose it, and we don't have to compromise on terms that were important to us."

"No." The word snaps out of me, but I take a deep breath and try to explain. "I want this for myself, and I don't think it would be good for our relationship if you were the owners of the company I was running. We tried that when I worked for Knox Bourbon after graduation, remember? I don't want to work for you."

Dad pushes back from the table and stands, ignoring it when his chair tips over behind him. "Lucky for you it's not an option anyway. You've proven yourself to be unreliable and unprofessional, and I'd rather throw my money into a fire than spend it on a business left in your hands." He turns to Mom and nods toward the exit. "Come on, Harriet. I can't look at her anymore."

I've heard those words so many times before. I keep waiting for the day they don't hurt, but today's not that day. My father knows where to land his punches.

Cami returns to the table with a smudge of chocolate on her mouth. "Why does everyone look so mad?"

Dad's eyes blaze with fury. "Because your mother is a fool and a disgrace."

"She is *not*!" Cami folds her arms and glares at him.

"Cami, baby . . ." But what do I say? *It's fine*? It's not, and I don't want her believing it's okay for people to treat others the way my father treats me.

Dad turns on his heel and stomps off.

Mom watches him, then shakes her head. "I wish you wouldn't provoke him so much." Then she too heads for the exit.

Cami fights a frown as she watches them leave. And I hate them for putting that hurt in her eyes.

"I'm sorry, baby," I whisper. "I shouldn't have told them here."

She shakes her head and pats my shoulder. "I don't think you're a fool."

A sob catches in my throat, and my eyes burn as I pull her against me for a hug. "Thanks, baby."

CHAPTER NINETEEN

BRINLEY

March 10th, before

"This has to be the most beautiful spot on the planet," I say, turning a slow circle and trying to take in the beautiful day. When I turn back to Marston, he's smiling up at me from his spot on the picnic blanket. "What?"

He shakes his head slowly. "I've never met someone like you. Most people walk around taking the beauty around them for granted, and here you are, seeing it in your own literal backyard." His smile seems to flicker.

"What's wrong?"

"This place gives you so much joy, and I think I'm just realizing what an asshole I am to ask you to leave."

My heart squeezes in my chest and I sink to my knees in front of him. "There are beautiful backyards all over the country." I take his hands in mine and intertwine our fingers. "Have you heard back from any of them?"

He nods, knowing what I'm talking about. College is all we talk about lately. "UCLA and Washington University both offered special financial aid packages since, you know, my mom and stuff."

"So that's California and . . ."

"St. Louis."

My heart sinks. Even if I follow him for college, two years apart feels like way too much. "Which do you like better?"

He laughs. "Based on their websites, you mean?"

"You should visit the one in St. Louis. You could drive that, couldn't you?"

"It's about eight hours away, so I could, technically, but I don't know if Uncle Henry's car could handle it."

"Wow. That's farther than I thought." I was hoping he'd go somewhere I could visit on the weekends, but sixteen hours round trip? Alone and hiding my real destination from my parents? I deflate as the reality of it hits me. We'll never see each other.

He cups my face in both of his hands and leans his forehead against mine. "I wish you could come with me. I'd do anything to get you away from him."

I stiffen at the mention of my father, and that old guilt for revealing private business to someone who's not family trickles like familiar poison in my veins. "That's not why I wish I could go with you."

"I know, but that's why it's so hard for me to leave."

I fold my arms. "And here I thought it was hard because you wanted to be with me."

He shifts, rolling to his knees in a posture that mimics mine, and then pulls my body against his. "I *do* want to be with you. I want us to be able to walk down the street holding hands and to sleep in the same bed." He sweeps gentle kisses across each of my cheeks. "I don't just want to *plan* a life with you. I want to *live* it. Someday, I want to watch you walk down the aisle toward me and know you're mine and I'm yours. But I want all that without having to sacrifice your heart to that fucking asshole."

I flinch, jerking back like he's hit me. Some days when I'm angry with my father it's easy to hate him for his cruelty, for the way he always cuts me down, for his inability to treat my sister like anything other than a porcelain doll. But some days, Marston's criticism of Dad feels like criticism of me. "He *is* my father, and I don't want to feel like I have to choose between having my dad in my life and having my boyfriend."

"Shit, Brinley. I'm sorry," he says, his face crumpling. "I'm gonna work so fucking hard that you won't ever have to make that choice. I'll be the kind of man he wants for his daughter. I promise."

CHAPTER TWENTY

BRINLEY

Present day

*E*ven after Marston left town, the south dock at Lake Blackledge remained my favorite spot for when I needed to think or be alone. It doesn't disappoint today. The sun sparkles on the water, and the sound of it lapping against the shore washes away my fears.

Right after Roman picked Cami up for their trip, I made the call to Mrs. Wright to let her know I wasn't getting married and therefore wouldn't have the funds to purchase The Orchid before her June deadline. She's done so much to give me the chance to buy it, and it didn't seem fair to put it off any longer. She was understanding and kind, just like she's been for years, but there was no offer to hold off on selling, no suggestion that she'd consider anything but a cash offer. Ending the call felt like closing the door on my dream, and I came straight out here. I've been staring out at the water ever since.

In truth, I never expected my parents to agree to give me my trust after I told them I was calling off the wedding. I wasn't even sure it was an option, and even if it had been, I knew they'd say no, but I had to ask. This way I'll never have to wonder.

Tonight when I meet the girls at Smithy's, I'll break the news to them, and when I'm back at The Orchid on Monday, I'll tell the rest of the staff. Maybe we'll get lucky and nothing will change, but I know they won't blame me if anything does. I'm annoyed with myself for even being disappointed. What kind of privileged jerk am I to even *have* a trust to ask for early? Any frustration I feel about having my parents keep it from me is tempered with annoyance at myself for relying on my family's money so much even now.

Gravel crunches behind me. Somehow, I know Marston's here before I ever turn to look at him, and his presence is a balm to my battered heart.

"It's as beautiful as ever," he says, lowering himself to sit beside me on the top of the cool concrete ramp. He's scruffier than usual today, as if he didn't bother shaving this morning, and I have to fight the instinct to reach out and run my fingertips over that dark stubble.

"I never knew about this spot until you took me here on homecoming night," I admit. "And then it became my favorite place to think and brood when I was sad."

He studies me, lips parted, eyes searching. He probably thinks I'm sad about my breakup.

I am, sort of. I'm sad I hurt Julian. I'm sad I didn't know myself well enough to see I was making a major mistake, and sad it took an impulsive marriage to a man I can't have to open my eyes. I'm sad I've spent years patting myself on the back for my independence and for going after my dreams with hard work and not my family's money, only to realize I've been leaning on the promise of it all this time. "I'm meeting up with the girls tonight, and I want to shake off this funk before I see them."

"Do you want to talk it out?" Marston asks softly.

I wrap my arms around my legs and rest my chin on my knees. "I spoke with my parents today to let them know we're canceling the wedding."

Marston's mouth draws into a thin line. "I wish you would've let me go with you."

I huff out a breath. "If you'd been with me, it would've been an even bigger disaster."

"I take it the news of our marriage didn't go over well?"

I wince. "I didn't tell them about that."

He cuts his eyes to me. "Why not?"

I shrug. "It'd only make everything worse. I didn't see a reason to upset them over something. . ."

"Something you plan to undo as soon as possible," he says. There's no judgment in his voice, only a quiet resignation.

"Those plans haven't changed. I told you last night." I just need to figure out why I can't bring myself to fill out the paperwork and then get over it.

He stands and tilts his head back, closing his eyes and lifting his face to the sun. "You always wanted to pretend you didn't care what they thought, but even now you let them dictate your life."

"I don't." I stand too and step in front of him so we're facing each other. "They haven't dictated my life in a long time. You don't get to pretend nothing changed just because you weren't around to see it."

He flinches then looks away again and nods. "Fair."

I reach for him but drop my hand before I touch his arm. "I guess *that* hasn't changed."

His eyes flick to me. "What?"

"The way the air between us goes tense and cold when the subject of my parents comes up."

He stares at me for a long moment, and I wait for him to say something else about them. He has every right to. They treated him terribly. "My mom used to like me to send her pictures of the lake," he says, surprising me. "She said she liked seeing that I was living in a little slice of heaven." He shakes his head and bends to pick up a pebble from the dock. "I never let her know that my year here wasn't all sunshine and roses."

I swallow hard at the reminder that Marston of all people understands what it's like to love and be loved by someone who's profoundly imperfect. "How's your mom doing, anyway?"

Marston stills where he's stooped.

Maybe I shouldn't have asked. I'm pretty sure the rules of etiquette my parents live by say you *don't* ask about the addict family member who's dropped out of rehab a dozen times. But I know it's important to Marston, and—inconvenient paper marriage or not—I care about him.

He swallows and stands, turning to me. "She passed away during my freshman year of college."

My stomach clenches. "Oh, Marston. I'm so sorry."

He tosses the pebble into the lake. "She'd been abusing

pills and alcohol for too long and stopped cold turkey—trying to do it on her own when she knew better. It was just too hard on her body."

I try to imagine what that was like for him, but I can only hope he had someone to hold his hand. "I'm so sorry."

"You know, it sucked, but I try to see the good in it, if that makes sense?" He rubs his fingers together, as if he can still feel the stone there, even though it's gone. "She was *trying*—she went out *trying* to be a better mom. They found her in bed, like she'd gone to sleep and just never woken up."

"That must've been awful."

"In some ways, it hurt like crazy. In my head, I had a hundred arguments with my dead mother where I yelled and screamed at her for being so stupid, for not doing it the right way. But I like to think that wherever she is now, she knows she went out trying to do the right thing for her kid—because it didn't matter how old I was, that was how she thought of me. I like to think she's found some peace knowing that."

I don't care that it's been ten years. I don't care that goodbye will be harder if I don't keep my distance from him. I *know* this man, and the grief in his eyes when he talks about his mom reminds me so much of how I still feel about my sister. I wrap my arms around his waist and hug him. I hug the friend I had and the man he became—understanding in the way someone who's only experienced loss can that he's both of those people at the same time, and they're both hurting. "I'm so sorry."

His voice is as rough as the gravel beneath my feet. "Thank you."

I bury my face in his chest. He's so damn tall, and it's

the only way I know how to give him a real hug. He strokes my hair, and for a beat it feels like he's comforting me. This is what I needed those days after Brittany died. My parents didn't know how to let me grieve, wouldn't or couldn't share their pain, and I needed them to help me but didn't know how to ask for it. I'm not sure I even realized how good a hug would've felt. "I hope you weren't alone," I whisper, remembering the isolation of loss. "I hope you had friends to carry you through."

"I had Aunt Lori. It was hard, but it wasn't a huge shock. And I dealt with my grief the way I dealt with all other too-big emotions. I threw myself into my schoolwork."

I pull back and wipe away tears I didn't realize I'd shed. I go to take another step back, but he grabs my chin and looks into my eyes.

"Thank you, Brinley." He drops his hand, but I don't move. "Most of the people who know about my complicated relationship with my mother think I didn't or shouldn't have grieved. It means a lot that you get it. I'm glad you found a family you could share your grief with too."

"Family?"

He arches a brow. "Savvy, Abbi, and Stella? They're your family now. I can tell. They're protective of you and love you unconditionally." He gives me a sad smile. "If I don't get to hold your hand through the shit the world will throw your way, I'm glad you have them."

How am I supposed to guard my heart against this man when he knows it so well?

CHAPTER TWENTY-ONE

BRINLEY

"*T*onight, drinks are on me," Stella says as we head into Smithy's.

"You don't need to spend your money on my drinks," I say. *Especially since, come Monday, all of our jobs are up in the air.*

She shrugs. "I don't need to, but I *want* to." She gives me a sad smile. "I just went through a breakup too. Let me treat you in solidarity."

"You ready to talk about that breakup yet?" I ask.

She ignores me. "Ooh! Ten-dollar pitchers tonight!"

I frown at my friend, who's rubbing her hands together as she studies the sign advertising the special. "I thought you didn't like beer."

"Hate it, and don't you go thinking it's a beer night for you either. You canceled your wedding. This calls for the hard stuff."

I'm thrilled to be spending a rare girls' night at Smithy's, but the truth is, thanks to my talk with Marston at the dock, I would've been okay if my girls couldn't get together. It's funny that my talk with Marston was exactly what I needed to knock off some stress when a few days ago, it felt like Marston *was* my biggest stressor. But it was good to connect with him today—good to know he understands where I stand on *us*, and good for us to open up to each other. It doesn't matter that he's leaving soon or that I need to file for divorce. He'll *always* be one of my favorite humans.

"I told you I'm fine." I spot Abbi and Savvy in a booth opposite the entrance and point their way. "They're already here."

Stella waves at them but saunters to the bar. "Smithy, baby, we need a pitcher of cosmos," she says, batting her lashes sweetly.

"I'm sure you do, baby girl," he says, "but that's not actually a thing."

Stella flips her hair over her shoulder and leans over the bar, giving Smithy a generous view of the cleavage already spilling out of her hot-pink halter dress. "But shouldn't it be?"

"I can make it, but the special applies to *beer*, not booze."

"Please? My girl had a shit week and a shittier day." She bites her red lip, and I snort at how thick she's laying it on. Stella has never been interested in my cousin, but she loves tormenting him. If I had to guess, I'd say he's a pretty big fan of her particular brand of torture.

"Fuck me, woman. You don't play fair."

Straightening, she beams. "You can bring it to the table. Thanks, Smithy." She throws him a wink over her shoulder as she saunters away, hips swishing, and my cousin doesn't take his eyes off her until she slides into the booth.

I slide him my credit card. "Charge us whatever is fair."

"Nah, I got you." Smithy pushes the card back to me. "Least I can do. Sorry everything's so messed up right now."

Smithy is *rarely* serious, and I want to squirm under his sympathetic gaze, but the word is out, so I'm going to need to learn to deal. "Listen, I run a business too. I know you can't give everyone special deals. It's fine."

Smithy takes my card. I have a sneaking suspicion he won't run it, but at least I tried. "Why don't you talk to Stella for me? Convince her to give me a shot?"

Aww. This poor guy. "I thought you wanted Savvy."

"Um, yes to either? Or preferably both—at the same time?" He winks at me, back to his fun-loving self.

"I'll let them know you mentioned it," I lie. I cast a glance around the bar. "Hey, have you seen Marston around tonight?"

"Nah. Haven't seen him since Julian took a swing at him."

I wince. "I'm sorry about that. I never would've expected Julian to come in here and make trouble."

His lips twitch. "I can handle him. In fact, after what Abbi told Kace about the way he's been acting this week, I'd *like* a chance to handle him."

"Don't do that." I smile. "Thanks again for your help with that. If Marston comes in, don't bring up anything about Julian? I don't want things to get ugly if they run into each other again."

Smithy grumbles something under his breath about Julian deserving ugly, but I decide it's close enough to agreement and head back to sit with the girls.

Savvy looks over my shoulder as I slide into the booth. "Please tell me Smithy's coming with the booze."

"I told you I took care of it," Stella says.

"You said you ordered a pitcher of cosmos," Abbi says. "That's not a thing."

Stella rolls her eyes. "It's totally a thing, ladies."

Savvy shakes her head and shifts her attention to me. Her mouth pulls into a grimace, as if she can see every bit of this morning's stress written on my face. "How're you holding up, Brinley?"

"I've been better," I admit. "Damn it, ladies, I feel like I owe you all a big apology."

"What?" Abbi squeaks. "Why?"

"Are you kidding? Look at this mess." I tick off the reasons on my fingers. "You all already bought your bridesmaid dresses."

"They're sexy, red, and knee-length," Savvy says, waving a hand. "Totally usable elsewhere."

I go to my second finger. "You took time off work for my bachelorette party."

Stella holds up a hand. "What? Why's that canceled?"

"God, you're *so pretty*," Savvy says, shaking her head.

Stella sticks her tongue out at Savvy. "Shut up. I've been looking forward to getting trashed in Atlanta with you bitches for *months*."

"There's no wedding," I say. "No wedding means no bachelorette party."

"So we call it something else," Stella says. "No reason to change plans altogether."

"Girls' weekend," Abbi agrees, nodding and pointing to me. "I like it. And you *need* it."

"Oh my God, you guys are spending all your free time

cleaning up my messes." I look toward the bar, totally ready for Smithy to save the day with a pitcher full of vodka.

"Yeah, a weekend drinking with you would be a hardship," Savvy deadpans.

"You know what I mean," I say. "I feel awful, and God only knows what's going to happen to The Orchid now."

Abbi frowns and studies me. "But you don't regret it, do you?"

"No. I don't. I regret agreeing to marry him in the first place. I regret not listening to my gut—"

"Was that your gut saying don't do it?" Savvy asks. "Because I could've sworn that was me."

"And I regret whatever reckless instinct made me marry Marston in Vegas and then forget it. But I—"

"Whoa, whoa, whoa!" Stella shakes her head. "I don't think so. I call bullshit."

My eyes go wide. "What? If I hadn't forgotten, I wouldn't have been able to say yes to Julian, and then I never would've been in this mess."

She waves a hand. "Not that. The part about *marrying* Marston? I call bullshit that you're regretting that. I think this whole thing with him has been a blessing in disguise. He showed up, and suddenly you had to take a real close look at what you were doing with Julian. He saved you from *that* disaster, and now you get to consider if maybe there's still a chance for you and Mars. Zero regrets."

"Is that what you all think?" I ask.

The other girls are suddenly very interested in their manicures.

But leave it to Stella to speak her mind. "You weren't marrying Julian for yourself, honey. Everyone knows that. Even *Julian* knows that. He was the choice you *should* want.

Your parents like him, he's financially stable, and you'd get to play savior to everyone at The Orchid."

I guess that's probably *partly* true, but again, embarrassing.

"But Marston," she says, her smile growing devious. "Even in the beginning, back when you were sixteen and innocent as a nun, Marston was *one hundred percent* for you."

I swallow. I don't want to think about that too much. As much as I'd like to give me and Marston a chance, I don't want to leave Orchid Valley, and he doesn't want to live here. I've worked too hard to make my life my own to surrender it now, and even if the whole living situation weren't an issue, I don't know if I want the kind of intensity and passion that come hand in hand with loving Marston. It scares me. "Anyway," I say, weaving around that landmine. "I'm really sorry."

"Have you told Cami yet?" Savvy asks gently.

I nod. "Yeah, and I don't think any of it was real to her. It was like we were planning to have this fancy party, and now the party's been canceled." Thank God I never let Julian ask her to call him Dad. He'd been pushing for that for a while, and I said it wouldn't be fair to Roman. But again, I think part of me knew. "Mostly, I think she's worried about me."

"She's a good egg," Savvy says.

"But what I want to know is have you told *Marston* yet," Abbi says, leaning forward.

I laugh. "Actually, Julian told him when he got shitfaced and tried to take a swing at Marston."

"Did Marston beat the shit out of him?" Savvy asks. "Julian must've been *plowed* if he thought he could win that fight."

I rub my temples. I don't like to think about it. Julian's been acting out of character all week, and I can't help but feel responsible. "Marston said he dodged the swings. I think he was too focused on getting to me to hand Julian's ass to him."

"Wait, Marston came to your house last night?" Savvy asks, eyes wide. "Details, please."

Oops. I scan the table, willing our martinis to appear. "I'm gonna need a drink first."

"Oh my God!" Stella cups her hands around her mouth and shouts across the bar, "Smithy, who do I have to blow to get those drinks?"

CHAPTER TWENTY-TWO

MARSTON

*W*hen I walk into Smithy's, Brinley is the first thing I see. She stands out like a beacon, sitting at a big table with her friends, her head thrown back as she laughs. She's changed out of the tight black pants and blouse she was wearing at the lake and now she's in a pair of jeans and a blue halter top that shows off her tan shoulders.

"You're staring."

I turn to Smithy and shrug. "Can you blame me? Look at her."

His brows disappear beneath his shaggy mop of hair. "Look at *all* of them. So much hotness in that corner. If insurance knew, they'd make me keep the fire marshal on standby."

I chuckle. He's right. Each woman in that group is beautiful in her own way, but I can't take my eyes off Brinley when she's smiling like that.

"Are you going to go over there or just stare all night?" he asks.

"I don't want to interrupt her fun."

"She and Julian *broke up*." He grabs me by one shoulder and gives me a shake. "This is the moment you've been training for, soldier!"

Grunting, I nod to the bar. "Get me a beer, meddler."

"Hey, Marston!" Kace waves me over from his perch farther down the bar.

I take the spot next to him while Smithy pours my drink. "How are you here every night? Don't you have a kid at home?"

"Hope's with her mom this weekend, and I don't like an empty house," he says, but he's distracted by something behind me. When I turn to follow his gaze, I see Stella, laughing with a group of guys by the back hall.

When Kace turns back to me, I arch a brow. "You and Stella?"

"No." He shakes his head. "Fuck no." There was something in the way he was just looking at her that says otherwise, but I'm not about to argue. "Her brother and I are business partners, and she's absolutely not my type," he adds.

"Methinks the lady doth protest too much," Smithy mutters as he taps an order into the computer.

Kace shifts awkwardly, so I pretend I didn't hear Smithy. "So how's the whole single-dad life treating you?" It wasn't until I ran into Kace at the grocery store a couple of days ago that I even found out he has a daughter. This is what I get for avoiding Orchid Valley all these years. I totally missed out on my friends' lives. It seemed like the only choice at the time, but now I wonder if Abraham Knox wasn't just manipulating me to his will.

"It's awesome in some ways, really fucking hard in others. I never expected to be a card-carrying member of the divorced-before-thirty club."

I grunt. If Brinley has her way, we'll both be part of that group in no time. "Can I ask what happened?"

Kace takes a sip of his beer and sighs. "I don't know. I worked too much? She didn't communicate enough? Whatever the reason, she was dissatisfied and didn't believe we could fix it." He shakes his head. "By the end, all that mattered to either of us was what was best for Hope. Amy looked at me one day and said, 'Is this the kind of marriage you want your daughter to have? Because whatever we show her is what she'll believe marriage should be.'"

"Damn," I whisper. "That's . . ."

"True," Kace says. "And it made a hard decision easy, or *easier*, at least. It helps that we see eye to eye on how to raise Hope. I think we've been doing a stellar job of co-parenting."

"That's awesome." I nod. I sometimes wonder what my mom's lack of even a halfway-decent partner did for my perception of relationships. I hate thinking about it too much, because it never goes anywhere good.

Smithy leans over the bar. "Bro," he says, tapping on my beer. "Don't look now, but Brinley can't take her eyes off you. You sure you don't want to be spending tonight with *her*?"

"I never said that," I say, turning on my stool to see Brinley.

"Dude, I said don't look." Smithy groans behind me. "You have zero game, I swear."

Fuck him, it's worth it. The moment I make eye contact with Brinley, she smiles and her cheeks turn pink. I wink at her and turn away again, even though every cell in my body tells me to go over there, even though there's nothing I want more than to feel that smile against mine. But I can be patient. She might think I've given up, but she hasn't even seen me try yet.

Two beers later, Stella wanders up to the bar on sky-high pink heels, a pink martini in one hand, and gives Kace a once-over. "Hello, gorgeous."

He stiffens. "Hey, Stella."

She bursts into laughter. "Oh my God, it's like you think I'm going to jump you." She squeezes his shoulder and whispers, "Don't worry, Kace. If it ever comes to that, I'm pretty sure you could fight me off."

His jaw twitches. "Quit reading something into nothing."

"Whatever. I'm not here for you anyway." She drops her hand and turns to me. "Brinley said you're a pool shark."

I slide my gaze to her table again, but this time Brinley's busy talking to Savvy and doesn't see me looking. "Not so much anymore."

"But you still have some skills, right?" Stella grabs me by the wrist and tugs at my arm. "I need someone to play eight-ball with me who doesn't totally suck at it."

I look at Smithy. "Surely there's someone around here who can play?"

"Nah." He shakes his head. "Nobody like you."

I put down my beer. "Sure, but I might be rusty."

Stella beams. "Not a problem." She grabs me by the wrist—I'm beginning to understand that she's become the touchy type since high school—and pulls me away from the bar and not toward the pool tables but toward the booth with her friends.

"You know, you can let me go," I say. "I'm not going to run away."

She winks at me as if I just told an inside joke only the two of us would get. "Table first. Then game."

"Whatever you say." I don't know why she thinks she needs to lead me by the hand, but she doesn't release me until we get to the table.

The girls stop talking when we stop at the booth.

"Brinley, I found you a teacher," Stella announces.

Brinley looks back and forth between me and Stella. "A what now?"

"Someone to teach you how to play pool."

Brinley rolls her eyes. "Stella, honey, for the hundredth time, I don't care about billiards."

Stella snorts. "Okay, Princess Brinley, but us common folks call it *pool*, and it's really just basic adulting."

Brinley turns her skeptical gaze on me. "You came over here to teach me how to play *poooooool?*"

Laughing at the way she draws out the word, I shrug. "I thought I agreed to play a game against Stella, but I can teach you if you want."

"She does," Savvy says. "She definitely *wants.*"

Brinley narrows her eyes at Savvy. "*Et tu, Brute?*"

I shake my head and offer my hand to Brinley. "Come on. Let's do this."

She takes my hand and I help her slide out of the booth, but as soon as she's standing, she pulls her hand away.

Still not a couple. Okay. *Message delivered.*

"You two versus me," Stella says. She's already headed toward the pool tables.

We follow her, and I grab a pool cue from the rack on the wall as Stella loads the table with quarters and sets it up.

"You didn't need to have your friend ask," I tell Brinley, chalking the end of the stick before handing it to her. "I would have been happy to teach you without the social gymnastics."

"I didn't. Stella's got a mind of her own."

"Some things never change." I remember Stella's antics in high school. Of all the people who hovered around Brinley all the time, Stella was one of my favorites. There was never anything fake about her.

"I'm sorry about this," Brinley says, watching Stella set up the table.

"Why?"

"You had your own plans tonight, and she pulled you away from them, from your friends." She drags her bottom lip between her teeth.

Damn. That'll always be hot to me. "The guys will still be here in ten minutes. Don't worry about it."

Stella rolls the cue ball to our side of the table. "Brinley, you break."

"Yay," Brinley mutters, and I chuckle.

"Come on. It's not that bad." I position the cue ball and motion for her to strike it. "Just hit the white ball into the cluster of balls at the opposite end of the table."

Brinley takes the stick and aims, but I stop her with a gentle hand on her wrist before she can take her shot.

"Hold it like this." I adjust her hand on the stick then position my body behind hers to show her how to line it up.

We lean over the table, and I guide Brinley's arm as she takes her shot. The cue collides with the other balls with a crack, and I look up just in time to see Stella give me a nod of approval, even though Brinley's break was too weak to sink a single ball.

Brinley straightens and turns to me with a smile on her face. "That wasn't too bad, was it?"

I tuck back a lock of her hair, brushing the shell of her ear with my fingertips. "Not bad at all."

Brinley holds my gaze for a beat longer than necessary before swallowing hard and turning away. "Okay, Stella. Show me what you've got."

Stella takes her turn and sinks a stripe first, followed by four more, before she misses her target.

"Solids, then," Brinley says, scanning the table. "Okay. Three ball, corner pocket."

She lines up the shot, and I step behind her to make adjustments, too aware of the heat of her ass against my cock when I lean over her. No doubt this is what Stella was after, but she has no way of knowing this takes me back to Vegas—back to that club with the poles and Brinley's giddy smile as she showed off her moves. *Free, confident, happy.*

I manage to focus enough to help Brinley sink the three, but she misses her next try. We go back and forth a couple of times before Stella's cleared the table of stripes and sunk the eight ball.

"That was fun," Brinley says. She turns to me. "Thank you for your help."

I duck down and put my mouth close to her ear before whispering, "I think your friend is trying to get me to touch you."

When she steps back to meet my gaze, she's smiling, and I feel like I won the lottery. "I think it worked."

"I'm gonna go grab another drink," Stella says. "Why don't you two play again?"

Brinley doesn't bother to stifle her laugh. She shakes her head and watches her friend walk away. "She's shameless."

"A little," I agree, "but not in a bad way."

"She only acts like she's still the party girl she was in high school and college. The truth is, she's grown up a lot. Kace can't stand her, but I think he's too tough on her."

Kace definitely wasn't looking at Stella like he *couldn't stand her*, but I'm not sure even he knows that. "Why doesn't he like her?"

"He still thinks of her as the high-school girl who crashed his college party and tried to seduce him when he was drunk."

"Oh. Shit."

She sighs. "I know, but like I said, she's grown up a lot since then."

"Right. I can totally tell." I nod solemnly, and she laughs.

"You're lucky she hasn't caught us together at The Orchid. She'd probably lock us in a room until we consummated our marriage." She seems to realize what she's said and looks up at me with wide eyes. "I mean . . . maybe consummate again or . . ."

I search her face, my chest aching at the reminder that she has no memory of a night that was so fucking important —so fucking *everything*—to me. "What *do* you remember?"

She draws in a shaky breath but keeps her eyes locked on mine. "I remember the nightclub, dancing with you, and . . . the booth?"

The memory of sliding my hand beneath her skirt in the crowded club sends blood pumping hard and fast to my dick. "Is that a question?"

"No, I definitely remember the booth. It . . ." Her

cheeks flare pink, and she bows her head. "I don't have questions about that part."

"What else do you remember?"

ॐ

BRINLEY

Does Marston hear the huskiness in his own voice on that question?

I swallow. "Shopping for shoes and lingerie, the booth . . ." I don't know what's crazier—that we're having this conversation or that we didn't have it sooner. In truth, I'm a little scared to remember the events of a night that led me to the altar. "And I remember the limo ride after."

Marston's nostrils flare and his pupils dilate. "Do you remember the next club? With Savvy and Alec?"

I close my eyes. This is where things start to get sketchy. "I have blips. Moments. I remember taking shots and laughing while Alec drooled over Savvy working the pole." I laugh then swallow hard and squeeze my eyes shut for a long beat. "I want to remember, Marston."

He slides his hand to the back of my neck and strokes his thumb along my jaw. "I wish you could. I want to plug you into my brain and show you everything. I want . . ." He swallows.

I don't need him to finish that sentence to be sure I want that too. Whatever it is. "This is crazy."

"I like crazy." He grazes his thumb across my bottom lip, and his eyes are pleading when he says, "Are you free tomorrow night?"

"Cami's with her dad all week. Disney World." I sound

as breathless—and possibly as desperate—as I feel. But then I come to my senses and blink at him. "Why?"

He smiles down at me. "Is it so strange to want to take my wife on a date?"

I take a step back without realizing it, but he grabs my hand before I can get far.

"Just give me a chance, Brinley. Give *us* a chance."

"You live in L.A. and I live here." I shake my head. "I won't let you give up the life you've worked so hard for—the success you've found—to move back to Orchid Valley."

"That's where we got this wrong," he says softly. "We did everything backward, and now you're giving me all the reasons this marriage can't work when all I'm asking for is a date. I want to take you out. Dinner, maybe a walk if the weather's nice. No expectations, just time together . . . for us."

For us. No expectations. When I think of saying goodbye to him next week without getting that, when I think of sending in those divorce papers and never seeing him again . . . "I want to," I whisper. His smile turns big and broad, and warmth floods my chest.

"Good. You won't regret it." He holds my gaze, and I think he might kiss me again. In the space between two heartbeats, I have to have a conversation with myself about why that would be a bad thing. First, we're in the middle of a crowded bar. And, right until last night, I was supposed to marry someone else. But finally, he nods once and backs away. "I can't wait."

I'm still staring after him when Savvy saunters up to my side. "Do you have the name of a good OBGYN?" she asks, waving a hand in front of her face.

I head toward the table to grab my phone. "Sure. I'll give you mine. Why?"

"Because I think I just got pregnant from watching you two *look* at each other."

I stop in my tracks and slowly spin to face her. "Bitch."

"Hussy."

"Troublemaker."

"Mother Teresa."

I prop my hands on my hips. "Mother Teresa wouldn't call you a bitch."

"No, but she would buy me a drink." She angles her head toward the bar's main room and starts striding in that direction. "Come on, Abbi and Stella are waiting, and I can't wait to see their faces when we tell them about your date."

I gasp. "You were eavesdropping?"

She flashes me a grin. "You think I'd miss that show?"

CHAPTER TWENTY-THREE

BRINLEY

Savvy's sprawled in the middle of my unmade bed, playing on her phone, when I step out of my bathroom in a just-this-side-of-appropriate little black dress.

"What about this one?" I ask.

"Super-hot. Love it," she says without taking her attention from her phone.

"Savvy, you didn't even look!"

With a sigh, she puts her phone down and gives me a once-over. "I didn't need to. You look absolutely fuckable, and he won't be able to take his eyes off you. I mean it, and I meant it for the last three outfits too."

I wrinkle my nose. "I'm just nervous, okay?"

Standing, Savvy opens her arms. "Come here."

I step forward and let her hug me, and after a stubborn beat, I hug her back. "I know I'm being dumb."

"You aren't being *dumb*. You're nervous because you

care, which is fucking fantastic, because I haven't seen you really care about a date since . . . Well, I'm not sure I have." She grips my shoulders and pulls back so she can look at me. "But you don't need to worry about what to wear. You're a hottie, and he's wild about you. You could show up in a potato sack, and the boy would be driven to distraction the whole meal as he imagined taking it off you."

I laugh. "I somehow doubt it."

"We both know these nerves aren't really about your outfit." She arches a brow. "Right? This is more about what this date *means*."

I wrinkle my nose and frown. "Why do you always have to psychoanalyze me like that?"

"Because I love you," she says cheerfully. The doorbell rings. "Sounds like Prince Charming is here to sweep you off your feet."

I tip my face up and take a few deep breaths, then I go to the door.

Marston is dressed in dark jeans and a white dress shirt that's rolled up at the sleeves, a single red rose in one hand. *Just like prom night.*

I'd gone with Roman to his senior prom at my parents' insistence. It would *shame* them if I refused, they'd said. Roman was such a nice boy, they'd said. Why did I have to fight them on everything?

So I went with Roman and spent my night texting Marston from a burner phone I'd bought at the gas station. Then, about an hour into the dance, when Roman had finally given up on me acting like the date I'd told him I didn't want to be, Marston texted and told me to slip out the back door. There he was, sitting on the hood of his aunt's Honda Civic in a stiff white dress shirt and a pair of black jeans, twirling a single rose between two fingers. He hopped off the car and strode over to me, offering me the flower. Then, as if on cue, the muffled opening chords of James Blunt's "You're Beautiful" floated out to us from the gymnasium. *Our song.*

I knew that somehow Marston had planned it that way.

"Dance with me?" he asked.

I nodded and stepped into his arms. We let our bodies sway to the beat, his arms wrapped around me, my cheek against his chest.

The memory grabs ahold of me, and I can hardly breathe as Marston takes me in slowly, from my strappy black heels to the nearly inappropriate hem of my sexiest LBD. Every inch of his visual perusal feels like a caress, and by the time his eyes meet mine, I'm a live wire.

❧

MARSTON

I give myself three beats to stare, to look my fill and memorize every inch of her. She's beautiful. I've known this since the night we met, but seeing her dressed like this and knowing she chose to doll herself up for a night with *me?*

I swallow hard and offer her the rose. I didn't expect to be nervous, but here I am. "For you."

Her lips part as she takes it, then she blinks up at me. "Like prom night," she says softly, and warmth floods my chest. *She remembers.*

"Ready?" I ask, gesturing toward the car.

Her eyes widen and she lets out a long, low whistle. "Trying to impress me, Marston?"

I grin as I follow her gaze toward my Porsche 911 Cabriolet. "I got sick of the rental. I'd had my eye on these for a while, and there happened to be one available nearby."

"She's gorgeous," Brin says, but she's looking at me again. She's having as much trouble not staring as I am. *Good.*

I turn to the car and rush to open her door before she can get there.

She laughs as she climbs in. "Such a gentleman."

"You don't mind a bit of a drive, do you?" I ask when I settle behind the wheel.

"Where are you taking me?"

I start the engine. "If you have time, I thought I'd take you into the city."

"Atlanta?" she asks, eyes wide.

"A business acquaintance of mine just opened a new restaurant there. A farm-to-table place. He said their soft-shell crab is excellent, so I thought we'd check it out." I cut my eyes to her. "If that's okay with you."

She seems to think it over, then shrugs. "I have nowhere to be. Why not?"

"You won't regret it," I say. I back out of the driveway and navigate my way to the main road. I've only driven to Atlanta a few times since returning to the OV, but it shouldn't be bad this time of day. Though it takes me more than an hour on a weekday morning, it should take us less than forty-five minutes tonight.

Brinley leans forward and flips between stations on the satellite radio until she lands on a modern rock station. She keeps the volume low enough that it's just background noise. "I don't go to Atlanta much," she admits. "Roman lives in the northern suburbs, so even when I take Cami or pick her up, I never bother going all the way into the city. We make time for a trip to the aquarium once a year or so, but that's about it. Though I can't deny it'd be easier for Cami if her dad and I lived closer—she spends too much time in the car getting back and forth between us."

"I've learned to appreciate my driving time. Especially when it's a beautiful night like this," I say, taking my eyes off the road for a beat to look at her. "Want me to put the top down?"

Her eyes light up but she bites her bottom lip. "My hair will be a disaster by the time we get there."

"Does that bother you?"

She shakes her head. "Not really, but I don't want to embarrass you."

I want to kiss her. I want to drag her over to me and kiss that idea out of her head. "You couldn't embarrass me." *And I'm sorry your parents taught you to always worry about that.*

But I push that aggravation aside, lower the top, and revel in the joy on Brinley's face as she rides with the wind in her hair.

§

BRINLEY SWIRLS the wine in her glass and tips her head to the side, studying me.

"What's that look about?" I ask.

Her smile says it's about something very specific, but she says, "What look?"

I prop my forearms on the table and lean forward, happily satisfied after a relaxing drive and a delicious meal. "Out with it. We're on a date. Ask me anything."

She takes a long pull of her wine, as if gathering her

310

strength. "Okay. I keep thinking how strange it is that you don't have someone back home." She chews on her bottom lip for a beat. "But you admitted in Vegas that you've had relationships."

I nod and laugh softly. "I have."

"Tell me about them?" She wrinkles her nose. "I promise not to go all jealous girlfriend on you. I'm just curious about your life."

"Okay." I lean back, trying to figure out how to condense a decade of romantic relationships. Do I start with college and move forward, or do I start with the most recent and work my way back? "I've been with several women, casually, I mean, but only with a couple of them have I had anything I'd qualify as a *relationship*."

"So mostly random hookups, or . . .?"

I shake my head. "No. I mean, a few in college, I guess, but I've never gotten much of a thrill out of sleeping with women I don't know on some deeper level. Even if that deeper level is just friendship, I needed more than sex for it to be worth it to me."

"Isn't that what I'm supposed to say?" she asks. "I mean, if we're going to be stereotypical about gender roles here?"

I laugh. "I don't know that it's a predominantly female trait. Alec is like me in that way."

"But he slept with Savvy, and that was just a one-night thing."

"Sure, but—" I catch myself, shake my head, and laugh again. "Oh, no you don't. I'm not going to analyze our friends' relationship."

"Party pooper," she says, grinning into her wine.

"Is that the way it is for you, though? You prefer your casual sex to be unburdened by emotion?"

"Oh, hell." She drains her glass, then sets it on the table and waits for me to refill it before speaking again. "Right after you left, obviously, yes. But that wasn't about pleasure so much as . . ."

I wait, needing to hear her explanation without tainting it with my own interpretations.

"After you left . . ."

"After you *asked* me to leave," I correct her, because it burns every time she refers to me leaving. I didn't fucking *want* that. But then I regret my words, because she sinks into herself almost imperceptibly. "Sorry," I whisper.

"It's fine. You're right." She swallows and swirls her wine, watching the eddies splashing up on the side of the glass. "That summer I felt like I was drowning in the middle of a crowded pool. There were all these people around me, and no matter how much I flailed, it was as if no one could see how much I was struggling to keep my head above water. The partying, the booze and sex . . ." She doesn't lift her eyes to mine, and I wish she would. I need to see the emotions she's trapped inside. "It was the only way I knew how to make them hear me."

"I'm sorry." I reach across the table and cup my hand over hers. "I'm sorry I let you push me away when you needed me the most."

Her eyes well with tears. "I'm not."

I've pulled my hand back before I even realize it. She's not sorry I left, and it's one of my biggest regrets. That burns.

"I can't regret Cami," she says, meeting my eyes. "I won't. Not ever."

I let out a long, even breath. "Of course not. She's a great kid, and you're an amazing mom."

She huffs softly. "I'm okay. Not the best, not the worst, but luckily it's not a competition." She forces a smile then sighs. "Obviously my pregnancy slowed down my hookups, and after Cami was born, there wasn't anyone for a few years. Then, yeah, it was easier to do the random hookup thing than try for a relationship. I remembered you talking about your mom's revolving door of boyfriends and—"

"It wouldn't have been the same. *You* are not the same as her."

She shrugs. "It made an impression, though, and I was fine. I have the best friends and I have Cami. I didn't need anyone else. Cami came first, and while I know there are guys who would've respected that, I couldn't do anything that might bring instability to her life, and I didn't see anything they could offer that would be worth the risk."

"Until Julian? Or was there a real relationship before him?"

"No. He was the first, but I don't know if I'd call it real."

I cough on my wine. I want to shout, *"I knew it!"* but I refrain. *Barely.* "Explain that to me?"

She wrinkles her nose like the subject smells bad. "You first. Tell me about these real relationships you had, and I'll explain me and Julian."

I brush some invisible crumbs off the tablecloth in front of me. I feel like I need to give her something good, but there's not a whole lot to share. Nothing has ever been as *real* as me and her. "The first was Dierdre, and I met her in college. We were friends, but we started dating our senior year. It was . . ." I drag a hand through my hair and try to remember those days with Dierdre. The study sessions, the parties, the wasted Sunday afternoons snuggling on the couch. "It was nice. Before she convinced me to give her a chance, I wasn't sure I wanted to be in a committed relationship again."

Brinley flinches. "That was my fault."

"And mine." I clear my throat. "I'd pinned so much on my first love that when I lost you, I felt like I'd lost everything. Dierdre showed me I could still have love and affection, that loving you didn't preclude me from loving someone else."

"What happened?"

I shrug. "We graduated. Alec and I decided to start our own company, and Dierdre got an assistantship in a graduate program in Oklahoma. We were young and didn't want to do the long-distance thing, so we decided to split."

"Just like that?"

I laugh. "It happens every day."

"But if things were so good—"

"I said they were *nice*. But it wasn't the soul-shattering kind of love. It kind of sucked to say goodbye, but we were both okay."

"You don't miss her?" She searches my face as if she might find some emotion there that I'm even hiding from myself.

"I used to, maybe, as a friend, but it's been so long. Mostly I'm just happy she didn't let me get in the way of her dreams. That would've been a disaster."

She squeezes her eyes shut and nods. "It's awesome that you get that."

And her dreams are in Orchid Valley. No questions asked. Fuck, I get that it's a problem, but I hate that she shuts down any talk of our future because of it. My first instinct is to brainstorm solutions, possibilities, but I know if I start, she'll push me away. "So . . . Julian?"

She wags a finger. "Not yet. You said there were two. Who was the second?"

I chuckle. "I can't decide if you're really this interested in my past romances or if you're dodging the subject."

"Maybe a little of both. Tell me about her."

I pause for a long time. Honestly, if I could skip this part, I'd like to. It seems unnecessarily dramatic, and that doesn't actually match up with my feelings toward the woman in question. "Her name was Bridget."

Brinley rolls her eyes. "And what was Bridget like?"

"She was . . . ambitious, which I could relate to. We both worked and traveled a lot, so she didn't resent my job, which was refreshing."

"What'd she do?"

"You know . . ." I take a sip of wine. "Some acting or whatever."

She blinks at me. "You don't mean Bridget Schaffer?" When I drop my gaze to the table again, she shrieks softly. "You were in a *relationship* with Bridget Schaffer? *How* did I not know about this?"

I shrug. "I don't know. The media found me boring and was more interested in reporting on every time she was spotted with her ex." Bridget's ex is a British pop star, so their possible reunion made a much more interesting story than her steady-but-quiet—and mostly secret—relationship with me.

"I don't know whether I should be jealous or impressed." She giggles and does a little hair toss. "I'm going to go with impressed. Look at me, on a date with Bridget Schaffer's ex."

I arch a brow. "Look at you, *married to* Bridget Schaffer's ex."

Her blue eyes go wide. "Right! Damn, I must be a catch."

My smile falls away. "You're better than a catch. You're . . ." I scan her face as I look for the word. *Catch* sounds like she's just another woman and this is just another date, when she's always been *the* one for me. "You're even more amazing now than you were ten years ago."

Her smile wavers, and she swallows. "I'd like to think so. I was just a kid back then." She shakes her head, as if not letting herself dwell there. "Tell me what happened with Bridget."

I suck air through my teeth. "Well, unlike me and Dierdre, it was *not* an amicable split."

"Did she break your heart?"

I study her and wonder if she understands, truly, that she's the only one who ever had the power to do that. "It wasn't like that. She was still in love with her ex, but she didn't want to give me up, either. It was ugly."

"She cheated on you?"

I turn up my palms. There isn't a single piece of me that still longs for Bridget. I'm where I want to be right now. But at the time? I was angry. So fucking angry. "They were caught making out in a club, and I didn't find out about it until the pictures were all over the gossip sites. She swears it was just that once and that nothing else happened but . . ." I study Brinley's parted pink lips and remember how I sat down with a bottle of bourbon and did a deep dive into some self-pity. It wasn't just Bridget—though the days those images were everywhere were some of the most embarrassing of my life—it was that I'd never felt anything for anyone that came close to what I'd felt for Brinley Knox when I was a teenager, and I wondered if I'd ever feel that again. "I broke it off with Bridget, told her to get the fuck out. Then, after inadvisable quantities of bourbon, I picked up the phone and called you for the first time in years."

Brinley lifts her hand to her mouth. "You did? When was this?"

"It was a couple of years ago." I close my eyes. "You still had the same number as when we were in high school. I couldn't believe I still remembered it, but it was imprinted somewhere deep in my brain, and even loaded and in no position to talk to anyone, I was able to dial your number."

"I don't remember . . . I didn't see a call from you." She shakes her head. "But I didn't have your new number until I saw you in Vegas."

"Exactly. Maybe that's why you didn't answer. Or maybe you wouldn't have if you'd known it was me."

"I would have," she blurts. "I don't answer calls from numbers I don't know, but if I'd known it was you . . ."

I shrug. As if it doesn't matter. As if I wasn't lonely as fuck that night and so many nights before and after. I called three times just to listen to her voice asking me to leave a message. *Hi! You've reached Brinley. Sorry I can't make it to the phone, but leave a message and I promise to get back to you as soon as I can.* She sounded so damn *happy*, sounded the way she'd *looked* the day I came back to Orchid Valley and saw her holding Cami on the patio behind her parents' house. "I didn't leave a voicemail," I say unnecessarily.

She bites the corner of her mouth. "What would you have said if I'd picked up?" She smiles. "Hey, this gorgeous Hollywood starlet just broke up with me; come over here and kiss me better?"

I have to laugh. "I like to think I would've done better than that, but like I said, there was a lot of bourbon involved." I swallow. "I imagine I would've just said I missed you every day, and I didn't think I'd ever love someone else the way I loved you."

She drops her gaze to her wine. "You always say sweet things."

More words lodge themselves in my throat—*sweet things* she probably doesn't want to hear. "Tell me about Julian."

She wrinkles her nose. "Do I have to?" When I just arch a brow in response, she sighs. "Julian moved to town about six years ago. We met at Smithy's and hit it off."

"Six years ago?" I lean back in my chair, fighting every possessive, jealous asshole instinct I have. I want to hear this story, but this isn't some random hookup she's telling me about, and unlike my old girlfriend, Julian's not just an ex I can process in an intellectual way. This is the guy she almost married. This is the guy I almost lost her to. *And they were involved for six years.*

"Like I said, a long-term relationship was never a priority to me. When I went home with Julian that night, he was supposed to be another random hookup. One and done. I wasn't looking for more."

"But he was," I say. "He's thought of you as *his* since that first time."

She rolls her head from side to side as if she needs to release tension in her neck. "I'm not sure how you know that, but yeah. It's becoming very clear to me that despite my warnings that I wasn't interested in more than easy hookups, Julian's been playing the long game since the beginning." She closes her eyes. "I feel like such an ass, in retrospect. I should have realized he was falling for me."

"But you did at some point—realized it and realized you returned his feelings? Or was it not that at all? Was there another reason you were planning to go through with this marriage?"

When she looks up at me, her eyes are guarded. "If you've already figured it out, please don't make me explain. It's mortifying."

I scoot my chair halfway around the table and brush my knuckles down her arm. "I haven't figured anything out. But I know you came home from Vegas and got engaged days or, at most, weeks after. When I first found that out, I made myself crazy thinking what we had that night was nothing more than a last-minute fling. Cold feet."

"In some ways, it was," she says softly, and when her eyes meet mine, there's something like shame there. "I went to Vegas knowing I needed to make a decision about Julian."

"But the woman I spent that night with wasn't in love with another man. I don't know why, exactly, you decided to marry me, but I know you weren't in love with anyone else."

"No," she says, and her voice is so low it's as if she wants to keep her secrets from all the strangers in this restaurant. "I wasn't in love. Not in the way you mean."

"So why did you agree to marry him?"

She looks around, and something like shame pulls at her features. "Can we get out of here?"

CHAPTER TWENTY-FOUR

MARSTON

*T*wilight has descended when we leave the restaurant, and the streetlamps cast the streets in a soft glow. "Want to walk or go to the car?"

"Walk, if that's okay?"

I nod. The restaurant is tucked in a charming little residential neighborhood. The two-lane street's lined with colorful craftsman homes, and the light breeze makes it the perfect temperature for a stroll.

We're two blocks down before she speaks again. "The spa," she says, turning to look at me as if those two words explain everything and she expects me to react to this somehow. "The owner retired years ago after training me, and now her kids are pushing her to sell. She doesn't do much with the place anymore. She would've sold sooner, but she was trying to give me a chance to be able to buy it from her. But . . . I'm not."

This surprises me, but then I remember that her father cut her off when she left the family company.

"If you're thinking of my sizable trust," she says, catching my expression, "you should know that my grandfather was as much of a misogynist as my father is—maybe even more. He never forgave me for getting pregnant—and worse, for keeping Cami when I could've gone to my grave with this shameful secret instead. After Grandma passed, he changed his will to read that I didn't get the money in my trust until I turned thirty or was married—and not just married, but married to a man my father approves of."

I bow my head. Part of me wanted it to be something like this, but I understand why she's so ashamed. I've been the one who needed to work the system before. But damn her grandfather for being a spiteful old man and who thought he needed to punish Brinley for getting pregnant. "Who's to say the man you marry will even be good with money?"

"I know, right? God forbid a woman have access to that much money without a man to manage it for her." She rolls her shoulders back as if she's trying to shrug off tension. "And I've gone to the bank to see about a business loan, but they can't offer me anything close to what I need. I screwed up my credit when I was younger, and now it's biting me in the ass. And I won't necessarily be out of a job if they sell to someone else, but . . ."

I get it. The place is important to her, and she doesn't trust it in anyone else's hands. In her parents' emotional absence, she's made a new family of her best friends, and they all work there and depend on their jobs. "You want to maintain control."

"I do. My parents love Julian—probably more than they

love me, if we're being real here. Before I saw you in Vegas, I joked with him that I should just marry him so I could have access to my trust and buy The Orchid before it sold to someone who might change everything or fire me and my friends. Or both. He shrugged and said he was up for it, but of course I laughed it off. I told him that wasn't fair to him and I'd find another way." She sighs and does nothing but breathe for a few long moments as the sidewalk leads us up a steep hill.

At the top, we stop to wait for the light to change. Cars whiz by as I turn to her. "What changed your mind?"

"A few weeks later, he had an opportunity to buy an apartment building, but the owner wanted to sell to a married couple. She'd owned it with her husband and he'd passed, but she believed a married couple would care more about the families in the units. That a single guy would be more likely to price-gouge and run them off, that kind of thing."

I gape. "Wow. People do business like that?"

"Small town." She shrugs. "So, suddenly I wasn't the only person who was going to benefit from this arrangement. He proposed we get married. I'd get The Orchid, and he'd get his new real-estate investment, and in the meantime we could both enjoy having a partner in life. Someone to talk to at the end of the day and take to business dinners."

"And someone to warm his bed," I say, my words too hard.

She cuts me a look and frowns. "That was a given. Julian and I had been sleeping together for years. Not regularly, but on and off. His plan made sense."

I want to tell her it was a *terrible* plan, but I know what it's like to fight loneliness. And I know what it's like to desperately want to create something of your own—and that's what The Orchid is for her. The only difference is, she's already built it, but now she might lose it anyway. "Where does Vegas fit in all this?"

The signal changes, indicating we should walk, and we cross the busy street before she speaks again. "I think I knew I was going to say yes when I came looking for you." She swallows. "I needed to see you one last time, maybe convince myself that whatever we had once was gone."

What we had will never be gone. Not as long as I draw breath. "And you were convinced? What you remembered of our night was enough to make you believe you could be happy with him?"

"Nothing was that simple." She stares off into the distance. "That night was enough to remind me that I forget myself when I'm with you. When I woke up with that ring on my finger, I realized I'd almost thrown away everything." She shakes her head, and a tear spills down her face. "There are so many people at The Orchid and in the OV who rely on me. I *love* what I've built. I have a good life here, and Cami goes to a great school. I didn't want passion that swept me away and made me as reckless as it did when we were kids. I wanted to keep my feet under me and do what's right for everyone who will be affected by my decisions."

The blow of these words knocks me off balance. I stop walking, and she turns soft, apologetic eyes on me.

If she'd told me she didn't feel anything for me, it wouldn't have hurt because I'd know she was lying. But hearing her say she's been avoiding the kind of intensity we had? "You'd rather live a life without passion?" I ask. She didn't want what she felt with me. She didn't want to be reckless like she'd been with me. Reckless like she'd been the night her sister died. *She still blames herself.*

She turns her palms up. "I thought so, but look at me. I'm here."

Yes. She is. "And what do you want now?"

She searches my face. "I want the water and the desert, the night and the day. I want things that can't exist together." She grimaces. "Rich-bitch problems, right?"

I stare at her for a long beat. "I've never thought your problems were trivial, Brinley." Leaning forward, I brush my lips against hers. "And if you want things you're not allowed to have, then we change the rules."

❧

BRINLEY

Slowly, he lowers his mouth to mine and flicks his tongue across my lips. I open to him instinctively. I know we're in the middle of the sidewalk and everyone who walks by is looking at us, but I want his kiss more than I want to avoid their notice.

I slide one hand into his hair and clutch his forearm with the other. It's not like starting over. It's like picking up where we left off in the foyer Friday night, and I'm as turned on as I was when he let himself out the door. Tonight, I don't want him to walk away. If I'm honest, I didn't want him to before, either. It's everything I crave in his kisses—warmth, affection, hunger, lust, and emotion shaken together in a cocktail I've never found with anyone else.

He breaks away before I want him to, and I instinctively

324

cling to his arm. "Ready to go?" he asks, and there are so many more questions tucked inside that innocuous one that my nod feels like a promise.

We hold hands on the walk back to the car and the whole drive home. It takes every bit of my restraint not to lean over the console and kiss his neck, rub my tight nipples against his arm. Maybe this is going too fast, or maybe he's my husband and I don't have to worry about slowing down. The truth is, I'm no closer to guessing what tomorrow will bring than I was before he asked me on this date.

"Then we change the rules."

It sounds too good to be true, and I'm not sure I even want to see if it's possible. The only thing I'm sure of is what I want tonight—those big hands on my thighs, those dark, greedy eyes all over me.

"Fuck me, Brinley, but I can practically smell your thoughts over here."

I shift in my seat, the pulsing ache between my legs growing more insistent.

The second he pulls off the interstate, I can't resist anymore. I pull my hand from his and press it against his thigh, stretching across the console until I'm palming his dick through his jeans.

A little moan escapes my mouth when I feel how hard he is. He lifts his hips off the seat, pressing into my touch. "Not yet, baby," he murmurs. "Just give me another minute."

"I need to feel you." I lean toward him, frustrated when my seatbelt stops me short. "I'm dying over here."

"I've got you." He takes my hand off his crotch and moves it back to my side of the console. I push my head back against the headrest. "Shh." He inches the hem of my skirt higher and higher, and I shift forward on the seat, desperate to get that hand where I need it. When he finally cups me between my legs, he curses. "You're so fucking wet. Goddamn, I want to feel this all over me."

He strokes me through my underwear, the gentle friction of the lace against my clit making me writhe in the seat. I need him inside me—if not his cock, then his fingers—and I'm about to beg when Marston takes a sudden turn into the parking lot at Lake Blackledge. He pulls the brake on the car, and I don't waste any time getting unbuckled and climbing over the console to straddle him.

"I've never felt like this with anyone but you," he says, his words husky and a little shaky. He's as desperate for this as I am.

His hands are on my thighs, sliding up and under my skirt, and mine are on his belt, clumsy and fumbling as I try to free him from his pants. He helps me, lifting his hips and helping me slide his jeans down just enough to free his cock.

I keep a hand between our bodies, stroking him, and he goes thicker and harder in the palm of my hand. I grip him tightly, and the wetness that's already gathered at the head slicks the path. He lifts his hips, jacking up into my hand.

"Christ, that feels good," he groans. "I need to touch you." He peels down my dress and my bra in one rough tug, freeing my breast. He's wild. Tongue, lips, teeth—flicking, kissing, nipping and sucking until I'm grinding myself on his thigh, desperate for release.

"Condom?" The word comes out breathless.

"Glovebox." He's already leaning over to open it. The box is unopened, and he tears it in his impatience to get inside. I take the condom from him, pull it from the foil package, then grip him at the base of his shaft as I slide it down his cock. I don't let go until I've shifted my hips over him, his dick notched at my entrance.

Slowly, I lower onto him, letting him fill me and stretch me. I don't breathe again until he's fully inside me, and then it's in an inhale so ragged my entire body shakes. He shifts under me, and we start to move together. "Marston." His name's a gasp, a prayer, a revelation. My body's clenched tight, and I'm barely holding off the release it so desperately wants. "I've missed you."

Maybe the words don't make sense. Maybe I'm drunk on pleasure, but his face softens like he understands. "Every fucking day," he whispers. His eyes are dark and heavy-lidded, but he holds my face in one big hand and locks his gaze on mine. "Promise me you'll remember this tomorrow. I can't have you forgetting this one."

My heart squeezes. "Yes," I whisper, arching as I rock on him. "I promise I'll remember."

My body ratchets tighter, even as my shoulders fall and the tension from my need drains away. He doesn't release my face, doesn't stop looking into my eyes, and I continue moving on him like that—his hand on my hip as I rock in tiny circles, gazes locked.

"So beautiful," he whispers. "I never stopped dreaming of this face. Never stopped—" He cuts himself off with a curse and a powerful upward thrust of his hips.

Pleasure spirals. Builds. Tightens. Crests.

I collapse forward, resting my head on his shoulder and rocking in desperate, jerky motions. The pleasure is too much and not enough. I want to slow down and make this last, but at the same time I want more skin, more friction, more *time*. A sob rips from me at the unwelcome reminder that this is temporary, but he presses his mouth to mine and swallows the sound, taking away the fear and grief with the slide of his tongue and nip of his teeth.

When he releases my hip, it's to slide between our bodies. His thumb finds my clit and he strokes. All the tension coils and loosens in a powerful spasm that has me muffling my moan in his chest.

With one more forceful thrust of his hips, he bites my shoulder and buries himself deep inside me, his cock swelling with his release.

I don't know how many minutes we sit there, half-dressed, a sheen of sweat on our skin, clinging to each other as we catch our breath. When I straighten, he looks at me and chuckles, shaking his head.

"What?" I smile. "You're not supposed to laugh right after sex. You'll give a girl a complex." I'm not really offended, though. I couldn't be with the joy I see in his eyes.

"I've been looking forward to tonight for a hundred reasons, not the least of which was having you in my *bed*. You deserve better than a quick fuck in my car or a finger fuck under the table. And here we are, ten minutes from either of our beds, and I've taken you like a horny teenager."

I press a kiss to his neck. "You say that like it's a bad thing."

He skims his hands up and down my back, soothing, gentle strokes. "Oh, it was *very* fucking good, but I want more with you. I want skin and space to spread your legs. I want you completely nude while I taste every inch of you, and I want the whole night to do it." My body clenches around him at those words, and he groans. "Come home with me. I need you out of this dress."

CHAPTER TWENTY-FIVE

BRINLEY

I nearly whimper when I walk into Marston's rental. This isn't a typical vacation property or temporary rental. This is an *event* property. The kind of place that's rented out for a hefty price tag to people who plan to have on-site destination weddings and want to provide their guests with a place to stay.

If I didn't know how filthy rich Marston's become in recent years, I'd think he was flexing by choosing this place, but the truth is he can afford it. He's become accustomed to a lifestyle of only the best. It's part of his brand. I used to live that life before I decided I wanted to prove to myself and my parents that I could do it on my own.

Our steps echo through the massive foyer as he leads me inside and into the massive kitchen. I shake my head as I look around. "Do I even want to know how much you're paying to rent this place?"

He takes my purse and sets it on the marble breakfast bar. "It doesn't matter."

I'm not sure if his evasion makes me feel better or worse, but I struggle to ignore the niggling in my gut that's trying to ring the alarm at the inequity between us. We're not at the point where it matters yet. *If* we get there, I'll figure out a way to move forward and maintain my independence. "Show me around?"

He quirks a brow. "To be clear, that's *not* code for *fuck me on the kitchen table*?"

I cackle and wink at him. "Not this time."

He blows out a breath. "Okay, the tour it is."

I have to walk quickly to keep up with Marston's long strides as he takes me through the living room with its wooden beam ceilings and massive stone fireplace, then up a gorgeous, winding staircase that overlooks the living room below. The sight reminds me so much of the room where we first kissed that my stomach pitches, but Marston isn't so affected. He strides toward a dark hall, and the overhead lights flick on as he enters. *Fancy.*

"There are five bedrooms," he says. "All have *en suites*, but mine has the best view."

Marston opens a door and waves me inside. Unlike in the hall, he uses the switch on the wall to control these lights, but a sigh slips from my lips when I catch sight of the wall of windows and the view of the lake beyond. The Orchid sits on the opposite side of the lake, the landscaping lights around it giving it a beautiful and regal air.

The bed and breakfast where we first made love had a view of the lake. I wonder if Marston remembers that. Remembers the way his hands shook as he positioned himself over me the first time and how scared he was that he'd hurt me. How it felt like our souls were connected that night . . . until the pounding on the door tore our love in half.

I press my hand to my chest and swallow hard.

"Are you okay?"

I nod to the view. "It's beautiful."

He studies me for a long beat, as if he's trying to decide if he should share something with me. "I'm glad you like it," he says softly.

My brain is going a hundred miles an hour. What would've happened if I hadn't spent that night with him? Has he truly forgiven me for the way I acted afterward? Could he be happy here if he could live in a place like this? Would I ever feel truly independent if I was married to someone who brought so much wealth to the table? Would he be willing to live a simpler life if I wasn't comfortable with *taking* so much?

"What's going on in that mind of yours?" he asks softly.

I shake my head. "Too much," I admit.

"Can I help?"

I don't want to ruin tonight by digging into those questions, so I unzip my dress and let it fall to the floor, relishing the heat that flashes in his eyes. "In fact, you can."

MARSTON

"I can't believe I finished that entire thing," Brinley says, pushing away her empty plate where a small puddle of syrup is all that's left of the French toast I had delivered for her this morning.

I shrug. "You said you were craving French toast, and I aim to please." The corner of my mouth twitches in a smirk. "Anyway, I shouldn't be the only one who got to eat my fill of something sweet."

Her cheeks blaze, and I wish I could take a picture of her like this. She's wearing nothing but her panties and one of my T-shirts. Her face is free of makeup, and her hair's piled on top of her head in a messy bun. Her expression is relaxed and happy, and if I had my way, I'd put that look on her face every fucking morning for the rest of her life.

She stands and stretches her arms over her head, giving me a view of her soft thighs and the black triangle of lace between her legs. I took my time kissing and touching her there last night, but I still want more.

"You keep looking at me like that, and you're going to make me late to work." She glances at the clock on the stove and groans. "I can't believe it's after seven and I still need to run home and shower."

Not bothering to stand, I wrap my arms around her waist and pull her to me, sliding the borrowed shirt up before nuzzling my face against her stomach. "You'd like the shower here," I say, running kisses across her abdomen. She shivers and slides her fingers into my hair. I fucking *love* when she does that. It reminds me of being between her legs, of the hungry whimpers and pleas as I licked and sucked. "And I need to fuck you again before I leave."

She freezes in my arms, and her hands go slack in my hair. I'm so busy sliding my hand between her legs and feeling how slick she is there that it takes me a minute to register why.

I pull back and look up at her. "Four days in Atlanta," I explain. "Alec's flying in today, and we have business meetings that can't wait." I stroke her between her legs, and her eyes float closed. She widens her stance to make room for my hand, but instead of giving her what she wants, I tug her toward me. "Come here."

She straddles my lap and loops her arms behind my neck. "You don't have to explain yourself. Of course you need to work."

"If our schedule weren't so crazy, I'd come back every night." I kiss her gently and groan as she rocks against me. She's so fucking wet. I can feel her through her panties and my boxer briefs.

I wrap my arms around her, holding her tight, and stand.

Brinley squeaks in protest but wraps her legs behind my back. "What are you doing?"

I head toward the stairs and the luxury shower waiting for us up there. "I'm making you late."

CHAPTER TWENTY-SIX

BRINLEY

*I*t's been a long freaking week. And it's only Wednesday.

My parents are still in town—not that they're talking to me. They're just *around*. Meaning there's potential for any public outing to turn excruciating if I happen to run into them.

Cami's having the time of her life at Disney World and sending me pictures that alternately make me smile and remind me of this missing piece of me. I never feel quite right when she's gone. Her birthday was yesterday, and after I sang to her over FaceTime, I indulged in a private little cry over not being there with her.

Every time I get a message on my work email from anyone in the Wright family, I go tense all over, convinced the ax is about to drop.

And Marston's still in Atlanta. He texts me between

meetings, calls me at night, and generally has me so wound up that I'm likely to jump him the second he walks in the door on Friday.

When I enter my condo after work Wednesday, Julian's keys are on the entryway table.

My stomach pitches. We haven't spoken since he stormed out Friday night. Maybe he's here to talk. Maybe he's going to apologize for the way he acted and admit he played a part in how all this unfolded. I screwed up, and I can forgive him for being hurt, but he lied to me to get me to agree to this marriage and then snooped through my things. I think there are apologies owed on both sides if we're going to maintain our friendship going forward.

I drop my purse by his keys and head toward the sound of steps in the bedroom, but when I step inside, I gasp.

The closet door's wide open, and inside are big boxes piled full of my clothes. On the bed, more boxes with all of my belongings piled inside.

Julian's stooped in the corner, taping shut yet another box, and when he looks up at me, his eyes narrow. "I'm done with Cami's room. You can help me with the kitchen after this."

I look around, taking in the boxes one at a time. "What?" I shake my head. I'm completely missing something. "What's happening here, Julian?"

He straightens and tosses the packing tape on the bed. "I've let you and your kid live here for less than half rent for *months* while you led me on. I have a waiting list of people who will pay more than list rent for this condo. I'm done losing for you."

"Losing what?"

"Money, time, my future, and my pride. I've given

enough, and you've given me shit-all in return. Nothing but empty promises. I'm done. I need you out yesterday so I can get someone in here who isn't going to take and take and never give back."

That feeling in my stomach turns to a full-on twist of knots. "You're the one who wanted me to live here," I say, my voice barely above a whisper. "I told you I couldn't afford it, but you *insisted*."

"I wouldn't have done that if I'd known you were married to that asshole, though, would I?"

He's right. I swallow back my angry retort and scramble to think of a solution. "I'll borrow money from—" From my parents? Unlikely. And my friends don't have it. Kace *might*, but he just bought a house that he's renovating and . . . I shake my head. "I'll borrow it from somewhere. Somehow. Let me pay full rent until I can find somewhere else."

"Even if someone would give you the money—and I *seriously* doubt that—I wouldn't take it." He looks around my disaster of a bedroom slowly, his disgust palpable. "You can't have everything handed to you your whole life and never expect to give something in return, Brin."

Handed to me. That's how he's seen this arrangement: him spoiling the rich girl who's never had to pull her own weight.

He said he wanted me and Cami to have a nice place to live. He said he wanted to take care of us and this was all part of being a family . . . and now my name's not even on the lease, so I don't have a leg to stand on. I knew better, but I told myself it'd be okay because Julian isn't like my father. Julian's kind. Julian cares about me.

History repeats itself. Only now, instead of finding myself at my father's will, I'm at Julian's.

"Where do you expect me to go?" I ask, my voice shaking.

"I don't give a shit where you go, Brinley. As long as it's nowhere close to me." He pulls out a dresser drawer and dumps it over an empty box, sending bras and panties all over the place. "Go live with that man you married. Then again, I hear he left town on Monday. Maybe he doesn't want you, now that he knows his wife's been fucking *me* for the last six years."

I flinch. "Julian, can we just—"

"Or go to Florida and move in with your mom and dad." He smirks and gives a condescending tilt of his head. "Wait. You can't do that either. Guess what? *No one* wants to take in the spoiled bitch."

I don't want his words to hit home, but they feel so true that I'm nauseated. "I am *sorry* I screwed up," I say. "Please listen. I—"

He holds up a hand, just like my father. "You're lucky I didn't send someone to get your shit out of here. I'm trying to do you a solid."

"By kicking me out?"

"By helping you pack."

<hr/>

MY DAY WAS A DISASTER, but luckily I have the best friends in the whole world. Once I decided I'd had enough verbal abuse from Julian, I promised him I'd be out by dark and suggested he leave before my cousin Smithy arrived. That was it. One final angry glare and Julian was gone, and shortly after that, my friends were there.

Savvy, Stella, Abbi, and I moved boxes into the U-Haul I

rented minutes before they closed, and Kace, Smithy, and Stella's brother Dean loaded my furniture into it.

We took everything but a couple of suitcases of necessities to Kace's garage for temporary storage, and now we're *all* exhausted.

I jump in for a quick shower while everyone cools off with beers in Kace's living room. Since Kace is the only one with two extra bedrooms, I'll stay with him for the time being. I considered moving into his pool house, but it's a studio, and as much as I love my daughter, I love occasional privacy too. Hopefully I can find a place quickly that can get us in right away, but I'm exhausted just thinking about it. I feel like I've been beaten from the inside out.

As much as I'd like to pretend Julian and my father are both wrong about me and my decisions, the truth rang clear in so many of the cruel things they said. I've made a fool of myself and my family too, and now my shitty decisions are going to throw another wrench in Cami's life.

I climb out of the shower and head to the guest bedroom to change out of my towel and into clean clothes. Stella's sitting on the edge of the bed, waiting for me. She gives me the kind of sad eyes people usually reserve for mutilated puppies. "Hey, baby girl. You okay?"

I want to be strong. I really do, but this week has been too much, so all I can do is shrug.

"I am so sorry."

"Why do people keep apologizing to me?" I ask, my eyes filling with tears. "I'm the asshole here."

She stands and frowns at me. "How do you figure?"

"I got drunk in Vegas, married a guy my parents hate, and then nearly committed a federal crime by accident to marry a guy I don't even love. Then we broke up, and I conveniently forgot he'd been giving me a break on my rent." I stretch my arms out to my sides to indicate the metaphorical disaster all around me. "And I don't even know what's going to happen with The Orchid."

"Right. That." She shrugs. "No, I'm sorry we didn't all tell you sooner that Julian's a big asshat and he doesn't deserve you."

To be fair, they did tell me. They just tried to do it nicely.

She takes my hands. "If we hadn't let you get engaged to him, this never would've happened."

"First of all, I'm a grown woman and it's not your responsibility to keep me from making mistakes." I blow out a breath. "Second of all . . . thank you. I'm not sure I deserve you."

"Pssh. No one deserves me," she says with a wink.

"I wish I had a crystal ball. I feel like I have no idea what my life is going to look like next week."

Her eyes go big. "Or one of those fortune-teller machines! Remember the ones they had at the fair when we were kids? Brittany was *obsessed* with those."

A familiar tug of loneliness pulls at my heart at the mention of my sister, and I have to swallow hard before I can speak again. "When the fair comes this summer, let's go find one. She'd like that."

Stella gives a sharp nod. "It's a plan. Now get dressed and come out there to have a beer with your friends. Everyone's worried about you."

"I don't know." I look at the ceiling, willing my eyes to dry. "I'm such a fucking mess right now, Stella."

She slings an arm around my shoulder and squeezes me tight. "Come on. You need your girls, and we need to see that you're okay—which you are, because you're fucking fierce and can handle anything."

I laugh at the modified mantra I share with Cami all the time and blink away my tears. I *am* fierce, *dammit.* "Thanks."

"Absolutely. Trust me—of all people, *I* get how much guys suck."

"Once again, I feel compelled to point out that in this situation, I'm the one who sucks, and *you* still haven't told me what happened in Jamaica."

"Hmm." Another shrug then she points at my overnight bag next to the bed. "Get to primping, baby boo. Your friends are waiting."

I wait for her to leave and shut the door before I pull off my towel and use it to dry my hair. On the nightstand, my phone flashes with a new message, and I pick it up.

Marston: I bought you something special.

"You can't have everything handed to you your whole life and never expect to give something in return, Brin." Julian's words are a living thing eating away at my confidence and sense of self.

Me: You didn't need to buy me anything. The
only gift I want is another night with you.

I stare at my phone after I send the message, realizing how complicated nights together are going to be once Cami gets home.

Marston: I want that too. I'm doing
    everything I can to make sure it happens.

I frown as I reread his message half a dozen times. Everything he can? Does that mean he might not be coming back? Even the possibility of that makes me feel too heavy. *Please come back. Please don't make me say goodbye yet.*

Julian's words gnaw at me again. *"I've given enough, and you've given me shit-all in return."*

I can't ask Marston to stay forever. He has a life on the other side of the country, a house, friends, and a business to run. I type, *I'm not asking you to stay forever,* then delete it. Then I type, *I don't want you sacrificing anything for me,* then delete that too. Finally, I manage a message I don't have to overanalyze.

Me: Cami's home Saturday, but Friday night is
    yours.

Marston: Just Friday? That's a start, but you
    know me better than to think that'll be
    enough.

I swallow hard. Because I do.

CHAPTER TWENTY-SEVEN

BRINLEY

*F*riday morning, after my staff meeting and just as I've sat down to fire up my computer, Marston stalks into my office in jeans and a fitted T-shirt, looking so good I want to eat him up.

"I didn't think I'd see you until later," I say, grinning.

He shuts the door behind him. *Locks it.* The heavy click echoes off my office walls, and I feel it between my legs—a clench, a vibration, a promise. "This morning's meeting got canceled last minute, so I canceled my lunch meeting because I was sick of waiting to see you." He stalks around to my side of the desk, eyes dark, intense. "How are you this morning?"

"I'm okay." I stand and smooth down my black-and-white wrap dress. I put it on this morning thinking of him, imagining what it would be like when I finally got him alone tonight and he untied the bow and . . . I'm too full of nerves to sit, but now that I'm out of my chair, I don't know what to do with my hands. "I've missed you," I whisper.

He trails his gaze over me and leaves shivers in his wake. My nipples tighten against the lace of my bra as I anticipate the feel of his mouth on mine. "You sleep okay?"

No. Kace's house creaks in ways I'm not used to and I just feel . . . weird staying there. "Not bad." I was up half the night thinking about him. *Wanting* him. The other half, I was worrying—about Cami and how our sudden move is going to affect her, and about what I'm doing with Marston. Can we make this work? Am I asking for heartache if I even try?

His nostrils flare as he takes in my heels—my *Vegas* heels —because of course I couldn't spend all night thinking about him and *not* wear these shoes today. "I didn't," he says, as his hand slides behind my neck.

"I'm sorry. Didn't wha—" His mouth crushes down on mine and his hands slide up my sides to my ribs, his thumbs skimming my breasts.

I kiss him back hard and tug his shirt from his pants, considering and dismissing the unlikely possibility of someone seeing us through the picture window. I've wanted this since that first time he walked into my office, and now that I can take it, I don't let rational thought deter me.

He tears his mouth from mine and kisses his way to my ear. "I went to sleep wanting you. I woke up wanting you."

I palm him through his jeans, and he thrusts his hips forward, pressing into my touch. "Same," I whisper.

He unties the bow on my dress but parts the fabric slowly, kissing his way down each additional inch of exposed skin. His mouth is open, wet, and hot—between my breasts, over the swell of each, across each nipple. When he reaches my waist, he circles my navel with his tongue and the dress falls to the floor. The muscles between my legs clench in anticipation.

He drops to his knees and his gaze zeroes in on my sex, covered only in the sheer white material of my panties. He licks his lips and hooks a finger at each hip before guiding them down my thighs.

He cups me with a firm palm between my thighs, and my legs shake as I step apart to keep my balance. "On the desk." His voice is gruff, thick with lust, and I don't dare ignore the command. I don't want to.

I push a pile of paperwork to the side and hoist myself onto the big walnut desk and reach for him, but he shakes his head and takes a seat in my chair. He parts my thighs with his hands. "This is mine today. I'm not waiting another minute to taste you again."

With the first stroke of his tongue over me, I have to bite back a moan, and a little whimper escapes instead.

Turning his head, he presses a firm kiss to the inside of my thigh. "Can you be quiet for me, baby? Let me have this?"

"Yes," I whisper, then I have to bite my lip again because he's sweeping his tongue over my clit, and I'm so sensitive that I tremble beneath his mouth, my hips making jerky little thrusts I can't quite control.

"Stop holding back," he growls. "I want to feel you unleashed." This time when he lowers his mouth back down, he slides a finger inside me. He moves in and out, adding another finger and fucking me with his hand as he sucks and licks my clit and the tender skin all around where his fingers are buried inside me.

I'm right on the edge, so close to coming when he lifts his head and withdraws his fingers.

"Not yet, baby. Hold on." Standing, he unbuckles his belt. He reaches for his back pocket, grabs a condom, and tears the wrapper. I shove down his jeans, freeing his cock, my mouth watering, my body desperate.

Sitting, I stare down at where he's sliding the latex over his shaft. I hook a foot behind each of his powerful thighs and tug him closer. I've never needed anything as much as I need him inside me.

He grips my hips hard. "Lean back."

I obey and prop myself up on my hands to watch as he guides himself to my entrance and slowly drives home. My body clenches tight around him. I'm right on the edge, but I need more. I reach between my legs and find my clit, circling it with two fingers.

Marston's hips jerk and his gaze is glued to where our bodies are joined, where my fingers are working. "Fuck, that's hot. Do it, baby. Touch yourself for me."

His fingers dig harder into my hips, and I savor each spot of near pain. He drives faster and harder into me and I rub myself until— "Mars!"

He pulls me up fast, crushing my chest to his, and his mouth crashes down over mine right as my orgasm hits in a bolt of pleasure that races hot and powerful down my spine.

He nips and sucks at my lips as the last waves of pleasure roll over me. "So beautiful. So sexy," he murmurs against my mouth. "I want you like this every fucking day. Forever."

MARSTON

Pissed. That's the only word for the way I felt when I found out that Julian kicked out Brinley and Cami without any notice. I wanted to find the sonofabitch and give him a lesson or two about what happens to guys who treat women like that, but luckily, Smithy was there and talked me down.

Now it looks like Julian's asshat behavior is going to work in my favor.

I smile as I read the text again.

> Brinley: I don't think Kace wants to hear us banging, so can I be uncouth and invite myself to your place tonight?

Truth is, since I had her in my bed Sunday night, I've thought of little else but having Brinley under my roof. I've done so much thinking, in fact, it would be fair to call it fantasizing.

Brinley in those tiny black sleep shorts . . . and then out of them.

Brinley in the middle of the four-poster bed in the master bedroom, her legs parted and nipples swollen as she watches me lower myself and push into her.

Brinley swimming in the heated indoor pool at the back of the house . . . I'm half hard and adjust myself at my desk before replying.

> Me: Tonight. Any night. You up for going to dinner first or want to get naked and stay that way until morning?

Brinley: Tough call, but we should probably
        carb-load before the naked-all-night part?
        Wouldn't want you to be short on
        stamina.

Me: Is that a fucking challenge, woman?

Brinley: Maybe. ;)

ACCORDING TO KACE, Bella's Café is the best Italian restaurant in town. I remember how much Brinley enjoyed pasta when we were younger, and she's the one who made the joke about "carb-loading," so it seemed like the obvious choice.

I open the passenger door for Brinley, helping her out of the car by the downtown restaurant. She takes my hand and smiles up at me. "Is this okay?" I ask.

"Of course. Bella's is my favorite, and since my trainer had me off pasta for the last two months, I could eat my weight in pasta carbonara." She gazes inside as we pass the big front window, then comes to a stop and back-pedals on the sidewalk, away from the doors.

"What's wrong?"

"My parents," she says, then winces. "I thought they were going to Atlanta tonight, but their plans must've changed."

I know I need to move toward the car, but I can't make myself do it. "I'm not afraid of them, Brinley."

She shakes her head, sadness darkening her blue eyes.

"It's not worth it, Marston. I've seen him tear you down before. I won't let him ruin tonight."

"I'm not afraid of him," I say again. I don't think she believes me. "You say the word and I'll walk in there and tell him we're married, or tell him nothing at all and just enjoy our dinner. Let him say anything he wants." I slide a hand into her hair and run my thumb along the edge of her jaw. "The night you agreed to marry me, we knew there'd be consequences. We don't exist in a bubble."

She rests her head on my shoulder. "I know, and as much as I'd love to see the look on Dad's face when we tell him, I'm not up for it tonight."

Then when? It's been over a decade since Brinley first told me she was mine, and we're *still* hiding from her parents.

CHAPTER TWENTY-EIGHT

MARSTON

May 28th, before

I'm so nervous I think my stomach is going to flip inside out.

"Marston!" Brinley's eyes go wide as I lead her into the candlelit room. Rose petals are scattered across the four-poster bed, and the jetted tub on the opposite side of the room looks out over Lake Blackledge.

I've spent weeks preparing for our single night here—our stolen time. I planned every detail, from the champagne Smithy snagged from his parents for us to the chocolate-covered strawberries waiting in the small fridge. Everything is perfect, but I've never been so nervous.

"Do you like it?" I ask.

"How . . ." She shakes her head. "We get to stay here?"

"Your parents think you're staying at Stella's tonight, right?"

"So does Stella," she says, laughing.

I slide my hands around her waist and pull her close to me. "No, Stella was in on my plans. She knows you'll be with me." I lower my mouth to hers and kiss her. And kiss her. And kiss her.

A whole night with Brinley. I've wanted this for so long, and I'm practically shaking now that it's finally happening.

When she breaks the kiss, she looks around the room again. "Marston, this is too much. You didn't need to spend—"

I cut her off with a hard kiss. "Shh. You're my girl, and I've loved every second we've stolen together, but I want your first time to be special. You deserve more than a blanket in the woods."

"I liked the blanket," she says, cheeks pinkening, and I know she's remembering the same thing I am—the first time I touched her, put my mouth on her. I told myself I'd wait, but we were there, and she was so sweet and responsive.

"I did too," I whisper. I hold her face in my hands. "But that doesn't change that you deserve better. Someday I'll be able to give you the fairytale every day, but until then, I'll settle for giving you a tiny piece of it tonight." I kiss her again. "Tell me you like it."

She grins against my mouth. "I love it, and Marston, it all feels like a fairytale with you."

※

I WAKE up to the sound of a scuffle in the hallway and low voices growing louder—a man and a woman. I close my eyes again and pull Brinley closer. Tonight was perfect, and I'm not going to let some loudmouthed jerk ruin it by waking Brinley and scaring her.

"*Sir*, I said you can't go in there," the woman says.

"The fuck I can't." There's banging and a scuffle. Are they outside our door?

"I tracked my daughter's phone, and this is where she is."

Shit. "Brinley," I whisper, stroking her hair back from her face. She's out. "Brinley, baby. Wake up."

"My guest reserved this room for the night and deserves privacy. He—"

"My daughter is a minor, and she's in there with your *guest*."

I shake her by the shoulder. "Brinley, you have to wake up."

"Now unlock the damn door or I'm going to kick it down."

Brinley's eyes open as the key scrapes the lock.

I grab the sheet and tug it up over her. "Your dad's here," I whisper, but then the door flies open and Abraham Knox storms in.

"You!" He points a shaking finger at me. "Get away from my daughter. Brinley, get dressed."

I start to move off the bed, but Brinley grabs my wrist. "No," she says. "Don't go. He needs to deal with this. With *us*."

My chest snaps tight with anxiety and warms with so much fucking love, and I'm so distracted by the chaos happening inside me that I don't even realize Brinley's father has come around to the other side of the bed.

He grabs her by the wrist and hauls her onto her feet.

"Get your hands off her." I lunge forward and try to wrap her in a sheet.

The woman squeaks and spins away from our nakedness.

"This was what was so important you couldn't answer your phone?" her father shouts, right into her face. "You're here fucking delinquent trash?"

Brinley tries to pull away and fails. "Let go."

Her father spits at me, and it lands on my bare feet. He releases Brinley and finds the pile of her clothes by the jetted tub. He scoops them up and throws them at her. "I hope you enjoyed yourself, because she's dead now. It's too late for goodbyes."

"What?" Brinley stares at her father, the tossed clothing forgotten at her feet. "What did you just say?"

"Brittany's dead." He backs away from her and into the hall, sneering. "My youngest daughter's dead, and you"—he looks her over, disgust curling his lip—"you might as well be. I lost two daughters tonight."

CHAPTER TWENTY-NINE

MARSTON

Present day

"You have the best view in the whole damn town," Brinley says. She props her chin on the edge of the hot tub and peers out over the balcony railing to the lake and mountains beyond. Her hair's piled on top of her head, and the water steams around her bare shoulders. "I don't think anything could make me want to leave this spot."

I grab the bottle of wine off the deck railing and refill her glass. "Sounds like a challenge."

She laughs. "I didn't mean it that way."

When we first got back to the house, we carried the ghost of her parents with us. I don't like that she's keeping

LEXI RYAN

me a secret from them, and it hurt to have her panic tonight when she thought they might see us together. In that moment, I saw clearly that she's not given me her whole self yet. She's not ready to. But we slowly shrugged off the weight of those worries, and finally it's just us again. Marston and Brinley.

I kneel behind her in the center of the spa and dip my head to press my lips against her shoulder. I take my time, savoring the slide of her sweat-slicked skin beneath my lips as I move to her neck and suck lightly. Moaning, she tilts her head to give me better access. "We can stay here as long as you want," I whisper. I slide my hands around her waist and stroke up to cup her breasts. I pinch her nipple, and she gasps, pressing back against me. I'm already hard—have been since she said she wanted to soak, stripped naked, and threw me a smile over her shoulder as she climbed into the hot tub. I love how comfortable she is in her own skin. How comfortable she is with me.

"Thank you for spending tonight with me." I trail my mouth up her neck and then down along her jaw. "I needed this after this week. I needed you."

"Same." She spins in my arms and wraps her legs around my waist under the water. When my cock notches against her sex, she groans and rocks gently. "If I recall, the view from your room is just as good."

I grin against her mouth. "No hot tub up there."

She slides her tongue between my lips in a kiss that's somehow both lazy and hungry. "Maybe you could keep me warm."

I kiss her again, drawing it out, needing the taste of her like I need water. I nip at her bottom lip when I pull away. "Definitely." I wrap my arms more tightly around her and stand, making her squeak. I climb out of the hot tub with her wrapped around me, and she buries her face in my neck as I take the stairs to the bedroom.

When I open the door, she casts a glance over my shoulder toward the path we came in. "I feel like the owner might freak if he knew the amount of water we just dripped across his hardwood floors."

"I promise he doesn't give a shit," I say, walking into the bedroom and kicking the door shut behind me.

I set her on the bed and step back, just to get a good look at her. Her skin is flushed from the hot water, her nipples dark pink and puckered. Her lips are kiss-swollen, and little tendrils of hair have escaped her high bun and curl around her face. "Christ, you're beautiful."

She leans back on her elbows and grins at me as she looks me over from head to toe. "Not as beautiful as you." When her gaze locks on my dick, she licks her lips and shivers. "Come here and keep me warm."

I climb on top of her, and she laughs as she lowers the rest of the way to the bed. "Wait, how would you know about the owner not caring about his floors?"

"Because he has more pressing concerns right now," I say, shifting my hips forward so she can feel the length of my cock cradled between her legs.

"You . . . bought it?" She holds my face in both hands and looks me in the eye. "You bought a house in Orchid Valley?"

I swallow, worried the truth will scare her away. Of course I bought a house. As long as she's here, I will be too. As long as there's a chance for us, I'll need a place to stay. "It seemed like the right choice."

She searches my face for a long time, and I wish I knew

what she was looking for. I wish I knew what she needed to be all in on *us*. "I don't know how not to be scared about what's next," she whispers.

"There's nothing to be scared of. I won't hurt you. I just want to . . ." I swallow down the word before it can escape. *I just want to love you.* "Give this a chance."

She threads her fingers through my damp hair and presses her mouth to mine in a kiss that's sweet and tender and . . . hopeful? It'd be easy to read too much into a kiss like that. Easy to slip and admit that love has already taken hold. That it never went away.

But I won't risk scaring her with my words, so I trail my mouth down her body and let my hands and kisses do the talking. *I love you. I've always loved you. I will die loving you.*

❧

BRINLEY

"Thank you for last night," Marston says, studying every inch of my face in the morning light.

I smile up at him, resisting the urge to plaster myself against him only because we're standing on Kace's front porch and there are likely little eyes watching us from inside. The night might've started rough, but after some Bella's delivery, a couple of bottles of wine, and a soak in the hot tub on the back deck, I didn't care about my parents anymore. Once he carried me to his bed, I didn't care about anything but him. "I'm pretty sure I should be thanking you."

His gaze drops to my mouth, and a bolt of longing zips through my body. I don't think I'll ever get enough of his kisses. "I can think of one way you can thank me." He pulls a set of keys from his pocket and places it in my hand. "Let me give you and Cami somewhere to stay."

I blink at the metal in my palm. "You rented us a *house*?" I can't accept this. Of course I can't—it's every old habit I'm trying to break. But the idea of getting out of Kace's guest bedroom is tempting as hell. "Without asking me?"

"They're keys to *my* house, Brinley. You know I have more space than I need."

The part of me that wants Marston no matter what, no questions asked, begs me to say yes. To ask no questions and jump in with both feet. "How long are you even going to be here?"

He draws in a sharp breath. "I'm working on some opportunities in Atlanta the next few months, and I can commute." He smiles, but it's tight. "That way I get time with you."

A few months. Marston is going to be here for a few months . . . and he wants me to live with him. I know if I spent *months* in his bed, it would change something in me. Julian hurt me, but Marston . . . Marston could shatter me.

"It's a split floor plan," he says, as if reading my mind. "I'm not trying to talk you into being my family right now. You and Cami will have the whole guest wing to yourselves."

I bite the inside of my lip. "That's too generous. I can't . . ." I shake my head and open my palm to give the key back. "It's not a good idea."

"Move in. I'll be gone in Atlanta half the time, and I promise not to pester you when I am around." His lips quirk. "Unless you *want* to be pestered."

"I'm not worried about that. I just don't want to be a

357

charity case." His eyes go shuttered, and I realize what I've said. "Shit, Marston. I didn't mean . . ."

"Yeah, you did, and I don't blame you. No one wants to be a charity case. That's why I worked so damn hard to get where I am. But this isn't charity."

I bite my lip. His offer is beyond tempting. We'd have more space than we'll have at Kace's, and his place is more convenient to work. Not to mention easy access to Marston himself. *Very. Fucking. Tempting.* "Can I think about it?"

"Take all the time you need."

❧

MARSTON

I knew giving her keys this soon would spook her, but I take it as a small victory that she didn't throw them back in my face.

I glance at the big bay window by the front door and the little towheaded girl staring out at us. "That must be Hope," I say, nodding.

Turning, Brinley grins and waves. "Hi, Hopey!"

Hope waves back, then runs away from the window.

"Are you going to invite me in to see your new place?" I ask, trying to play it cool.

Brinley shakes her head. "Cami will be back soon."

Something sharp lodges in my chest at that. If she doesn't want me here when Cami gets home, how the fuck do I expect her to agree to move in with me? I ignore the burn and focus on the positive: here and now. I respect that she's protective of her daughter and needs time before inviting me into Cami's life. *I can be patient.*

I brush a kiss across her mouth, savoring the smell of her and the instinctive parting of her lips. "See you soon."

"Not soon enough." She lifts onto her toes, and I think she's going to kiss me again when she jumps back, eyes wide and focused behind me. "Roman! You're early."

Roman Humphries stands on Kace's front sidewalk, hand raised in an awkward wave. Cami's right behind him, fingers flying on her phone. Roman looks back and forth between us, confusion creasing his brow. "Jesus, Marston Rowe. Is that you?"

I don't think this guy did anything *but* sneer at me the year we went to school together, so I'm taken aback by his smile. It even seems genuine. "Hi, Roman."

"Hi, Mom," Cami says, looking up from her phone. "Do we for real get to stay with Uncle Kace and Hope for a while?"

"For a little bit," Brinley says, nodding.

"Yes!" Cami says, weaving around us to get into the house. She grins at me as she turns the knob. "Hi, Marston."

"Hey, Cami," I say, returning her smile. "Did you have a good time at Disney World?"

"It was awesome," she says. "How was your week?"

"It was . . . fantastic." *Why lie?*

Cami swivels to face her mom. "I'm going to go play with Hope."

Brinley nods. "Sure, sweetie. That's fine."

Cami reaches around me, and I step out of the way as she gives her dad a one-armed hug. He kisses the top of her head. "Love you, Daddy. See you in a couple of weeks."

"See ya, kiddo." He squeezes her one last time before releasing her, and then Cami's off.

Roman looks back and forth between Brinley and me. "So, you two . . ." Smiling, he shakes his head. "Hell, it was inevitable from the start, wasn't it?" He sounds almost happy about it, which throws me, to be honest.

"We're still figuring it out," Brinley says. Then more softly, "Don't say anything yet. I don't want to confuse Cami."

"Julian's a tool," Roman says, then says to me, "Whatever part you played in saving my daughter from Brinley's awful choice in husbands, I commend you."

"Stop it," Brinley growls. "Julian's a good guy. Or . . . was until recently." She frowns. "Everyone can be a little dickish when in the middle of a breakup."

Roman grunts as if to say, *Yeah, right. Whatever you say.* "What matters is it's over."

Brinley sighs. "It wasn't meant to be, but don't blame that on Julian. I feel bad enough without him being unfairly maligned."

Roman throws up his hands. "I won't say another word."

"Thank you," Brinley says. "Was Cami able to work on her history project on the drive at all?"

He nods. "Almost done. She said she wanted to color the cover sheet here, but the rest looks good to me."

"Good. One less thing to get done before Monday." She smiles.

"It's no problem." He tucks his hands into his pockets. "You can trust me with more of that stuff, you know. It doesn't have to be all fun and games when she visits Dad."

I look back and forth between them, gauging the dynamic. For all Roman's faults in high school, he does seem to take co-parenting seriously and have a solid relationship with Cami.

Brinley wrinkles her nose. "I'm working on it. Trying to cut the apron strings a little at a time."

Roman chuckles. "I'll be patient." He shifts awkwardly. "Brin, you think you could give Marston and me a minute alone?"

She turns her wide eyes on me. "Um, I . . ."

"I was on my way out." I give Brinley's shoulder a reassuring squeeze. "I'll walk with you."

Roman's shoulders fall. "That'd be great. Bye, Brin."

She looks back and forth between us—her husband and the father of her child. "Please don't kill each other."

"I think we've grown out of that," Roman says. He winks and heads to the driveway.

Roman doesn't scare me, but for his sake, I sure as fuck hope he's not planning to give me a "don't hurt her" speech. While I might appreciate it from anyone else, it wouldn't sit right from the guy who left Brinley to raise a baby alone while she worked her way through college.

"I owe you an apology." He huffs out a laugh. "Fuck, I owe you *much* more than that, but I figure we can start with an apology."

"I . . ." I shake my head and let out a hoarse laugh of my own. "I did not expect that."

Roman rubs the back of his neck. "I was such a punk kid. For so many reasons, but there's really no excuse for the hell I put you through. I was jealous and thought I was entitled to whatever I wanted. I saw the way she looked at you and knew she liked you more than me, and . . ." He shrugs. "Like I said, a bunch of excuses but nothing to justify what an ass I was."

"I forgive you." I'm surprised how easily the words roll off my tongue, but they're true. "It takes a big man to apologize for what he did when he was young. I appreciate it, and I'm sorry for slashing your tires on prom night."

Roman chuckles as we stop by his car. "I knew that was you, but I couldn't prove it." He clears his throat. "I figure you and Brinley are gonna end up together, and since Brin is a big part of my life because of Cami, I want to do whatever I need to for things to be cool between us."

"It's history, man. Don't sweat it."

His face tenses as he looks back toward the house. "I wasn't there for her, and I really regret it. I found out she was pregnant and made myself scarce just in case the kid was mine. I didn't know for sure until Cami was two and a half. I regret missing those early years." He shakes his head. "I regret it so much."

"Judging by what Brinley says, you're more than making up for it now."

His gaze is distant. "Her parents sure didn't make it easy on her. I've tried to help, but Brinley's proud. She's always been willing to let me buy clothes and shoes and whatever for Cami, but it took me *years* to get her to take child support, and I know damn well she's squirreling most of it away for Cami's college fund." He smacks me on the back. "I'm glad she's got you to help out, but word of warning? Don't expect her to ask for help when she needs it. That's just not how Brinley works."

I nod. I picked that up the moment I came back to town. "Thanks. And . . . thanks for the apology, too. I'm glad as fuck those years are over."

Roman laughs. "Man, me too. Me too." He opens the door and climbs into his car. "See you around, Marston."

CHAPTER THIRTY

BRINLEY

"*M*rs. Wright," I say, pulling my office door wide for the owner of The Orchid. "It's good to see you. Come on in."

I've been preparing for this meeting since Mrs. Wright's housekeeper called me this morning and asked to set up a private meeting with me. I already know I've lost my chance to buy the spa, and as a result we may all lose our jobs, but part of me is grateful that things have moved so quickly. Too much of my life has been stuck in limbo lately, and knowing what's to come on the professional front will be . . . well, it's one less thing to think about, at least.

Mrs. Wright grips her cane in a white-knuckled hand as she lowers into the upholstered chair opposite my desk. I stand there until she's safely seated then take a seat myself in the chair right next to her. I owe this woman for *years* of the best job I've ever had. I'm not going to speak to her from behind a desk.

"You've been busy, haven't you?" she asks, a devious smile twisting her lips. "A husband and a fiancé. That sounds like something I would've tried to get away with in my day."

I laugh. I have no idea where she's getting her information, but I'm not surprised. Mrs. Wright always seems to know what is going on. "I can only plead ignorance, as embarrassing as that is."

She waves a hand as if my knowledge of my near bigamy is irrelevant. "You know my kids are anxious for me to sell, and I promised them it'd be done by summer."

I bow my head. "I know. I'm so sorry."

"I wanted to give you as much time as I could, but I'm not getting any younger, so when you said you couldn't buy in May as we planned—"

"I understand." I wince. I shouldn't have cut her off, but this is literal torture.

"I've been selective with my buyer, and since I know you worried about what any of the national chains might do if they took over, I tried to avoid the big names."

I nod and smile politely, but tears press behind my eyes. Owning The Orchid has been my dream for years, but I have to let it go. I can see now that my belief that I could eventually buy it is a sign of how spoiled I've been my whole life. "It was kind of you to consider my wishes. You certainly didn't have to."

She huffs. "Well, you *have* made me a great deal of money over the years, so that's worth something, isn't it? My kids just see this place as the money pit it was before you came on. They have no idea what it's been making me in recent years." She winks and whispers, "Can't let them know too much, or they'll come around looking for their share."

I laugh. "Well, I'm glad you thought my efforts were worthwhile."

"Indeed. And it was easy to prove that with the numbers as well. As a result, the company that's taking over has agreed to let the current staff stay on."

"Who's the buyer?"

"The name of the business is BEK, LTD." She gives me a grim smile. "I know it's not the same as making The Orchid yours, but it's the best I could do, Brinley."

My eyes well with tears, but I take a deep breath and tighten that string that seems to be all that's holding me together these days. "You did more than you had to. You have for years. And I'm grateful."

❧

I RARELY CLOSE MY door when I'm not in a private meeting, but after Mrs. Wright leaves, I do. I close it and curl up in a ball in my chair, looking out over Lake Blackledge. I won't cry. No. I'll save that for later. But I need some quiet moments—my chance to say goodbye to my dream.

We got off easy. My friends and I will still have jobs. There's more here to be grateful for than not . . . but still I need to grieve.

When there's a knock at my door, I ignore it and keep staring.

The door opens anyway. "Hey, baby boo," Stella says. "I wanted to check on you."

"Hey." I force a smile. "I have good news. The new

owner is going to keep us in our positions." I don't add *for the time being*, even though the pessimist in me knows it's easy for them to make those promises now and then change the rules the moment something suits them better.

She lowers herself into a chair across from my desk and sighs. "Well, that is good news, but it's not the reason I was worried about you."

"Oh?"

"Promise you won't freak out." I nod, and her brow wrinkles with her frown. "I'm friendly with Mrs. Wright's finance guy, and he just called to give me the scoop on who bought the spa."

"BEK, LTD," I say. "Whoever the hell that is." It's not like I'm privy to all the companies and individuals who've been considering the purchase, but I know enough about some to know who to be on the lookout for. That one wasn't on my radar.

Stella gives me a sad smile. "Honey, it's Marston," she says. "He's BEK, LTD."

My heart squeezes hard and sinks just as suddenly. "Marston?"

She stands and wrings her hands. "You said you wouldn't freak out."

Swallowing hard, I shake my head. "I'm not." I don't trust myself to say much more. My hands are already trembling. He did this for me, I have no doubt.

Just like my parents paid for my first house and first car.

Just like Julian cut me a deal so I could live in a condo I couldn't afford.

Marston's not like them, but a slick, slimy feeling coats my skin as I realize what this could mean—for me, for my friends, for any future relationship I might've tried for with Marston.

Nausea rolls over me, and I bring the back of my hand to my mouth.

"I wanted to tell you before he did. He's out in the lobby chatting with Savvy, and I don't think he understands you might not like this."

Might not like this. It makes me feel like the spoiled little rich girl again. The fragile thing who couldn't do for herself and messed it up any time she tried. The *trapped* girl who only had one thing that was ever really hers—and when she panicked and pushed him away, she didn't even have him anymore.

I look up when Marston steps into my office.

"Hey, Stella!" He's grinning and looks so damn handsome. I could almost forget my worries if they weren't sitting on my chest like a five-ton elephant. He's dressed down today in jeans and a dress shirt rolled to his elbows, no tie, and when he turns to me, his eyes brighten with joy. "Good morning, beautiful," he says softly.

I lift my chin, but everything inside me is too tight. Like I'm made up of thousands of tiny strings that are all about to snap. "Morning."

"I'll just go," Stella says, sidestepping him.

Marston flashes her a confused smile, but she waves and pulls the door closed behind her as she goes.

He strolls toward me and walks around to my side of the desk before leaning against the edge. "Remember when I was in Atlanta and told you I bought you a gift?" He pulls a skinny box from his pocket and puts it on the desk in front of me.

I close my eyes as each of the strings holding me

together is pulled a fraction tighter. Pretty soon they'll snap and I'll fall apart. "I told you I didn't want you to buy me anything." When his knuckles brush along my cheek, I open my eyes again.

"Don't be sad, baby. You'll want this. I promise." He lifts the lid off the box, revealing a delicate blown-glass orchid inside.

I don't speak. I can't.

"I know how important this is to you, and I realized that by canceling your wedding to Julian, you were giving up something you've spent years working for."

"So you bought it for yourself?" I barely recognize my own voice. It sounds hollow. I should be grateful for his generosity, but . . . I thought Marston understood. I thought he *knew* me.

"For you. I bought it for you." He tilts his head to the side, studying me. "Because you couldn't."

"So it's mine?" I hate myself for the words, for the sneer in my tone, for the panic that's making me turn to ice and shove him away. "On what condition?" I ask, my voice shaking.

"I don't understand what the problem is. There are no conditions. There are no stipulations. I formed a shell company I can transfer to you at any time."

"You bought me a multimillion-dollar business for nothing? You're just going to hand it over?" I shake my head. "Don't condescend me. I'm not a child."

He stands, irritation clear in his face. "And I'm not your parents."

"What if I told you I still want the divorce? That I don't want to move to L.A. with you? Would I still have my job here, or would the new owner take it away?"

"I don't expect you to move to L.A. Alec and I were in Atlanta scoping sites for a new office. Our business has grown. We can have dual headquarters now, and Atlanta makes sense. I can commute for the time being, and then when you're ready and you've trained someone to run this place, we can buy a place there."

I shake my head. "Tell me you aren't making plans for my life without me."

He takes my hands and pulls me out of the chair. "I'm making plans *with* you. And I've been listening. You want Cami to be able to see her father more. You want your friends who work here to be secure in their jobs, and you want to own the business you've worked so hard for. I'm giving you all those things."

I press my hand to my chest. "All I want is to be independent. I want to take care of myself so I can control my own life. You took that away from me when you bought this place."

His jaw is tight. "That's such bullshit, Brinley. You were happy to let Julian put you up in that condo, but you couldn't move in with me. You were planning to take that trust from your parents, but you wouldn't take money from me. You say you want to be independent, but what you really mean is you don't want anything from *me*."

I straighten and back up a step as if it might help me dodge the blow of his words. "Julian *wanted* me and Cami to live there. It made sense when we were about to get married."

"You and I are *already* married," he snaps. He scoops the box with the glass orchid off the desk and sneers down at it. Then it's his turn to back away. "But I guess just on paper, right? Have you even told your parents about me yet? Were you ever planning to tell them about *your husband*, or did you keep me your dirty little secret like you always have?"

I wrap my arms around myself, but it does nothing to soothe the hollow ache I feel there. "They're still trying to come to terms with me canceling my wedding to Julian."

"So, you'll tell them next week? Next month? Next year? Will it ever be a good time to admit that you want to be with a piece of shit like me?"

I choke back a sob, wishing he'd never come in that door, wishing I'd had *time* to get my feelings in line before I had to explain them to him. "They don't see you like I do. They look at you and see . . ." My stomach heaves. I'm going to be sick.

"Finish that sentence," he says. But I can't. He knows I can't. When I bow my head, he huffs out a breath. "Yeah, that's what I thought."

"You're not being fair."

"Fair? I'd do *anything* for you. Anything at all. And that's always been true. I told myself you'd do the same if circumstance hadn't been in the way." He pulls the glass orchid from the box, and I can't tear my eyes away, convinced the neck will snap at any moment in his angry hands. There's too much hurt in the air, and it's too fragile. "I'm realizing now I've been lying to myself."

He tosses the orchid onto my desk, and it shatters into a million little pieces. I stare and stare and stare. I stare, knowing the answers would be there if I could put it together again. I stare, knowing I can't.

They'll always look at you and see the reason they lost their daughter.

I can't make myself look up, but Marston's footsteps echo in my ears as he walks away.

CHAPTER THIRTY-ONE

BRINLEY

June 4th, before

*M*y parents said I didn't have to go to school today, but I didn't see the point in staying home. I don't want to sit around and think about Brittany. I didn't want to watch my mom hide her tears or the whole staff walk on eggshells around my father, who's been more prone to outbursts than usual.

I don't want to be here, but I don't want to be anywhere else, either. Except maybe home with my sister, hiding in a blanket fort in her room and saying goodbye one last time. *That's* where I want to be.

"I've been calling you," Marston says beside me.

I blink up at him. He has dark circles under his eyes, and his skin's pale, like he might be sick.

And all I can think about when I look at him is that I wasn't there for her. I turned off my phone and I missed my chance to say goodbye. I disobeyed my parents and wasn't there for my sister the night she decided she'd finally had enough and stole those pills.

Marston looks me over, and his gaze snags on the bruise on my wrist. His nostrils flare. "That asshole put his hands on you again."

I pull the books for my first two classes out of my locker. "It's not his fault."

"Brinley, there are fingerprint bruises on your wrist. Don't lie to me."

I slam my locker door shut and turn to Marston. "It's not his fault," I whisper. "It's my fault because I snuck out. It's my fault because I wasn't where I was supposed to be, and I made him worry." *It's my fault because I wasn't there to stop her and she died.*

He shakes his head. "None of that gives him the right to—"

I push past him. "I'm gonna be late for class."

I don't hear a word my teachers say all day, but none of them call me on it. I can't look at them, because the pity in their eyes is a reminder I don't want. I barely register the whispers all around me. At lunch, I'm vaguely aware of Stella yelling at some people to stop staring, but I can't blame them.

I'm the girl with the dead sister. I'm the girl who didn't even answer her phone when her only real family was calling to say goodbye.

❧

MARSTON

I don't have money for a suit, but Aunt Lori pulled Uncle Henry's old one from storage for me. It's too tight across my shoulders and the pants are a couple of inches too short, but it's the best I can do.

Lori texted me to tell me Brinley didn't come to the funeral home with her parents and would arrive at the start of the visitation, so I wait outside until her car pulls in.

I rush to the driver's-side door to help her out. Only as I reach for the handle do I realize Brinley's not driving. Roman is.

I stumble back as he swings the door open and climbs out of the car. He looks me over, a sneer curling his lip. "What are you doing here, Death Rowe?"

"Don't start with me today, Humphries," I growl.

The passenger door opens, and Brinley climbs out of the car. I scramble around to help her. She's in a long-sleeve black dress and simple black heels. Her makeup is heavier than usual but still doesn't hide her puffy eyes.

I offer her my hand, and she shakes her head. I wish she'd just kicked me in the nuts.

I want to ask what I did, to know why she won't look me in the eye. I want to ask why the fuck she had *Roman* bring her, but I shove the question deep down. My jealous insecurity is the last thing she needs to deal with right now.

"What can I do?" I ask in a whisper.

For the first time in five days, she meets my eyes. "You can stay away."

I swallow. She's right. If I go in there, her father will

373

make a scene, and the entire day will become about how much he hates me when it's supposed to be about Brittany and her life. Brin's right, but it still burns.

A crowd is gathering in the parking lot as kids from school arrive.

I take a deep breath and try to ignore this panicky feeling in my gut. This feeling I've had since her father found us and told us the news. Brittany's the one who ended her life, but Brinley's the one who's being punished for it. "Okay. I'll call you tonight."

She shakes her head. "Don't. Please." Then she turns away and walks toward the funeral home.

"Burn!" Roman laughs. "Dude. Get a clue. She had her fun and now she's done."

I lunge forward, and Smithy appears out of nowhere and grabs my arm. "Don't do something you'll regret," he whispers.

I yank from his grasp and go for Roman again, but someone else already has me wrapped up, arms crossed over my chest to hold me back.

"He's not worth it," Kace says.

Roman smirks at me, but my eyes are on Brinley as she steps inside the funeral home to say goodbye to her sister.

※

THE NIGHT OF THE FUNERAL, I go to the south dock at the lake. I know Brinley, and after a day like today, she'll want to be out in our spot to find some peace.

I wait for hours. She finally shows up just after dark.

"We need to talk," she says when she spots me.

"Brinley." I swallow hard and step toward her.

She shakes her head and shuffles back. It's dark out, but even in the little light from the distant streetlamps, I can see she's been crying. The sight tears me apart inside and makes me reach for her. "Don't touch me."

I flinch. "I would *never*—"

"It doesn't matter, though, does it?" she asks, her voice small. "If you did it or someone else. It doesn't matter if I love you. Our relationship *hurts* my parents."

"Who cares what hurts your father? He—"

"Don't. Please don't. They're my parents. They're not perfect, but are you going to stand there and tell me *yours* are?"

The blood drains from my face. I can handle a lot of angry words, but I never expected such a low blow from Brinley.

"My sister is *dead* because I wasn't around to save her. She's dead because I was with *you*, and there's nothing I can do to bring her back. My parents lost a child, and I won't be responsible for causing them more pain." She presses her palm to her chest. "Because it hurts *me* to see them hurting like this."

She's cutting me in two. Right down the middle. I can't *breathe*.

"Okay." I lift my hands. "Okay. Tell me what you want to do. Tell me how to fix this."

She hangs her head. "You should leave."

I nod. "I can do that. I'll go. Just call me when you're ready to talk and—"

"No. Leave Orchid Valley. Go to college and don't come back."

I feel like she just punched me in the chest. "What?"

"For me," she whispers. "I won't be strong enough if you're still here. Do it for *me*."

"Don't you get it? This isn't what love looks like. You're *here*, Brinley. *You* didn't die. You didn't even do anything *bad*. You just fell in love with a guy they don't like."

"I fell in love with the *last* guy they'd want to see me with. I fell in love with the guy I can never have anything real with."

I shake my head. This can't be happening. "I'll give you space, and we'll talk about this later."

"No." Her chest shakes with her sob. "Every time I look at you, I see my sister in that casket. I should've been there, and I was so lost in you that I failed her."

I take a step back, but the blow still lands. "I know you're hurting, but don't push me away for good. I love you."

She nods, tears rolling down her cheeks. "If you really love me, you won't make me hurt like this. You need to go, and you need to stay gone."

CHAPTER THIRTY-TWO

BRINLEY

Present day

"More ice cream?" Savvy asks. She hoists the carton in the air from the spot next to me on Kace's couch, where I've spent most of my day, and where she joined me after she finished with her classes and clients at the spa.

I lick my spoon and shake my head. I have a stomachache from too much sugar, a headache from too much crying, and a heartache from too much damn pride. More ice cream can't fix that.

"You could call him," she says gently.

I pull my knees more tightly to my chest and shake my head. "He's right," I say in a whisper. "I want to believe I'm so independent now, but I've never been able to do it on my own."

Savvy carefully sets down the carton of ice cream and straightens in a way that tells me a Savvy lecture is incoming. She folds her arms and huffs out a breath.

"Say it," I mutter.

"Do you think *I'm* a failure as an adult? A loser who doesn't have her shit together?"

I pull back like she's slapped me. "Of course not. I'd never—"

"But I need you. I rely on you for so much. You cover my ass at work when shit goes down, you're there for me when I need someone to talk to, and you've been personally responsible for keeping my lights on more than once."

I bite back the obvious objection—that's what friends do—because it's a trap. I know where she's going with this.

"Abbi and Stella are the same. They need you, and you do so much for them. But they're still inde-fucking-pendent women. And so are you." She takes my hand in both of hers and squeezes it. "No one does it alone. Not even Marston."

I study our fingers as she laces them together. All my strings are busted, but my sister by choice is holding me together the way she has so many times. "You don't know that."

She laughs. "Yes, I do. Alec isn't just Marston's business partner; he's his best friend. He bails Marston out all the time—maybe not financially, but still. Marston's been on the phone with him like crazy since he came back to town."

I frown. "You keep in touch with Alec?"

"Don't change the subject." She pats my hand. "Then there's Marston's Aunt Lori, who's like a mom to him to this day. She still makes him cookies at Christmas, and she's the one who took care of him when he broke his ankle in college."

I tilt my head to the side and gape. "Where did you get all this information? Have you been holding out on me?"

She gently smacks my hand this time. "Focus. She takes care of him, and he takes care of her in return. Because that's what family does—whether it's the family we were given at birth or the one we put together ourselves." She sighs heavily. "Think back to the time in your life when you needed someone the most."

I close my eyes, but not before a tear rolls down my cheek. I needed someone so badly after my sister died, and my parents were too emotionally crippled to give me anything more than money. *They still are.* "When Brittany died," I whisper.

"Your world fell apart, and you've told me how that felt, but think how it must've been for Marston. You were falling apart, and instead of letting him help, you pushed him away."

I swallow hard, and more hot tears spill onto my cheeks. "I thought I was doing the right thing."

She squeezes my hand again. "I know, baby girl, and no one blames you for the mistakes you made as a grieving sister, but you've gotta be bigger than that now. Marston wasn't calling you out for never doing anything on your own. His issue isn't that you rely on other people. It's that you won't rely on *him*."

Sniffling, I open my eyes and see that Savvy's crying too, and my heart is buoyed by the reminder of the family I've found despite everything. "I haven't told my parents about the wedding or even that I'm seeing him. I thought I was saving him from drama, but . . . he thinks I'm ashamed of him."

"Shit," Savvy whispers. "Well, at least you can fix that, right?"

"Can I? I'm not *ashamed* of him, but I don't want to tell my parents. I can't rip that wound open all over again." I snag the carton of ice cream off the coffee table and stab the melting contents with a spoon. "They aren't even speaking to me, so what do I care if they disapprove of me dating Marston? I don't *want* to care. It's dumb."

She shrugs. "It makes sense to me. They're your parents. But honey, love shouldn't be conditional. If Marston makes you happy and your parents love you, they'll find a way to be happy for you. If they don't . . . well, I know it's hard, but maybe that means you're better off letting them pull away." She squeezes my shoulder. "We make our own family, right?"

I nod, my eyes filling with tears. "That's what I keep saying."

"And you know I'm yours until death, whether you want me or not." She smiles. "What's the worst that happens if you tell your parents the truth? They cut you off? Already done. They emotionally blackmail you into doing their bidding? Wait, no, that's what they've done for twenty-seven years, and it's why we're in this mess now."

I release a dry laugh, but it sounds as hollow as I feel. "I wish I could argue."

"You know they're going to be disappointed. They'll probably give you a lecture, tell you some bullshit that makes you feel like a bad mom, and then give you the silent treatment for six months to a year. Right?"

I nod. I hadn't thought it through, but I've disappointed

my parents before, and Savvy's litany of "punishments" sounds on point.

"Fuck them, Brin. There's still a part of you who holds their opinion of you and your life above your own happiness, and I get that—they *are* your parents, and we're, like, programmed to let them fuck us up more than any other. But I think it's time to stop. You don't owe them shit, and you're a fucking *fabulous* mother, and you have an amazing *husband* who'd fetch the stars for you."

"And what do I do about The Orchid?"

"I mean, Alec said Marston planned to sign it over to you. So if this is just about having the control, having it in your name, it's practically done. What do you think the BEK in BEK, LTD stands for?"

Brinley Elizabeth Knox. I close my eyes. I can't believe I didn't see it before.

She studies me for a beat, then sighs. "But that's not going to work for you, is it? You didn't want him to buy you a company."

I shake my head. "I don't want that to be part of our relationship—something I always feel hanging in the balance."

"You'll figure it out," Savvy says. "You *and* your pride."

I frown. "What do you remember about that night? In Vegas?"

She chuckles and throws her hair back. "A lot that I'm not going to share with you."

I roll my eyes, though I do appreciate her levity. It's one of the things I love about her. No matter how serious a situation is, she can always find a way to laugh—not to brush off your problems or ignore them, but as a waypoint so we can catch our breath in the middle of the hard times. "I mean with *me*, bitch. What on earth happened to give me the courage to marry Marston?"

"Other than some good booze?" She shakes her head. "I don't know. After the second bar, we parted ways. You got that fortune from the machine by the bathroom and practically dragged Marston out of there by his collar. You were a woman on a mission, though I had no idea that mission's destination was a *wedding chapel*."

My heart stumbles into a faster beat and I have to force myself to breathe. "Fortune. What fortune?"

She turns up her palms. "It was one of those machines. You know, you ask it a question and it spits out a card that supposedly answers whatever you asked. I told you it was a waste of money, but you said Brittany had been obsessed with those things when you were kids and insisted on feeding singles into the machine."

I stand and slide on my shoes.

"Where are you going?"

"To the garage. I need to find my purse from Vegas."

She gives me a blank look. "Why?"

"I had that little black clutch with me, remember?" When we got home, I never cleaned it out. I just retrieved my ID and credit card and dropped the clutch into the drawer with my spares. Maybe, just maybe, there's an answer in there.

"Wait a second," Savvy says, but I'm already on my way to the garage, and before she catches up with me, I've found the box I'm looking for.

I drop to my knees and dig through it until I find the black leather clutch I carried that night. I hold my breath as I open it, and the first thing I see is a long, thin jewelry box.

I'm an idiot.

I should've known he'd end up buying The Orchid for me, should've seen it coming a mile away. The first thing he did after not seeing me for more than a decade was try to buy me everything I could possibly want and more. It was as if somewhere in his mind he still had to prove to himself he wasn't the poor kid. The orphan. The *help*. He had to prove to himself he could give me all the things my parents had made him believe I needed.

He's been so focused on *giving* to me that I don't think it ever occurred to him I might not *want* it. And it never occurred to me just how much he needed me to accept his gifts.

My hands shake as I set the jewelry box to the side then dump the purse onto the cold concrete floor.

Lipstick, loose change, and a few bills fall along with a blue ticket the size of a playing card.

"There it is," Savvy says.

I lift the card that came from a fortune-teller machine, the machine I no doubt used thinking of my dead sister. And when I read it, I know exactly why I married Marston that night.

"Does that smile on your face mean you're going to run and beg for his forgiveness now?" she asks.

I shake my head. "There's something else I have to do first."

CHAPTER THIRTY-THREE

BRINLEY

*O*nly after I left a message at their hotel claiming I had an "urgent matter to discuss" did my parents finally agree to meet me. They chose breakfast, at the country club, of course—*their turf*—and I came here right after dropping Cami at school.

"What was so urgent?" Mom asks after we're all settled in a private dining room.

"Do you remember when I went out to Vegas for my twenty-seventh birthday?" I don't wait for an answer before barreling forward. "I spent that night with Marston Rowe."

My father grunts. "Never expected that kid to make a damn thing of himself."

I straighten. "Well, he did, and I always knew he would. But that's not what I need to tell you. That night, we got married."

"What?" Mom squeaks, and Dad stays silent, nostrils flaring, his face going red.

"And since I'd taken my anxiety meds and had a couple of drinks, I didn't remember it the next day."

"How long have you known?" Mom asks.

I lift my chin. "Marston found out about my engagement to Julian and came to town to stop the wedding. That's when I found out."

Dad glares at me, anger and disgust in his blue eyes, but it doesn't cow me like it used to.

I've spent so much of my life wanting those eyes to see me. To accept me and be *proud* of me. I never realized how freeing it would be to let go of that dream. "You married that punk at some walk-in chapel like a piece of low-class trash?"

There are so many words in that question that I take issue with, but I don't bother to argue. "I did." I swallow. "Because somehow, for that one night, I found the courage to give myself what *I* wanted without worrying about the consequences."

"That's right. You didn't think about the consequences," Dad growls. "Only yourself. Only *ever* yourself."

"And he didn't tell you?" Mom asks in a whisper. "He never thought to mention it until you were lined up to marry someone else?"

"He assumed I regretted it and was giving me space."

"He was waiting to hold it over you when it served him best," my father says, pushing out of his chair. "And now he can use it to embarrass this entire family—my surviving daughter, a teen mom and soon-to-be divorcee. No wonder Julian walked away from you."

I don't even flinch. His angry words are sleet against the

walls I've put up around my heart—walls I've put between me and my parents in order to protect myself. I should've done it years ago.

"Everyone calm down," Mom says. "Abraham, no one needs to know. This doesn't have to mean anything. We'll get our lawyers on it right away. They can see about expediting an annulment."

"No," I say, and now it's my turn to stand. "I love Marston. I've loved him since I was sixteen, and I pushed him away because I thought loving him was hurting you." I turn to my dad. This isn't the man who scooped me into his arms the first time I fell off my bike or the one who stroked my hair when I couldn't sleep. That man left us the first time Brittany's cancer recurred, and if he hasn't come back by now, he never will. Tears well in my eyes. "I cut Marston out of my life and told him not to come back because I was grieving and hurting, and I needed my dad."

"I won't let you use your sister's death to manipulate me."

I shake my head. "But I'm not. I'm not here to ask for your forgiveness or for your blessing. I'm here because I've finally accepted that you can't be the father you used to be. You can't be the *dad* I need. And no matter how hard I try to be perfect or how badly I screw up, you can't find it in yourself to be him." I blink back the tears I promised myself I wouldn't cry today. "I forgive you for that, but I'm not going to keep hurting myself trying to make you love me the way parents should."

Dad sets down his untouched coffee and pushes himself out of his chair. He stops just before he reaches the double doors to the hall, and when he turns on me, his eyes are hard. "You're no longer my daughter."

I swallow. "You've said that a few times before." I shrug. "I've finally decided to believe you."

Mom presses a trembling hand to her mouth. "Abraham, maybe we can talk this out."

Dad's eyes blaze. "Don't make me repeat myself, Harriet." Then he storms away.

Panic glistens in Mom's eyes as she turns them to me. "Why do you have to provoke him like that? You *know* how he's going to react."

I shake my head. "If you ever decide you need to get away from him, or that you just can't bend to his will anymore, I'll help you leave."

She gasps and jumps up from her seat. "I have *never* once tried to leave your father."

"I know, Mom. But if you change your mind, I'm here for you."

She holds my gaze, and her bottom lip trembles and a single tear rolls down her cheek. "I have to go." She follows my dad, and I sink back into my chair, feeling light and heavy all at once. Untethered but grieving for the parents I so badly wanted them to be.

§

MARSTON

Brinley's the last person I expect to see at my door at ten a.m. on Tuesday, but there she is, looking half angel, half temptation in a gauzy white dress that barely reaches the middle of her thighs. My chest is a traffic jam of emotions when I see her, and I wonder if I'll ever get to the point where I just feel *lucky* that, for part of my life, I got to know what it was like to be loved by her.

"Is this an okay time?" she asks.

"Sure," I croak, then clear my throat. "Sure, it's fine. Come in."

The echo of her clicking heels fills my too-empty home and makes my gaze drop to her feet. She's wearing the *Vegas* shoes.

I swallow hard. I want to believe she wouldn't wear those if she wasn't here with good news, but hell—they're just shoes.

She stops just inside the foyer, and I have to shove my hands into my pockets to resist the urge to pull her against me. She's all business with a red tote slung over her shoulder, some files sticking out the top. She pats it with her hand. "Could we sit somewhere? At a table, I mean? I have some paperwork from my lawyer."

If anyone else would've asked, I would've told them my heart was as broken as that blown glass orchid in her office, but I guess there were some pieces left to break, because they shatter under the weight of those words. *Paperwork. From her lawyer.* "Whatever you want," I say. Because that's what I've promised myself. I don't know any other way to prove to her that I'm not her father. That I'm not Julian. That nothing I give her has any string, stipulation, or ulterior motive, aside from giving her what she wants. Even if it's a divorce.

"Do you want coffee or anything?" I ask as she sits down at my dining room table. "Wine? Bourbon? Brandy?"

She shakes her head. "I'm good."

I drag a hand through my hair. "Do you mind if I

drink?" Because I'll do this for her, but I'm not sure I can get through it without a little liquid courage.

She smiles. "Sure."

I feel her eyes on me as I walk across the dining room and pour myself a snifter of brandy. One might say it's a little early in the day for hard liquor, but I'd counter that it's a little early in our marriage for divorce papers, so fuck it.

I take a generous sip as I stroll back to the table and take my seat across from her.

She's already pulled a manila folder from her tote, and she taps her fingers on it nervously, no doubt as ready to get this over with as I am.

"Listen," I say, "I'll sign whatever you want me to sign. I'll give you whatever you want, but can I apologize first?"

Her head snaps up and she meets my gaze. "I think I'm the one who owes *you* an apology." She sighs. "I overreacted, and while I stand by what I said when I told you I didn't want you to buy me anything, it wasn't fair for me to imply that you'd use the spa as leverage in our marriage."

I lean back in my chair. "Thank you. I'm sorry I didn't *hear* you all those times you told me you didn't want me to buy you anything. But, Brinley, in my mind, the only difference between the guy who was in love with you then and the guy who's in love with you now is *money*. I have it, fucking plenty of it, but in every other way, I'm the same person. I love you as much as I did then and in the same way—with every fucking piece of me. And I say this knowing damn well it probably indicates I need some serious therapy sessions, but I need you to understand." My whole body feels like it's vibrating, as if my brain is so determined to deliver these words that it's putting physical energy behind them. "Who I was then, in high school—he wasn't enough, and this is the only way I could bridge the gap between who I was and the kind of guy your parents always wanted for you. The kind of guy I thought maybe you wouldn't have shoved out of your life."

"I figured that out," she says, staring at her hands.

Then why are you here with fucking paperwork? "You were right to be angry with me. I see that now. I shouldn't have made any assumptions about our life or about whether or not you even wanted to be with me . . . let alone where we'd live or where you'd work if we did. It's just . . ." I take another sip of my brandy, willing its warmth to calm some of this frenetic energy that's making it hard to stay seated. "You were so convinced we wouldn't work because of where I live. I thought if I could fix *that* . . ." I take another sip of my brandy to stop my own rambling.

It's over, and I need to let her go. I don't want her walking out of here feeling heavy with guilt. I've had enough chances with Brinley Knox. If I haven't made it work by now, that's on me.

She lifts her gaze. "I want to circle back to this—the gifts and the plans. But first . . ." She taps the folder in front of her. "Can we look at this?"

My stomach cramps hard. "Whatever you want."

She squares her shoulders and blows out a breath, then opens the folder.

I frown at the heading on the top of the first sheet. It's a business proposal. For the purchase of The Orchid.

"I've wanted to buy The Orchid for years, but as I'm sure you know, the original owners refused to consider anything but a cash offer, and my credit is worse than shit."

"This is about *The Orchid*?" I ask. Because if I *hope* and I'm wrong, it might destroy me.

"Hear me out?" she asks, flashing a tentative smile. I nod, and she continues. "I spoke with Alec, who was able to give me good information about market rates and what kind of return you might expect on an investment like this. Since he had the information in your system from your work at The Orchid, he was also able to help me by doing a quick analysis and providing me with a conservative time frame in which the spa could pay for itself." She lifts her eyes to mine. "I didn't want you to buy me the spa. I wanted to buy it myself. But since that didn't work out, I'd like you to sell it to me on contract, essentially acting as the seller and the bank, and allowing me to use The Orchid's profits over the course of ten years to buy it. Of course, there are substantial risks to you agreeing to a deal like this, including any unforeseen economic downturn that could profoundly affect business or a competitor coming in."

"I know the numbers," I say. I'm practically staring a hole in the damn contract, because I need to know what's beneath it. "You run a tight ship, and your growth trajectory is incredible. What you're describing is feasible and done frequently when small businesses are sold."

"That's what Alec said too," she says. She turns her head to look out the dining room windows, and her earrings catch in the light. "It's important to me that this is the kind of deal you'd take from anyone and not a special concession you're making for me."

"It . . ." *Those earrings. That necklace.* She's not just wearing the shoes I bought her in Vegas. She's wearing the jewelry too, and hope makes my chest swell.

I shove my chair back and stalk around to her side of the table. I stand behind her chair and lean over her as I pick up the stack of papers and slowly flip through the contract. This is all business paperwork. Every page about a deal between my subsidiary company and Brinley.

I toss the stack back on the table and swallow hard. "I thought you were bringing me divorce papers."

She hops out of her chair, gripping the edge of the table. "I don't have a personal interest in pursuing those, but if you'd like—"

"Not a chance." I kick the chair out of the way and slide my hands around her waist, pulling her back to my front and relishing the way every one of her soft curves feels pressed into me. I nuzzle her neck until I'm drunk on the smell of her perfume and the feel of her perfect skin under my lips.

"I need our relationship to be separate from my business. I need to be proud of what I've made for *myself* there, and I don't ever want any part of what we have to feel burdened by business."

"Not a problem." I breathe her in again. *She's real. This is real.* "I love you. Fuck, do I love you. So much I don't know who I'd be without that love."

She turns in my arms and lifts her chin. *God, she's beautiful.* "I love you too."

My breath snags in my chest, right alongside hope and joy and my quickly mending heart. "Say it again."

She smiles. "I love you, Marston Rowe."

I can barely breathe, I want this so much. "I want a *shot* at this marriage, and I know I'm asking the impossible since your parents—"

"I don't care what they think. I made my choice before we went to that chapel in Vegas."

"But you don't even remember why you decided to marry me."

392

"Now I know why." She shakes her head. "No, I've always known why I married you. I love you, and I want to spend my life with you—*that's* why. What I didn't know was how I found the courage to do it, but that mystery's been solved." She reaches into her tote and pulls out a blue piece of paper the size of a playing card.

"What's that?"

"Savvy told me you and I left the second club after I used one of those fortune-teller machines they have in touristy gift shops and at fairs. Brittany used to love those, and apparently on my birthday I insisted on playing in her honor. I don't know what question I asked, but I went digging and found this in my purse from that night."

She hands it to me, and I flip it over and read the small print on the back.

Let go of the relationships that cause you only pain. We make our own family.

"Isn't that what Brittany told you once? *We make our own family?*" I lift my eyes from the card, and Brinley's smiling at me, tears in her eyes.

"I'm not saying my sister spoke to me from the grave," she says, then clears her throat and blinks away tears, "but as soon as I found that card, I knew why I walked down the aisle to you."

I blink down to the words that brought her back to me, and my chest feels crowded—too full of warmth and sunshine and love to allow me to speak.

"I'm sorry I let them win," she says, her eyes brimming with new tears. "After Brittany died, I felt like I was drowning, and I thought my family could save me. I thought I could make them love me the way I needed them to love me. I thought . . ." She bites her lip hard. "I'm ashamed I forgot my little sister's wisdom so soon. I needed you, my family by choice, and I pushed you away."

I pull her body tightly against mine and nuzzle her neck. "I shouldn't have let you, but my pride . . ." I shake my head. "My fucking pride had me convinced it was best for you."

"My family—the only one that's ever counted—is Cami, Savvy, Abbi, Stella, Smithy, and Kace. But I'd really like to include you at the top of that list. Marston Rowe, my husband, my friend, my lover."

I press a hard kiss to her soft mouth. "As long as you'll take me, I'm yours."

She smiles against my lips. "I have video evidence to prove we already agreed on forever."

EPILOGUE

BRINLEY

*T*he patio behind The Orchid and overlooking Lake Blackledge makes the perfect setting for intimate weddings. Once the tables are cleared out, we can seat as many as forty for a ceremony and then open the doors between the restaurant and patio for the reception.

I peek out the window from inside the bridal suite. The guests take their seats in white folding chairs. At the front of the aisle, an arbor covered in red roses and dark green ivy overlooks the lake. The groom and his best friends laugh together, waiting for the bride.

Every wedding we've held here has been breathtakingly beautiful, but today's is my favorite.

"Stop!" Cami grabs my hand and pulls me away from the window. If you ask me, she's going to steal the show in her hunter-green junior bridesmaid dress. "He's going to see you, and that's bad luck."

I wrinkle my nose at her. "You think so? Even though we're already married?"

She props her hands on her hips. "I *know* so."

On the other side of the room, my bridesmaids, Savvy, Abbi, and Stella, have their heads together and are whisper-arguing about something.

"Girls?" I pick up my short lace train and make my way to them, trying not to get distracted by my new, super-hot wedding night shoes. "What's going on?"

They jump apart faster than teenagers caught at the drive-in.

Savvy steps forward. "There's someone here to see you."

I laugh. "Okay, then, send them in."

Savvy looks to the other two then back to me before shrugging and opening the door.

"Grammy!" Cami says, bouncing on her toes beside me.

My hand goes to my mouth immediately at the sight of my mother, dressed for the occasion in the signature beige lace of mothers-of-the-bride everywhere.

She grips her purse in both hands and her eyes fill with tears as she looks at me. "Oh, Brinley, you look just lovely."

I've been planning this day for months and made every decision for every detail with love and anticipation. I thought I'd planned the perfect day. I'd dismissed the heartache over walking down the aisle alone, but now that she's here, I can't deny how much I'd like her by my side.

"I'm so sorry," Mom blurts. "I've never been strong like you, but I left him. Finally, I did it, but I understand if it's too late. If you can't forgive me."

She's imperfect, and she enabled my father's verbal and emotional abuse for years, but she's my mother, and by being here, she's asking to be part of this family I made for myself. *We make our own family.* Maybe Mom needs to learn that as much as I did.

She draws in a breath and her shoulders tremble. "It's up to you whether I stay or go, but I'd really like to see my daughter get married."

"They're already married," Cami says. "They just wanted to make their promises again, since they did it *without me* last time!"

The tension in the room breaks, and we all laugh.

I nod. "Would you want to walk me down the aisle?"

She covers a sob. "Yes. I'd like that very much."

The processional music starts on the patio, and Savvy says, "That's our cue!"

All the bridesmaids grab their flowers and file out, one by one. Then Cami takes her turn, tossing me a final grin before she pushes out the doors.

When the music changes, I take Mom's arm, and my staff opens the double doors wide for us. I see the shock on Marston's face when he sees Mom at my side, but he smiles and nods. Because he's my family and he loves me, even when it's hard. It's the sight of him—that nod, that easy smile, that warmth in his eyes—that roots me in the moment and unfurls love in my chest.

We stop under the arbor, and Mom kisses my cheek before taking a seat at the front.

Marston steps forward and bends to whisper in my ear, "You are *stunning.*"

I whisper back, "Wait until you see me in nothing but my new shoes."

His gaze drops to my feet, hidden beneath my lace gown, then slides to the doors. "Is now an okay time for you?"

Laughing, I grab him by the tie and tug him down to kiss me, and my daughter shouts, "It's not time for that part yet!"

I laugh and kiss my husband anyway. And there, in front of our lake and our family, I promise to love Marston Rowe forever. With every little piece of me.

❦

THANK you so much for joining me in Orchid Valley for Marston and Brinley's story. I hope you'll return for Stella's story in my next release, *Every Sweet Regret*. If you'd like to receive an email when I release their book, please sign up for my newsletter: lexiryan.com/signup

I hope you enjoyed this book and will consider leaving a review. Thank you for reading. It's an honor!

OTHER BOOKS BY LEXI RYAN

Orchid Valley

Every Little Promise (Brinley and Marston's prequel)

Every Little Piece of Me (Brinley and Marston's story)

Every Sweet Regret (Stella and Kace's story, coming late 2020)

And more to be announced later!

The Boys of Jackson Harbor

The Wrong Kind of Love (Ethan's story)

Straight Up Love (Jake's story)

Dirty, Reckless Love (Levi's story)

Wrapped in Love (Brayden's story)

Crazy for Your Love (Carter's story)

If It's Only Love (Shay's story)

The Blackhawk Boys

Spinning Out (Arrow's story)

Rushing In (Chris's story)

Going Under (Sebastian's story)

Falling Hard (Keegan's story)

In Too Deep (Mason's story)

LOVE UNBOUND: Four series, one small town, lots of happy endings

Splintered Hearts (A Love Unbound Series)

Unbreak Me (Maggie's story)

Stolen Wishes: A Wish I May Prequel Novella (Will and Cally's prequel)

Wish I May (Will and Cally's novel)

Or read them together in the omnibus edition, *Splintered Hearts: The New Hope Trilogy*

Here and Now (A Love Unbound Series)

Lost in Me (Hanna's story begins)

Fall to You (Hanna's story continues)

All for This (Hanna's story concludes)

Or read them together in the omnibus edition, *Here and Now: The Complete Series*

Reckless and Real (A Love Unbound Series)

Something Reckless (Liz and Sam's story begins)

Something Real (Liz and Sam's story concludes)

Or read them together in the omnibus edition, *Reckless and Real: The Complete Series*

Mended Hearts (A Love Unbound Series)

Playing with Fire (Nix's story)

Holding Her Close (Janelle and Cade's story)

OTHER TITLES

Hot Contemporary Romance

Text Appeal

Accidental Sex Goddess

Decadence Creek (Short and Sexy Romance)

Just One Night

Just the Way You Are

ACKNOWLEDGMENTS

I'm so thankful for everyone who helped me as this book grew from an idea to a reality. As always, to my family first. Brian, Jack, and Mary—thank you for believing in me and inspiring me to be my very best. To my mom and siblings— thank you for all of your support and for making me want to write big casts of characters forever.

I'm lucky enough to have a life full of amazing friends. Thanks to my writing friends who sprint with me and talk me off the ledge when the book looks like a disaster. To my hand-holding, hair-stroking, and pep-talking best bitches, Mira Lyn Kelly and Lisa Kuhne, my eternal gratitude to you and to unlimited texting plans. To the Goldbrickers and the ladies in my Slack group, thank you for helping me remember the power of consistency.

To everyone who provided me feedback on this story along the way—especially Heather Carver, Samantha Leighton,

Tina Allen, Lisa Kuhne, Dina Littner, Nancy Miller, and Janice Owen—you're all awesome. I appreciate you all so much!

I have the *best* editorial team. It truly takes a village. Lauren Clarke and Rhonda Merwarth, thank you for the insightful line and content edits. You push me to be a better writer and make my stories the best they can be. Thanks to Arran McNicol at Editing720 for proofreading. I've worked hard to put together this team, and I'm proud of it!

Thank you to the people who helped me package this book and promote it. Sara Eirew took the gorgeous cover photo and Hang Le did the design and branding for the whole series. Nina and Social Butterfly PR, thank you so much for all your work! I love working with you and your awesome assistants! To all of the bloggers, bookstagrammers, readers, and reviewers who help spread the word about my books, I am humbled by the time you take out of your busy lives for my stories. My gratitude will never be enough, but it is sincere. You're the best.

To my agent, Dan Mandel, for believing in me and always believing the best is yet to come. Thanks to you and your team for getting my books into the hands of readers all over the world.

Finally, the biggest, loudest, most necessary thank you to my fans. Because of you, I'm living my dream. I couldn't do it without you. You're the coolest, smartest, best readers in the world. I appreciate each and every one of you!

XOXO,
    Lexi

ABOUT THE AUTHOR

Lexi Ryan is the *New York Times* and *USA Today* bestselling author of emotional romance that sizzles. A former academic and English professor, Lexi considers herself the luckiest girl around to make a living through storytelling. She loves spending time with her crazy kids, weightlifting, ice cream, swoony heroes, and vodka martinis.

Lexi lives in Indiana with her husband, two children, and a spoiled dog. You can find her on her website.

Made in the USA
Coppell, TX
19 October 2020

39941732R00246